IDLE BLOOM

JEWEL E. ANN

Copyright © 2014 by Jewel E. Ann

ISBN 978-1-7359982-1-3

Second Print Edition

Cover Designer: Jennifer Beach

DEDICATION

*To my husband ... my always, you fill my heart with love and
my belly with laughter.*

CHAPTER ONE
IVY LEAGUE DOUGHNUTS

Vivian

WAKE. Stretch. Shower. Then navigate through the bustling morning crowd to the subway via the corner coffee shop. A kaleidoscope of colors and the inviting bittersweet aroma of America's favorite pick-me-up dazzles my senses.

No offense to Paul Revere, but when I think of Boston and its exhausting list of historical figures, William Rosenberg is the name that warms my chest and tempts my tummy. It's my firm belief that his inspiration and influence in the business world fed my ambition to achieve the high merits that earned my acceptance into a well-known university north of the Charles River.

"Boston Kreme and a medium Dunkaccino, please."

I ignore the piercing glances, rolling eyes, and subtle head shakes behind me. Yes, at five foot eleven inches I can eat whatever I want and not gain a pound. Long, wavy, ink black hair and green eyes, a runway model on the outside. Yeah, yeah, I've heard it all before. My personal assessment of the reflection in my mirror includes the words lanky, bony, witchy hair, monster eyes, and freaky freckles. A tiny grin tugs at the corners of my mouth as I focus on my phone, moving my thumbs over the screen with effortless strokes to send off a text.

Me: *Up, bitches? 2 hrs. to study then get your asses to work. The real world awaits.*

Judgments are nothing more than presumptuous thoughts, flawed opinions at best. What lies beneath my veiled "perfection" is the ugly truth—my truth, my reality, my destiny. Though, for now, I grab my decadent treats and sashay out the door with a wicked smile.

Two years after I nailed the admissions interview, I have yet to see the inside of a Harvard lecture hall, but it won't be long now. Instead, I take the Red Line at Harvard Square to Central Square every morning while my two bitches enter the coveted black iron gates to "Grow In Wisdom." Since my hopes of love and marriage were snuffed out like a torch my senior year of high school, I have my whole life to focus on becoming a successful entrepreneur.

The air grows thick and musty on my final descent to the subway. And then I see him, my new visual indulgence. He first captured my attention a week ago. A sky scraper among the diverse sea of heads bowed and drawn into their handheld technological gods. But then again, when you're my height the bar for being considered tall is set pretty high. He must be at least six foot four with lean muscles, short sandy blond hair, and cornflower blue eyes. Sipping my Dunkaccino, I peek over the lid and worm my way through the morning crowd, positioning myself to get on the same car. Everyday he's dressed in faded jeans, an old T-shirt, and leather work boots. Maybe he's married, or has a girlfriend, but it doesn't matter. My infatuation will go no further than basking in his sexy aura and taking mental pictures to use for my own pleasure.

The train screeches to a stop and the whoosh of the hydraulic doors sets the crowd in motion. Most mornings I find a seat opposite my rugged blue-collar worker. We play a flirty game of peek-a-boo where I unabashedly stare at him until he glances at me then diverts his shy eyes, taking a deep swallow. I eat my Boston Kreme doughnut and sip my coffee keeping my eyes fixed on him. *Click, click, click*—I take my mental pictures.

This morning, however, the car is herded to capacity. I find myself next to him with my drink in one hand and my doughnut in the other. As the rest of the passengers cram in, I glance up and smile. He returns a hesitant smile, and for the first time I can see his straight white teeth and dimples. *Holy crap!* He has dimples. My heart rate increases exponentially as I lift my doughnut toward my mouth. *Dimples!* The doors fold shut and the train jerks forward before my legs have a chance to balance and root into the floor.

"Oh shit! Oh my gosh, I'm so sorry!" I'm drowning in horrid humiliation while peeling my half-eaten doughnut off his gray T-shirt. I can't look at him.

Through my squinted eyes, all I see is a smeared glob of chocolate frosting in the middle of his shirt. Risking a glance, a grimace takes over my face while meeting his raised brows, eyes darting back and forth between me and his shirt. Depositing the doughnut back in the bag, I retrieve the wad of napkins I shoved in my purse and begin to wipe his shirt like a mother would do to a child. He doesn't say anything, he doesn't move. My brain registers the faint giggles and snickers from a few of the lucky commuters who have witnessed this embarrassing mishap. I may have to start taking the bus from now on, or dress incognito so I'm not recognized as the clumsy doughnut girl.

"It's fine," a deep voice sounds. Long fingers encircle my wrist, halting my frantic strokes. "It's just a shirt."

Biting my lips together, I nod unable to make eye contact. He releases my wrist and I shove the napkins into my bag.

"I, uh … I'm just so, very clumsy … embarrassed, and uh, again … sorry." I. Will. Not. Move. I shall stay bowed in shame until I leap from the train at the next opportunity.

"It's really okay, no need to feel bad."

"*Central Square*," the speaker sounds as the train's piercing brakes pull to a halt.

My frantic dash to the door threatens to take out a few unsuspecting passengers. I can't concern myself with that; sometimes casualties are unavoidable and necessary.

"Is this your stop?" Mr. Frosting Shirt says with a questioning tone, probably because for the past week he's gotten off the train before me.

It is today!

Without looking back I nod and sprint off the subway.

LUCKY FOR ME, when the white sign with the green planter's pot becomes visible over the hill, there isn't a line of miffed people waiting under it to get in the door.

"Maggie, I'm so sorry," I say with a genuine apologetic tone as I shove my bag under the counter and tie on my green apron over my fitted T-shirt and frayed denim shorts. "I had to take the bus and walk the last mile."

"Vivian, dear, why are you apologizing? I told you to

take the day off anyway." Maggie shakes her head while arranging the packs of seedlings into cardboard flats.

I take over while she rings the customer's order up on the register. "I know, but this is the busiest time of year and who knows if or when Alex and Kai will show up to help."

Maggie, proud owner of The Green Pot nursery, originally started her business as a front for growing marijuana. She's not a law-breaking pothead, per say. She's a ten-year cervical cancer survivor.

"You don't see me looking too concerned do you?"

I laugh. Maggie has saintly patience and I love working for her. The Green Pot has become a legitimate greenhouse —one of the top suppliers for local landscaping companies— but she still has a stash of wacky tabbacky for those who don't want to jump through the hoops to get it legally. Her only request is that these VIP customers don't all come on the same day with their scarf and bandana wrapped heads asking for the Brown Bag special.

"Chance should be here soon if you want to go out back and double check to see if his order is all there."

Ah, Chance Konrad, the horny green jack-of-all-trades owner of The Handy Hunk. Chance is a real player and, in his eyes, I am the World Series of his playboy game. For two years he has tried to sweep me off my feet and into his bed. For two years I have rejected his often times outrageous efforts to win my affection.

The familiar red flatbed truck backs into the loading zone as I finish double checking the order. "Vivian." Chance's velvety voice caresses my name as he strips me with his usual lustful gaze.

I give him the eye roll he's come to expect while shaking my head. "Chance."

I'm not naive enough to think that he has been waiting

in patient celibacy for me to succumb to his advances. In fact, I can't imagine him going a single night without some gullible girl's naked body wrapped around his. Not that I too don't find him physically appealing, but I've resigned myself to believe that all my orgasms will be self-induced. Chance is eye candy, another visual for my private moments. *Click. Click. Click.*

"Hate to disappoint you, I know how much you look forward to our sexy banter, but my brother is working with me now so you'll need to use a little more discretion with your advances," Chance says as he leans against the back of his truck with his arms folded over his chest.

Uncontrolled laughter erupts from my chest but halts in my throat, nearly choking me, as the other door to the truck opens and a very tall guy steps out with a chocolate stain stamped in the middle of his gray T-shirt.

Kill. Me. Now!

"Viv, this is my brother Oliver. Don't mind his shirt. Some chick on the subway rammed into him with her doughnut."

My eyes are so wide I think they're locked in this position. "That uh, really sucks. She must have felt awful."

"Yeah, what did you say?" Chance looks at Oliver. "That she scurried off at the next stop with her tail between her legs?" Chance laughs.

Oliver grimaces, glancing at me. "I don't think that's exactly what I said."

"Yeah, bro, it was. You also said——"

"I'm sure she gets the point!"

I nod and cross my arms over my chest. "Oliver's right. I get it. I can totally imagine it. But I'm sure she didn't run off with her *tail between her legs*. It was probably just her stop." I give Oliver a tightlipped grin and offer my hand. "Anyway, Vivian Graham, nice to meet you."

Oliver stares at my hand for a few moments then meets my eyes. "Nice to meet you, Vivian." We shake hands and my grip cinches to convey my unspoken displeasure with his interpretation of what happened this morning.

"Mind if I use the restroom before we load up and head out?" Chance asks, not waiting for my response before he heads into the building.

Oliver and I divert our gazes away from each other as an awkward silence closes in on us. I glance at his shirt and an uncontrollable giggle bubbles up and out.

"What are the chances?" I laugh, shaking my head and meeting his gaze.

He grins and chuckles.

"I really am sorry. I'll get you a new shirt."

Wiping his hand over the dried chocolate stain, he licks his lips and smiles so big his dimples steal my attention. "Not necessary. It will probably come out and if not, I'm quite certain I have at least twenty other old T-shirts just like it."

"Load 'em up!" Chance emerges from the building as we slip on our work gloves and start arranging the plants into the back of the truck.

When everything is loaded and secured, Chance hops in the truck, starts the engine, and rolls down the window. "Let's go, Oliver, no need to flirt with my girl. After two years of rejecting yours truly, I'm pretty sure she's a lesbian. And for some reason that makes my dick even harder."

Oliver closes his eyes and shakes his head as I laugh. "Please excuse my vulgar brother. He doesn't have a delay button between his brain and mouth."

I wave a dismissive hand. "I've been putting up with

him for two years. His potty mouth is the highlight of my lesbian day."

Oliver furrows his brow with a slow nod. "All right then, I guess I'll see you around."

"Later, guys." I hand the order receipt to Oliver with a wink and walk away to check on Maggie.

***

Oliver

"Now I KNOW why you're taking on so many landscaping jobs instead of sticking to mowing and home repair." I flash Chance a knowing glance.

"She's hot as hell, isn't she?" He grins, pulling out of the back parking lot.

I shake my head. "It's been two years. I think it's safe to say she's not interested."

He lifts his shoulders. "She's baiting me, slowly reeling me in."

"She's stamped rejection on your head so many times you have brain damage and can no longer see you make her skin crawl with your dick talking."

"She's a nice girl. We have a good thing going. Didn't you notice how she defended the doughnut chick from this morning?"

"Shit." I laugh and run my hands though my hair. "She *is* the doughnut chick from this morning, dickhead."

"What the hell are you talking about?"

I roll down my window and pull my Red Sox baseball cap on. "Vivian was the one on the subway who fell into me with her doughnut. Thanks to you, now I look like a real asshole because you had to run your mouth about the whole tail between the legs comment."

Chance laughs. "Damn, you lucky son of a bitch! I should start taking the T. I'm probably missing out on a huge untapped population of hot women. They're wasting their time bumping into you, the one guy who won't ever give them the time of day."

I sigh. "You're right. I couldn't care less."

———

At the chance of risking what's left of my manhood to some philosophical bullshit, I have to admit that digging in the dirt and being in the sun all day is somewhat therapeutic. I can't help but mentally pat myself on the back for coming to that conclusion without the help of a psychiatrist. Lord knows in an effort to save one hundred and forty dollars an hour, I can ask myself how I'm feeling and why I think I'm feeling it with less resentment than I felt from those damn therapists in Portland.

We're adding raised-bed gardens to a hotel in the Seaport district so they can use the fresh vegetables and herbs in their restaurant. Just one of a million reasons I love this town.

"Wanna go out tonight?" Chance asks while mixing the compost into the soil.

"Nope."

"Tara is going to bring her sister. We're going to some new Italian place by the wharf then to Mike's for Cannoli."

"Who's Tara?" I sit back on my heels and wipe the sweat from my brow with the bottom of my chocolate-stained shirt.

"The girl I took to Mom's birthday dinner."

"Not interested."

"Oliver, you need to get out."

"You don't know what I need and I told you never to mention a fucking second of my past!"

"Jeez, dude! I'm not talking about your past. I'm talking about *now*! Nothing more than dinner with a pretty woman. She just graduated from MIT and she's brilliant. A nerdy scholar like yourself. It's okay to let a nice piece of ass make your dick twitch every once in awhile. Gives your hand a break."

"Bite me!"

"Nobody says that anymore, but whatever, your loss."

I hate that he's right, but I'd rather gnaw off my own arm than admit it out loud.

"Sorry, Chance, I'm just ... shit, I'm just not ready. I'm not saying never, just not now."

He pats me on the shoulder. "Don't sweat it, Bro."

With a deep sigh, I close my eyes and try to shake the image of the one person who does make my dick twitch. And when that fails, I decide to call it a day. It doesn't appear that my hand will be getting a rest anytime soon.

I'VE BEEN BACK for two months settling into my new life. I feel like a zombie most of the time. Food lacks taste, I see the sun but I can't feel it touch my skin, comedy is void of humor, and the monotonous play of life in all its muted colors doesn't catch my eye. At least that was the case until last week when I started working with my brother.

Living in Cambridge, I take the Red Line to South Station. Every morning for the past week, I've sat across from this long-legged woman with raven hair falling in unruly waves around her slender shoulders and down her back. Soft green eyes peek through sexy long lashes, casting a spell on me, and I've found myself locked in a trance watching her eat her cream filled doughnut with chocolate frosting. She makes a complete mess of it, and by the time she's done every guy in the subway car is sporting a boner from watching her lick her full lips and suck the sticky sweetness off her long fingers one at a time like a fucking Dunkin' Donuts porn movie.

So now the only thing I smell is a mixture of coffee and doughnuts. I can taste sweet cherry red lips that I will never kiss. It's absurd I'm so fucking enthralled with her just the thought of the subway elicits a pathetic schmuck grin, and the vision of her lingers like a drunken haze even when I close my eyes. But most disturbing is the part of my body she awakens that I swore I'd never use again.

I'm so screwed.

CHAPTER TWO
THE WELCOME WAGON

Vivian

"**H**EY, bitches, it's about time you showed up." I give both Kai and Alex a big hug.

"Sorry, Flower. Sean and Kai were late." Alex pins Kai with a gimlet-eyed stare before hugging me.

"I hate when you call her that," Kai clenches his jaw.

"She calls us her bitches, yet you think calling her flower, like we both don't know what's tattooed on her back, is somehow what? Disrespectful?"

I link my pinkie to Kai's then playfully nudge him in the shoulder. "I can think of worse things to be called."

The scowl on Kai's face refuses to fade. Alex thinks she knows everything about the events that led to my inked backside, but she doesn't. Kai was there and as much as he would like to forget how that night forever changed my life, he can't. I hope someday we can remember what we were and not what we've become.

"I hate that fucking tattoo," he says.

"Well good thing it's mine and not yours. Besides, Kate has an infinity symbol tattooed on her ankle."

"Ah, Kai and Kate. It's bad enough that you two look like Ken and Barbie, but seriously, hearing your names together is just too much." Alex mock gags with her finger in her mouth.

"I don't look like Ken."

"Maybe not blond Ken, but you could pass for the pretty boy dark-haired doll, and Kate is definitely Barbie. I've never seen her in anything but heels. Are her feet permanently molded to that shape? Does she walk on her toes even when she's barefoot?" Alex laughs.

"Suck me, Alex."

"Afraid not, babe. Sean's idea of a threesome is with me and Flower."

"Timeout, you two!" I make a T with my hands. "I'm going home while you two help Maggie close up. Try to play nice."

"I won't be home tonight," Alex says as I sling my bag over my shoulder.

"You never are. Tell Barbie ... I mean *Kate,* I said hi." I giggle, giving Kai a wink.

He scans the crowd for onlookers, then waves goodbye with his lone middle finger.

I STICK in my earbuds and float away with Ed Sheeran as I take the Red Line back to Harvard Square. At South Station an all too familiar face steps through the doors. We make eye contact, sharing mirrored grins.

"You're haunting me today," I tug my earbuds out.

Oliver takes the seat next to me. "I could say the same about you."

"Your obnoxious brother let you off early?"

Oliver laughs. "I didn't ask. I pretty much decide when I'm done. What's he going to do? Fire me?" His gaze dips, heating my skin. "So why are *you* going home so early?"

"Wasn't really my day to work so I left my friends to clean up the mess and close up shop. Besides, I skipped lunch and I'm starving."

"You think it's because you skipped lunch? Or maybe it's because you left half of your breakfast with me." Oliver pulls at his chocolate-stained shirt.

"Funny guy, huh? I'm starting to feel less and less badly about this morning's little incident."

We both stand as the train stops at Harvard Station. "Come on." He signals with his head as we step off. "I owe you a doughnut."

I hesitate as commuters shuffle past us. "That's a ridiculous comment, but I'm starving so yeah, I'll let you buy me a doughnut."

We navigate up the stairs and make our way out to Harvard Square. I hold up a finger and duck into the corner shop returning just a few minutes later. "Here, we're even." I toss him a Harvard T-shirt. "Now you can pretend you went to an Ivy League school."

He shrugs off his shirt leaving me with a gaped-mouth stare as I look around to see if anyone else is watching. Drool-worthy, carved muscles hug his lean frame, and I can't hide the blush that creeps up my neck as he slips on the new shirt before tossing the old one in the trash.

"What makes you think I didn't go to Harvard?"

I shrug. "Well, probably the leather work boots. Why? Did you go to Harvard?"

Oliver cruises ahead toward Dunkin' Donuts. "It's possible."

I can feel his smirk as I roll my eyes and jog to catch up.

"After you." Smirking, Oliver holds open the door.

"Why thank you, Mr. Konrad."

We order doughnuts and iced coffee then take a seat by the window.

"So, are you?"

"Am I what?" He arches a sly brow.

"A Harvard graduate."

"Ah, piqued your curiosity, have I?"

"A little." I remove the lid from my coffee.

He stares into his drink as if he's waiting for his next words to float to the top. "Yes, I went to Harvard."

"Cool," I reply, sticking my finger into the cream-filled hole then licking it off.

With cow eyes, Oliver watches me suck the filling off my finger. He clears his throat. "Yes, I guess it is *cool*."

Sticking my finger back in the hole to scoop out more filling, I laugh. "I don't mean it dismissively, I'm just trying to not make a big deal of it. You're obviously not using your degree, that is if you received one, so I don't want to make you feel bad for doing something else in life."

Sliding my tongue along my cream-covered finger, I wait for his response. He's staring at my mouth again with his lips parted and he takes an exaggerated swallow when his eyes meet mine.

"Uh, that's um, an interesting way to eat a doughnut."

I lick my lips and grin. "I like to savor it. You know, the way some people lick the frosting from the center of an Oreo before eating the cookie part?"

He nods and clears his throat. "I graduated with a degree in Law."

"Really? Did you ever practice?"

His forehead tenses into valleys of lines, almost looking pained. "For a short while, but ... life became too demanding so I had to give it up." He says each word with slow calculated precision.

"Do you think you'll ever start practicing again?"

He keeps eye contact, but his gaze becomes glazed. "A few years ago I would have said no, but now I hope I find my way back."

"Sounds like you're lost."

Oliver leans back and laces his fingers behind his head. "I think I am."

I pull the straw from my cup and chew on the end giving thought to his comment. "Lost is a state of mind. You'll find yourself when you acknowledge you're exactly where you need to be in this moment."

He laughs. "At Dunkin' Donuts?"

"Nope, just alive." I smile but it falters as I watch the color drain from Oliver's face. "Did I say something wrong?"

The legs of his chair screech along the floor as he stands. "No, I just should get going."

I grab my drink, shoving the straw back into it, and stand. "Okay, well, thanks for the late afternoon treat."

"Yeah, sure. So I'll see you around." He doesn't wait for me and before I can say anymore he's out the door.

Now who's scampering away with their tail between their legs? What the hell just happened? How can Chance be so transparent, as in, "I'd do you in the back of my pick-up," but Oliver such an enigma? I climb the front stairs to my building while fetching my keys.

"Hey, Oliver, how's it going?"

I whip around and see Oliver waving toward an open window of a condo across the street, then he digs his keys out of one pocket while holding a paper grocery sack with the other. He unlocks the door next to the one with the open window, enters, and closes it without a single glance in my direction.

No way! Oliver is my neighbor?

I have nothing to offer this tall sexy man, yet I feel compelled to march across the street like the welcome wagon lady with a chip on her shoulder.

Knock knock knock!

He opens his door and his brows sink into a scowl. "Did you follow me?"

I make a fist and point my thumb over my shoulder. "See that red door?"

He nods.

"That's where I live. I heard your neighbor greet you as I was getting ready to unlock my door. How long have you lived here and why did you drop me like burnt toast then run out of the doughnut joint?"

He jerks his head back. "Um, two months and I didn't drop you like *burnt toast*, I had to get going."

Crossing my arms over my chest I widen my stance, jutting my hip out. "How have I not seen you coming or going? And yes, you did drop me like burnt toast, and then you ran out the door with *your* tail between your legs."

He rests his free hand on his hip and bends down to my eye level. "I don't exactly have a front yard or porch swing to lounge in, so it's not a big surprise that we haven't run into each other. And I *didn't* run out with my tail between my legs."

"Well ... whatever. Welcome to the neighborhood."

Turning on my heels, I sally forth down the stairs.

"Wait!"

I stop, keeping my back to him.

"Thank you for the shirt. You said something that hit a little too close to home and I didn't know how to react so ... I left. It was a dick move and ... I'm sorry."

I nod once and continue across the street.

"Hey! Do you want to come in for a drink or something?"

"Not today."

"Are we good?" he yells.

Unlocking my door without looking back, I flash him the A-OK sign with my left hand.

***

Oliver

I POUR myself a scotch and collapse on my back deck. Normally I wouldn't turn to hard liquor before five o'clock, but the black magic my new neighbor across the street weaves requires something stronger than a Sam Adams. I had the upper hand when she nearly choked on her own saliva as I shrugged off my shirt in the middle of Harvard Square. It was completely unnecessary, but I wanted to see how she'd react. I'm not sure why, since I have no intention of acting on any of my dick brain impulses. The impulses she feeds like blood to sharks. The crazy part is I honestly don't think she has a clue what she does to me and probably every other straight guy she encounters. Seriously, what was that today? Finger fucking her doughnut then sucking it off like she was giving a tutorial on blow jobs?

I don't even recognize the voice in my head. I'm depressed, agitated, lost, starving, and horny as hell. It's been over three years since I've had sex. *Three. Years!* Chance thinks I need to get laid, but I've never been the guy who easily indulges in one night stands. However, a relationship is not an option, so I guess I'll keep my Playboy subscription and hand lotion to save the poor women of Boston from falling prey to my selfish needs and lack of ability to ever commit again.

The scotch is numbing, infiltrating my blood with the ease of molasses. In moments like this I feel outside of my body, a stranger observing the mere shell of the man he used to be. I miss that Oliver Konrad. He was full of life, confident, kind, aspiring, and driven. But mostly he was connected, rooted in this world and thriving in his environment, taking all life had to give.

Lost. I'm lost in this moment. I'm lost in every moment, floundering around as one day blurs into the next. I won't look back, but I can't see forward. Stuck—that's it—I'm stuck. Am I waiting to be rescued? Will I dig my own way out and move forward? Or, will I perish in this dark hole?

I HAVEN'T MISSED many sunrises in my adult life. It's my favorite time of the day. It used to be symbolic of living to see another day, but now it's the reminder I need that time isn't standing still. For a brief moment I actually feel the earth moving beneath my feet, inching me away from my past.

Several months ago I agreed to move back home under

one condition—my family would never mention my time in Portland. It's asking a lot of my mom, who is a psychiatrist, to pretend her son is not fucked-up in the head, almost to the point of insanity. My dad, however, is a cardiologist and he openly admits the only matters of the heart he cares to deal with are the ones behind the closed doors of a sterile OR.

"Are we still on for dinner, sweetie? Your brother is bringing a 'friend' so feel free to do the same. Love you!"

I delete the voice message off my phone with a deep sigh. My family is the best, really. Growing up in Boston our house was the gathering point for all our friends, and when it wasn't overrun with kids, my parents hosted dinner parties and wine tastings. Now the once *Leave it to Beaver* house is haunted by the ghosts of my past and the only thing more awkward than the impersonal and random dinner conversation is the blinding pain in their eyes. It says so much more than words ever could.

Me: *I'll be there, no plus one for me. Love you.*

I send off a quick text and head to Harvard Square. Leaning against a concrete post in the underground transportation dungeon, I see the doughnut queen come down the stairs. Curious eyes find me as she masks her smile behind the lid of her coffee cup. It should be illegal for someone with legs that long to wear shorts that short. I wait for her to make her usual navigation in my direction, but instead she stares at the MBTA map like she hasn't seen it a million times before.

Worming my way through the growing crowd, I stand behind her without saying anything.

"Hey, neighbor," she says, and I think I can hear the grin on her face.

"No doughnut today?"

She turns, both hands cupping her coffee inches from her mouth. "I already ate it. Thought it was in all the other commuters' best interest."

I grin and nod. I'm sure I won't be the only guy disappointed that the 7:30 a.m. doughnut porn show has been cancelled.

We board the subway and stand facing each other again. I look at her coffee with a single raised brow, then at her eyes.

"No worries." She smiles, securing a firm grip on her hot drink as the train jerks to a start.

"I wasn't thinking anything." I chuckle.

"You were thinking I was going to owe you another new shirt. Your eyes say it all. It must be a Konrad family trait because your brother's eyes don't lie."

"Well, you're wrong. I was actually wondering what you eat when you're not sucking down caffeine and sugar."

"If that's your sneaky way of asking me to dinner, then I'll stop you right now."

Glancing over her head I shake mine, rolling my eyes. "I'm not asking you to dinner or looking for a date. I was just making conversation."

"Good, because I don't date."

I shrug. "Neither do I."

"Good."

"Good."

"Fine."

"Fine," I say back as we approach my stop. "Well, see you around."

She nods.

"Indian!" I hear her call as I maneuver my way to the doors.

I glance back.

She lifts her shoulders with a goofy grin beaming across her face. "Since you wondered ... I like Indian food."

"Me too." I match her grin and jump off as the doors start to shut.

CHAPTER THREE
A NUN'S LIFE

Vivian

3 Years Earlier

"WE DON'T HAVE TO," *Kai reassures me.*

"I know. Don't you want to?"

"Yeah, of course I do ... I just, you know ... I don't want to hurt you."

I slip off my sundress and wait for him to make the next move. His eyes explore my body and I feel it. Desire. I didn't know if I would feel it, if I even could, but Kai wants me and when he pushes down his shorts exposing his tented briefs, my hopes are confirmed.

"Are you sure your parents won't be home until later?" he whispers as if there's someone else in the house.

"I'm sure. Besides, I'll be nineteen in another month. What could they possibly do to me?"

Kai nods, shrugging off his shirt. He's the epitome of tall, dark, and handsome with his olive skin, dark brown hair, hazel eyes, and muscles defined from relentless laps in the pool. I can't believe the boy I've known since kindergarten, the one who used to call me skeleton girl because my early growth spurt made it nearly impossible to keep an ounce of fat on my body, stands before me ready to take my virginity.

It's taken twelve years for our friendship to blossom into something beautiful. There have been a spectrum of emotions and drama between us. But after years of choosing every girl except me, it's finally my turn. Kai wants to be with me, not as a friend, but a lover. I push back the thoughts of his jealousy. Whether I need it or not, I don't want to be reminded that he chose me after I showed interest in someone else. A little competition is good. It's what he needed to see, the only girl for him has been by his side all along.

My legs shake as I step closer to him. I rest my hands on his bare chest, and he weaves his fingers through my hair. Our lips connect and a silent chill ripples through me as my skin tightens, erupting with goose bumps. We've been intimate in every way except having sex. My hand makes the familiar journey along his stomach, slipping under his briefs. He moans into my mouth as I stroke him. I love how firm he gets for me.

Kai moves his hands to my shoulders, gently pushing me down. Freeing him from his briefs, I take him in my mouth like I've done so many times before. His head falls back as he sucks in a tight breath. We've done this, and as much as I like pleasing him, I want more. I want to feel him inside of me. I want him to take what I've saved just for him.

"Kai?" I release him with my mouth but continue to stroke him with my hand.

"Don't stop, baby."

"Kai, I want more." I stand, reaching behind to unclasp my bra. As it falls to the floor, I watch his eyes. "Touch me."

Kai's never given me an orgasm. I want that to change tonight. Maybe if there are no boundaries, he'll take his time with me. Our intimacy usually ends as soon as he's had his release. Maybe the feeling of him penetrating me will allow me to let go of my own pleasure.

"Please, Kai, touch me."

He's still. I slide down my panties, step out of them, and take his hand. As I turn to lead him to my bed, I hear his breath catch in his throat and his grip on my hand tightens. I shouldn't look back, because I know what I'll see and it will crush me.

My body deceives me. Turning my head, I see it. Pity.

"Kai?"

"Viv..." he shakes his head "...I'm so sorry. Does it hurt?"

Yanking my hand from his, I sigh. "No, it doesn't hurt! What hurts is the look in your eyes. Jeez, Kai, you've touched it before!"

"I know, it's just ... this is the first time I've ... seen all of it. I didn't think it'd look so ..."

"So what? So gross? So disgusting? So deformed? What, Kai? Tell me!"

Tears swell in his eyes.

"Don't you dare. Don't you dare cry!"

"I'm sorry, Viv. Maybe we should wait—"

"No." I pull my hair over my shoulder so he has an unobstructed view of my back. "Take a good long look because this is the last time you'll see it. The last time I'm going to put up with that pathetic pity in your eyes."

"Viv, don't."

I grab my dress and slip it back on.

"What are you doing?" he asks.

"I'm taking my virginity and what's left of my pride as

*far away from you as possible. Hell, I'm taking my freakin'
virginity to my grave someday!"*

"Vivian!"

*"Take your sorry ass someplace else. I'm not going to be
part of your pity party. Not now, not ever! I can't change
what happened and neither can you. Your incessant apologies have been eating me alive, but that look ... you gutted me
with that ONE! Single. Look."*

Present Day

"KATE'S LEAVING for Italy with her parents in the morning.
I'm yours for a month." Kai swaggers in the house and
plunks himself down on the couch.

"It's laughable that you think I want to hang out with
your boring ass for the next month. And come on in, by the
way, have a seat, make yourself at home."

He laughs while propping his feet up on the coffee
table. "Thanks, I think I will. Why don't you grab me a
beer?"

"Get it yourself, bitch." I smack his feet off the table.
"It's been a long day. I just want to fall into bed not babysit
you. What are all your frat boys doing tonight?"

"Vacationing or getting laid."

"Who's vacationing or getting laid?" Alex asks, tossing
her bag by the door.

"Apparently, everyone but Kai." I give him a gleam of
devilry.

"And Viv." He smirks back.

Harnessing all the maturity I can find, I stick my tongue
out at him. "Who put you in charge of my hymen? Maybe

I've already gotten laid. It's not like I'd send out a text or anything."

Kai rolls his eyes.

"Flower, is there something you're not telling me?" Alex raises a single brow.

"No, there's nothing she's keeping from you. Trust me, if there were, she sure as shit wouldn't let you call her that damn nickname!"

I walk toward the front door, smacking Kai on the back of the head. "Don't be so sure."

"Hey, where are you going?" Kai jumps up ready to follow me like the lost puppy he'll be for the next month.

"I need tampons, but I'd love the company."

He collapses back down on the couch with a dragged-his-blanket-in-the-dirt look. "I think I'll stay with Alex."

"I'm just grabbing some clean clothes and heading back to Sean's. Sorry, Kai Pie." Alex sticks out her pouty lower lip as she passes him to go upstairs.

Kai grabs his bag and follows me out the door. "You know the only name I hate more than Flower is Kai Pie. Pencil me in for dinner tomorrow."

I waltz off in the opposite direction. "Sorry, I'm busy."

"See you at seven," he yells.

I amble around the block and head back inside. The tampons were a decoy. I needed to ditch Kai for the night. As much as I love my best friend, he's still selfish and needy, especially when Kate is gone. I'm not ruling out dinner tomorrow, but tonight I don't have the energy or patience to deal with my clingy friend.

"For someone who's known you for nearly sixteen years, I find it ironic that he doesn't know you stock tampons like survivors of the depression stock food." Alex laughs, grabbing a bottle of wine out of the fridge.

I lean against the kitchen island. "I'm a terrible friend aren't I?"

Alex hugs me. "Not to me, Flower."

"I'm hungry and tired."

"Then eat and sleep. I'll see you Sunday." Alex snatches her bag and gives me a wink.

My hunger can wait. Pulling my canvas bag out of the entry closet, I head out front and sit on the steps. This isn't my usual location, but now I have this desire to people watch. Okay, maybe *person* watch. Pulling out my ball of yarn and needles, I resume my recent knitting project: mittens. I took up knitting after I declared to keep my virginity indefinitely. It's not sexy, but it keeps me focused, and I like the euphoria I get from completing a project. My family and friends are usually the lucky recipients of my crafty work. My dad said he felt like an eighty-year-old man when I gave him a blanket for Christmas, but I know he uses it to keep warm while he lounges in his leather recliner watching his Giants play.

Minutes morph into hours and it's nearly too dark to see what I'm doing. I'm sure I've dropped more than one stitch. Just as a twinge of disappointment hits me, I see Oliver. He's getting out of a black BMW in front of his condo. Yes, I've been waiting hoping to catch a glimpse of him, but now that he's here I feel ridiculous. As he looks in my direction, I drop my head back to my project.

A rapturous buzz seizes my nerves as he nears.

"I'm not sure what's most odd about this situation."

I glance up with owl eyes as if I'm really surprised to see him. "Excuse me?"

He sits down beside me as I shove my yarn back into the bag. His clean pine and sandalwood scent wafts near my nose, and in spite of the cool breeze that's crept in over the past hour, my skin flushes with heat from his close proximity.

"I wouldn't have taken you for a knitter."

I shrug. "A lot of younger women knit these days. It's therapeutic, like meditation."

"You always knit in the dark?" He edges closer, giving me a toothy smile that pulls in those damn dimples.

"Well, um ... Most of it's by feel and it hasn't been dark that long. I was just getting ready to go inside." My stomach growls in angry protest; it's a beastly noise. I squirm while my crimson face prunes.

"Whoa!" He laughs.

Hugging my arms around my stomach, I try to physically strangle it into silent submission. "I'm a little hungry. I sort of skipped dinner." It's possible my decision to skip dinner in favor of the late neighborhood watch shift was a teensy bit rash.

"Come on." He stands and gestures toward his condo with his head. "I just had dinner at my parent's house and my mom sent me home with way too many leftovers. You like Tilapia, new potatoes, and asparagus?"

A wary smile escapes. "Yes, but—"

"It's not a date, Vivian. It's leftovers. Nothing I haven't done for stray animals."

Standing tall, I cock my head to the side. "Are you implying I'm a stray animal?"

He shakes his head and offers his hand. "Come on, stop reading into everything I say."

Staring at his hand for a brief moment, I place mine in it and let him guide me across the street. I'm trying hard not to *read into* the myriad of physical sensations that his touch evokes. My pulse pounds, heart gallops, and butterflies awaken in my stomach as the warmth from his hand sends a tingling sensation up my arm. Rarely do I not feel tall and lanky, like I want to slouch down to keep from standing out in a crowd, but right now I feel petite and feminine in his lofty presence. He grabs a brown bag out of the back of his car before we head inside.

"Would you like a glass of wine?" he asks while spooning out food onto a plate.

I smack my lips together. "No, I'd better not. I'm kind of a lightweight and there's the long trip home and all ..."

I love the sound of Oliver's laugh; it's genuine and spontaneous, like he's trying to hold it back but can't. "Water, then?"

"Yes, thank you."

He sets my plate on the woven gun metal gray placemat and pulls out a chair for me.

"This is weird eating by myself. Are you just going to watch me?" My lips set into a grim line.

"Nope."

I hear the bag rustling, then he sits down across from me with a square glass container and a spoon.

"What's that?" I ask after swallowing a bite of the best fish I have ever tasted.

"Strawberry-rhubarb cobbler. I was full after dinner so I took my dessert to go."

"Mmm, looks good."

"It is. My mom is an amazing cook," he mumbles behind a napkin while wiping his mouth.

"I'll second that." I gesture to the plate with my fork. "This is the best Tilapia I have ever had."

We eat in comfortable silence for a few minutes, both of us enjoying the culinary orgasms in our mouths. I sneak nervous glances at him while he spoons bite after bite of the cobbler into his mouth, releasing a few humming sounds.

Finishing the last bite on my plate, I give him my best puppy dog eyes as I notice there are only a few bites left of the cobbler.

He grins. "Looks like you enjoyed it."

"Yes, it was very good."

He nods. "God, this cobbler is amazing. It's still warm, too."

"It must be good, you're really hogging it down." My comment comes out a little harsher than I intend.

He scoops up the last big bite and lets it hang in the air a few inches from his mouth.

My eyes tighten as I glare at him.

"Oh ... did you want to try a bite?" he asks with a devilish smirk.

"No, that's fine. It's yours not mine." I scoot my plate to the side and rest my elbows on the table.

He shrugs. "Okay, then."

Never before have my eyes felt so close to popping out of their sockets. My mouth falls open as I gasp. "Oh my God! I can't believe you ate the last bite!"

Oliver's brow tenses as he inches the spoon out of his mouth wiping it clean with the tight seal of his lips. "What? I just asked you if—"

"I may have said no with my mouth, but my eyes were begging you for just one bite! Jeez, you can't go on and on about how good it is and make those ridiculous sounds and not think that maybe I might want one little taste!"

His laughter cracks through the air and I fight my impending grin.

"Here." He shoves the container in my direction. "You can lick the bowl."

I roll my eyes. "Like I'm really gonna lick the bowl."

"Suit yourself."

He reaches for the bowl, but I snag it and pull it closer to me, wasting no time swiping my finger inside and sucking it off with my own heavenly moan.

"My God! You sure are a handful, woman." He scoots back in his chair with his arms crossed over his chest watching me clean the bowl like a starved animal.

I flip the switch as if I didn't bite his head off two seconds ago. "So can you cook?"

His gaze stays on my mouth and he looks like he's starving too, but not for food. It's the same look he had at the doughnut shop. I'm not sure why he gets so captivated watching me eat. *Weird*.

He clears his throat and takes a deep swallow. "Yes, I can cook. My mom made sure both Chance and I could cook, do laundry, and sew on a button."

"Wow, had I known all this time what a great catch your brother is, I might not have shot him down so many times."

"Says the girl who doesn't date."

"Says the guy who doesn't date."

"Touché, Vivian."

"So do you have dinner with your parents often?"

He nods. "Once a week since I moved back from Portland."

I tap my fingernail on the table. "Maine?"

"Oregon."

"Oh, how long did you live there?"

He purses his lips to the side. "Three years."

"Why'd you move there?"

He clears his throat, diverting his gaze while adjusting his sitting position. "I took a job with a law firm there."

Digging my teeth into the corner of my bottom lip, I wait for his eyes to meet mine. "I'm being nosy, I apologize."

Oliver stands and grabs our dishes, clinking them

together with wavering control. I sense it's time for me to leave so I stand and follow him to the kitchen.

"Well, thanks for dinner. I feel like a mooch. Tell your mother it was wonderful ... or not. It's possible you might not want her to know you fed her leftovers to *stray* neighbors."

His back is to me, hands pressed against the counter and head bowed. The air feels thick, almost suffocating. This isn't how I saw the night ending.

"Okay ... so I'll just—"

"Stay."

I'm not sure I heard him, so I wait for confirmation. My inner voice chastises me for not acknowledging the absurdity of this situation. I'm drawn to this man and I can't give him what other women can, but every look, touch, and soft laugh makes it difficult to not want him. Maybe, just maybe he could be what I need—a relationship based on emotions without the need for physical gratification.

Oliver

MY MIND SAID "GO" but my mouth said "stay." Vivian has this innocence to her that is not of this world, and when I'm with her neither am I. We're transported to some alternate universe where the past doesn't exist and the future doesn't matter. I need her to leave because I don't trust myself around her. The hunger I feel for her touch is painful. When she placed her hand in mine I had to fight every urge to throw her in the backseat of my car, strip off her clothes, and taste every inch of her body. It's possible I should be on meds or maybe I do need therapy. I wasn't like this before.

It's just her, but I don't know why. Yes, she's beautiful—stunning actually—but it's more and I don't have a word for the *more*.

Maybe, just maybe she could be what I need—a physical release without the emotional investment.

I face her, allowing my eyes to drink in her soft features: silky skin, full lips, emerald eyes, and black hair that flows in endless waves down her back and over her breasts. The image of those perky breasts peeking through the thick black layers as she sits naked astride me stirs my dick. If her eyes drift a few degrees south, she'll know how I react to her. I should care and try to hide it, but I don't.

"Stay. Have some wine or more water, just ... stay."

"Wine, but only if you promise to carry me home when I pass out after two sips." She brushes her hair back and wets her lips with a nervous graze of her teeth over the top one.

I've become my brother, imagining everything she does and says is an invitation into her pants. I'm the "nice" guy; the kiss goodnight on the cheek, opening doors, lavishing with flowers and jewelry, waiting until the third date to kiss on the lips and a month before copping a feel. The old Oliver would insist that sex is at least six weeks out, but my dick hasn't gotten the memo. This new, completely lost Oliver is ready to tie her up and spank her ... I'm not sure why people even do that, but I think modern women like it, so sure, I'd give it a try.

"So wine it is." I grin while grabbing two glasses from the cabinet. "Do you live alone?"

Vivian laughs. "Why? Are you planning on stalking me and sexually assaulting me?"

Okay, so I think I'll hold off on the spanking. I probably wouldn't do it right anyway. "A little paranoid?"

"My roommate, Alex, her parents own the condo. They're rich, I guess. Anyway, her boyfriend and my friend Kai are good friends so they introduced us when I needed to move to Cambridge. Alex is rarely there, so she was thrilled to have a roommate to look after things and one who needed a job. Maggie, her aunt, owns The Green Pot and needed some help running the nursery since she's been battling cancer off and on for years. Alex's parents agreed to keep the condo instead of having her move into student housing with the agreement that she'd work part-time for Maggie. So I get a job and cheap rent, and Alex helps out occasionally at the nursery, but mostly she makes her spending money off my rent payments. It's a win-win."

I hand her a glass of wine and motion to the couch. "Alex's parents are okay with this arrangement?"

She sips her wine. "They don't know. I make myself scarce when they come to visit."

"And you're okay with deceiving people you don't even know?"

She waves her hand in the air dismissively as she swallows. "I know them. I come to 'visit' every time they're in town. They love me, of course, because I'm such a good influence on Alex."

"So why not just tell them the truth?"

Vivian tucks her legs underneath her. "They want Alex to stay busy with school and work so she doesn't get distracted by guys."

I shake my head. "It's quite the con you two have going."

"You don't know half of it." She takes another sip of her wine, and another, and another.

I anticipate having her naked within the hour. Reaching over, I fill her glass back up before it's even halfway down.

God! What the hell is wrong with my brain?

"So why did you *need* to move to Cambridge?" I ask.

She giggles and I adjust myself because I'm already imagining her glazed over eyes calling to me. "My parents think I'm getting my business degree from Harvard." She giggles some more.

My dick has officially taken a backseat to this conversation. As much as I want to avoid too much personal detail, her comment has my naturally curious mind turning its cogs. "Why do they think that?"

"Because I got accepted."

There's no way I could have seen this coming. Vivian doesn't just surprise me, she knocks me on my ass leaving me speechless with everything she says and does. "To Harvard?"

"Yes, Oliver, to Harvard. Don't look so surprised."

I set my drink on the coffee table and adjust my body to face her. "Let me get this straight. You were accepted to Harvard. Your parents think you're attending Harvard. You moved to Cambridge so they would believe you're going to Harvard, but you're not going to Harvard?"

She massages her temples with her thumb and middle finger then drags her fingers across her forehead "Yep, I've had way too much to drink." She laughs. "So I'm not sure I caught all of your questions or statements or whatever, but ... yes, yes, yes ... and yes." Full lips curl into a large and oh-so-proud smile like she just aced some big test.

"I don't understand."

"Oh, Oli-ver, you don't have to understand everything." She leans her head back and closes her eyes. "I need to pee."

"The bathroom is upstairs, first door on the right."

She doesn't move.

"Do I need to carry you upstairs?"

She opens her eyes and grins, swinging her feet to the floor. "Nope, I just wanted to see if you'd offer. After the cobbler hoarding incident I wondered if you were much of a gentleman."

She stands with a slight sway. I grab her waist and bright eyes sparkle with hidden wonder as she fixes them on mine, pressing the palm of her hand to my cheek. Every indecent thought I had about her vanishes leaving a murky residue on my conscience.

"You're alarmingly handsome. Do you know that?" she whispers, feathering her thumb along my lips.

I close my eyes willing myself to hold still, to resist the urge to cup her hand, taste her thumb, pull her closer—so close there's no space for the rest of the world between us.

She's gone, but my breath remains hostage in my chest. Opening my eyes, I release it. Okay, maybe I need something more than her body.

CHAPTER FOUR
BLURRED

Vivian

THE STAIRS PROVE to be more challenging than I expected. I'm not sure how much I've had to drink. Not much, at least I don't think so. Oliver kept refilling my glass before I ever finished the previous refill. *First door on the left.* I ram into the solid wood door as I make a clumsy attempt to turn the knob and push it open. It's locked, as in *seriously* locked. It seems a bit odd to have a bathroom door with a dead bolt. I look right. *Ah ha!* Yeah, he might have said right not left.

A tingling numbness prickles my skin, including my ass, as I sit on the toilet. I like Oliver. He's so handsome, especially tonight with that copper-blond hair doing its own thing and a day's worth of sexy stubble along his strong jaw. I had to touch it and those lips ... so kissable. For a moment I forgot that our relationship can't go there. Alcohol does that to me. I should just show him what lies beneath and get it over with, but the problem is I like the way he looks at me. Giving myself to the possibility of someone looking at me, all of me, with nothing but desire is the most amazing feeling until I'm stolen from the moment back to reality—my reality. If Kai, my best friend and the person who loves me unconditionally, can't see past it, then no man ever will.

Exiting the bathroom I stop and study the door across the hall. It's not like all the other doors and something about it is *off*.

"Everything okay?" I startle at the sound of his voice. He's halfway up the stairs.

"Uh, yeah, I'm just ... out of it."

He waits for me then follows behind.

"I should go." I focus on each step to mask my jelly-like legs.

Oliver hands me my knitting bag. "I'll walk you home."

"It's just across the street."

"Yes, but you've had more than your limit of alcohol and that's my fault, so now I'm obligated to make sure you make it home without incident."

I step past the threshold forgetting that there is about a three inch drop to the stoop, just enough to make me look tipsier than I already do.

"Watch it. See, the trip across the street could prove to be more difficult than you think." He laughs, grabbing my hand, this time interlacing our fingers. I wish it were a longer walk, but it's not and I have to release his hand to get my key.

He waits for me to unlock my door. "Goodnight, my lightweight neighbor." He smiles while brushing my hair behind my ear on one side.

I want his kiss right now more than doughnuts, coffee, or his mom's incredible cobbler. My mouth works on its own accord. I wrap my hand around his wrist lingering behind my ear. Pulling it toward my cheek I whisper, "You could kiss me. Just tonight ... just once."

He smiles and mimicking my moves from earlier, brushing his thumb along my lips and shaking his head. "No, I don't think I can kiss you, just *tonight*, just *once...*" his touch fades as he steps back "...sweet dreams."

My gaze clings to the subtle curves of his tall frame as he drifts across the street with long, smooth strides. Okay, maybe I need something more than an emotional connection.

THE GREEN POT's bustling crowd has infiltrated every inch of the greenhouse. Alex is MIA with Sean, but Kai is here and today I'm genuinely glad to see him. Maggie and I would be buried otherwise.

"Good morning, old knitting neighbor lady." I grip the flat of asters tighter, knowing that smooth voice makes me weak in the knees and everywhere else.

"Hey!" I turn, greeted with Oliver in his rugged work attire, Red Sox hat on backwards, and another day's worth of facial hair growth. I continue walking to the front counter as he follows me. "Did Chance call in an order because I don't recall seeing it?"

"No, we're just about finished with the hotel's garden, but we need another dozen red chard and six Italian parsley."

I deposit the asters in the customer's cart and ring her up while Oliver stands behind me.

"Sir, you need to wait in line," Kai says.

"I'm waiting for Vivian," Oliver replies.

"He needs a half dozen Italian parsley and a dozen red chard," I say while swiping the customer's credit card through the machine.

"Well, *Vivian* is busy so I'll grab them, but you still need to go to the back of the line, sir." Kai's losing his politeness and I recognize the possessiveness in his voice as he says my name.

I sigh with a scowl. "I'll get them. Take over the register."

Kai huffs but bites his tongue while the corners of Oliver's mouth pull up into a sly smile.

"Don't act so cocky, everyone in that *long* line is shooting daggers at you." I worm my way to the back.

"Yeah, well just think of this as returning the favor."

"Excuse me? For what? Getting me drunk?" My voice elevates an octave.

"For sharing my mom's cobbler."

I stop and turn so fast Oliver nearly bowls me over with his forward motion. "You did not share! You took the last bite and made me lick the bowl like a dog!" I feel numerous sets of eyes on us and hear a few snickers in the background.

Oliver surveys our audience with a hesitant grin. "I didn't *make* you lick the bowl."

I turn and push through the backdoor to where the vegetable and herb seedlings are kept. "I only have ten red chard, but I do have six parsley." After arranging them in the cardboard flat, I shove them into Oliver's chest. "I'll add these to Chance's tab and now you owe me a favor."

He chuckles. "What's that?"

I shrug. "I'm not sure yet, but I'll let you know."

He wets his lips and explores my face with those intense blue eyes. "I wanted to kiss you."

My nose wrinkles. "You did?"

He nods.

The calm façade on the outside masks the exuberant

celebration going on inside my body. "Well that moment has passed and you can't get it back."

Oliver cocks his head to the side. "I can't get it back?"

"Nope, it's like the cobbler ... gone forever. But I might let you lick my hand or brush my hair sometime, you know, as a consolation prize."

He raises his brows and I wish I could read his mind, but he's mastered the arcane expression.

"As much as I'd love to decipher what that look means, I have to get back to work."

Oliver gives me a lopsided grin. "Later, neighbor."

***

"So who's the guy getting preferential treatment?" Kai asks as we piece together what's left of the greenhouse after the tornado of people that tore through here today.

I sweep a pile of leaves and dirt into the dustpan that he's holding. "Chance's brother."

"Oh jeez, another Konrad to fight off." Kai shakes his head.

Unsure how to respond, I shrug my shoulders. I don't want to fight off Oliver. Attack him? Yes. That's the problem. I'm so intrigued by him I can't see straight. My vision and my mind are blurred.

"Oliver is not Chance."

"How do you know?" Kai stands dusting off the front of his shirt.

"Well, he hasn't asked me out or tried to feel me up behind the compost pile."

"Yet," Kai deadpans.

"Yeah, well maybe I want him to."

He empties the dustpan in the garbage and turns, resting one fist on his hip. "What's that supposed to mean."

It pisses me off that Kai acts like it's absurd that I might be interested in Oliver. "It means exactly what you think it means."

He shakes his head. "He doesn't deserve you."

"You don't even know him!" I cross my arms over my chest, toe-tapping a staccato.

"Is everything okay?" Maggie flips her pin-straight platinum blond hair away from her face while digging her keys out of her purse.

"Everything's fine," I mumble.

"We'll I'm pooped so I'll see you Monday." She pushes her studious, red-framed glasses up on her nose. I see that loving twinkle in her baby blue eyes as she leans in to give me a quick hug then shakes her finger at Kai. "Be nice."

"Mags, I'm always nice." Kai winks at her as if his boyish charm is going to work on someone who is older than his mom.

The crazy part is Maggie blushes every time Kai flashes his flawless smile. She's never been married. Maybe she's a closet cougar. I'd say she looks good for fifty, but truthfully she looks good for any age. She's completely changed her lifestyle since her first cancer diagnosis by eating a plant-based diet and exercising every day. She's thin and petite, the top of her head barely reaching my chest. Basically she's Alex thirty years from now except Alex has larger breasts and her long blond hair falls to her butt.

"You're unbelievable." I roll my eyes at Kai as Maggie walks to her white Prius.

"Unbelievably charming? Unbelievably handsome?"

"Unbelievably arrogant." I give him a playful shove.

"So where are you taking me to dinner?" Kai drapes his

arm around my shoulders as I lock up the back door. For some reason, maybe self-preservation, my mind erased the promise of dinner I made to Kai this morning when he agreed to help out Maggie and me.

"Since you drove today, I was thinking a quick trip through McDonalds, my treat of course."

Kai, showing off his manners, opens the passenger door to his grey Honda Pilot. "Superb idea! That will save us plenty of time to find some good porn on Netflix to watch while you give me a hand job on the couch. After all, I think that's the best friend's responsibility when the significant other is out of the country."

Before I can respond he shuts my door and swaggers around to the driver's side.

"You're right, I'll call Sean and see if he can fit you into his hand job schedule tonight. I have to believe that he knows how to stroke a dick better than I do. I'm sure Alex could please me better than you."

"God, Viv! Talk as much as you want about you and Alex pleasing each other ... I dig that shit, but if you ever mention Sean and my dick in the same sentence again, I will seriously lose my lunch in your face. Yuck!"

"So Casa Romero, you watch porn at your place and no hand job it is." I laugh as Kai pulls out of the parking lot.

THERE's nothing typical about my relationship with Kai. I hate him almost as much as I love him. The decision to never be more than friends again was mine and I haven't regretted it once. However, I still get a pang of jealousy when I see him with Kate. The lucid part of my brain knows it's what they have, not who they have. Kai is my comfort. He's familiar and as much as we joke around, I never feel the need to impress him. I know he would have chosen me, stayed with me, and eventually we may have been able to forget and love each other the way every human deserves to be loved.

Lately there has been a shift. The face I once couldn't wait to see is the same one I now avoid, for instance, fake tampon runs. Kai looks at me with glasses from the past. He assumes he knows me better than anyone so if I try to take a new path, he's the first one to remind me that I'll most likely get lost. Kai is the mother that yells to her daughter as she heads out the door for her first date, "Don't forget your acne medication, sweetie, don't want you waking up with hamburger face in the morning." There's nothing worse than trying to make a good first impression when someone who knows your darkest secrets and biggest fears is standing behind you with a megaphone.

"What are you doing tomorrow?" Kai asks, pulling up in front of my condo.

"Washing my hair." I open the door and he clutches my arm.

"What's been up with you lately?"

I deflate a little with regret. "Nothing, I'm just ..."

"PMSing?"

I laugh because Kai may be a brilliant student and he'll probably be an equally brilliant doctor someday, but when it comes to reading women who don't want sex from him, he has the skills of a toddler.

"Yeah, sure, I'm probably just *PMSing*."

"Well, take some Advil and eat some chocolate or something. I'll call you tomorrow." He smiles, once again oblivious to what's really happening in my life.

"Bye, Kai Pie."

"Stop calling me—"

I slam the door and grin at his huffy scowl. He pulls away from the curb allowing my gaze to lift to the set of steps across the street. I glance both ways then walk toward my insanely handsome neighbor.

"You're a ball of yarn and a set of knitting needles away from looking like a complete dork sitting out here with only a few minutes left of daylight on a Saturday evening."

Oliver takes his time allowing his eyes to explore me while brushing his index finger over his bottom lip. "I can't say that I've ever been called a dork before."

"Not to your face anyway." I giggle.

His eyes find mine and he shakes his head, relinquishing a slight grin. "Come in for some wine." He holds out his hand.

"Thanks, but no thanks." I gesture to my clothes. I'm a mess from today, in desperate need of a shower, and it's a little creepy that you're so quick to try and get me tipsy."

"So invite me over and take a shower while *I* get a little *tipsy.*"

Gathering my hair in my hands, I pull it off my neck, feeling sweaty on this balmy evening. "You really think that's a good idea?"

Oliver scrubs his hands over his face. "Probably not, but I'm all out of good ideas tonight."

Releasing a deep breath, I offer him my hand. "You're more dangerous than your brother."

He takes my hand and stands. "Why do you say that?"

"Because it's easy to say no to him."

I'm in the shower, naked, and Oliver's downstairs. I'm in the shower naked, and Oliver's downstairs.

My mind reels. I'm alone in the shower having the most erotic moment of my life. Desire blossoms and just his proximity downstairs heightens all my senses. It's *his* hands massaging shampoo into my hair, sliding down my neck and over my breasts, teasing my erect nipples. Closing my eyes I feel *his* fingers dip between my legs, parting me and teasing me.

"Oh God!" I moan, resting my other hand on the shower wall while my fingers, *his fingers*, pulse over my most sensitive area.

Knock, knock, knock!

"I'm going to run home and grab my phone, be right back." Oliver's voice drenches me in cold water.

"O-okay." The frog in my throat croaks.

I skip the orgasm—wouldn't be the first time that opportunity has gone down the drain. After drying off, I pick out a pair of light pink lace panties and a matching bra. Not to look sexy—that would be a lost cause—just to feel sexy. There really is something to be said for feeling sexy. I know it changes my whole persona. One day I wore a long sundress without any underwear and Alex commented on me having an extra bounce in my step.

Lotion, perfume, a little makeup, and a partial drying of my hair expedites my return to Oliver. Turning my back toward the full-length mirror, I glance around to see how much of my ink shows along the straps of my tank top. Not much, just enough to make me look mysterious, sexy, and badass. Okay, that's Alex's quote, but I like how she thinks.

"Looking for a better offer?" I tease, skipping down the stairs seeing Oliver messing with his phone.

"Yes, but it appears you're as good as it's going to get tonight."

"Funny guy, huh?"

"Not usually."

"You tipsy yet?" I grab my purse.

"Not yet. You haven't exactly been the most gracious hostess."

"Let's go then." I open the door and wait.

"Go where?" He stands and hesitates a moment before walking to the door.

"J.P. Licks for mango sherbet."

"You want me to come watching you eat ice cream?"

"What did you just—"

He scratches his stubbly jaw. "Shit, I didn't mean or what I meant was coming ... uh, crap! I just meant we're coming together ... dammit!"

It's quite possible I could wet my pants I'm laughing so hard as he stumbles through his self-induced awkward moment, rubbing his face and tugging at his hair.

"Never mind, let's just go," he mumbles, walking ahead of me.

I wipe the tears from the corners of my eyes. Hurrying to catch up with him, I grab his hand and interlace our fingers. He looks down at our hands and then at me.

"Thought you could use a hand."

"Hilarious," he says, focusing on the sidewalk in front of us.

"I think so."

"First kiss?" I ask.

"Jenna Reed, second grade. You?"

"Milfred Mumford third grade. First heartbreak?"

"Wait just a minute ... your first kiss was with a girl?"

"No, Milfred is definitely not a girl. He ended up being the biggest jock in our graduating class and a total stud on the rugby field."

"Milfred?"

"His mom thought for sure he was a girl and she wanted to name him after his grandmother, Mildred, even after he came out with a surprise penis. His dad liked the name Fred, so after much dispute and a week of him being called Baby Boy Mumford they settled on the name Milfred."

"Well, good God! Didn't he have a middle name to go by instead?"

"Hazel."

"You've got to be kidding me."

I shake my head and giggle, sucking the sherbet off my spoon. Oliver willingly plays my game of firsts as we enjoy our cold treats. I know his first trip to the hospital was for a broken leg from soccer. His first time on an airplane was to Michigan to visit his grandparents when he was six months. First car was a red Camaro. His first time breaking the law was in his Camaro when he had his license revoked for driving over one hundred miles per hour on the interstate just outside of Boston at 2:00 a.m. when he was seventeen.

"First Ivy League college you pretended to attend?" Oliver taps his spoon on his teeth.

"Ah, I've got you on this one. It's driving you crazy not being able to figure out why I'm not in school."

He doesn't respond, just keeps tapping away like a ticking clock.

"Fine." I stab my spoon into the melting scoops. "Shortly after I got accepted my dad lost his job and then we had some unexpected medical expenses that were paid with the money they had managed to save for my college education. My guidance counselor was confident that I would receive a fair amount of scholarship money, but when that fell through I didn't have the heart to tell my parents that I could no longer afford to go to Harvard. It's not that my parents are dumb or anything like that. They just trusted their 4.0 GPA-child, who was planning on getting a degree in business, would have all the financial details figured out and arranged. They also made such a big deal about their baby going to Harvard, to say they were proud is a monumental understatement. So when my best friend Kai got accepted too, we both thought it might be in everyone's best interest for me to appear like I was going to Harvard until I saved up enough money to actually *go* to Harvard ... which has to be this fall."

"You're starting school in the fall?"

"Yep, they gave me a two year deferment which is nearly impossible to get unless you're in the Peace Corp or something like that. However, given the job loss, medical, and financial issues my family encountered, I managed to get two years instead of one."

He purses his lips to the side and the cogs in his head are so loud I'm certain the people across the street can hear them. "Has it ever occurred to you that there might be a special place in hell reserved for you and Alex for the great deception you both have going on with your parents?" Oliver raises a single brow.

"Without a doubt." I laugh. "But if you feel like you've already been to hell and back, then for some reason a return trip in the afterlife doesn't seem like such a big deal. You know what I mean?"

Oliver's face falls somber. "Yes, I think I know what you mean. How long did it take you to get back?" His words are soaked in anguish; they're heavy, sucking the air from the room.

I shrug, leaning back in the chair, still feeling ghostly remnants of my trip to hell. "A little less than two years."

"How'd you know you were back?

I peek up at his tensed face and smile. "One morning I didn't recognize myself in the mirror."

Oliver nods, maybe pondering my statement as a metaphorical one, but it's not. I mean it in the most literal sense.

"So have you always lived in Cambridge?"

He smiles. "Yes. Born and raised. I was the over-achiever, steadfast in my determination to follow in our parents' footsteps to graduate from Harvard and conquer the world. Chance, suffered from ADHD and while his grades were okay, he had no desire to sit in another class-room after he graduated high school. Our parents were disappointed, but they have always been loving and supportive of our decisions and they didn't hesitate to help Chance get up and going with his own business."

"Do you like working with Chance?"

"I like playing in the dirt. Working with Chance..." he grins "...that's yet to be determined."

"Do you miss Portland?"

"No. Shall we go? You still need to get me tipsy then make inappropriate sexual advances at me that we'll both regret in the morning." His eyes light up, maybe too much.

I'm. In. Trouble.

He's sexy, irresistible, and ... *guarded.*

Oliver

Clueless. I have no idea what the hell I'm doing wandering around chasing a young woman who does not need the head case that is Oliver Konrad. There's only one problem: I can't stop. Vivian is so plain she's wildly interesting. I've never seen her pull out a compact or reapply lipstick. People stare at her because she is truly stunning, but she's oblivious to every set of admiring eyes. When she clasps her hand with mine it feels as natural as folding my own together.

I deserve nothing, yet I want her every word, every smile, every laugh ... and tonight I want her every touch.

"Which car is yours?" I ask as we approach her condo.

"I don't have a car. I'm the queen of public transportation. It's better for the environment, sometimes entertaining, but mainly it's cheap." She laughs. "Maybe when I'm CEO of the company that pushes Amazon off the map I will at least purchase an old beater so I can buy more than two bags of groceries at a time."

"Pushing Amazon off the map, huh? That's a mighty ambitious dream."

She releases my hand to unlock her door. "Maybe, but I watched an interview of Jeff Bezos and he admitted that eventually another company would come along that would be better than Amazon because that's just life. Nothing lasts forever and at some point the next best thing will happen." She tosses her keys and purse down as we enter. "So why not me? Why can't I be the next best thing?"

I follow her into the kitchen, trying not to stare at her legs that stretch to infinity.

"Beer or wine?"

"Water's good."

She gapes at me. "Water? Really? How are you

supposed to get tipsy on water? How am I supposed to make *inappropriate sexual advances?*"

"You're dangerous. I think I'd better keep my wits about me," I say with a slow wink.

She laughs. "Yes, because I'm such a sexual predator. If you only knew." Vivian hands me a glass of water and, as usual, she leaves me hanging with her mysterious comment.

A chime sounds. "Have a seat while I find my phone."

She tosses a strange assortment of things out of her purse, such as yarn, a tank top, two Snickers, and a bottle of hot sauce before finding her phone at the bottom.

"What is it, Kai?" She rolls her eyes. "No, Alex has her car ... well, get a cab. I thought you were going home. How stupid are you to go to the bar by yourself?" She turns her back to me, lowering her voice. "No, I'm busy. No, I have company. Not a date, just company. Well, then take the subway and go get your car in the morning, dipshit."

She tosses the phone back in her purse and buries it again with her unusual necessities.

"Sorry, my friend's girlfriend is out of town and I'm pretty sure she took his brain with her."

"Do you need to borrow my car to go get him?"

"Hell, no! Kai is a bloodsucking leach. He takes and takes and loves to be coddled. He won't drive home drunk, he just doesn't want to leave his car overnight, but that's just too damn bad."

"You're a little fiery tonight. Must be all that hot sauce you keep in your purse for *whatever* reason."

She grins and her whole body relaxes as she sits next to me on the couch with her feet tucked under her. "I acciden-tally picked it up at a Mexican restaurant. I've been meaning to return it."

"You can't be serious." I chuckle.

"Totally, it's the difference between borrowing and stealing. I do have morals, you know."

I'm hearing her, as evidenced by the uncontrollable grin on my face, but I also find myself counting the light freckles that dot the bridge of her nose and high cheek bones. If I connect them in the correct order will they uncover the secret of her addictive personality?

"Are you listening to me? Why are you looking at me like that?" She tilts her head to the side.

"Yes, borrowing, stealing, morals. Got it." My hand moves to her face on its own accord. There's an audible catching of her breath as I brush the back of my hand along her cheek. "Not a date, huh?"

She shakes her head. "We don't ... date. Remember?" Each word comes out as a shaky whisper.

I nod. "That's unfortunate because if it were a date, I'd kiss you ... like this." I'm being a selfish prick. At some point over the past few days I've convinced myself that I *need* to taste her mouth. Lust-filled eyes fall to my lips as I lean into her. It's all the permission I need. I brush my lips over hers, moving my other hand up to cradle her face. She melts into me as I tease my tongue over the seam of her lips. She opens for me and all the blood from my brain drains into my dick. I feel the slow throb building at a record pace.

"Mmm ..." She vibrates over my mouth as I consume every inch of hers.

I'm dying to move my hands away from her face, down her neck, and over her breasts ... breasts that I imagine are heavy with firm nipples. Just the feel of her nipples budding out from my touch would cause me to lose it. It's been too long since I've touched a woman and Vivian is not like any other woman.

It's the slow rip off of a Band-Aid as I pull away from

her. She's wide-eyed and breathless. I need to get the hell out of here. The entrance to the danger zone has been breached and the warning sirens pierce my ears.

Her tongue peeks out to brush along her lips like she's savoring the taste of me on her.

"It is unfortunate." She grins and my dick continues to strain against my jeans with no relief in sight as I see naughty intentions dancing in her eyes. "Because if it were a date and you kissed me like *that,* I'd want to crawl up on you ... like this." She sits up on her knees and straddles me with a leg on either side.

Oh fuck!

My hands rest on her hips as she lowers herself onto my lap. Those sexy green eyes shut when the apex of her legs meets the bulge in my pants. Her mouth goes slack as her breaths come short and quick with each prominent rise and fall of her chest. "And then I'd run my hands through your hair ... like this."

Her fingers lace through my hair. "And ... oh God..." she licks her lips and swallows as her eyes shut for a brief moment "...the feel of your *hard* body against mine would make me want more of this." She clenches her fingers in my hair, and with a firm tug she pulls my mouth to hers again.

I'm a caged animal ready to break out and attack her. It takes everything I have to not rip off her clothes and bury myself in her.

Shit! Shit! Shit!

Her hungry tongue strokes mine as she rocks her pelvis with the same subtle motion against my dick. I dig my fingers into her hips as she grinds against me. *What the fuck is she doing to me?* The sensible voice in my head speaks up. It always does, but I don't call it the voice of reason. I call it the voice of ruin because it's ruined so many moments that promised such pleasure.

I pull back. "If it were a date, I'd stay longer but ... since it's not I should—"

"Touch me," she whispers through her labored breathing. "Show me how you'd touch me if this were a date." Her words aren't teasing or seductive; they're a desperate plea. I watch her and through the silence between us I hear her with absolute clarity. My hands move up her sides and slide to her breasts. The thin material of her top does little to hide the equally thin layer of her bra covering erect nipples.

"If this were a date ... I'd touch you like this." My voice breaks on the last word as she rests her hands on my shoulders, eyelids fluttering for control. My untamed needs fade into the background as I knead her breasts, circling my thumbs over her nipples with a slow firm motion.

Mesmerized. That's all I am right now. As Vivian gives in to my touch, her face tenses and her head falls, hair long and flowing down her back. I don't know how, but I'm allowing this to be about her, for her. Even as her hips rock into me over and over, I remain still. Only my hands move with the sole purpose of bringing her pleasure.

"Oliver ... *please* don't stop." The vulnerability in her voice is raw.

Her eyes blink open just as her nails dig into my shoulders. She presses her hips against me one last time, and her eyes roll back into her head. "Oh ... My ... God," she moans in ecstasy.

I swear the image of Vivian coming apart from my touch will forever be etched in my memory.

Her forehead rests against mine and I move my hands to her head as I kiss her just once, long and slow.

"Thank you." She smiles against my lips. "I owe you one."

I chuckle as I lift her off my lap and stand. "No you don't. If it were a date, maybe, but it's not so everything that just happened was ... *hypothetical*."

She stares at the floor with a smile that's still overwhelming her face.

I open the door. "I had a nice time."

"Liar." She looks at me and rolls her eyes. "A nice time shouldn't end in a cold shower."

"I'm not going to take a cold shower." I kiss her cheek and inhale her addictive scent. "Good night, Vivian."

"Good night." She blushes.

I didn't lie. I'm not going to take a cold shower. I'm going to sleep with my balls in a bucket of ice.

CHAPTER FIVE
JEALOUSY

Vivian

I'M NOT certain what the protocol is after what happened last night. Sure, I've been touched by guys before ... Okay, just one until last night, but Kai touched me like it pleased him. Oliver touched me like it pleased me. And Oh. My. God ... did it *ever* please me.

"Hey, Flower, how's the cat toy?" Alex grins as she and Sean stroll in the front door.

I return a snide look. "They're mittens."

"Mittens for the kittens." Alex giggles.

"Something to keep her pussy warm," Sean says in a low voice as he follows Alex into the kitchen.

"I heard that, *Simpleton*."

"Yeah, well, *Simpleton* is going to be graduating from Harvard Business School way before you." Sean sticks his thumbs in his ears and wiggles his fingers around while sticking out his tongue.

"Yeah, well, someday you'll be fetching me coffee when

I'm the only successful CEO willing to offer your pathetic ass a job."

"Play nice, kids." Alex hands Sean a Coke.

"We're just kidding." Sean opens the can and takes a swig while giving me a wink. "I can't wait for Viv to be my boss, those long legs in a mini-skirt suit, cracking a whip at me all day." He takes another swig.

Alex smacks him in the junk and he spits pop out of his mouth. "What the hell?" He bends over a few degrees, holding his crotch.

"Oh sorry, honey. I was swatting a fly and didn't see you. Maybe if I had *longer legs* I could have seen you better."

Sean's not entirely stupid. He's been with Alex long enough to know when to take his punishment like a man and shut the hell up. He sits in the recliner and she hops on his lap facing me like nothing happened.

"So who was your *company* last night?" she asks.

I don't dare take my eyes off my knitting because my face will never hide the truth. "Company?"

"Don't try to buy time by acting dumb. That's a guy's game and you know it."

"Hey, now—" Sean says.

"Zip it, dick brain." She reaches back and fists his junk again.

"God, woman! Stop pulverizing my balls!"

Alex ignores him and I can see out of the corner of my eye that she's smiling at me, waiting, not so patiently.

"How did you know I had company?"

"Kai called Sean last night to pick his drunk ass up from the bar. Now spill."

I shrug not missing a beat in my knitting rhythm. "Our neighbor across the street."

"A guy?"

I nod. I'm pretty sure I've dropped a stitch, but I keep going anyway.

"*Really?*" She drags out the word. "Did I miss out on a block party or something? How'd you meet him?"

"At the greenhouse. He's ... well he's Chance's brother."

"Chance Konrad's brother?" She jumps up. "Out." She tugs at Sean's arm until he stands."

"What?" he questions.

"I said out. I need to talk to Flower in private. I'll call you later."

"But I thought we were going—"

"Something's come up, now out!"

I can't help but laugh as a buck-five Alex shoves all two-hundred and twenty some pounds of rugby player Sean out the front door.

"So you're dating now? That's great!" She jumps on the couch next to me.

"No, not dating."

"Then what was he doing here last night?"

Getting me off.

"After Kai dropped me off I saw him, Oliver, sitting on his front steps so we ended up at J.P's and then back here for a drink. That's all."

"How old is he?"

"I don't know, but I'm pretty sure he's older than Chance."

"He lives alone?"

"Yes, well, I think so."

"Does he have a girlfriend?"

Alex asks some brilliant questions. It's just now occurring to me that these might have been a few of the basic things to ask before requesting that he fondle my breasts until I exploded with my first male-induced orgasm while dry humping his crotch.

"I'm going to say, no."

"So you asked?"

My face wrinkles. "No."

"Then why do you assume *no*?"

"Because we ... kissed."

"Eeeeee!" Alex squeals standing up, bouncing on the couch and clapping her hands like a circus monkey.

Finally, she sits back down. "Did he see your—"

"No."

"But you're going to let him see—"

"No! I mean ..." I shove my knotted-up yarn in my bag. "I don't know, I like him and he looks at me like a child does the first time seeing Disney World. I just want to enjoy it for a little while before I have to face the look that is inevitable."

"You don't know that, and your tattoo is beautiful, Flower. He might not even notice." She strokes the back of my hair like the big sister I never had even though she's only six months older than I am. "So, is he as hot as Chance?" She giggles, lightening the mood.

"Hotter." I beam.

I SHOULD HAVE WALKED over and knocked on Oliver's door yesterday to get the awkward post make-out encounter over with before the start of another work week. Now I'm nervous with equal parts fear and anticipation as I get ready to take the stairs down to the subway where I know he'll be standing looking all sexy in his worn jeans, T-shirt, work boots, and if I'm lucky, a nice five o'clock shadow.

He's so tall it's nearly impossible to miss him, but this morning I don't see him anywhere. Perfect. He's probably chosen a different route just to avoid the pathetic neighbor who begs him to give her an orgasm but does absolutely nothing in return. Why'd I have to be so damn greedy?

The doors snap open and I shuffle onto the subway car grabbing a rail among the morning crowd. I don't have his cell number or know if he'll be by the greenhouse today. The more I replay Saturday night in my head, the thicker the cloud of insecurity becomes.

"I'm thinking of asking my neighbor out on a date. Do you recommend flowers or chocolates?"

The whisper of his voice in my ear steals my breath. I bite my lips together to control the emanate grin that's becoming a tangible emotion smeared across my face.

An uncommon phenomenon occurs: My body boils over with heat at the same time chills trickle down my neck and spine from his breath across my ear.

"Neither, unless you're like fifty years old," I reply and turn.

A lady sitting to the right of where I'm standing, probably in her fifties, grins with a growing blush as she buries her nose in a bouquet of red roses. The guy next to her, dressed in some sort of security uniform, holds a box of chocolates and shrugs when I look at him.

Oliver has a Cheshire cat grin on his face, making a poor attempt at looking casual and innocent.

"Hi," he says.

"Hi." My grin wins over. "So this neighbor of yours, what do you think the chances are of her saying yes?"

He rolls his eyes up to the ceiling and scratches his chin. "Um, I'd say fifty-fifty. She's unpredictable."

The train slows approaching his stop. He leans down

and brushes his lips from the corner of my lips to my ear. "Have a good day," he whispers, leaving me in a puddle on the floor of the subway car.

"I THOUGHT you requested that your VIPs not show up in large groups." I smile over clenched teeth as Maggie exchanges her seventh brown bag special in a row for cash and no receipt.

"You think there's some sting operation set up across the street or something?" She laughs.

"No, I think law enforcement officials landscape around their own homes too, and I don't think they'll wear their uniform just to warn you to stash your grass."

"You do realize, dear, that a few of my VIPs are in law enforcement, right?"

"That's not going to make your case any stronger in court."

She shoos me away with her hand. "Your Handy Hunk will be coming by soon, go check his order."

And just like that, I've forgotten about Maggie's eminent demise. A warm, fluttery giddiness swells in my chest as I skip to the back. Never before have the words Handy Hunk made my heart race. I wonder if Oliver has said anything to Chance. My ability to count plants and check them off the order sheet is nonexistent.

As the truck backs in, I attempt casual: work gloves on, work gloves off; stare at the truck, stare at the sheet; pen behind my ear, pen clipped to the front of my shirt.

"It's official, Monday no longer sucks." Chance leaps into flirt mode in record time, as if he has any other mode.

"Hi, Chance." I smile trying to look at him and not the other door of the truck.

"Well, don't you sound chipper today. Is that happiness to see me I detect in your voice?" He reaches for the pen clipped on my shirt to sign the credit slip.

I squint my eyes, peering at the back window of the truck. I'm surprised Oliver hasn't gotten out yet.

"So ... still working at the hotel?" I feign nonchalance.

"Yep, last day. Oliver will probably have all the holes dug before I get back there. He's working with some extra energy today, wish I could say the same."

Fireworks ignite inside me thinking about Oliver having extra energy because of me.

"I have no doubt it's because of the hot waitress from the hotel's lounge that keeps bringing out cold drinks to him. I offered to stay and do the digging, but he insisted I come get the plants. It's about time he decided to get dirty with something other than actual dirt." Chance chuckles as he starts to load up the back of the truck.

The fireworks fizzle out. I could easily dismiss the waitress comment from Chance, after all, I'm sure he thinks all men are like him, but I can't figure out why Oliver sent Chance to get the plants, knowing I'd be here.

"You make it sound like Oliver's a monk or something."

"Might as well be. I can't share why, but I can say he hasn't had sex in ... years. So naturally he has to be ready to explode and that waitress is definitely the spark that could set him off."

"I didn't need to know that." I try to sound offended by yet another brash comment from Chance, but the truth is I do need to know this. Shit! It hits me how close to losing it Oliver probably is especially after what I did to him, or *didn't* do to him last night.

"Yeah, well don't mention it to him. It's a sensitive subject," he says while loading the last plant.

"Because you know I have a habit of discussing people's sex lives, especially those I've known less than a week." I shake my head trying to not overshoot my why-would-I-bring-it-up-to-Oliver attitude.

"Fair point." Chance smiles. "Stay gorgeous."

I want to be pissed and rant about how all men are the same, but I was the one who had the orgasm the other night. Hell, I asked for it! The pang of disappointment is from cracking the door to let in the possibility that Oliver is different, that his eyes could see me and not my scars.

Oliver

I can't remember the last time I wanted time to fly. That's probably the reason I feel stuck and lost. When I stopped running from my past but hadn't yet looked to my future, time stood still. I've heard that's considered living in the moment, but I think that requires a certain amount of appreciation for that moment. So for me, looking at my watch and anticipating something in my future, even if it's only a few hours into my future, should be considered real progress. Once again, I'm self-diagnosing and self-treating my screwed-up mind. It's money in the bank.

"What the hell has gotten into you today?" Chance asks. "You've been working circles around me and still have energy to burn."

"I always work circles around you." I chuckle.

"Maybe, but not like this. Are you taking something? Should I be worried? Should I be taking it too?"

"I had a good weekend, that's all."

"Good, as in your favorite scotch was on sale or good as in good company?" Chance leans on the handle of his shovel stuck in the ground while I continue to work those circles around him.

"I met one of my neighbors and we went for ice cream."

"A *female* neighbor?"

I laugh. "Yes, I believe *she* is of that gender."

"Well, shit, Oliver, is she hot?"

"How about is she nice, fun, what does she do? Not, is she hot?"

"You're right, how could I be so insensitive. Is she nice looking? Fun in bed? What does she do in bed?"

"I think this conversation has expired and so have I for the day." I toss the tools in the back of the truck and grab my water bottle.

"Okay, fine. Just tell me if I would like her?" Chance removes his gloves and wipes his brow.

"You do realize that doesn't take much. In fact, as I recall, two breasts and a vagina are usually the only *mandatory* requirements. Except if you've had too much to drink, in which case a transvestite with a padded bra can turn your head or *heads* as well."

"Fuck you!" He makes an attempt to look offended, but it's a futile one.

Even Chance can't spoil my giddy mood today, so I go ahead and get in a good laugh. "Sorry, man, I couldn't resist. The answer to your question is yes. Something tells me you would undoubtedly like her."

I'm not trying to hide the truth, but rather I'm trying to protect my fragile and undefined relationship with Vivian for a little bit longer.

"When do I get to meet her?"

We both get in the truck. "I'll *reveal* her if and when the time is right."

"Reveal? What the hell does that mean? Damn, Oliver, is she under age?"

"Yep, you got me. Figured I'd add statutory rape to the Konrad family rap sheet."

Fuck! I can't believe I just said that.

"Oliver—"

"Don't, please, just forget I said that. Okay? Just … don't."

Chance nods and we ride the rest of the way in silence.

WE HAVEN'T EXCHANGED numbers so I can't call her, but since I'm dying to see her, a knock on the door feels perfectly appropriate.

"Just a minute." I hear her muffled voice. "Oh God, what are you doing here?" she calls from the other side of the door. I assume she's looking through the peephole.

"Well, if I were God my answer would be, 'I'm here because I'm everywhere, my dear child,' but since I'm not actually God, then I'm going to go with I'm here to see your lovely face." I smile big in front of the peephole.

"Ugh!" She moans. "Can you just say you're here to see me?"

"O–kay. I'm here to see you."

The door cracks open and I see a curtain of black hair covering her face as she looks down. "See me? Now can you come back next week?"

"Vivian, what's the—" I brush her hair away from her face. I've seen enough in my life that very little shocks me. The downside is my mind has an endless stock of images to use when my brain decides to conjure up a good nightmare. The upside is I have unwavering control over my reactions to certain things, Vivian's face for example. It's bright red, puffy, and raw in several places. It looks like she found a hole in the ozone layer and stood under it too long. However, I know from a few legal cases I helped with in school, that she probably had a chemical peel today.

"I thought we could get some Indian food tonight. We could go out or order in, doesn't matter to me." I find a comfortable neutral with my look.

"Are you blind?"

My brow tenses. "No, I've never even needed glasses."

She points to her face. "This. Is this the *lovely face* you came to see?" The tone to her voice doesn't say anger, it's more incredulity.

"Yes, it is."

She shakes her head. "I don't know what your game is but whatever. Alex will be home soon so we can eat at your place. Apparently you don't see why, but I'd prefer to stay in tonight."

"Whatever you'd like."

CHAPTER SIX
NO TAKE BACKS

Vivian

Growing up with little money makes me a sucker for a good deal. Intending to own my own company someday makes me a stickler for a real deal. LivingSocial has some genuine deals if one does their research. I did mine and found a reputable place to get a chemical peel for half off. Alex has had several over the past few years, but she thought, given my history, it was odd that I wanted to try one. I did and now I'm dealing with the "minor" redness and swelling, and it's because of my history that I am an expert on it and it is, relatively speaking, minor.

Oliver, however, should not see my face as minor. He should have run across the street and locked his door behind him. I look like the villain in some superhero movie. Instead, he didn't so much as flinch when he brushed my hair back. Now after dinner and dessert, we're lounging on his deck which overlooks a vibrant colorful community garden, and he still hasn't mentioned my face. I can't even detect his eyes wandering from mine to inspect the hot spots that will take longer to heal.

"Chance thinks we might get the bid on part of the campus beautification. It would be a great job for us and some hefty sales for The Green Pot as—"

"Enough! I can't do this anymore."

His head jerks back.

"Say something, anything, but stop looking at me like you don't notice my face!"

Oliver's lips slide into an easy smile. He sits up and holds out his hand. I look at it waiting for him to say something, but he doesn't. Sighing, I take it. He pulls me over to him and I straddle his lap like I did the other night.

Brushing my hair back, he finally takes an obvious look at my whole face. "I notice everything about you, but I only see the things that matter."

What. The. Hell?

He has no idea what those words mean to me, there's no way he could. There's also no way I can hold back the tears that fill my eyes.

"Hey, no, don't cry."

I wipe away the tears. "Sorry, it's just ... sometimes ordinary words have such extraordinary meaning. You know what I mean?"

With gentle hands he cups my head and pulls me into his body, pressing a soft kiss into my hair. "I think I do."

I sit up and relinquish an I-should-know-better smile. "I got a chemical peel. I know it looks like something went horribly wrong, but it's supposed to be like this. By next week I'll have the most radiant skin you've ever seen."

"Well you didn't need the peel for that, but whatever floats your boat."

I nod, contemplating asking the question that has been dancing in my head all day. "What 'floats your boat?'"

Oliver traces his finger along my collar bone then dips it down to brush the exposed swell of my breasts, sending familiar jolts through my body in the most intimate places. "As of lately ... you."

I watch his finger, mesmerized by how it makes me feel, threatening to distract my thoughts. "Not sexy waitresses bringing you cold drinks while you're working?"

He stills, meeting my gaze. "No." He smirks. "It's impossible to float a boat in a puddle when it's already set sail in the ocean." He presses the pad of his finger to the underside of my chin and tilts my head back.

I swallow hard as he leans in and kisses my exposed neck, teasing his tongue along my sensitive skin. "However, it was nice of you to indulge my brother in his twisted take on reality."

"He said you told him to come instead of you. Why didn't you want to see me?" I whisper with a shaky voice as he reduces me to a nearly incoherent pile of needy lust with his touch.

He stops, rolling his shoulders back. "I *did* want to see you, that's why I stayed. I knew he would stand around and flirt with the waitress instead of working and we would end up staying there until dark just to keep on schedule. So I sacrificed a few minutes with you earlier for a few hours with you now."

How is it possible for someone to say the right words at the right time and have it sound so seamless and effortless?

I wrap my arms around him and play my fingers through his hair at the nape of his neck. "You're smooth. I mean, Chance is smooth too, but he's Nestle Crunch smooth. You're Godiva chocolate truffle smooth."

He squints one eye. "Is that a good thing?"

I give him a slow repeating nod. "Yes. One is mildly tempting during an extremely weak moment, the other is flat-out irresistible."

"You just made my night." He squeezes my thighs with his large hands.

You just made my entire year!

"Listen, I know we've only known each other for less than a week—" I start to say.

"Two weeks if you count the week on the subway that you stalked me before the doughnut *mishap*."

I squint my eyes, shaking my head. "Any–way ... as I was saying ..." I take a deep breath because I'm getting ready to say something I *need* to say, but *can't* explain, and he *won't* understand. "What you said earlier ... about noticing everything but only seeing the things that matter."

"Yes," he whispers.

"Will you promise not to take it back?"

"What do you—"

I move my finger to his lips. "Just ... promise?"

He nods, kissing my finger. "I promise."

AFTER TWO WEEKS of facial skin regeneration and casual dinner dates at my place or Oliver's, hope has popped its head over the horizon. Physically we haven't made it past kissing and hand holding; it's like the orgasm night never happened. I know he wants more, but never once has he tried to take the moment beyond my lead. It's almost too much to imagine or *hope* that I might not spend my life as the eternal virgin.

We talk about everything and nothing at the same time

with such ease of conversation. Oliver is twenty-nine, which originally I guessed he was a few years younger than that. He, however, doesn't want to think about my age: twenty-one.

There's an indescribable connection between us; it's first-time excitement and aged comfort all in one. Then there is the door. That Fort Knox door across from his bathroom. I haven't gathered the nerve to ask him about it, but I know he senses my curiosity as he's seen me staring at it on more than one occasion. Truthfully, I fear just my asking about it will change what's between us more than what's actually behind it.

Oliver is ninety-nine percent outgoing, funny, sexy, caring, and spontaneous, but on occasion I see that one percent that's a man consumed by something, someplace, or someone else. The blank stare or forced smile that comes from nowhere and leaves just as quick reminds me of the part of him that is closed to me.

"You're staring," Oliver says as I sit cross-legged on his counter while he scrubs the kitchen floor.

"I like the view." I grin.

On his hands and knees, he looks up at me. "Do I need to put my shirt back on?"

"That's like a Broadway director asking the audience if he needs to bring down the curtain in the middle of a Tony Award-winning show."

He shakes his head and continues to scrub the sand-colored tile.

"Are we going to your place later so you can scrub your floor, topless?"

"Hmm, let me think ... no."

Oliver keeps his head down. "Am I ever going to see the tattoo on your back?"

He doesn't skip a beat in his motions nor does he look at me. Good thing because I'm certain all color has drained from my face.

"I've seen the edges of the ink when you wear tank tops and pull up your hair."

I used to make sure all my shirts covered the tattoo, but in the past few months I've allowed parts of it to be revealed in exchange for getting to wear the shirts I like best. I'm sure other people have noticed it, but no one else has ever asked to see it.

"Only an elite group of people have seen it."

Oliver looks up again. "What are the qualifications for the group?"

"Basically you have to be my tattoo artist, my doctor, Alex, or Kai."

"Kai's seen it?"

I nod.

"How did he get in the group?"

I'm looking at the exception to every other man alive. Oliver can handle it—at least that's what I'm trying to convince myself. I should have showed him when we first met. A proverbial laying down of the cards to say take me or leave me. But I didn't. Now I'm too scared that I could be crushed because not only do I like him, I've built him up to be the man I want him to be. What if he's not? What if it's too soon?

"Kai was ... *inspiration* for the tattoo." That sounded different coming out of my mouth than it did in my head.

"Lucky guy." Oliver continues with the task at hand. If I knew him better I'd say he's mad, but I haven't seen Oliver's mad side yet, so I'm not sure this is it.

"I think he would disagree." I cringe at the thought of Kai hearing Oliver's words of envy.

"Yeah, well no girl has ever permanently marked herself for me."

Closing my eyes I shake my head. "It's not for him, it's because of him. Anyway, it doesn't matter. I'm sure he'd rather be in your shoes of not knowing than his."

Oliver dumps the bucket of dirty water in the sink. "It's no big deal. Some doors are better left unopened."

O–kay.

This coming from the guy who has a mysterious locked, *unopened,* door upstairs. Secrets. That's what we're agreeing to without saying the actual words.

"Are we talking about my door or yours?"

He pauses with his back to me. "I need to take a shower before I go to my parents' house for dinner. You want to grab some breakfast in the morning?"

I hop off the counter. "I'm leaving in the morning to stay with my parents in Hartford since Alex's are coming to visit for the next week."

He turns. "You're leaving for a week? Don't you have to work?"

"No, I'm leaving for two days, and no I don't have to work. That's the upside to Alex's parents coming to visit. They think she works for Maggie so she actually has to when they're here." I flash a smile and a wink.

"So where will you stay for the rest of the time?"

"Kai's."

He folds his arms against his chest and widens his stance. "Kai's? Doesn't he have a girlfriend?"

"Yes, but she won't be back for another week and they don't live together anyway. She's fine with me staying there. I do it all the time."

"I see. Have the two of you ever been ..."

I'm relieved he's curious, maybe even jealous. "Yes, and

no. We've been friends since kindergarten, but we were never more than that until our junior year in high school. But that only lasted a couple of years."

"So you've been ..." He looks at me with big questioning eyes.

"We've been ... what?"

Oliver rolls his eyes. "Intimate."

"You mean sex?" I laugh because the alternative hurts too much.

"I don't need to know." He turns and heads upstairs.

"Wait!"

He looks back at me.

"We haven't had sex—"

Oliver holds up his hand. "I said I don't—"

I walk partway up the stairs to meet him. "I know what you said." Wrapping my hand around his neck, I pull him to me. Our lips connect for a slow kiss. "But I needed you to know. I haven't been with Kai ... in fact, I haven't been with anyone."

Yep, that did it. Frozen, eyes wide with slow exaggerated blinks, Oliver is in shock. I could wait to see if he finds his voice, but I'm not anticipating that happening anytime soon.

"So ... enjoy dinner with your parents. I'll call you when I get back in town."

Nothing.

I smile and walk down the stairs with an occasional glance back at the stone statue that is Oliver.

Oliver

I LIKE this amazing woman that's eight years younger than I am. She's an adult and old enough to drink. Age shouldn't matter, *until* she flashes her V card! I'm not that old, but I'm too old to be taking anyone's virginity.

My head yelled at her to stop because we needed to discuss the bomb she dropped on me, but my mouth could not move. Now she's leaving for the next two days and I'm going to go crazy. Chance would think I hit the jackpot, not the case for me. That damn V card has too much fine print on it.

Expectations.

Words like love, cuddling, fairy tales, forever, marriage, babies, and minivans are stamped all over it like a passport to Hell. I can't be Vivian's Prince Charming, and even if that's not what she wants, it's what she deserves. It sounds so shallow, as if looks are all that matter, but twenty-one-year-olds that look like Vivian are not virgins. Was she abused? Is she religious? What is her story?

"Hi, Mom." I give her a big hug as she greets me just inside their front door.

"I was hoping you'd bring your neighbor *friend*." She rubs her hand up and down my arm as we walk out back to see Dad and Chance.

"Someone has a big mouth," I say loud enough for Chance to hear as my mom hands me a beer.

Chance tips back his bottle taking a long pull while hiding his grin. "You've been blowing me off to spend every night with her, so I assumed this would be the week we'd get to meet her."

"We're just friends and that's all it's ever going to be. She's too young for me and bringing her here could give her and everyone else the wrong impression."

"Oliver, a few days ago you acted like the age difference

didn't matter. What's all of a sudden changed?" Chance asks.

I take a swig of my beer. "She's just young and has a lot to *experience* in life, that's all. Can we talk about something else?"

"Your dad and I are thinking about flying out to Portland next week. Would you like me to get you a ticket too?" My mom is talking to me with the ease and confidence she would have while spewing off a grocery list to my dad over the phone.

"No."

"You do realize it's the—"

"Yes, Mom, I *realize!*" I drain the rest of my beer. "Find a new subject or I'm out of here."

She sips her wine and looks at my dad. He gives her a slight head shake and takes the food off the grill.

"You boys both going to the game with me?" My dad knows how to change the subject and keep the peace.

"Yep," Chance and I reply in unison, relaxing the tension that's heavy in the air. This is what I need: no-brainer emotionless conversation.

Vivian: *On my way to my parents'. Hope you had a nice time at yours. Call you when I get back :)*

THIS IS NOT how I want to start my day, but I need to make a clean break. A text seems like the coward's way, but the last thing I need is Vivian building *us* up in her mind over the next two days.

Me: *I think we should stick to being neighbors/friends. Okay?*

Vivian: *Did I do something wrong?*
Me: *No. The age difference is not going to work for me.*
Vivian: *WTF?*
Me: *Please don't be mad.*
Vivian: *Am I not old enough or do I not have enough experience?*
Me: *I don't have what you want.*
Vivian: *I don't recall telling you what I want, but UR right, UR an ass and that's not what I want!!!*
Me: *I'm sorry, don't be this way.*

I wait for a response, but receive nothing. As much as I want to call her, I don't. She's pissed and rightfully so. I have to keep reminding myself that I'm not worthy of her. The hardest part is figuring out if I'm worthy of anyone. The past few weeks I haven't felt alone, which is all I've felt for the past three years. Now, it's back and so is the shell of the man I've become. Maybe my mom's right. Maybe I need to join a support group for "healing". Although I know everyone in those groups is there for the same unspoken reason: misery loves company.

I know just a few miles away my dad is watching the sunrise too while my mom continues to sleep. He'll be here soon to pick me up. Unless he gets called into the hospital, this is our new routine: sunrise, coffee, and rowing. My dad has rowed his whole life. In college he was on the heavyweight crew and I followed in his footsteps in college after he introduced me to sculling in high school. He's been a member of the Cambridge Boat Club for years and quickly moved through my membership application as soon as I came back to town.

"Looks like a perfect morning," my dad comments as we

stare at a few other sculls already gliding along the river while we finish our coffee.

"Yep."

"You're quiet this morning." He's always been a man of few words but very direct.

I shrug. "Tired, I didn't sleep well." We both continue to stare at the water.

"This about Portland or the girl?"

I give him a one-grunt laugh. "Neither, both, hell if I know."

"Let's go, then. You just need to clear your head." He finishes the last of his coffee and gestures toward the water.

It's been four days since I've seen Vivian. Uncontrolled nerves have hijacked my body like a goddamn smoker having withdrawals. I'm short with Chance—fidgety, unfocused, and miserable. It doesn't help that my mom keeps reminding me that they're leaving in three days for Portland.

"Easy, bro, that's the fifth paver you've busted today." Chance shakes his head. "What the hell is going on with you? Did you tease your dick with that girl one too many times?"

I toss the rubber mallet to the side and grab my water. "We never had sex, dipshit."

"What? Why the hell not?"

Wiping my brow, I shake my head. "Virgin."

Chance drops to his knees, bends over, and pounds his gloved fists on the ground. "Why, why, why does everyone think you're the smart one? You are a total dumb fuck!"

I grab another brick and continue working. The only

thing surprising about Chance's reaction is that it's not more extreme. I expected him to beg for her phone number.

He stands back up and grabs his shovel. "It doesn't change your fucking moron status, but I'll let it slide today since I have a date this weekend." Chance grins and I see the canary feather sticking out of his sly cat grin.

"A date, huh? As in you called a girl and planned something in advance as opposed to the usual last minute drunken pick up?"

"Yep, well, actually she called me. But that's not the craziest part. As you know I'm not really a wine and dine 'em kind of guy, but the one girl who I'd like to take to dinner and savor my time with, told me dinner was the optional part of the date."

"She sounds like a real gem, the kind you bring home to meet the parents." I chuckle.

"That's just it, she is that girl. You know her."

I sit back on my knees and squint at him. "Who?"

"Viv." He grins.

"Vivian?"

"Yeah, Vivian Graham from The Green Pot."

I shake my head in disbelief or maybe to clear it, because there is no way I'm hearing him correctly. "You're full of shit."

Chance laughs. "Sometimes, but not about this. She called me last night and said my years of annoying but diligent nagging are about to payoff. She said 'one night' and dinner is optional. Now, I may not have a degree from Harvard, but I know when a girl is offering up sex and nothing else."

How does she do it? How does she blow my mind over and over again? This is ridiculous and beyond stupid on her part.

"Chance, you can't sleep with her."

"Um, now see, that's the difference between you and me. *I* don't have an issue with consensual casual sex. Have you taken a good look at her? Man, those long legs wrapped around—"

"Yes! I've seen her. Just shut your goddamn trap about her. Show a little respect would you?"

He holds up his hands. "Chill, dude! You don't have to be so touchy. What's your deal lately?"

"Just stop talking and get back to work." I sigh.

CHAPTER SEVEN
MOVING ON

Vivian

Oliver deserves the biggest prick award. What guy doesn't want to be a girl's first? Claim her. Plant his flag. Make his mark. Maybe he's just selfish and assumes I won't be good in bed, that I won't be able to satisfy him. I put him too high on a pedestal way too quick.

My poor mom thought I was still depressed about the accident and my dad—typical guy—assumed I was PMSing when I sulked around their house for two days. I've felt hurt then angry then back to hurt again, finally settling on pissed, bitchy, and out for redemption. Oliver made me believe for a moment, a small moment, that I could be with a man someday. He reminded me that beauty is not skin deep. Then he made it clear that sexual experience matters.

So just like getting an unsightly mole removed, I'm going to get rid of my virginity. It's so overrated. It's not like I feel special still having mine. I can't put it on a résumé or anything like that. The first time will be a stick, a pinch, and a burn just like getting my ears pierced or a shot at the doctor's office. I didn't make a big deal out of getting my ears pierced. It's not as if the specialist who put two holes in my ears sends me Christmas and birthday cards. Heck, I don't know if she ever even told me her name.

As always, Kai is letting me stay with him until Alex's parents leave. And, as always, I've been invited to dinner with Alex and her parents at the place I call home ninety percent of the time. The timing is good. I need to grab another change of clothes to get me through the rest of the week.

"Do you have your key?" Kai questions as I get ready to leave.

"They're going to be there, why do I need my key?"

"No, to your bedroom."

I always lock my bedroom door before Alex's parents come to visit. She told them that she's taking up painting but not ready to share her masterpieces with the world. The crazy part? They believe her.

"Thanks, and yes, I have my key."

"Well, you know where I'll be." He sighs.

I don't even acknowledge him before closing the door behind me. Kate is coming home in a week and Kai promised he'd repaint the living room while she's gone because she can't handle the fumes. He's just now taping everything off. The downside will be Kate reaming his ass because she'll still smell it and know that he waited until the last minute to do it. The upside is Kai has something to do that doesn't require me entertaining him.

It's only a mile to our place from Kai's. I've walked it so many times over the past two years I think I could do it blindfolded. The first thing that I notice is Alex's parents' black SUV parked by the curb with its New York license plates. Then I notice my *neighbor* walking in the opposite direction toward his place. He's still dressed in his work clothes so I imagine he's just gotten off the subway train. When he spots me I make a quick diversion with my eyes praying he doesn't say anything before I can hurry into the house.

"Vivian?"

Too late!

Keeping my eyes to the sidewalk I give a quick wave.

"Vivian, wait!"

Out of the corner of my eye I see him heading across the street. Taking a courageous breath, I stop and look up at him, crossing my arms over my chest.

"Yes, *neighbor*?" Smiles don't get any more fake than mine.

He sighs. "Listen, I'm sorry about the text. It was pretty shitty of me to not just call you or tell you in person. I just—"

I hold up my hand. "Save it. It's fine. I'm fine. Whatever." I brush past him.

"Vivian, wait!"

I stop, keeping my back to him.

"Did you really ask my brother out this weekend?"

"Does it matter?"

"I think so, since he has the impression you're looking for a one-night stand."

"Does it matter?"

"Jesus, Vivian! He's just going to use you."

I whip around. "No, I'm using him."

Oliver plants his fists on his hips. "To make me jealous?"

Shaking my head I laugh. "Get over yourself." I walk up the steps to the front door and look back. "Besides, Chance is closer to my age. He'll have more stamina to keep up with me when I ride him like it's the Kentucky Derby." I knock on the red door and just as it opens I throw him one last smile. "Later, *neighbor*."

I'm not sure if the look on his face is horror or shock, but either way, I feel the bittersweet satisfaction.

"Viv!" Alex's mom greets me with open arms as I step in and shut the door.

"Annabelle, nice to see you. Mmm, something smells good and I know it's not Alex's cooking."

Annabelle smiles. "You're right, it's not Alex's cooking but not because she doesn't know how. Don't let her make you think I didn't teach her how to cook."

"Is that so ..." I glare at Alex as she watches TV with her dad.

"For the record. I never told you I can't cook, I said I *don't* cook."

"Hey, Viv." Her dad smiles.

"Hi, Mark. What's the score?"

He grunts. "Zero-three."

Alex scoots closer to him, nudging his arm. "You mean zero your team, three mine."

"Watch it, young lady, or I'll have your butt transferred back to where you remember what it means to be a Yankees fan."

"Yeah, yeah, whatever." Alex hops off the couch. "So I finally got to meet the older Konrad brother today. They were picking up some shrubs and holy moly, how did I not know he's our ... uh, I mean, *my* neighbor?" She makes a quick recovery. Luckily her mom is enthralled with dinner preparations and her dad is drowning in the misery of his team falling behind in the always heated rivalry.

"I'm not sure, but he's no longer on my radar."

Alex hoists herself up on the counter and starts picking at the colorful salad her mom's making. Annabelle smacks her hand away. Alex pops a cherry tomato in her mouth and smirks.

"So spill, what happened?"

I hold up two fingers to make a V.

"Seriously? That's a problem?"

I shrug. "Apparently."

"What's a problem?" Annabelle asks.

Both of our eyes widen and Alex giggles. "Nothing, there's this guy that Flower likes but he's being weird about her ... height."

I roll my eyes.

"Viv, you're a beautiful young woman. I'd love to have your long legs, sweetie. I'm sure you just intimidate him, which means he's not the one for you."

Alex nods. "Yes, he's just intimidated by your *height*. Those long legs of yours and the way they form a perfect V." She giggles some more.

Annabelle smacks Alex's butt. "Why are you acting so goofy today? Hop off and set the table."

Alex hops down and we both carry the plates and silverware into the dining room.

"He really dumped you because you're a virgin?" she whispers.

"*Dumped* is a little extreme, but yes, he decided we should be neighbors or friends because of the age difference and him not having what I want. Which is total code for I'm a virgin, especially given the fact it was the last conversation we had before he decided to ... well, yes, dump me."

"Ahem." Annabelle clears her throat as she and Mark stand a few feet behind us with their hands full of serving dishes.

Great! The knowledge of my virginity just keeps spreading like a virus. I need to get rid of it before it goes any further.

"You asked Chance out?" Alex's screech bounces off the walls of my bedroom as I gather some spare clothes.

"That's what I said." I laugh.

"Yeah, but … why? Is it to make Oliver jealous?"

"No, definitely not that." I plop on my bed. "If I tell you, can you keep it to yourself?"

"Of course. You know me." Alex flips her hair back like my question is ridiculous.

"Sure I can. That's why Sean knows everything I've ever told you."

"Not *everything*."

"Mmm hmm, whatever." I grimace as I take in a deep breath. "I'm just using Chance to lose my virginity."

"What? Flower, are you serious?" Alex sits down next to me.

I nod. "I'm not doing it to get Oliver back. Obviously if that were the case I wouldn't choose his brother. It's just that Oliver made me believe that maybe I'm not destined to be an eternal virgin, and if that's the case I want to know that when the right guy comes along I'm not dealing with this virgin issue again."

Alex giggles. "I love the way you're referring to it as the 'virgin issue,' like a yeast infection or something."

"Well, if you would have seen the way Oliver looked at

me when I told him, it might as well have been a yeast infection or an STD for that matter."

"Are you sure Chance is the best choice? I didn't think you were interested."

"I'm not. That's what makes him ideal. He's a total player and one-night stands are his specialty. He's good looking and relatively nice, even if his kindness is often misplaced as inappropriate advances."

Alex picks at her bottom lip. "But ... don't you want your first time to be special?"

"Was yours?"

She shrugs. "No, but ..."

"But what?"

"I don't know." She laughs. "I just said it because I thought it was the right thing to say. You know, like talking someone off the edge of a cliff."

I chuckle. "Thanks, but I'm twenty-one, not fifteen."

"Does he know?"

"Chance?"

Alex nods.

"I don't think so. Not unless Oliver told him. I just asked him out and basically alluded to the fact that he was going to get laid and it would be a one-time deal. I didn't say 'Hey, can I interest you in dinner, a movie, and my virginity?'"

"You should have."

We both chuckle.

"What about your back?"

"That's another reason I picked Chance. Something tells me that if I wear the right skirt or dress, sans panties, he's the type of guy who can happily get the job done without removing all our clothes. I'm thinking a button down, open in the front bra, and knee length skirt."

"Only my brainy business friend would approach losing her virginity like a strategic business transaction."

"So help me, God, if you tell Kai I will murder you right after I tell your parents about our little housing and work arrangement."

"Me—ow, put your claws away. Save the catfight for all the women who are going to hate that you're officially putting yourself back on the market."

I shove her off the bed. "Shut up. I'm just getting rid of my *yeast infection*, nothing more."

She stands back up with a goofy grin. "Oh, by the way ... my parents are leaving tonight. My dad has to get back for a meeting and I'm going to Sean's as soon as they leave. So no need to pack more stuff." She gestures to my bag. "You'll be here by yourself to bask in your non-virgin glow. Unless you stay the night at Chance's."

"Yeah, not happening."

***

Oliver

ANOTHER SELF-DIAGNOSIS. I'm reverting back to childish ways of discarding a toy and deciding I want it again when my younger brother claims it for his own. The difference is I don't want Vivian, I need her. Not because I want to. I don't. The last thing I ever wanted was to need someone again.

"Where should I take Viv to dinner tonight?" Chance asks as we load up the truck.

He's managed to go the past two days without mentioning his date, until now.

"I don't know. Where do you usually go ... oh, that's

right, you usually just have meaningless sex and send them off with cab fare and a gift card to Panera."

"I'll have you know I give them a Charlie Card for the subway or bus because cab fare is ridiculously expensive and the gift card is to 7-Eleven, not Panera." We both get in the truck and he adjusts his baseball cap with his familiar dumb-shit grin smeared across his face.

"You're an idiot."

"I'd rather be an idiot taking Viv back to my place tonight than a nerd going home by myself."

"Whatever." I sigh looking out the window. I should tell him Vivian is my neighbor, the girl I was seeing, the virgin, but I can't. He wouldn't understand why I broke things off with her, and he wouldn't understand why I need her. I can't even explain it to myself. Maybe he'll get sick. Maybe she'll get cold feet. Maybe I'll lose the last bit of my sanity sitting alone in my house imagining them together.

Most likely I'll get drunk and pass out because my mind has nowhere to go that isn't painful. I'm barely holding it together knowing my parents are in Portland. Everywhere my thoughts travel, there is a road block. I could find a detour and deal with each problem one at a time, but it's easier to just idle until I run out of gas, stalled in the middle of nowhere, completely alone.

"What would you think about swapping vehicles for tonight?" Chance asks, pulling up to the curb in front of my house.

I look across the street and dream of Vivian stepping out of her door, Chance making the connection, and maybe their date tonight getting cancelled. No such luck.

"Don't you think she'd wonder why you're driving my car?"

"How would she know it's yours? Do you have the title taped to the dash?"

"Why would she think you drive a BMW?"

"Duh, because I'm a successful business owner. It would only make sense that I have a non-work car."

I open my door. "Then why don't you?"

Chance's eyes widen and he juts his head toward me. "Because I'm not *that* successful, but she doesn't need to know that."

"Uh, yes she does. Drive your truck. Maybe she'll tell Maggie how poor you are and we'll get a good deal on our next order. So, see ya, and don't be a jerk tonight." I slam the door.

I'VE SPENT YEARS STUDYING, observing, and dealing with the legal consequences of self-destructive behavior. Anyone else in my shoes would run and take cover knowing that the fuse has been lit at both ends. Not me. I can't control my emotions, not the ones that have bloomed and are waiting to die, or the ones that are opening up and waiting to be acknowledged. They're becoming tangled in my head and creeping into my every thought.

Mom: *They bloomed, Oliver. Oh my goodness, they bloomed! Maybe they've been waiting for you.*

I look down at my phone.

Me: *Maybe they've been waiting for the sun.*
Mom: *Yes, my son.*

I shut off my phone for a while so she gets that I'm not discussing this with her. Then I look at my couch and see the small blue and gray striped decorative pillow my mom bought last month. It's survived longer than any other. I think of her message, then I think of Chance, then I think of Vivian. It's thin cotton with weak stitching, and I usually open these flimsy pillows like a bag of chips, but for some reason I grab a knife from the kitchen and stab it over and over until there's nothing left but an empty tattered shell and white polyester fiber filling everywhere.

Fuck it! Fuck her! Fuck everyone!

Tossing the knife on the coffee table, I collapse on the couch and rake my hands through my hair, breathless from my pent up anger. Reaching in my pocket, I pull out my phone and turn it back on.

Mom: *You're exactly where you need to be. In your own time, dear.*

I notice the time: 7:00 p.m. Grabbing my wallet and keys, I rush out the door, driven by something that doesn't yet make sense in my head. Maybe *it's* where I need to be at this time.

I ease my car to a stop along the street at the opposite end of the alley from where Chance parks. Within a few minutes I see his truck stop along the curb and like the gentleman he is not, he opens the passenger side door. His chivalry pisses me off more than if he'd just grope her ass and show his true colors. Vivian's knee-length skirt flows in the light breeze, as does her long raven hair, while he guides her into the alley with his hand on her back. They stop at his door and he bends down with his mouth next to her ear. Vivian's head falls back in laughter as he unlocks his door.

My knee bounces out of control while my fists clench at a steady rhythm. I could call him and fake an emergency, but it wouldn't be more than a temporary fix. This same scene would play out another night. I watch the clock on my phone, trying to decide if I'm here to stop her or pick up the pieces when she walks out his door later. God, that's the million dollar question. If I want her, then I should see if she goes through with it and maybe that will be the answer for me. But if I *need* her, then there's no way in hell I can let Chance have her tonight.

Tick-tock.

Knee bouncing.

Fists clenching.

Heart racing.

Fuck it! I need her.

I'm not sure how many paces are between my car and Chance's front door, but I'm certain I just halved it.

Bang, bang, bang!

Chance opens the door with his face contorted in confusion. "Bro, what are you doing here?"

I brush past him. Vivian sits on the couch holding a glass of wine—she's probably already drunk—and there's some soft music playing through his speakers. Her daring eyes widen as I approach.

"Oliver, what are you doing?"

"Dude, what's going on?" Chance calls behind me, but I keep my eyes on Vivian as I hold out my hand to her.

She stares at it, then me. "No." She shakes her head.

"Oliver, do you mind telling us what's going on?" Chance rests his hand on my shoulder, but I shrug it off.

"Vivian is my neighbor." I grit my teeth.

"Your ... what? She's who you've been—"

"Yes, and now she's coming with me."

Vivian sets her wine down and stands, crossing her defiant arms. "I'm not going anywhere with you."

"Viv, you're the *virgin*?" Chance asks.

Vivian throws her hands in the air. "Oh. My. God! Has it gone viral online too? Does *everyone* know I'm a virgin?" She grabs her purse, storming to the door. "Why is it such a damn big deal?" she yells.

Chance doesn't move. It's apparent his mind is playing catch-up. I follow Vivian out the door.

"Don't touch me and don't follow me!" She waves her finger at me when I attempt to grab her arm.

"Where are you going?" I call as she stomps up the alley.

"I'm going to get my cherry popped, dickhead!"

What?

"Vivian, wait!" I jog after her. "Don't be ridiculous." I reach for her hand. She yanks it away.

"Oh, that's rich coming from the guy who ditched me because my hymen's still intact." She turns and strides away.

"I'm sorry."

Still walking away.

"I was stupid."

Still walking away.

"Dammit!" I chase after her. Grabbing her waist, I pull her to me as she twists and flails to escape. "Just listen to me."

"No!" She wriggles in my arms, jerking her elbows side to side.

Leaving me no choice, I hoist her over my shoulder and she screams. "Stop, my skirt ... I'm not wearing—"

I reach up to pull her skirt down over her ... *bare ass*!

"Where the hell are your underwear?"

She punches her fists against my backside. "They're at my house. Now put me down!"

"Are you behind on your laundry?"

"No! Are you really this dense?"

I deposit her in the passenger's seat.

"Buckle up."

She crosses her arms over her chest. "Why would I go with you?"

My head drops and I rest my hands on the top of my car. "Because I need you."

She gapes at me with an unrelenting stare as I shut her door.

"Why do you need me?" she whispers as I pull away from the curb.

Keeping my eyes on the road, I shake my head. "I don't know. That's what I'm trying to figure out."

WE TRAVEL HOME in a thick cloud of silence, my voice held hostage by my emotion laden tongue. I anticipate her making a dash across the street for her door when I stop the car, but she doesn't. She waits for me to open her door. Taking her hand, I lead her to my place and she follows without hesitation.

Vivian stops just inside the door as I continue forward, tossing my keys on the counter.

"Do you want something to drink?" I hate the uncertainty that's in my voice, like I just made a huge mistake and now I don't know what to do about it.

She shakes her head as intense eyes full of uncertainty track my every move. My phone chimes in my pocket. There's a missed call and a message from an unknown number. I listen to it as Vivian continues to watch me, gauge me, unravel me.

It's not the voice on the message, or the words, it's the timing. I can't hear anything past my own pounding pulse and all I see is red. Three years later and I hate her with every fiber of my being. I slam my phone on the counter shattering the face of it. Vivian jumps while standing in the middle of my living room. At some point she made her way to the mess of pillow filling and ripped fragments of material still strewn about the floor and couch.

"I'm … sorry. I should not have brought you here." My feet take me to the stairs on their own accord because I'm so numb right now the only thing I feel is the suffocating compression on my sternum as my lungs fight for air. "Sor– sorry." I stumble to my room and slam the door, ripping off my shirt because even the light weight of cotton feels like lead against my chest. Sitting on the edge of my bed, I hunch over with my head in my hands and cry. The pain pours out like a mix of blood and acid. The hate is all consuming and the pain is crippling.

The door creaks open. My emotions stall in my throat. I can't look up, so all I see are her bare feet facing away from me.

"Please … go." My voice cracks.

She doesn't budge. Her shirt falls to the floor by her feet. I can only see the back of her legs from the knees down. *What is she doing?* Her bra joins her shirt on the floor.

She waits.

Her back is to me and then it hits me so hard—her *back* is bared to me.

Releasing my hands from my face, I move my gaze up to her back one slow inch at a time. She's shaking like a delicate leaf and her hair is pulled off to one shoulder. I blink away my tears—twisted branches with flowers. Flowers everywhere and not one ... single ... one ... is bloomed.

Oh. God!

Every intricate detail covers what's lying beneath: scars —everywhere. Then she turns her head and glossy green eyes meet mine as she bites together her trembling lips.

"Vivian ..." I whisper. "... beautiful, you're ... *perfect*."

Tears spill down her cheeks. "No take backs?"

I smile, taking her hand in mine. She turns around and moves between my legs, brushing her hair off her chest. Pressing my lips to her palm, I close my eyes and crash. My whole world collides and she has no idea that in this moment she's throwing me a lifeline. "No take backs."

It kills me that someone so stunning inside and out has lived in fear of people changing their mind about her beauty. I wonder how long she's lived with such insecurity. Even more, I wonder if any man has made her feel less than perfect. The pain in her eyes when she looks back at me tells me the answer is yes.

She begins to slip her skirt past her hips but I grab her wrists.

"Not tonight. I'm just ..." I sigh. "I have too much on my mind, but soon. Okay?"

She pulls her skirt back up and nods while grabbing her bra and shirt. With a weak smile she turns away from me to finish dressing.

"Vivian?"

"Hmm?"

"You're not upset are you?"

She shakes her head. I stand and walk in front of her as she buttons the last button.

"Are you sure?"

She looks at my chest. "Yes. I'll just see you tomorrow or something."

I cup her face and kiss her soft lips. It's taking everything I have to let her go tonight, but she deserves my full attention and right now I'm being pulled apart.

"I'll walk you home."

"Don't be stupid. It's across the street." Her voice is void of emotion as she turns and walks down the hall to the stairs.

I sense she's at least a little disappointed, but I don't know what more I can say or do tonight. Looking out the bedroom window, I watch her sprint down the front steps of the building and across the street. As she fumbles to get her key in the lock, I notice her arm keeps rubbing her eyes.

Shit! She's crying.

CHAPTER EIGHT
TIME STANDS STILL

Vivian

THERE'S APPROXIMATELY twenty strides from Oliver's front door to mine, but I make it in less than ten. Holding myself together until I reach the safety of my sanctuary is excruciating, but not as much as yet another rejection. I saw his pain, but I couldn't see past it. The message on his phone, the massacred pillow, the aching sound of his sobs, I wanted to take his pain away and I thought he could do the same for me. Letting my guard down, letting him see me ... all of me.

I laid my heart on the floor in his bedroom; with his words he held it in his hands and with his eyes he gave it back to me. It was the first time someone has looked at my back and not had pity in their eyes. Doctors, my parents, Kai, Alex, they all had the same look, but not Oliver. In his eyes, I became a woman not a victim, and in that moment the scars faded and my heart felt reborn. Then he took it all away. Racked with nerves shaking my entire body, I needed him to wrap me in his arms and wash away the pain, insecurities, and ugliness that has plagued my body and mind.

He left me with nothing and I left him with a vision that will fester in his mind until he wakes up and sees what everyone before him has seen—too much to bear. I know that moment was real, but that moment has drifted away and I fear we can never get it back.

Locking the door behind me, I wipe my eyes. The room feels cold, bare, and lonely. Alex is gone, but I wish she were here. I need someone's arms, anyone's arms.

A pounding against the door startles me. My heart surges against my chest as the rest of my body stills against the door. I inch it open to see Oliver.

He's here!

He holds my purse up, letting it dangle from his finger.

Oh, I just forgot my purse.

"Um, thanks." I try to grab it without completely opening the door. He has his own problems; I don't need to be one of them.

He pulls it away as I try to grab it.

"Vivian?"

"Hmm?"

"Open the door."

I wipe my eyes and open the door with a defeated sigh. Oliver tosses my purse on the floor and frames my face in his hands. My brain wants to protest his touch, but my body can't. Fragile blue eyes steal my breath so I surrender my words, leaving them for another time. Right now I take him in: disheveled copper-blond hair that usually has order, his strong angular jaw with a soft stubble shadow below prominent cheek bones, and faded crimson lips that I can't stop craving. Oliver is beautifully handsome.

He shakes his head, relinquishing a sad smile as he

wipes the moisture away from my cheeks. "Vivian, I told you, no take backs."

Oliver kisses me and the earth stops moving beneath my feet, as if our lips meeting trumps anything else the over seven billion other people in the world are doing at this exact moment. Time just ... stops.

Somewhere between now and forever, he carries me up the stairs bumping our bodies from one wall to the next as I refuse to let go of his lips.

"This one," I murmur into his kiss as we start to pass my room.

He kicks the door shut setting me on my feet. Brushing my fingertips over my bruised lips, I grin. Oliver raises a brow, staring at my bed.

"A twin bed?"

I nod, then he nods. "O–kay." He pulls down the covers and tosses my pillow on the floor.

He has some real pillow issues.

"I've had a shitty day ... until you." He unbuttons my shirt. "With you..." he pushes my shirt off my shoulders and unfastens my bra "...everything's better."

My body trembles and I hate that my nerves are so obvious. Oliver kisses me. It's the only part of our bodies that touch. Our tongues tease and our lips caress. My eyes fight to stay open as he trails his lips and tongue along my neck and down my chest, stopping between my breasts, lingering right over my heart. Each blink is heavier than the one before, but I don't want to miss one second of this. Every look we share is filled with a million wordless emotions.

He pulls down my skirt and looks up at me with a tiny grin as if he just remembered I'm not wearing any panties. I shrug and smile.

Standing, he backs me to the bed until I sit. Lying back,

I pull my feet up on the bed and part my shaky knees while he shrugs off his shirt.

Stick, pinch, burn, stick, pinch, burn.

My chest rises and falls in rapid succession.

Stick, pinch, burn, stick, pinch, burn.

Oliver unfastens his jeans and pushes them down leaving on his boxer briefs. He's turned on. Oh. My. God! He's turned on by me. I look at him and he grins. He's watching me stare at his tented briefs.

Sucking in a deep breath, I swallow hard and squeeze my eyes tight while my hands grip the sheets.

Stick, pinch, burn, stick, pinch, burn.

"Don't worry about me, I can take it. You don't need to hold back, just ... do it!" I clench my teeth together and fight to keep my legs spread for him.

I wait.

And wait.

Nothing.

Peeking one eye open, I see Oliver standing before me with his briefs still on. His brows knit together and he smiles, releasing a soft chuckle. He kneels on the bed between my legs and grabs my right foot. Bringing it to his mouth, he kisses the pad of my big toe and then my arch, keeping his eyes on mine.

My fingers relax their death grip on the sheets. His lips and tongue ignite a blazing fire along my skin as he works his way up my leg. About three inches beyond my knee, he brushes his tongue against my inner thigh and makes a slow move to continue up my leg.

I snap my legs together against his head like a vice, preventing him from going any farther.

"Vivian? What are you doing?" His voice muffles against my leg.

"What are *you* doing? Whe–where are you going?"

He grips my knees and pries my legs open, releasing his head. "I'm preparing you."

I swallow. "For what?"

"For me."

"Oh ... um ... uh ..."

He takes my hand and guides it between my legs until I'm covering myself. His lips press against the back of my hand, kissing my knuckles and each one of my fingers. Then his tongue repeats the same pattern and my hand twitches. My pulse takes flight and my mouth falls open as my breathing becomes heavy. I curl my fingers and touch myself. Oliver slides his tongue between my wet fingers and grazes my sensitive flesh. He sucks my finger into his mouth and as I pull it from his mouth, I slide it up my belly and relax my legs exposing all of myself to him.

"Ahh!" I cry, jerking my hips off the bed when his mouth covers me.

He doesn't stop and it's embarrassing how quickly I'm seeing stars. "Ol–Oliver ... stop ... I'm ... I'm going to—" I grab his hair and fist it so hard I'm pretty sure he groans, but he doesn't stop his relentless assault.

"Oh God! Oh God! Oh ... Oliver!" I yell, thrashing my head from side to side as my orgasm sucks the life out of me in thundering waves.

There's not a tense muscle left in my body. In fact, I feel like I could pass out from exhaustion. Oliver kisses his way up my abdomen to my breasts and hums as his mouth closes over my nipple. Releasing it, he sits up and removes his boxer briefs then goes right back to my other breast.

"Did you like that?" he asks while working his way up my neck.

"Yes." I start to find my breath. "Ung!" I cry as his

mouth takes mine and he pushes into me with one hard thrust.

Stick, pinch, buurrrnn! Goodbye, virginity.

Oliver stills while his tongue invades my mouth. My fingers dig into his firm butt muscles, then he starts to move —slow at first. His mouth never leaves my body; it's on my lips, neck, ear, and breasts, distracting me from the torpedo invasion down below.

I don't really have anything to compare him to except books and movies, but Oliver is not very vocal during sex. He must think I'm a real screamer. Then there is my twin bed that I've had since I was six, the frame on it squeaks and squawks like a rusty wagon being pulled along a cobblestone road. I'm so grateful that Alex is not home to hear the symphony of Vivian and her childhood bed getting seriously nailed by the hottest guy to ever walk the planet.

"Ouch!" I yell.

Oliver distracts my thoughts as he stills deep inside me and bites my nipple a little harder than necessary. I glare down at him and he smiles with my nipple still between his teeth and sweat beading along his brow.

"Sadist, huh?"

He releases my nipple and kisses it shaking his head. "Not hardly."

Easing off me, he inches out and I can't hide the slight grimace on my face. His mirrors mine. "Sorry."

I shake my head. "It's fine." I sit up on my arms, look down, and see a little bit of blood on him and something else that's not there. "Oh my God! Where's your condom? Please tell me you used a condom? I don't remember you putting one on! Oh. My. Go—"

He kisses me and I relax, a little. Releasing my lips his

gaze falls and he stands pulling on his pants. "I can't have children, sorry."

Wrapping the sheet around my body, I sit up. "Why are you sorry?"

He runs his hands through his hair. "Because I should have told you before things ... went this far."

"You're assuming I want kids and being with me would just be leading me on?"

He nods and the pain in his face is so disheartening. I stand letting the sheet fall from my body. Resting my hands on his chest, I look up at him. "Before I met you I had resigned myself to the idea that my fate was to be an eternal virgin." I press my lips to his chest and his hand cups the back of my head with tenderness. "So really, kids haven't been on my radar since I played dollies as a young girl. Okay?"

Oliver kisses the top of my head. "But you deserve—"

"I deserve this." I wrap my arms around his neck and pull him to me. "No take backs."

He nods with a sad smile as he wraps me in his arms. I can't get enough of him. He's ice cream on a hot summer day, peanuts and the Red Sox, popcorn at the movies, and a candlelit cake on my birthday. My lips find his and become demanding as my hands move to the button of his jeans.

"No way." He grabs my wrists. "You're going to be sore. You should think about taking a hot bath." Interlacing our fingers he moves our hands behind my back. "I'll see you in the morning. Okay?"

My lips pull into a forced smile so he doesn't see my disappointment. It's not about the sex. He's right, I'm a little ... okay, *a lot* sore right now. I just don't want to leave the comfort of his arms, and my twin bed isn't too inviting so asking him to stay would be ridiculous.

He kisses me again, and again, and again.

"Bye." He smiles and kisses my forehead.

"Bye." I wait until he closes the door, then I sit down on my bed hugging my knees to my chest. There's nothing worse than being alone with my thoughts. I should be thrilled. Earlier today I planned on handing my virginity to Chance in the least romantic way possible: half clothed on his couch. Instead, I ended up with Oliver and he made me feel beautiful, sexy, and amazing. So why am I sad?

I look up as I hear my door open.

Oliver grins. "You could throw some clothes in an overnight bag and come take a bath at my house ... with me."

Once again, the world stops turning. It's just us.

Oliver

VIVIAN INSISTS ON A BUBBLE BATH. I insist my non-SLS soap would not make very many bubbles. Nearly a full bottle of body wash later, we have a weak layer of bubbles floating around us, but Vivian seems nonetheless pleased.

After our bath, I'm equally as pleased to have her naked body next to mine in my *California king*-sized bed.

"I should have brought my pillow."

I offer her my arm. She rests her head on it as I pull her close.

"Can I ask why you have such an aversion to pillows? Bad neck or something?"

"It's something from my past to be shared in the future, just not now."

She tilts her head up and kisses my jaw, a non-verbal

acceptance of my vague explanation. I know that won't always be the case. I can't remember the last time I felt this content ... maybe never.

Creatures of habit like my dad and I don't need alarms. The sunrise calls to me, so I reluctantly leave the naked woman next to me to go out on my deck and welcome a new day. After I feel the official beginning, the end of another darkness, I run to Dunks and get doughnuts and coffee.

Vivian is still asleep by the time I return, and I can't believe the way she's managed to spread her long body diagonally across my bed. I assumed someone who slept in a twin every night would stay huddled on the edge. So much for that theory.

I set breakfast on the nightstand and remove my shirt and shorts before finding a small section of the bed in which to lie next to her. She's sleeping on her stomach with her tangled hair hiding her face. I have an unobstructed view of her back. Of course I'm curious about her scars, but I won't ask. That might be her past to be shared in the future, just not today. I lean over her and kiss one of the closed blossoms hiding a scar, then another, and another.

"Oli," she says in a groggy voice.

I move lower and kiss the soft curve of her ass. "Did you just call me Oli?"

"Mmmhmm." She draws in an audible breath then flips over and sits up. Her nipples are pebbled, and her raven hair is everywhere and so damn sexy. My already hard dick pulses. I tried to play it cool last night, like bathing with her and sleeping next to her naked wasn't torturing me. How stupid am I?

"I smell doughnuts." She whips her head around and grabs the box.

"Doughnuts? Only you would smell doughnuts in a box before steamy coffee."

She flips open the lid and grins so big.

Thump, thump, thump ... my dick pulses.

"Boston Kreme." She swipes some chocolate frosting off the top and sucks it slowly off her finger. "Mmm ..."

Thump, thump, thump.

I grab my coffee and take a sip, hoping the caffeine will counteract the effect she's having on me.

She sticks her finger in the hole and moves it around before pulling out the creamy filling and sucking it off with a soft moan while she closes her eyes.

THUMP, THUMP, THUMP!

I choke on my coffee as it scorches my tongue and the roof of my mouth.

"You okay?"

I nod, setting the coffee back on the nightstand while clearing my throat. She sticks her finger back in that damn hole.

"Stop!"

Her eyes go wide and she sticks her coated finger in her mouth again. "Stop what?" she mumbles around it.

Her innocence in the matter only makes things worse. There's nothing sexier than a woman who doesn't know she's sexy.

"This!" I pull her finger out of her mouth and stick it in mine then ease it out rolling my tongue around it. "Finger-fucking your doughnut. Stop. Finger-fucking. Your. Doughnut."

She giggles. "That's not what I'm doing."

"Yes, that *is* what you're doing and it's ..."

She takes a slow, seductive lick of the frosting off the top. "It's what?" I swear she purrs the words.

"Nothing." I shake my head.

Vivian cocks hers to the side. "Does watching me eat this doughnut turn you on, Oli?"

"What's with the Oli? And what do you think?" I gesture to my erection straining against my briefs.

She wets her lips and grins while pushing me back on the bed. I see the mischief dancing in those alluring eyes as she frees me from my briefs. Straddling my legs, she sits up straight and swipes her tongue through the frosting on her doughnut again.

THUMP, THUMP, THUMP!

Then she sticks her finger in the hole and pulls out a glob of cream filling and wipes it on my dick.

"What? Ah, don't do that—" I start to protest until she licks me and ... oh God ... sucks ... it ... off me. "Yes, oh ... do that ... please ... do ... that ..."

WE SIT in bed and finish our coffee, and Vivian finishes her doughnut like she didn't just lick and suck half of it off my dick. There must be some serious health code violation that just happened, but she left me with too big of a smile on my face to really give a damn.

"I fell into the smoldering embers of a campfire my senior year. It was an accident. I lost six inches of my hair and had third-degree burns."

Um ... okay. I guess we're talking about this.

Speechless. I didn't think she'd open up so soon. In a way relief washes over me. My mind had conjured up so many different scenarios, some of them involving abuse.

"Skin grafts were an option, but they weren't needed to prevent infection so I chose not to have the procedure. The donor tissue would have been from my legs, leaving a whole new area of scarring."

I take her cup and set it down next to mine then pull her between my legs so her back is to me. She gathers her hair and pulls it to one side in front of her shoulder, and I feel this whole new responsibility.

Trust.

Vivian has let me into her life and shown me a part of her that very few people have ever seen. She's given me her trust and now she's showing me everything because she *trusts* that I will accept her and protect the most vulnerable part of her.

I trace my fingers along the branches and over the blossoms, feeling the uneven terrain from her scars. She turns and looks at me. A hint of uncertainty still lingers in her tensed eyes. I smile and kiss her shoulder.

"No take backs," I whisper.

⁂

Vivian freshens up in my bathroom while I clean up the pillow disaster and assess the damage to my phone. It's amazing that she's still here. My behavior yesterday had to be a little frightening to someone who hasn't known me for long.

"You working today or buying a new phone?"

I look up to see her coming down the stairs in her very short shorts, a tank top, and her hair tied back into submission. "Both." I hold up my shattered phone. "This isn't me. What you saw yesterday ... I'm not usually a violent person."

She shrugs and hops up on the counter, grabbing my shirt while pulling me between her legs. "This morning, what I did…" she grins "…I don't usually lick Boston Kreme filling off my neighbor's cock."

I devour the skin on her neck, working my way up to those lips, the same lips that, yes, were wrapped around my cock an hour earlier. My hands can't resist cupping her breasts and when she moans and leans her head to the side inviting more of my touch, I realize I'm starting something that I don't have time to finish, and said cock is not going to be too happy with me.

"We should get going." My words don't sound very convincing.

She wraps her legs around my waist. "Are you sure?"

I grab her ankles and free myself from her suggestive proposition. "Unfortunately, yes, I'm sure."

"Dinner later?" Her hopeful eyes widen.

"I have dinner with my parents later. Maybe you could come over after I get back."

She purses her lips and nods once. "Actually, it slipped my mind. I have plans tonight."

"You do?"

She hops off the counter. "Yep."

"Okay, well I'll be at the Boat Club with my dad in the morning, but we could do something in the afternoon."

She stretches up on her toes and kisses me. "Sounds good. So I'll see you tomorrow unless we run into each other before then."

"You taking the T this morning?"

She opens the door. "I catch a ride with Alex on Saturdays."

I nod, a little perplexed by her aloof attitude.

CHAPTER NINE

ALL IN THE FAMILY

Vivian

Never underestimate a woman whose goal in life is to be the next Amazon. Oliver is smart and has the paper certificate from Harvard to prove it, but I'm driven and right now that trumps his law degree. The most successful people in life know there's more than one way to get invited to the exclusive events. Today, that's me.

"So my brain's a little fuzzy. Let me just see if I have this straight." Alex watches me water the fruit trees while she sips her drink and lounges in one of the display Adirondack chairs. "Oliver swooped in and took you away from Chance last night to take your virginity himself. And now you're crazy about him, but he didn't invite you to dinner at his parents' tonight so you're going with Chance since he did invite you?"

"Basically."

"How did you get Chance to agree to still take you?"

"I baited him. I called and apologized for last night and as expected he said he'd see me tonight, naturally assuming

Oliver would be bringing me. When I told him I hadn't received an invite he *reminded* me that I had received one from him at dinner last night. I acted unsure about going, but he insisted and said Oliver sometimes needs a little nudge."

"I've gotta say, I underestimated you, Flower."

"Everyone does." I throw her a sly grin.

"Do you think Oliver is going to be mad when he finds out?"

"Maybe, but I've got that covered."

Alex rolls her eyes. "I expect a full report tomorrow."

I spray the water at her and she squeals. "I expect you to get off your ass and help out today!"

"Okay, okay, okay!" She leaps out of the chair and scurries off.

CHANCE PICKS me up at the end of the street. Of course I am secretly thrilled he wants this to be a surprise to Oliver as much as I do.

"Hey, Viv, has my bonehead brother left yet?" Chance asks as I get in his truck.

"No, his car is still in the street. Did you two get along today?"

Chance laughs. "Yes. I didn't even give him shit about cock blocking me last night, but you really should have told me about the two of you."

I grimace. "I know, sorry. He's just so ..."

"Stubborn? Frustrating? Bullheaded?"

I giggle. "Yes, yes, and yes. Yet, I like him ... a lot."

Chance gives me a quick sideways glance and smiles.

"He likes you too. The idiot looked like the Joker from Batman today with a stupid smirk plastered to his face."

"Really?"

"Really."

We arrive at their parents' house and a bad case of nerves creeps up on me as Chance leads me up the cobblestone drive to their all brick two-story hidden by a forest of tall trees. My heart pulses in my throat and my palms are sweaty—great for first time introductions.

"Don't be nervous. They're going to love you, and when they find out you're really with Oliver they're going to love you even more."

I squint at him. "Why would that be?"

"He needs you more than I do." Chance opens the door and ushers me in before I get the opportunity to say anything else.

His parents are out back sipping wine and relaxing in an outdoor oasis that resembles something I've seen on Home and Garden TV—a jungle of flowers, ivy, bird feeders, and illuminated lanterns hanging from tree branches.

"Hey, this is my friend, Vivian. She works at The Green Pot where I get most of my supplies. She also lives across the street from Oliver."

His mom greets me first as they both stand. "Vivian, lovely to meet you. I'm Jackie and this is my husband, Hugh."

She curls her blond-highlighted chin-length hair behind her ear. Her tall, lean frame resembles mine, and her blue eyes match both her sons'. Hugh smiles down at me from his even taller stature. He has a completely bald head and hazel-gray eyes.

I shake both of their hands. "You too. You have a lovely home. Thanks for having me."

Jackie waves off my comment. "We're so glad Chance invited you. It can get a little boring around here with my three guys talking baseball and rowing. This place could use a little more estrogen."

I laugh as the nervous tension evaporates.

"Can I offer you some wine?" Hugh holds out a glass of red wine.

I take it. "Yes, thank you."

"Please have a seat, dinner will be ready soon." Jackie gestures to the circle of floral pillowed chairs surrounding a stone-masoned fire pit.

"Ah, here he comes." Hugh stands and walks into the house leaving the porch door open.

"Your brother brought a mutual friend, she's out back." I hear Hugh say to Oliver.

"Who's that?" Oliver comes to an abrupt halt at the back door when his eyes meet mine.

I smile and try to read his face, but tonight it's void, not a hint of emotion.

Chance hands him a bottle of beer and pats him on the back. "Yesterday I invited Viv to dinner. I assumed she was coming with you tonight, but when we chatted on the phone earlier she said you hadn't mentioned it. I assured her it was an oversight on your part and insisted she come."

I thought this was a good idea, but now Oliver's brow tenses. He looks shocked and maybe ... disappointed? My heart plummets into my stomach.

"Have a seat, sweetie," Jackie says to Oliver. "I'm going to bring the salad out while Chance helps your dad with the grill.

Chance squeezes Oliver's shoulder then walks over toward Hugh by the grill. Jackie leans up and kisses Oliver's cheek as she passes him on her way back into the house.

He walks toward me where I now sit alone by the fire. I wish he'd smile or say something to let me know that last night happened and I'm not his dirty little secret. He takes a swig of his beer, sets it down, and holds out his hand to me. I take it and he pulls me to my feet, but then he whispers in my ear and my feet no longer touch the ground with his words taking me so far beyond the confinements of gravity.

"You look beautiful." He kisses my ear. "I'm an ass. I should have invited you." Then in a move that leaves me speechless, he kisses me. Not a quick kiss, a slow kiss that makes a statement. "I'm so glad you're here."

I smile and blink back the tears. This was my game and he's turned the tables and taken control of the night. Fine with me.

I hear someone clear their throat and we both turn. His parents and Chance are all watching us.

"I didn't tell Mom and Dad that Viv is more than just your friend, but I think they know now." Chance grins and to my surprise, and relief, so do his parents.

Oliver pulls me into his arms and looks down at me with mischief playing across his lips. "Yes, we're more than friends. We're *neighbors*." He winks at me.

"Well, let's eat," Hugh says.

Oliver holds my hand and leads me to the table. Jackie stares at us both, and I swear I see tears in her eyes as she smiles. He is the perfect gentleman, pulling my chair out for me and refilling my glass of wine. I raise my eyebrow at him since I'm already feeling a buzz and one more glass could cause unnecessary embarrassment in front of his family.

"Are you originally from the Boston area?" Jackie asks as she passes around the serving dishes.

"No, I'm from Hartford. That's where my parents still live."

"What brought you to Cambridge?" Hugh asks.

I take a sip of my water. "I'll be attending Harvard Business School in the fall."

"Your first year?" he asks.

"Yes, I had some unexpected expenses come up so I wasn't able to start right out of high school. My best friend is in Harvard Med and he introduced me to my roommate who then introduced me to her aunt who owns the nursery where I've been working over the past couple years. Sorry, I'm probably confusing you." I realize my nerves are getting the best of me.

"No, not at all." Hugh smiles.

I don't look at Oliver because I'm afraid he's giving me the you-left-out-the-part-about-your-parents-thinking-you're-in-school-now look.

"Viv? How have I known you for two years but never knew you were waiting to be a Harvard snob too?" Chance says as his parents give him disapproving looks.

"You might have known if you'd have spent more time getting to know her instead of hitting on her." Oliver shakes his head.

Chance shrugs and shoves in a mouthful of food. "You're probably right," he mumbles.

A perfectly relaxed dinner segues into more easy conversation around the fire pit. I'm envious of Oliver and Chance having their parents not only close but available. I have wonderful parents and when we're together we have a lot of fun, but growing up, one or the other—and often times both—worked just to make ends meet. We didn't have dinner parties and wine around a fire pit.

I try to pace myself on the wine by eating plenty of food and drinking lots of water, but that only serves to make me need to use the bathroom every twenty minutes. This time when I return, Oliver pulls me onto his lap before I get to my chair. His family watches us with adoration on their faces that can be seen through the soft illumination of the fire and tree lanterns.

"I think we should leave soon," he whispers in my ear.

My mildly inebriated body is warm already, but his breath against my neck elevates my temperature to a near sweat. "But I'm having such a nice time." I rest the back of my head against his shoulder and gaze at the mesmerizing flames.

"I think you'll have a *nice time* at my place too." His lips brush my bare shoulder next to my sundress strap and his tongue wets my skin making me squirm in his lap.

Sliding me off his lap, we both stand. "We're going to take off."

"Yeah, I'm going to stay for a little bit yet, would it be too much to ask for you to drop Viv off at her place for me?" Chance tips back his beer bottle to mask his smart-ass grin.

Oliver doesn't acknowledge him with words. Instead, he grabs his beer and empties the rest in the grass.

"Hey, what the hell?" Chance yells.

"If you don't ease up you won't even be driving your own ass home." Oliver smacks the back of his head.

"Thank you so much for dinner. It was incredible and I've had the best time tonight." I address both Jackie and Hugh with sincere thanks.

"It was our pleasure. Hope to see you next week. You have a permanent standing invitation in case either one of our sons forgets to show their manners and invite you."

Oliver shakes his head.

"Are we still on for the morning, Son?" Hugh asks Oliver.

"Absolutely, see you bright and early."

Jackie stands and gives us both hugs.

"Bye, Chance. Thanks for the invite." I lean down and kiss him on the cheek.

Oliver is quick to tug my arm and pull me away from his brother.

"Bye, Viv. Tell my big bro to chill. We can share you. It's all in the family."

———

OLIVER USHERS me to the car with his hands all over me. Even my numbing buzz can't mask the sexual tension sparking between us. Somewhere between a step, a breath, and a blink, he's managed to pin my body facedown against the passenger door of his car. If we're role-playing good cop-bad cop, he's definitely not the former.

"Did I mention how much I like this dress?" His voice is deep, breathy, and teetering on the edge. I feel his erection pressed against my ass as his hands snake up my sides and cup my breasts.

"Yes," I whisper.

"No bra?"

"No, straps would show." My eyes roll back in my head. The wine, his hands, his voice, and those hips pulsing into me dissolve all coherent thoughts. I could pass out.

And in the same time-stealing instant, he's no longer pressed against me. I'm nothing more than a lifeless bug splattered on his car.

"Let's go."

I peel myself from the window as he opens the door. My body collapses in the seat, someone with more dexterity than I, fastens my seat belt, and the door is closed. Oliver starts the engine then leans over and sucks the last breath out of me with his greedy lips and demanding tongue. His hand slides up by bare thigh and my nonexistent nerves do nothing to stop his approach as I unabashedly spread my legs for him.

He freezes just as my panting reaches the red alert mark. "Where the hell are your underwear?"

My eyes pop open and my lips pull into a sexy grin. "I'm not wearing any."

"Obviously! Why not?" There's an edge to his voice.

I shrug. "I feel sexy without them."

He sits up and fastens his seat belt then shoves the car into reverse. "News flash, Vivian, you're a walking wet dream in a sundress without panties or in a full suit of armor!"

Pinching my lips together I try to hide my smile. He doesn't say any more until we're parked on our street. Opening my door, he holds out his hand. Something tells me I'd follow this man anywhere.

He flips on the lights as we walk through the front doorway. "Did you get the extra warranty?" I gesture to his new phone charging on the counter.

Oliver turns to me with a soft smile. His gaze caresses my skin.

"How do you do that?" I whisper.

"Do what?"

"Make me feel everything with an invisible touch."

He closes his eyes. In this moment I would crawl through the desert, drink the sand, and risk being eaten alive by snakes and scorpions, just to have one glimpse into his thoughts.

"Tell me what you're thinking." I rest my forehead against his chest.

"I'll show you."

Naked. I step from the pool of cotton at my feet. Lanky legs, bony hips, witchy hair, and a canvas of ink camouflaging the riddling of scars on my back, but it all disappears under his gaze. I see my perfection in his eyes.

He removes his shirt and grins. It's a little cocky, a tad boyish, and a whole lot of sexy. I sit on his enormous bed, scoot to the middle, and cross my legs. Oliver looks at me with a wrinkle of question on his forehead.

"Keep going." I bite on my thumbnail and grin.

He turns around, unfastens his pants, then slides one side down, looking at me over his shoulder while biting his bottom lip.

I giggle.

He eases the other side down.

Another sexy look back at me.

Another giggle.

He continues to make a meal out of undressing for me, and I eat every bit of it up—one deliciously teasing move at a time. Once he's completely naked, he interlaces his hands behind his head and flexes his hard glutes for me. His whole body is cut to a beautiful perfection and his skin ... flawless.

Oliver glances at me over his shoulder again with a playful grin that fades when he sees my face.

"Hey." He turns and crawls up on the bed, pulling me into his arms. "What's wrong?"

"You. You're ... confident and sexy and ... perfect." I swallow back my emotions. "And your skin, it's—"

Oliver presses his finger to my lips and shakes his head. Then his lips replace his finger. Hands of gentle strength glide over my body one small curve at a time.

He's showing me.

Somehow Oliver knows when words are inadequate. I feel his passion and carnal need harnessed with incredible control as he explores my body with his, bringing me to the edge. My body begs for his, every millimeter of space between us is unbearable.

"Oli ... please!" My voice is breathless as his incredible lips brush over my nipples, up my neck, finding home with mine as he sinks into me.

I wrap my legs around his waist, my arms around his neck, and I hold on. Oliver can take me *anywhere*.

Oliver

I'm in a bit of a quandary. The plan for my relationship with Vivian to remain solely physical is failing at a catastrophic level. The physical part is not even in this dimension. It's as if she's starving and I'm the only one in the entire world that has what she needs to survive. Will she wake up one day and realize that I've poisoned her? Will I survive if she does?

My nearly six and a half foot long body curls into a five by two foot space while Vivian sleeps in her greedy diagonal position across the bed. She was on top of me until I slid out at sunrise. My dad will be here soon anyway, but I can't pass up the few spare moments I have to watch her sleep. I'm up to twenty eight on her freckle count.

"I can feel your stare," she mumbles.

"Hold still, I'm not done."

She cracks open one eye, but just a squint. "Done with what?"

"Counting your freckles."

"Oh God!" She throws her arm over her face. "Yet, another undesirable trait of mine."

I pry her arm away and kiss her freckled nose, cheeks, and then her full, delicious lips. I have to adjust my hard-on because she's so damn sexy I can't even think about her without standing at full attention.

"Vivian, I swear I'm going to make it my life's mission to make you see that your brightness blinds the sun."

She brushes her palms over my face. "I don't deserve you."

I kiss her and stand, slowly releasing her hand. "You're right. You deserve better."

"I LIKE HER." My dad pants as he grips the water with his oars.

"I like her too." I exert all my effort while extending my legs and flexing my arms. "Maybe too much."

"And that's a problem?"

"She's so young and she doesn't know anything about me." I grind the words through clenched teeth as rivulets of sweat trickle down my face.

"What do you know about her?"

"She's smart as a whip, has impeccable work ethic. She wants to take over the world, yet she doesn't have a pretentious bone in her body." I suck in another labored breath. "She's kind with a childlike innocence, and seventy-five percent of her back is covered in third-degree burn scars that have been tattooed over."

My dad stops and looks back at me. "I saw part of the tattoo near her neck and shoulders, but her hair covered most of it. I had no idea—"

I shake my head. "She fell into a campfire. God, Dad, it's scarred her in more ways than one."

He nods. "Have you met her parents?"

"No, of course as you know, they don't live around here, but I don't know if I'm ready to be that person in her life—as in, the guy she takes home."

"You might be right, or you might be being a little hard on yourself. But she deserves the truth, Son. As much as you don't want to acknowledge it, it doesn't change what happened and all secrets get revealed in time."

I take a swig of water and sigh. "Yeah, I know."

I DON'T THINK we make conscious decisions as to what images get burned into our brains. Some of mine will forever haunt me, but this one, I will take to my grave and save it for my next life too.

"Hey, Oli."

Long bare legs extending beyond one of my Harvard Crimson T-shirts stretch out on my couch and cross at the ankles. That sexy mess of raven hair is piled in a knotted bun on her head, and she's wearing black thick-rimmed glasses while reading a paper—an actual newspaper. This naughty school girl image is a keeper.

"What are you doing?" I ask, grabbing a glass of water without taking my eyes off her. Not that I could even if I wanted to.

"Reading the paper, specifically the business section. Why, what does it look like I'm doing?" She folds the top of the paper down and peers at me over the rims of her glasses.

"Where'd you get the paper? You know you can get all

that info online now." I drain my water, wiping the back of my mouth with my wrist.

"I got the paper from my house. I subscribe. And, yes, I'm aware that this information is available online." She brings the paper to her nose and sniffs. "Ah, but this smell. You can't get it online. I love the smell of newspapers and books. I rarely use my Kindle. Besides, it reminds me of my grandparents. They used to live near us and I'd stop by their house on my way to school. My grandma would pour me a cup of orange juice in one of those little juice glasses with the flowers on the outside and I'd sip it and watch her and my grandpa drink their coffee and read the newspaper. It still smells the same."

I'm conflicted right now. I should feel the urge to share one of my own childhood memories. But I'm a guy ... with *her* looking like *this* on my couch so the only urge I'm feeling is the one to bend her over the back of the couch and make her scream in ecstasy. I'm not proud of it.

I walk closer. "Glasses, huh?"

Vivian nods. "I only need them to read, otherwise I get a headache."

I lift the hem of my shirt she's wearing. *No underwear, again!*

"Did you walk to your place wearing this?"

She gives me the over-the-glasses'-rim look again. "Yes, why?"

God! The neighbors must love her. I shake my head, roll my eyes to the ceiling, and sigh. "No reason, I'm going to shower."

A very cold shower!

"I'm going home to shower and get dressed," Vivian yells into the bathroom while I'm in the shower.

"It was a perfect morning on the water. We should go boating," I call over the water.

"Boating?" she says with uncertainty in her voice.

"Yes, my parents own a boat. We can take it out, pack some lunch, make a day of it."

"Um ..."

"I'm not taking no for an answer. Go grab your suit, pack a bag, sunscreen, whatever."

I lather my hair and wait for a reply, but I don't hear anything. Maybe she's left already. Peeking my head out, I see her leaning against the door frame picking at her lower lip, eyes downcast.

"What's wrong?"

"Nothing ... Well, I don't have a swimsuit. They're back at my parent's house. I'll just wear a sundress or shorts and a tank."

"You don't have a swimsuit?"

Vivian shakes her head.

"How can you not have—"

Her gaze falters and I physically feel the pain radiating from her.

"In that case, shower, get dressed, and I'll be over to get you in an hour."

She squints at me.

"No questions, just go." I give her a simple wink and a smile.

Her shoulders slump and she nods a few times before turning and walking out like an errant child. I want to chase after her, wrap her in my arms, and squeeze all the painful insecurity from her body, but I don't. The intricate details of her self-doubt that are woven beneath her surface cannot be unraveled in a day. I know this, but it still won't stop me from trying.

———

"Where are we going?" Vivian asks as we turn onto Soldiers Field Road.

"Shopping."

"For?"

I give her a sideways glance and a grin. "Necessities."

"There's more than one 7-Eleven in Cambridge."

"Not quite the necessities we need." I rest my right hand on her bare leg.

"*We?*"

"Yes, *we.*"

Vivian shakes her head and stares out her window. By some miracle I find a parking spot and parallel my smaller car in between two SUVs.

"Newbury Street? Hope you brought your black card."

"Funny coming from the woman who will probably own Newbury Street someday."

Vivian opens her door before I have a chance to get out. "Wall Street, Oli, not Newbury Street." She grins and hops out.

We both slip on our sunglasses, I take her hand, and we walk down the sidewalk scoping out the multi-level stores and boutiques.

"Why do you call me Oli?"

"It's short for Oliver, doesn't anyone else call you Oli?"

"Not since I was a kid."

She looks up at me. "You don't like it?"

"I didn't until ..."

"Until what?"

I can't hide my grin. She stops and faces me. "Tell me."

Bending down I brush my lips against hers. "Until you begged me last night, 'Oli ... please!'"

Her skin flushes and she shoves my chest. "Jerk. How do you like that instead? That's your new name because you're making fun of me."

I palm the back of her head and pull her back to me, tasting every inch of her mouth until her body melts into my touch. I'm sure people are staring, but I don't give a damn.

"I'm not making fun of you," I whisper as she rubs her lips together. "Now let's get what we need and get out on the water."

CHAPTER TEN
I COULD LOVE YOU

Vivian

"I'M NOT WEARING THIS." I yell from the dressing room.

"Let me see." Oliver chuckles sitting on the bench outside.

"No. Tell the clerk to bring me a one-piece that's not cut low in the back.

"Vivian, you're twenty-one, not fifty. You're not getting a one-piece. I'm the only one who's going to see you in it."

"Oli—*Oliver*, it doesn't cover—"

He opens the door and slips in the dressing room with me.

"Get out!" I try to cover myself.

He smirks. "It's *Oli* to you, and I've seen you naked. What? Are you trying to hide from *me*?"

I huff, letting out a sigh as I release my arms to my side. His seductive eyes consume my body as his tongue slides out to wet his lips.

"Turn around."

I shake my head.

He cocks his head to the side. "Really?"

"Fine!" I turn around.

He moves my hair off my back and kisses my neck as we stare at each other in the mirror. "Alluring, captivating, divine, elegant, exquisite, mesmerizing, radiant, ravishing ... stunning," he whispers.

"What are you talking about?" I roll my eyes.

"You. In case you're tired of hearing me call you beautiful. I have at least a hundred more. I could go on."

I stare at the simple white string bikini Oliver picked out. It barely covers my most private parts, let alone anything on my back. But for some reason, I want to please him today.

"I'll get it. Now get out of here."

Oliver lights up like the Fourth of July. Simultaneously, he pulls the ties on my hips letting the material fall to the ground. I raise a single brow.

"Just testing it out ... for later." He smirks. "I approve."

"Pervert."

"Not yet." He pulls the ties to my top revealing my naked breasts. "Now I am." He winks. "See you in a few minutes."

He looks all too pleased with himself as I exit the dressing room.

"Here." He holds out his hand as I exit with the flimsy material.

"You're not buying this."

"Yes, I am."

"Would you like me to add that to the rest of your stuff?" the clerk asks.

"The *rest* of my stuff?"

"Yes, Miss. The gentleman has some undergarments for you as well."

I sling the squinted death look at Oliver. "Panties? You're buying me panties?"

He motions for the clerk to take my bikini and he hands her his credit card. It's not black.

"I don't need panties."

"I disagree," he says with his back to me as he signs for the purchase at the counter. He takes the bag in one hand and grabs my hand with his other. "Shall we?" He leads me out of the store.

"*A,* I have plenty of panties. *B,* I told you I don't wear them sometimes because it makes me feel sexy."

He opens my door and sets the bag by my feet after I get in. Then he leans down and brings his face a breath away from mine as his hand slides up my leg. His thumb eases past my shorts. He stops and shakes his head as the pad of it meets my bare sex, no underwear.

My face contorts into a grimacing smile as my shoulders rise into a guilty shrug. He presses his thumb to my now wet center. My mouth relaxes as I suck in a breath and try to close the distance between our lips. He moves his head back just enough to deny me. He grins then moves his thumb a little higher. I moan as he rubs slow circles.

"How do you feel?" he whispers.

"G–good." I grip the side of the seat and let my head fall back.

"What else?"

"Turned ... on." I close my eyes.

"What else?"

I tilt my hips up as he works me up so high I fear my own reaction to the impending fall.

"Oli ..."

He speeds up, pressing his lips to my neck, and when his teeth graze over my sensitive skin I lose it.

"What. Else?" he whispers in my ear as the blinding sensation rips through me.

"Sexy ... I feel ... sexy." I try to catch my breath while my head's still spinning.

He kisses me hard then shuts my door.

I hate that I have no self-control to deny him giving me an orgasm while parked with the door open on a public street. Now he's sporting a ridiculously smug grin as he pulls out into traffic.

"What was the point of that?" I break the silence.

"I wanted to prove that *I* make you feel sexy. Now that you know that, you can start wearing underwear."

"What does it matter if no one else can see that I'm not wearing underwear?"

"First, some of the dresses you wear are awfully short. Second, *I* know you're not wearing underwear and I don't like walking around saluting everyone I pass."

"Saluting?"

He shoots me a you-know-what-I-mean look.

"Whatever, you're just being weird."

"I'm being a guy."

"That's what I said. You're being weird."

"CAN you believe I've never seen Boston from the harbor like this?" I say, sitting on his lap as he takes us farther away from the coastline. I'm wearing *the* bikini and he has on his board shorts with no shirt.

"Are you serious?"

"I know, it's crazy. There are tons of boat tours, even the whale watch, but I've never gone. I haven't even been over to the airport."

He nuzzles his face in my hair and kisses the back of my head. "What do you think?"

I laugh. "It's amazing. When you think about all that land that was manmade and the tall buildings sitting where there used to be water ... it's incredible."

"I think you're incredible." He kisses my shoulder, squeezing me tighter.

"I think you've lived here so long you're taking it all for granted."

He slides his hand over my stomach and up to my breast, slipping his fingers under my top. "I think we need to throw out the anchor and go down below."

"Oli ..." My breath hitches as he cups my breast.

"I can't wait. You in my shirt with those sexy glasses this morning, and now this bikini ... God, I'm dying, Vivian."

"How many women have seen this view with you?"

His body stills against mine. We're one with the rhythmic sway of the ocean.

"Does it matter?" His hand moves from my breast back to my waist.

"Of course not. It doesn't change anything, I'm just curious." I'm twenty-one with enough insecurities to sink this boat, and while I'm too smart to really think this is a good conversation for us to share, I'm too young to not have a burning curiosity.

"I can't really say. It's not my boat, so I've been on here with my parents' friends and Chance's friends ..."

"That's not what I mean."

He brings the boat to an idle on the choppy water. "Then what do you mean?" He stands, forcing me off his lap. Lifting the cooler lid, he grabs a beer. Keeping his back to me, he takes a pull and looks out into the saltwater abyss.

I sit back down and wait. There's really nothing else I

can do. I'm seeing the one percent of Oliver that is consumed by something else—something that scares me. There's this inferno of anger he falls into sometimes, but I think it's fueled by pain. I see it in his eyes like the night he shattered his phone. The man crying in his room was an Oliver I don't know. Where do we stand now and where can we possibly go from here if he can't show me his scars— bare himself to me?

"We should go back."

"No!" His voice cuts through the air with a sharp edge. "I just ... need a minute."

Everyone has a crazy button and it's usually hidden like a land mine waiting to be detonated by some poor unsuspecting person who just happens to take a wrong step. Oliver should have watched his step ... he just hit mine.

"Absolutely! Take all the minutes you need. I'll just wait here with my heart on my shoulder because I don't have a sleeve to wear it on since you picked out these ridiculous string pieces of nothing that leave me completely exposed to the whole fucking world! Or maybe I'll take a dip in the water and get eaten by sharks since I look like shark bait anyway and you'll be let off the hook of having to answer one *simple* question about your past!"

Oliver turns. "Two. Two women before you have seen this view with me—my mom and a girl I dated in college."

He lifts the top to one of the back seats and takes my sundress out of my bag. I uncross my protective arms as he slips it over my head. Shoulders slumped, head bowed, he pulls me into his arms and we collapse on the seats as the midday sun gets lost in the overcast gathering of clouds. The wind begins to cast a chill upon my skin and Oliver holds me closer, shielding me from the breeze, the world ... myself.

"I used to love going to Michigan to visit my grandparents. They had Tupperware and glass containers everywhere filled with candy and cookies. We only had candy at our house on Halloween and Easter, so Chance and I would drain their stash until we were doubled over at the toilet in misery. But by the next morning, we'd be feeling better and ready to raid the pantry, which was stocked with all the good cereals that we saw on TV but rarely got to have. Fruit Loops was my favorite. I'd eat the entire box with a half-gallon of whole milk." He laughs. "Milk never tasted so good—sugar and FD and C numbers one through a million."

I turn in his arms and rest my head against his chest. "I'm sorry."

"Don't be, we loved it so it was worth the stomach ache—"

I press my lips to his. He smiles against mine. "I'm sorry too," he murmurs.

Draping my leg over his hip, I move my hands to his face and deepen our kiss. He slides his hand up my leg and under my dress palming my ass with a firm grasp.

I moan into his mouth, sliding my tongue against his. Oliver draws emotions from me that I never knew existed. I'm the go-with-the-flow girl, a survivor, a lover of life. Burying my emotions, veiling them behind the façade I want people to see is my specialty. But I can't with Oliver. I want him to see me, all of me, even the ugly. He takes all of it and makes it better.

Oliver's mouth moves along my jaw as I draw in a deep breath.

"We should throw out the anchor ... and go down below." My words are anxious, my body desperate.

Oliver chuckles while grazing my earlobe with his teeth. "Brilliant idea."

Fighting the sway of the boat, we navigate the stairs to the bed. I pull my dress over my head and find admiring eyes watching me. I reach for my bikini ties. Oliver shakes his head and I grin. He tugs the hip ties at the same time and then repeats with my top. I don't give him another second to look at me. With one leap I'm in his arms, legs wrapped around his waist.

He takes two steps and we fall to the bed. The pillows are tossed to the floor as his eager mouth explores my breasts and he works his board shorts over his hips. I reach for him, wrapping my hand around his erection. He sucks in a breath, mouth slack, eyes heavy as I stroke him.

"Oli, I love your body." I look down to watch him make small thrusts into my hand. His arms, abs, and legs are tense; lean muscles ripple with every move. I push him onto his back and straddle his stomach. "You're beautiful." I run my fingers over his chest. "I know you probably don't like to be called beautiful..." I reach behind and continue to stroke him more "...but you are. You're flawless."

His eyes sear me and his jaw clenches as I scoot back and sink onto him. I take it slow, one inch at time as he stretches me. My eyes close with the intensity. He sits up and captures my mouth as our bodies move together. I seek pleasure in his touch as much as I crave giving him pleasure with mine.

"Oh God, sex with you ... is so ... amazing!" I suck his neck and tug at his hair before finding his lips again and kissing him like it's the last time we'll ever kiss.

He moans into me, but no words. He speaks with hands that clench my ass, hips that rock into me again and again, and lips that devour my skin. I'm not chasing my orgasm, I'm basking in this sexual journey, focusing on the way my flesh feels against his. I don't ever want it to end.

Oliver

I'м in so deep with this woman I don't know which way is up, and honestly, I don't care. I could drown in her and die happy. Her passion sucks me into a world I've never known. I think it may be Heaven.

"Are you sure you need to sleep in your own bed tonight?" I ask, walking Vivian to her red door.

"Alex is home tonight and I have laundry to do. I've been distracted lately and I've fallen behind on a few things." She snakes her arms under mine, resting her head on my chest. "You could stay with me tonight."

I laugh. "Sleep with you in your twin bed?"

She looks up at me with a grin. "Good night, handsome."

I stare at her—windblown hair, sun-kissed skin, and freckles that I find innocent and yet incredibly sexy. Then I can't hold back, so I kiss her until I'm certain she's no longer standing on her own. It's not my intention, but every day I feel like that's what is happening. I'm taking everything she gives and one day it could be too much.

"Good night, Vivian."

She opens the door then turns back for one more kiss. "Thank you for today. It was perfect."

I grin and nod.

Lately I have this problem. The grin on my face ... it's permanent. I reach my door and turn back. Vivian and Alex are staring out the window at me. They jump back and shut the blinds. I shake my head. What I'd give to hear that conversation tonight.

Grabbing a glass of water, I head upstairs to bed. I stop

and touch my hand to the door. Shame, regret, and so much anger hides behind it. Some days I can justify it in my own twisted way. They're just things and I know I shouldn't need them and I probably shouldn't have them, but I can't get rid of them. If Vivian ever found out she wouldn't understand. A rational person doesn't do this, but I'm not rational ... not anymore.

I haven't opened the door once since I first locked it. Tonight is the night. Vivian has made me stronger. Maybe I don't need it anymore. Lifting the cobalt vase off the hall console table, I turn it upside down and a lone key falls out. Unlocking both the knob and the dead bolt, I rest my head on the door. God, how did this happen? How did such darkness creep into my life?

I turn the knob like a dial to my heart; the thunder racking my chest becomes more painful with each turn. The door creaks as I inch it open. I close my eyes, the feeling alone is nearly unbearable. I can't look. One step in, that's enough. I lean against the wall just inside the door and slide to the ground. The strength I thought I had vanishes. Hugging my knees to my chest, I squeeze my eyes shut even tighter, but I can still see it. The hate has swallowed up the love and that makes me hate her even more.

Despite the restless night that will catch up with my body in a few hours, I wake with the sun and muddle my way through my morning routine. Lacing up my leather work boots, I laugh to myself. Who would have thought that I'd trade my three-piece suits and boardroom coffee with the firm's partners for leather boots and gloves?

When I open the door the anguish from eight hours ago

disappears like waking from a bad dream. Vivian sits on her front steps resting her elbows on her knees with her chin in one hand while her other twists a few long raven locks.

My grin is back and it feels amazing. She stands, blinding me with her own perfect smile before running across the street and leaping into my arms. I kiss her, once again taking everything I can, everything I need.

"Good morning," she whispers against my lips.

"It is now." I give her one more kiss and ease her body down mine until her feet are back on the ground. "Did you get your laundry done?"

"Yes, Mom." She moves her arm around my back and slips her hand in my back pocket then nudges me to start walking.

"Are you wearing underwear today?"

"Wouldn't you like to know?" She squeezes my ass.

"You'd better be."

"What are you going to do if I'm not? Spank me?"

I about choke on my own tongue. Does she want me to spank her? "Uh ... I ..."

She glances up and I can feel the heat in my face. I'm sure she can see it too. "I'm kidding."

"Boston Kreme and a Dunkaccino?" I open the door to Dunks for her, anxious to change the subject.

She nods wetting her lips then biting them together with a smile so seductive I could combust in the damn doughnut shop.

We have ten minutes so we take a seat so she can at least finish her doughnut before catching the T.

"Coffee black and no doughnut? How boring, Oli." She runs her tongue through the chocolate frosting.

"I ate at five this morning."

"I can't believe you watch the sunrise every morning.

And that was almost three hours ago. Aren't you hungry again?" She sticks her finger in the filling hole.

I rake my hands through my hair then scrub them over my face while releasing a frustrated groan. "Just eat the damn doughnut, Vivian!"

She sucks the cream off her finger. "A little *testy* this morning?" I start to shift in my chair, but her bare foot slides between my legs stopping me cold.

"Vivian ..." I look around to see if anyone is watching us.

She doesn't. Her eyes stay on me as she continues demonstrating her R-rated version of breakfast.

I grab her foot. "Put your shoe back on."

Curling her toes into my crotch, she shakes her head and slides her finger out of her mouth. "Nope," she says, popping the *P*.

"I'm serious."

"Oli, do you want to spank me?"

"What?"

Her foot strokes me. "You seemed ... flustered when I joked about spanking me."

For fuck's sake, woman, you're really sitting here trying to get me off in the middle of Dunkin' Donuts while asking me if I want to spank you! "I hadn't ... given it ... much ... thought." God, I can't think. I'm hard as steel and trying to gain some composure, but I can't. Instead, I'm guiding her foot with my hand. In between my thoughts about licking that frosting off her tits and my memories of her licking it off my dick, I manage to squeeze in a few rational ones. What will I tell my family when they're called to bail me out of jail because I've been arrested for lewd and indecent behavior?

She shrugs. "Okay. Well, Alex and her boyfriend, Sean, are going to stay in Cape Cod this weekend. His parents have a vacation home there. Alex asked me if I wanted to go and she invited you too." Her foot continues to bring me so close to losing my junk I can barely hear her. Vivian, however, continues to eat her doughnut and sip her coffee as if nothing is going on under the table. "Kai and his girlfriend are going too."

I'm not sure I could speak if I wanted to. Just keeping my eyes open has become an incredible challenge. My brain is trying hard to make sense of what she just said. I think something about cock ... or maybe it was cod, Cape Cod and Kai?

"I know it's short notice and this is a busy time of year for you and Chance, but maybe you could check with him and see if you can get this weekend off."

My hands tense, one around my coffee cup the other around her foot. I swallow hard as each breath becomes more labored.

"So do you, Oli?" She sucks the last bit of frosting off her finger, in and out, in and out. "Do you think you can *get it off?*"

"Shit!" I yell, through clenched teeth as I fist my coffee cup sending hot liquid everywhere and my dick does the same damn thing in my pants.

We both jump to our feet as a few other people around us whisper and gawk.

"Oh my gosh, sir!" One of the employees rushes over with a towel. "Are you okay? Did you burn yourself?" She makes fast moves to clean up the table.

"No ... um, I'm sorry." I glance up at Vivian. She's trying hard to hide her sadistic smile. I grab her hand and drag her out the door. She gasps as I pin her to the side of the building with my whole body. "Did you enjoy that?" I fight to control my anger that has been fueled by humiliation.

She doesn't answer. Wide green eyes stare at me refusing to blink.

"Well the answer to your question is *yes*. I want to spank you so fucking bad right now and I've never wanted to spank anyone before." I move my mouth next to her ear. "So congratulations, you'll be my first," I whisper before walking off without her and without looking back.

CHAPTER ELEVEN
ME AND MY DOM

Vivian

JUST A TYPICAL MONDAY MORNING. Alex invited me and my Dom to Cape Cod this weekend. I had my usual doughnut and coffee for breakfast. Then I showed up fifteen minutes late to work because my Dom threatened—scratch that, he *promised*—that he would spank me, therefore causing me to hide from him like a child and take the next train.

Me: *Have you ever been spanked?*
Alex: *Yes, my parents were all 'spare the rod spoil the child.'*
Me: *Not what I mean.*
Alex: *Not following …*
Me: *Has Sean ever spanked you … in bed.*
Alex: *Um … NO!*
Me: *Okay, just wondered. Have a good day!*
Alex: *NFW! Did Oliver spank you?!*
Me: *No … not yet.*
Alex: *?*

Me: *There was an incident at DD this morning involving dough-nuts, coffee, and cock stroking. Long story short, it didn't end well. I'll explain later, bye!*
Alex: *My naughty little Flower! Can't wait!*

I don't even know who that guy was this morning. My Oli is sexy with a dash of spicy but a sweet aftertaste. The guy who pinned me to the wall this morning was one hundred percent Habanero on steroids.

"So how's that new guy of yours?" Maggie asks while preparing her brown bag specials to be divvied out today.

"Hot, he's very, very hot."

She purrs like the cougar I've always suspected her to be. "Sounds like you have your hands full. The times he's been in here he seems like the sweetest young man, a real gentleman. I think you definitely got the better one of the two Konrad boys."

I'm not sure the *gentle*man she's referring to still exists. Everyone has their breaking point, and I may have found Oliver's this morning. He took the first train without me and he hasn't called or texted since. I'm sure he's thinking the same thing about me. It is possible that I'm the one who should be making contact first; an apology might be the proper protocol at this point.

Me: *Did the coffee burn you this morning?*

I decide to ease into things, showing concern for his wellbeing before jumping into any details—testing the water.

Oliver: *No.*

Not the elaborate answer I was expecting.

Me: *I'm sorry, looks like I owe you another new shirt.*

I wait but don't receive a reply. He's mad, of that I am certain. I finish all the outdoor watering, then check my phone again.

Nothing.

Me: *Was the yes just to the spanking or this weekend as well?*

I hesitate a moment then press send.

Oliver: *Both*

What do I say to that? He's planning on going which thrills me, but what about the other part?

Me: *Will one take place before the other?*
Oliver: *Wouldn't you like to know.*

Shit!

Me: *You're welcome for the orgasm.*

"So what happened?" Alex tramples me the moment I walk through the door.

"Nice to see you too. How was your day?"

"I don't have time for this. I'm meeting Sean for dinner and studying, so spill."

I get a drink of water while Alex hops on the kitchen

counter. "I sort of *got him off* at Dunkin' Donuts this morning and he crushed his coffee cup when he ... *released.* I think he was a little embarrassed and on the way there the subject of spanking came up, but only jokingly ... I think. Anyway, after the coffee incident he basically said he planned on spanking me and that's the last I saw of him."

"Oh my God, was he serious?"

I shrug and finish my water. "I don't know, I mean, maybe. He sounded really mad; I didn't even recognize his voice when he said it. Up to this point he's been the shy sexy type but this morning ... I could almost feel the metal handcuffs cutting into my wrists and hear the slap of his hand hitting my bare ass. He was *that* serious."

Alex chews her nails. "Wow, Flower, just ... wow! I mean you jumped in the deep end of the sex pool with Oliver. Sink or swim, what are you going to do?"

"I don't know. He wouldn't hurt me, I do know that. But I wasn't raised the way your parents raised you. I've never been spanked. Hell, I don't think they ever put me in time-out. It's not the pain part either. I've dealt with pain that was far worse than what having my ass slapped could ever be. I think it's the humiliation part of it. I mean, isn't it kind of degrading?"

Alex hops off the counter. "I've heard it's about dominance. Some men think they need to establish it and others do it because they think it turns women on to be controlled by a strong man. There's a role-playing factor as well. Men threaten to spank, women defy them on purpose so their man will in fact spank them. Personally, I prefer to be the dominant one. Maybe I should start smacking Sean on the ass. Lord knows he deserves it."

"Well I don't deserve it and I sure as hell wasn't role-playing with him."

"Flower, you molested him in a freakin' Dunkin' Donuts and then he spilled hot coffee all over himself because of it. Jeez, *I'm* half tempted to paddle your ass for that one." She grabs her bag and opens the front door. "Do what I used to do. Take it like a 'man' and move on. By the way, are you coming this weekend?"

I nod. "Yeah, my Dom and I will be there."

Alex laughs. "Night, Flower."

"Night."

Had the coffee mishap not have happened I would be knocking down Oliver's door to see him. I'm not afraid of apologizing, I'm afraid of rejection. In spite of all the confidence Oliver has given me and all the fears he's taken away, there's still lingering remnants of insecurity that hold their own memories and may never go away.

He might not be home. His car is out front, but he takes the T and walks to so many places, I can't rely on his car to give away his location. I can surge over to his door and breach the frontline, or I can grab my knitting bag and wave the white flag from my front steps. If he's home it might draw him out, if he's not, well, at least I'll get something accomplished.

By eight o'clock my ass is numb and I'm thinking I might need to unravel the mittens and start over. Ever since I met Oliver, this project has turned into a nightmare. I have dropped too many stitches to count and there's no place for the thumb. I could always keep them for myself. On really cold days I move my thumb in with all my other fingers anyway.

Just as I start to stand up, thinking my white flag is being ignored, Chance pulls up and drops off Oliver. Before he drives off he waves and gives me a smile that makes my skin crawl—a dirty *knowing* smile.

Oliver doesn't look in my direction. Instead, he stumbles up his front steps. He's still wearing his coffee-stained work clothes and he appears to be drunk. Great way to start the week.

I watch him make one failed attempt after another to get the key in the lock while spewing off a few profanities. My brain tells me to go inside and let him work out his issues, but my heart won't listen.

"Give me your key." I grab it from his clumsy hand.

"Viv-i-an ... I missed you ... today." I try not to laugh, but the way he slurs his words and tries to act sexy at the same time is cute, funny, and very entertaining.

I open the door and he drapes his arm around my shoulders as I help him inside. "You smell like dirt and beer."

"I do?" he asks with incredulity.

I laugh. Drunk Oliver is playful. "Yes, you do. Up the stairs you go." We pinball between the wall and the stair rail.

"Viv-i-an?"

"Yeah?"

"I came ... so hard ... in the coffee shop."

I bite my lips together to keep my giggle contained. "Yes, I know." I push him next to the bathroom sink so he has something to lean back on while I turn on the water to the shower.

"I'd like to fuck you ... in the shower. We haven't done ... th-at."

Focus, Viv!

How can his drunken words sound so seductive? I turn and realize he's already doing it with his eyes. I'm fully clothed yet he's undressed me. As he fumbles with the button and zipper to his jeans, I see evidence that his mind has done more than remove my clothes.

"Here." I push his hands away from his pants and pull his shirt over his head then squat down to remove his boots and socks.

"Do you know ... how many positions ... I've had your body in ... in my mind?"

I can't hold in my laughter. The guy who's a mute during sex is sharing all his uncensored thoughts with me. If only Maggie could hear my "gentleman" right now. I'm not sure whether I should just listen or if I should probe him for all his secrets, including what the hell is behind that locked door in the hall.

"My, my, Mr. Konrad, you sure are chatty tonight." I tug his shorts and briefs down.

"I can think of other things..." he grabs my ass and yanks me against his naked body "...I'd rather be doing ..." His eyes are heavy. "... with my mouth."

"Yeah, well, as tempting as that sounds ..." *And, oh my, does it ever sound tempting.* "... I think we should get you showered first."

"Yes, we should." He pushes me back and into the shower.

"Oli! My clothes!"

"Take them off." He attacks my neck and gropes my breasts over my wet T-shirt. "Then bend over. I'm taking you from behind."

Even in his drunken state he has the power to make my whole body blush. Oliver Konrad is one kinky bastard. I shove his hands away and push on his chest until he stumbles back landing on the corner seat of the large tile shower. "Just behave for a minute, will you?" I lather up my hands and wash his hair and then work my way down his body, making each move quick and to the point. I skim my hands down his legs.

"Did you forget something?" He smirks while grabbing my hand and moving it to his erection.

I shake my head and slide my soapy hand up the length of it just once then continue down his legs again.

"Oh sure, *now* you don't want to stroke my dick. You only like it when we have an audience, huh?"

I smile feeling the giggles building again.

"You think this is funny?" He laughs which makes this whole conversation that much funnier.

"I think you're an adorable drunk." I take the handheld showerhead and rinse him off.

He grabs my hand and directs the showerhead to my crotch. "Do you do this to yourself at home? Do you like the way it vibrates your pussy?"

Hilarious! Oh my God, Oliver is going to have me peeing in the shower, and with my luck he'd roll around in it because right now nothing he could say or do would shock me. When he looks up at me, I raise an eyebrow because I wonder when he's going to realize that the showerhead pressed against the crotch of my thick fabric shorts does nothing for me.

The locked door in the hall is high on my curiosity list, but before this truth serum wears off there's one more thing for which I *need* an honest answer. I massage my fingernails along his scalp as he looks up at me.

"What did you really think of my back when I first showed you?"

He looks into my eyes and smiles. "I thought you were a gift, an apology from God."

I stand corrected. He just shocked me.

I'm not sure what it is, but I know he just revealed a huge piece of his past to me. However, his puzzle is still too jumbled to figure out what any of it really means.

"I'm soaked." I spray him in the face. "Let's get out." Shutting off the water, I wring out my hair then grab a towel.

"You're such a cock tease today." He shakes his head while struggling to his feet.

I shove the towel into his chest then grab one for myself. He doesn't dry off. Instead, he wraps the towel around his head. I can honestly say I have never seen a guy do that. The water glistens against his skin and I feel my nipples strain against my lace bra and wet T-shirt. What do I find attractive in a guy? Oliver. His name is now synonymous with handsome, thoughtful, funny, and scorchingly sexy. He is the official litmus test for all other men.

He sways a bit then takes a few unsure steps past me. I check out his firm, bare ass and can't help myself.

Smack!

He freezes, not even turning to look at me. "You. Did. Not. Just. Spank. Me."

I open my mouth then close it. My face scrunches into a nervous grimace. "I ... I didn't spank you. I ... just *patted* you on the butt."

"You spanked me."

"It was a playful ... smack."

"It was a spank."

"A spank is bending someone over your knee and hitting their butt. This was a ... I don't know, sort of a ... high five to your ass, like athletes do to each other."

He turns and I see the devil in his eyes—wicked. As he steps closer, I look left then right to assess my situation and plan my escape route. I notice he's still swaying a bit. His inebriated state should give me a slight advantage.

I fake right then go left into the bedroom toward the door. He rams into the wall at first then lunges for me as I round the corner.

Crash!

"Goddammit!"

I turn. "Oli! Oh shit, oh no ..." He's on the floor and there's blood running down his face. "What happened?" I take the towel that's fallen off his head and hold it to the gash next to his eye.

"I tripped and hit the fucking corner of the dresser!"

"It looks bad, I think you're going to need stitches."

"No shit!"

I don't appreciate his attitude, but given the circumstances I let it slide.

"Uh ... hold this to your head while I get you some clothes." I run into his closet and grab the first things I see. Dressing drunk Oliver with my shaky hands, his lack of coordination, and blood freely flowing from his head proves to be a challenge.

I help him down the stairs. "I'm so very sorry, Oli."

"Grab my keys."

I help him out the door and down the stairs. He plods to the driver's side.

"Oliver, you're not driving."

"Well, neither are you."

I open the passenger door and dangle his key. "Yes, I am. Now get in!"

He collapses in the seat showing more coordination than I expected. The alcohol must be wearing off. I slip in the driver's seat and fasten in.

"Ahh ... you're wet! My leather seats!"

I glare at him. "Really, Oli? You're drunk with blood still running down your face, but you're worried about your leather seats?" I pull out onto the street and he grips the arm rest with his free hand.

It's possible I've been told that I drive like a maniac.

"Slow down!"

"Pipe down."

"I'm serious."

I speed up taking the corner much faster than I should.

"Jesus! Slow down!"

"Chill out, Oli. I got an A in Driver's Ed."

Oliver

VIVIAN IS dangerous to my health. She should come with a huge warning label and a list of side effects. I thought all three of us were going to perish on the way to the hospital—her, me, and my car. Indie drivers look like *Driving Miss Daisy* compared to Vivian.

My drunken brain has tapered off to a light buzz, just enough to still feel a little punchy.

"I think eight stitches should do it." The ER doctor finishes sewing my head back together. "How did this happen?"

"She spanked me while I was naked and then I fell into the corner of the dresser."

The doctor smiles. He's clearly amused by my comment. Vivian ... not so much.

"Oh my God! I ..." Her eyes bug out and her jaw plummets to the floor. "He's kidding ... that's not what happened."

As the saying goes, if looks could kill ... yep, I'd be dead.

The doctor turns and grins at Vivian. "Is it raining out?"

She looks down at her wet clothes and grabs a few strands of her wet hair. "Um ... no ..."

"She couldn't even wait to take her clothes off before jumping in the shower with me."

Another fatal glare. "I'll be in the waiting room!" She huffs.

"You're not the *son* I imagined seeing in the ER." My dad enters the room.

"Hey, how'd you know I was here?"

He steps closer and looks at my cut, shaking his head. "I'm listed as your emergency contact, and while this isn't an emergency they made a professional courtesy call to me anyway. How'd this happen?"

The ER doctor grins. I'm sure he's waiting to see if I give the same explanation to my dad.

"Too much to drink with Chance tonight. I face-planted into the corner of my dresser."

"Don't you think you're too old to be spending your Monday nights at a bar?"

"Probably. What can I say ... it's been a rough day. You off?"

"Just got out of surgery, so yes, I'm heading home. Do you need a ride?"

"I have my car." I ease off the table.

"You're in no condition to be driving."

I point toward the waiting room. "Vivian's here."

"Oh, come on. I'll say hi before I leave."

I follow him out realizing the upper hand I had ten minutes earlier is slipping fast.

"Vivian!"

She stands with a mix of a smile and grimace on her face. "Mr. Konrad."

"Please, call me Hugh." He hugs her which is very uncharacteristic for him. I get the feeling that if there were teams tonight he would be on Team Vivian.

He pulls back looking her over. "Is it raining out?"

She rolls her eyes then looks at me with her jaw clenched. "No, this is a side effect of taking care of your drunk son." Her lips curl into a see-how-it-feels-to-be-thrown-under-the-bus smile.

My dad turns, giving me a wide-eyed look. I shrug.

"Well, thanks for taking care of him. Make sure he treats you right."

It's my turn to roll my eyes. If he only knew what this woman has put me through today.

Vivian smiles. "Oh, I will."

Dad pats me on the shoulder. "Looks like you're in good hands."

He wouldn't say that if she drove *him* home.

"Mmm, yes. See ya, Dad."

Vivian dangles my key again. "Shall we?"

WE MAKE it back in record time, the screech of the tires and the whispering of my desperate prayers the only sounds breaking the silence.

She tosses my keys on the counter. "Um ... so, is there anything else you need before I go home?"

I chuckle and stare at her, loving the way she squirms when I look at her. She's fidgety, unsure of where to look and what to do with her hands.

"As a matter of fact, there is *one* more thing I need." I

move closer, backing her up against the wall.

She risks a quick glance up and swallows. "What's that?" she squeaks.

I peel her damp top off and my dick goes from hard to concrete when I see her firm nipples pressed into red lace. Her shorts go next. I love seeing her chest rise and fall like a strong tide as full red lips part and soft eyes gaze at me on my knees. Pressing my nose to her matching lace panties, I inhale her scent and smile when I hear her breath catch.

I don't recognize myself with her. Thoughts and desires that I used to suppress have been unleashed and can no longer be ignored. Gripping her thighs, I clench the waist of her panties with my teeth and drag them down her legs.

Her hands fist my hair. "Oli ... your head—"

"Is fine."

I devour her. She is the antidote for the poison that is my past. Spreading her open, I take *everything* until all that's holding her up is the wall and my hands on her legs. She yells my name over and over, desperate words fade to soft whimpers in my ears as her sweet taste infiltrates my mouth.

Then I remove my clothes, turn her around, hands pressed to the wall ... and I take *more*.

***

Here I am, once again. The sun peeks over the horizon and despite the humiliation, the hot coffee that threatened to singe my nuts, my excessive intoxication, a gouge to my head, and a near-death ride to the hospital ... I'm alive. My head, however, wishes that weren't the case. There's nothing quite like blunt trauma to the head to make a hangover feel like a jackhammer on my brain.

"Hey," a sleepy whisper sounds behind me. Vivian squints her eyes behind her matted hair that seems to be at war with itself.

Wearing only my T-shirt, she lifts her slender leg and straddles mine stretched out on the lounge chair. Her lips brush against the colorful border of my eye and stitched skin. "I'm sorry."

"You have a tattoo, and I'm Scarface. We're a real badass couple."

She smiles so bright, it feels like she's saying, *"Take that, sun."*

"You're up early." I rub my nose against hers.

"I was lonely in bed."

I chuckle then grimace as it intensifies the throb in my brain. "I doubt that. You have a habit of stealing the covers and crowding me out of my own bed."

She kisses my forehead and rubs gentle circles along my temples. "I think you're exaggerating."

I slide my hands up her thighs. "I'm really not, but it's okay. I like seeing your naked body sprawled out on my bed, even if my view is from the floor."

She shakes her head. "I'm going home. I need a shower and dry clothes."

Another grimace as I attempt to smile.

"Have you taken something for the pain?"

"I took you against the wall last night and then two more times in bed."

"Sex? Really? That's your analgesic?"

I skim my hands over her stomach to her bare breasts. "Yes, and my last dose is wearing off."

"I have to get ready for work." She grinds against me, proving her body doesn't agree with her words.

"I'll be quick." I slide my thumb down between her legs

and circle over her sensitive, wet skin.

"But people can see us." She closes her eyes and I know she's throwing out random excuses that won't change what's happening.

"Didn't stop you yesterday."

She's gone. Her lips collide with mine as she rocks her hips into me. "Mm-my phone." She pulls away and climbs off me.

I reach for her, but she's too fast.

I sigh. "Have you heard of voice mail? What are you, on call or something?"

"Nobody calls me this early in the morning unless it's an emergency."

Apparently a swollen penis doesn't qualify as an emergency in her category.

"I have to go." She gives me a quick kiss on the cheek.

"Whoa, wait! Where are you going?"

"Kai needs me."

I fight through the beating drum in my head to stand up and follow her. "Kai, as in your ex-boyfriend?"

"As in my *best* friend." She grabs her wadded up damp clothes off the floor next to *the wall*.

"Is he hurt or in trouble?"

"Sort of hurt."

"I don't follow."

She opens the front door. "Kate, his girlfriend, left him."

I laugh. "You can't be serious. That's the *emergency*?"

"Don't be so insensitive. I'll see you after work."

"Wait! You're not walking across the street wearing only my shirt."

"Chill, Oli. I have dresses that show more leg than I'm showing right now." She blows me a kiss and shuts the door.

I didn't need to know that.

CHAPTER TWELVE
THREE'S COMPANY

Vivian

I HATE LEAVING OLI, especially when we were getting ready to have sex again. I love sex with Oli. If I had a car I'd get a bumper sticker that said so. Maybe I should get a tattoo that says it. Maybe not. Then again, what if it's not Oli? What if I just love sex? I mean, sex addiction is real. Could I have it? How would I know?

I tiptoe down his front steps in my bare feet and halt when I look up. Across the street Kai sits on my steps.

"I said I'd come to your place." I stop at the bottom of the steps in front of him.

His eyes search the length of my body. "You also said you were at home."

"No, I said I was getting ready to take a shower."

Kai clenches his jaw, dark eyes glaring at me. "Please tell me you didn't give him your ..."

"My what? Virginity?"

Kai doesn't respond.

"It's none of your business." I march up the stairs, past

him, to the door. "Did Kate kick you out of your own place? Is that why you're here instead of waiting for me to come to you?"

He follows me inside and shuts the door. "No, she moved out two days ago."

I turn. "What the hell? Then why did you call me at five-thirty in the morning acting all pissed off and distraught like she literally *just* walked out on you?"

"Were you at his house all night? Is that his shirt?"

I shake my head. "Wh-what are you talking about? Why are you asking me this? I thought you *needed* to see me right away."

"Just answer the question!"

"What question?" I'm so confused. We're supposed to be talking about Kate but he's not said her name even once.

"Did you sleep with him?"

"Yes! Jeez, why do you care?"

He paces the length of the room. "I don't want you to get hurt."

Crossing my arms over my chest, I laugh. "You do see the irony in *you* saying that to *me*, right?

He sighs. "God! I'm sorry, I messed up. I've said it a million times. What more can I say? What more can I do?"

"Nothing! That's just it. I don't expect you to do anything. I'm not asking for you to apologize anymore. But don't ask me to spend the rest of my life reassuring you that it's *okay*. I'm fine. I'm moving on and so should you."

"Viv—"

"Don't Viv me. Now, do you want to talk about Kate?"

He shakes his head.

"Go home, Kai. I have to get to work."

When my dad was too busy working, Kai taught me how to ride my bike without training wheels. He lived four houses down from us, and I'm pretty sure I loved him from the moment he split his grape twin Popsicle with me after I took my first two-wheeled spill. We were inseparable. I played ninjas with him and he played house with me. He was my first kiss and I was his. We were seven and our moms had us kiss for a photo on Valentine's Day, but it still counted. I wanted to be Kai's first everything and him to be mine.

Me: *Sorry I skipped out so early. I REALLY wanted to stay :)*
Oli: *Lunch?*
Me: *Can't, Maggie is gone today.*
Oli: *You're alone?*
Me: *Just me and the Cannabis.*
Oli: *What?*
Me: *For medicinal purposes of course.*
Oli: *Funny*
Me: *It is?*
Oli: *I'll see you in an hour.*
Me: *:)!!!!!!*

"I had to bring my sidekick. We'll have to reschedule our nooner. Sorry, Viv." Chance comes through the door first, carrying a pizza box.

I untie my green apron and wink walking past him and straight into Oliver's arms. He hugs me and lifts me off the ground laying a long, sound kiss on my lips. "Hi."

"Hi." He grins.

I kiss one dimple and then the other.

"What are you doing?"

"Kissing your adorable dimples."

He shakes his head and releases me to the ground. "Not the dimples."

I slip my hands into his back pockets. "Oli, you *count* my freckles for heaven's sake. I think that entitles me to kiss and swoon over your dimples."

"*Oli?*" Chance turns around with a huge grin. "You let her call you Oli?"

"Zip it!"

I look back and forth between them. Oliver frowns with a scowl of warning while Chance feigns innocence with his single-dimpled grin.

"Would someone please explain what the big deal is? Oli is the common nickname for Oliver."

Chance moves his gaze to me. "Oliver's first girlfriend when he was ... What were you? Nine? Ten?"

Oliver continues to glare.

"Anyway, her name was Molly. Oli and Molly sitting in a tree—"

Oliver begins to close the distance with his fists clenched at his sides.

Chance holds up his hands. "Okay, okay ... I digress, said tree is still in our parents' backyard with O plus M equals heart carved into it. Molly broke his heart a week later when she left him for Tommy who was a year older and, in her words, 'had grown out of his boyhood name and was now going by Thomas.' That's the day Oli became Oliver and he threatened to beat up anyone who ever tried to call him Oli again."

I laugh. "Is this true?"

Oliver looks down at me and nods just once.

"My point ..." Chance speaks up, "... is that you must have some serious pussy power over him if he's letting you call him Oli."

"Shut up. You're so crude."

Inside I'm rolling around, holding my belly. After last night, I know that both the Konrad boys have the same dirty thoughts going through their mind. The only difference being Oliver is more refined, showing restraint and using a filter for his thoughts before they reach his mouth—except when he's drunk.

Chance folds his slice of pizza toward the middle and shoves half of it in his mouth.

"So did you get this weekend off?" I pick the black olives off my slice of pizza.

They both look at me in confusion.

"Cape Cod? This weekend? Alex and Sean invited us to go with them?"

Oliver chews in slow motion, squinting his eyes.

"I asked you yesterday at Dunks."

Chance chokes on his pizza. Oliver shakes his head and rolls his eyes. I see what I'm not supposed to hear.

"You told him?"

Oliver shakes his head while swallowing what's in his mouth. Chance snickers, refusing to make eye contact with me.

"You told him!"

"No, I didn't. I only told him I knocked over my coffee, that's all. I swear. I don't know why he's acting like a dumbass who knows something he really doesn't."

I glare at Chance. He holds up one finger as he swallows. "True. When he showed up for work he told me he spilled his coffee."

Oliver lifts his shoulders with a wide-eyed I-told-you-so look.

"*But* ... he shared a different much more interesting

story after his fourth beer last night." Chance wiggles his eyebrows and I want to die.

Now Oliver chokes. "I did ... not!"

"Yeah, ya did, Bro. And I suspect there's more to the cut on your head story, but we'll save that for the next round of beers. By the way, Viv, you can take me out to breakfast anytime you want." He winks.

I don't question Chance because I too got quite the earful of Oliver's uncensored beer lips last night.

Oliver shakes his head and chuckles. "How is it that I'm getting so much grief about this, like I did something wrong? Was public humiliation, hot coffee in my lap, and a trip to the emergency room not enough to warrant a pardon for the few indiscretions I may have had?"

Grabbing the neck of his T-shirt, I pull him closer and kiss his cut. "I forgive you, Oli."

"Gee, thanks."

"So, what I was trying to tell you yesterday is that Sean's family has a place in Cape Cod and we've been invited to go with him and Alex to stay there for the weekend." I look at Chance. "That is, if your *boss* will give you the weekend off."

"Oliver doesn't ask me for anything. It's not up to me if he goes." Chance tosses the pizza box in the trash. "Wrap it up, I'll meet you in the truck. Thanks for the nooner, Viv."

"Bye, Chance." I look at Oliver, trying to decipher what his expressionless face means. "So you'll go this weekend?"

"I don't know. A weekend away with your friends, that's ..."

"What? Fun? Relaxing?"

"Serious."

"Serious?" I twist my lips to the side and take a step

back, leaning against the checkout counter. "Okay, well I'm still going."

He nods. "You should. They're your friends and you'll probably have a lot of fun."

"I'd have more fun if you were going." I'm disappointed and hurt, but I'm only letting him see the disappointment. Somewhere over the past few weeks I thought we'd established an unspoken understanding that our relationship was *serious*—evidently not.

He holds out his hand, I take it, and allow him to pull me into his arms. "I have to go, but I'll see you later."

With a kiss and a smile, he's out the door. I berate myself for feeling so let down. Oliver is everything I never expected. Asking for more is slapping mercy in the face. I'll take every look, every touch, and every whisper he's willing to give me. The problem is the only place I have to keep them is my heart.

Oliver

THE MORNING SUN has become the opening act for the real star of my days—Vivian. She's this blinding light that makes me forget where I've been and not care where I'm going. I don't know what we are, we just *are*.

"You're going to miss me." She slips on her sundress, without underwear. I prop my head up with my hands laced behind my head, enjoying the view from my bed.

"I am, so you should stay tonight so I can get my fill before you leave."

She slingshots her lace panties at me. "Keep those as a

souvenir. I can't stay, I have to pack tonight. Kai is picking me up at six in the morning."

"Kai?" I prop up on my elbows and can't help but grin as she wets her lips with her gaze on my flexed abs.

"Uh … yes, I'm riding with him because Alex and Sean left yesterday."

"So just you and Kai?"

"Yes. Kate was supposed to go too, but since the breakup she's obviously not going and you're not going, so it will be the four of us." She kisses me and I harden again with the simple slip of her tongue. "Bye, Oli," she whispers.

She's on her back and I'm hovering over her in a breath of time that doesn't exist between us.

"Oli!"

"I changed my mind." My hands slide up her silky legs, taking her dress with them. "You don't need to spend time with your friends." The moment my lips find hers, she relaxes her legs and I sink into her. A soft moan escapes as she wraps her long legs around my waist. It feels like her body is telling mine to lead the way, that she'll go anywhere I go.

After I take her with the same depraved greed with which I stole her innocence, I watch her walk out my door. She looks back just once and I see stars in her emerald eyes. They're filled with dreamy illusions, like she knows me, but … she doesn't. I wish to God she did.

I NEVER KNOW what the sunrise will reveal. Sometimes the bright blue sky brings a sense of clarity. Sometimes I see hidden messages in the dull reddish-orange horizon. Other days the clouds morph into a question mark, no doubt symbolic of my recent state of being. Today, however, the message is clear. The woman who has infiltrated my life in every way possible is *not* going to Cape Cod with Kai and not me.

My bag is packed and loaded into my trunk. I lean against the driver's door as Kai pulls up in his gray Honda.

"Kai, is it?" I offer my hand as he gets out. "I'm Oliver Konrad. We met at The Green Pot."

He stares at my hand a moment before shaking it. "You up early just to tell Viv goodbye?"

"Actually, my schedule has changed and I'll be going with you." If it makes me a dick that I enjoy wiping Kai's smug expression off his pretty boy face, then so be it. After treating me like a complete nobody when we first met and taking Vivian away from me with his needy, emotional, my-girlfriend-dumped-me saga, I think I've earned the right to dish out a little payback.

"Does Viv know? I just talked with her and she didn't say anything."

I can't hide my smirk, and as if on cue, the red door across the street opens. "Hey, gorgeous!" I meet her as she tugs her bags down the stairs. She looks at Kai and it pisses me off to see her holding back. If he weren't here she'd already be in my arms, tongue down my throat, and grinding against my always-hard-for-her dick. Instead, she gives me a chaste kiss on the lips and a weak smile.

"Hey, Oli. You didn't have to get up just to see me off."

I take her bags and walk them to my trunk.

"What are you doing?"

"Well, Viv, it looks like your *friend* is coming after all," Kai says.

I don't look at him in spite of the way he's working over-time to set me off with his pissy cocksucker tone.

"You are?"

I toss her bags in with mine. "Yes, I am." She rewards me with a high-pitched girly squeal and hugs me the way I had expected her to a few moments ago.

"What changed your mind?"

I look at Kai while hugging her to my chest. "Nothing in particular. I just didn't want to be without you this weekend."

Kai squints at me. It's slight, but I can see it.

"Throw your bags in back, Kai. I'll drive." I wink.

Vivian walks to the passenger door and opens it. "Is this okay, Kai?"

My tongue has tripled in size from biting it so damn hard. I can't believe she's asking him if it's *okay*. She coddles him like a child.

"Whatever, Viv."

I don't miss the roll of his eyes as he grabs his bag and sunglasses.

"You just made my whole weekend." Vivian grins as I get in the car.

I squeeze her bare leg. "You made my whole night before you left last night."

Her eyes bug out at my words as Kai gets in the backseat. "Not in front of—" she says between gritted teeth while motioning toward him with her head.

That's sweet, it really is. I suppose a woman in this same situation would tear up and call her BFF to cry over the other woman vying for her man's attention. On top of that she'd hold a gigantic grudge against said man like it's his fault and withhold sex out of spite and jealousy. That's not how things work in a man's world.

There are no tears and BFFs waiting with tissues. There are dick measurements, pissing contests, and marking of territory. By the time we reach Cape Cod, Kai will not only know how many times I've had Vivian spread out on my bed, he'll know how loud I make her scream. And there will be *no* withholding sex tonight. Just the opposite. I'll take her so hard that the bed will be busting through the drywall while the mirrors and windows shatter into a million pieces.

Okay, it might not go *exactly* like that.

CHAPTER THIRTEEN
TESTOSTERONE

Vivian

THE HOUR and a half drive to Cape Cod has been exhausting. I should feel elated having my two favorite guys with me for the weekend. I *should,* but I don't.

As soon as the car stops, Kai jumps out and opens my door.

"Uh, thanks." I smile.

"I'll get the bags." Oliver opens the trunk.

Kai follows me toward the house.

"Help him carry in the bags." I turn back and glare at Kai.

He rolls his eyes and sulks back to the car.

"Flower!" Alex runs out the front door, nearly plowing me over with her enthusiasm. "How was the drive?"

"A nightmare. I should have left them both behind."

"Cock fight?"

"Yep, and I have a feeling it's not over."

Alex giggles, looking over my shoulder. "I think you're right."

I turn to witness my sophisticated Harvard men playing tug-of-war with my bags. "See what I mean? Kai shared everything there is to know about me, I think he might have even mentioned my blood type."

"Why?"

"I guess to prove he *knows* me."

"What did Oliver do?"

"He groped me the whole way. Even my anger couldn't stop my reaction to him. I almost had an orgasm from his possessive hand constantly feeling me up. It was embarrassing."

"Like Dunkin' Donuts embarrassing?"

"Touché. But anyway, I'm starting to see why Kate broke up with Kai."

"What are you talking about? Kai broke up with her."

The wrinkle of confusion on my face is obvious. "What do you—"

"I call dibs on the green room," Kai says, walking past us and up the porch stairs.

"In your dreams. There's no way the single guy is taking the largest room with the en suite bathroom. Sean and I already claimed it last night. Flower and Oliver can have the blue guest room and you'll be in the den."

"I'm not sleeping on that damn sofa sleeper!"

"Then pitch a tent on the beach, buddy, because that's your only option."

Oliver snakes his arm around my waist. "Alex, good to see you again."

"Hey, Oliver. Glad you could make it." She winks at me. "Come on inside, I'll introduce you to Sean."

As we walk inside I glance at my bags slung over Oliver's shoulder. "I see you won."

"Won what?"

I grin and shake my head. "Nothing."

"Oliver, this is my boyfriend Sean."

They shake hands. "Nice to meet you."

"Thanks for the invite. What a great place."

"It's really not." Kai emerges from the den. "There's only two bedrooms, two bathrooms, the floors creak, and it's old as sin."

Sean laughs. "Well, for those of us who weren't pampered growing up..." he gestures to Kai and Alex "...it's paradise. My grandparents used to own it and when they died my parents decided to keep it for a vacation home. Occasionally they rent it out. Kai is right. It's small and old, but the view is just as amazing as it is from the Kennedy compound."

"It's amazing." I tug Oliver's hand and lead him to the covered deck butted up to the grassy sand with a long boardwalk leading to the sprawling beach and breathtaking panoramic ocean view. The old gray house with white shutters isn't the most visually appealing house on this stretch of land, but it's cozy, charming, and ours for the weekend.

Oliver sets our bags down and walks to the edge of the deck with his hands on his hips.

"Not what you expected?"

Oliver chuckles. "I didn't have any expectations." He turns and pulls me into his arms. "My *neighbor* has been full of surprises, so I'm learning to go with the flow."

"She sounds amazing."

"She's unpredictable and dangerous..." he points to the cut by his eye "...but, yes, in the most amazing way."

Lifting onto my toes, I kiss him. His hands cup the back of my head as his tongue slides against mine.

"Get a room!" Kai's grumbly voice infiltrates our private

bubble. "Oh, that's right. You already have one. *I'm* the poor schmuck who will be sleeping in the den."

"Kai Pie, I'm sure you'll find some old rich lady to hook up with this weekend."

"Shut up, Alex."

"Is that why you broke up with Kate? Was she not mature enough for you?" Alex loves to prod Kai for a reaction, and he always goes for the bait.

"No, that's not why I broke up with Kate." Kai looks straight at me and his piercing stare and suggestive tone make me shudder.

"Let's take our bags upstairs." I nudge Oliver toward the door, avoiding all eye contact with Kai.

———

"ARE you going to play nice this weekend?"

Oliver sets our bags on the bed. "With whom?"

I walk behind him and rest my cheek on his back while wrapping my arms around his waist. "With Kai."

"What am I, a child?"

"It seemed so in the car."

He chuckles. "What will you give me if I play nice?"

I slip my hand below the waistband of his shorts and stroke him. "I'm sure I can think of something?"

He thickens in my grip as his breath catches in his chest. I start to remove my hand, just intending to tease him a bit.

"Don't stop." He grabs my wrist and pushes my hand back down.

"It's just a preview."

"Well, I need a longer preview. Don't stop until you get to the *coming* attraction."

I laugh. "They're waiting for us downstairs."

"Then hurry up." His words are tense and needy.

"Turn around." I pull my hand out and this time he doesn't protest.

Kneeling, I unfasten his pants as I look up at him and we both share sexy, naughty smiles. I run my tongue along his entire length and circle it over the head. His hips jerk forward and I smile in complete satisfaction.

"Take your shirt off."

His forehead wrinkles. "For this?"

I nod and stroke him while my tongue continues to tease the head. He shrugs off his shirt and I look up at his firm, defined chest while a pleasurable smirk tugs at my lips.

"You like looking at me?

I nod and he smiles.

"Well I don't," Kai says from the doorway.

"Kai! Get out!"

Oliver turns and fastens his pants while I scramble to my feet, crimson with embarrassment.

"Sorry, Viv, didn't mean to interrupt. Alex wants you to go with her to the store."

I stomp my way to the door and shove Kai's chest. "Tell her I'll be down in a minute. Out!" I slam the door and turn around, leaning against it. "I'm sorry."

Oliver slips on his shirt. "Don't be."

"I'm embarrassed."

He feathers his fingers over my face and smirks. "You weren't the one caught with your pants down."

"I know, it's just—"

"What? Are you embarrassed of me? You think I have a small pecker?"

"What?" My eyes widen.

"I'm kidding. I know you don't have a comparison, but trust me—"

"Wait what do you ... oh, the virgin thing." I grin. "Oliver, I was a virgin in the literal sense, not the broad spectrum never-been-kissed way."

His head juts back. *"Really?"*

"Really, and no, I don't think you have a small pecker." I start to wrap my arms around his waist, but he grabs my wrists and steps back.

"You'd better get going. I'm sure Alex is waiting for you."

I squint my eyes. "You're not upset are you?"

He turns and puts his hands on his hips with his head bowed. "No ... just ... it's fine."

Grabbing his arm I pull at him until he turns back to me. "You slammed on the brakes the second you found out I was a virgin and now the knowledge that your cock isn't the first I've seen is an issue?"

He pulls away from me. "I said it's fine ... just go."

"Unbelievable. You're a real head case sometimes."

"Don't!"

I jump from the snap of his firm tone.

"Don't ... ever ... call me that."

The verbal slap stings. There's that one percent again. The part of Oliver that is so foreign to me. It's a part I don't want to know, but I need to because it could make or break us. One percent seems like nothing, but I have a feeling it could be everything for us.

I hate that he can't even look at me. "I'll be back."

KAI IS the lucky recipient of my drop-dead look as I grab my purse. "I'll be in the car, Alex." Kai smirks and my hands clench, fighting back the urge to wipe that stupid grin off his face.

"What's going on?" Alex asks getting into the car.

"My best friend is an ass and my boyfriend is a jerk."

"Yikes. What now?"

"I can't figure out what the deal is with Kai. Why did he tell me Kate left him? Why is he acting like such a dick to Oliver, and why does he look at me like he owns me?"

Alex cringes.

"What?"

She chews on her lip.

"*What?*"

With a quick sideways glance, she sighs. "He told Sean that he has feelings for you. That's why he broke up with Kate."

"Feelings? What's that supposed to mean?" I cross my arms over my chest.

"You know what that means."

"No, I don't. Kai just got tired of Kate and he's bored so he thinks he wants me, but he doesn't. He just wants *someone*, anyone."

Alex lifts her shoulders. "Maybe, but Sean made it sound like Kai came to some life-changing decision that you're the one and only one for him."

There is no response to that. I stare out the window, releasing a deep breath.

"What did Oliver do?"

I roll my eyes. "Nothing, everything ... I don't know. He's hiding something, but I have no clue what it is."

"Hiding what? Like a wife or something."

I laugh. "No, more like something from his past that haunts him. I've met his family. They wouldn't welcome me with open arms if it were some deal breaker."

"Why don't you ask him?"

"I can't. Whatever it is feels like the line between Jekyll and Hyde."

"You're afraid of how he might react if you ask him?"

"I'm afraid of everything—his reaction, mine, losing him, losing us. He has this door down the hall from his bedroom and it's locked with a dead bolt ... a freaking dead bolt. Who has a deadbolted door to a bedroom or closet or whatever the hell it is?"

"Did you ask him about it?"

I shake my head. "He's caught me more than once staring at it, but I've never asked. That's when I see a slight glimpse of Hyde in his eyes. Well that, and given my own secret-filled past, I have trouble prying into his. I think he'll tell me, hopefully sooner than later."

Alex pulls into a parking spot. "Sean and I dated a year before he told me about his uncle."

A sad smile pulls at my lips. Sean and I give each other shit all the time, but I genuinely like him and his past breaks my heart. His uncle sexually abused him for over ten years before anyone found out. I've met his parents and they are the best. I can't even imagine what it must have done to them when they found out.

"I'll give him time. As much as I'm dying to know, it has to be on his own time."

We get out of the car.

"Maybe he has a weird fetish like a collection of porcelain-faced dolls, or teddy bears. Maybe he's into some kinky shit and he's hiding his whips and canes behind that door. I bet he has one of those sex swings suspended from the ceiling. Seriously, he did say he wanted to spank you."

"Yeah, I'm sure that's it." I laugh and at the same time

the spanking threat lingers like a neon light in the back of my mind.

Oliver

I HATE HER. I fucking hate her. It feels like a one-night stand with HIV as the parting gift. She's the poison in my veins. A poison that will infect everyone I ever touch.

"Hey, there's some drinks in the fridge and maybe a few cereal bars on the counter. The women should be back soon with some grub. Alex just texted me and said they're on their way back, but Viv wanted to stop for her doughnuts."

"Thanks, Sean, I'm good right now." I sit in the lounge chair next to him on the deck not giving Kai so much as a glance.

"So Alex said you graduated from Harvard Law."

I nod. "Yes, I did."

"But you're working with your brother right now?" Sean tips back his can of Red Bull.

"I am. How about you?"

"I'm getting my MBA just like Viv."

"What are your plans when you're done?"

"Wait for Viv." He laughs. "You do realize she plans on conquering the world? I can think of worse coattails to ride."

I chuckle. "Yeah, she's definitely driven."

"How would you know? You've known her for what ... two seconds?" Kai decides to open his piehole and add his two worthless cents.

Sean looks at Kai and shakes his head with a warning

glare. I'm missing something, but right now I couldn't care less.

"My relationship with her is none of your damn business."

Kai stands and smirks. "Whatever. She gives good head, doesn't she?"

I see red, hear my thundering pulse, and feel nothing but Kai's face against my fist.

Sean helps him up as Kai uses his shirt to catch the blood flowing from his nose.

"Thanks for the invite, but I think I'll head back to Cambridge. You'll bring Vivian home on Sunday?"

"Fuck, I think you broke my nose!"

Sean looks at me and nods once before tending to his asshole of a friend. I grab my bag from upstairs and pull out of the drive without a second thought about it. Vivian's lips wrapped around Kai's dick is an image I'm not going to forget all too soon—not without a little help from Jack Daniels.

CHAPTER FOURTEEN

Vivian

Oliver's car is gone. Maybe he took the guys for some lunch. I shouldn't have insisted on stopping for doughnuts, but we left early and didn't stop on the way.

"Did Sean say they were going somewhere?"

Alex hands me two bags of groceries from the back. "No, but they're guys, you know, forgetful and unpredictable."

"True."

We carry the bags into the kitchen.

"What the heck?" Alex says.

Kai sits at the kitchen table, holding an icepack to his bloodied nose, and Sean leans against the counter.

"What happened? Where's Oliver?"

Kai glares at me behind his icepack. "Real nice, Viv. I'm sitting here with a busted-up face and all you can say is 'Where's Oliver?'"

I set the bags down on the table. "No, I also asked what happened."

181

"Kai stuck his foot in his mouth and got a bloody nose." Sean smirks.

I look from Sean to Kai. "What happened?"

"Hey, babe, maybe we should take a walk and leave these two to talk."

"Then hurry up and help me put away these groceries," Alex replies.

"Kai?" I step closer looking down at him.

"He hit me."

"Why?"

He shrugs. "I don't know. He just lost it."

Sean clears his throat.

Kai glances at him and sighs. "I may have said something."

"What?"

He continues to look over at Sean, then finally back at me. "I said you give good ... head."

Smack!

"FUCK! My nose!"

Kai's icepack crashes to the floor and I stare at his blood on my palm.

"Yeah, let's go, Sean." Alex grabs his hand, leaving the rest of the groceries on the counter.

I toss a roll of paper towels at Kai. Eyes watering and hands shaking, he struggles to tear off a wad.

"What the hell is wrong with you?"

"Me?" he questions in disbelief.

"Where is he?"

Kai eases down to pick up his icepack with one hand while holding the paper towels to his nose with the other. "He went home."

My heart shatters. Oliver left thinking ... God knows what, and I can't get to him. I huff toward the stairs.

"Viv, wait!" Kai follows me. "You don't understand."

"You're right, I don't." I shake my head. "Friends don't do this." I start up the stairs.

"I love you, Viv."

I stop.

"I know the timing seems wrong, but I love you. I think I always have and I've just been too blind to see it … to see you."

Tears flood my eyes as I turn around. "Why? Why now? Do you have any idea how long I've waited to hear you say those words? God … I've loved you for as long as I can remember." I sniffle and wipe my tears. "It's too late, Kai." I shake my head.

"No, Viv, it's never too late. You know we belong together. I know you feel it in your heart."

I can't even see Kai, all I see is Oliver. All I want is Oliver. All I need is Oliver.

I love Oliver.

"I'm not your toy, not anymore. You only want me when you think you can't have me. But I don't love you that way, not anymore."

"He doesn't deserve—"

"Don't! Don't you dare say that to me. *You* don't deserve me, Kai. You broke me and I let you."

"Viv, you promised—"

"I don't care!" Tears of anger replace my tears of sadness and they're like dripping acid. "I don't care that I promised never to blame you. I do! I blame you for my fucking lot in life. You were drunk off your ass that night and if those other campers wouldn't have been watching I might have died. Do you get that?"

Kai looks at me with a world of remorse in his eyes, but it's too late.

"Do you, Kai? Do. You. Get. That?"

He nods once and swallows with renewed tears in his eyes.

"I can't do this anymore. At some point this..." I wave my hand in the air "...us, what we had, became toxic and we've been too blind and stubborn to see it. But it's over ... we're over. Stop calling me, stop coming over, just ... stay away from me." I turn and walk the rest of the way up the stairs.

"Viv?"

I keep going, even as I hear the foreign sound of a rare sob from Kai. I've seen him cry once before—when I woke up in the hospital after the accident.

Where are you?

I text Oliver and wait, but he doesn't respond so I call him. It goes to his voice mail. "Oli, I'm so sorry. Kai had no right to say that to you. Please call me back."

Next, I text Alex.

Come back. I need a ride to the train station.

Alex arrives back within minutes and follows me to the car. She refrains from saying anything right away, but finally breaks the silence as we get closer.

"Sean said Kai was an ass."

"I don't want to talk about Kai."

Alex nods as we pull into the train station.

"I'm sorry. Hope you can still have a nice weekend."

Alex hugs me. "Don't worry about it. We'll get Kai drunk until he passes out and then we'll go do our own thing."

I smile. "Thanks, Alex, for everything."

"Good luck, Flower."

"Thanks, I may need it."

THE TRAIN RIDE BACK IS EMOTIONALLY DRAINING as I grieve the loss of my best friend. I never dreamed the moment Kai would declare his love to me would be the moment I would let him go. It shouldn't be this way. Friends shouldn't have to choose. As angry as I am with him, I feel a painful emptiness inside. Will the man I love fill that void ... will he love me back?

His car is here and so is he. I feel it like my own heart beating in my chest. My hands tremble. I can barely make a fist to knock on his door. I've never wanted to rip myself open so completely to another person. If Oliver doesn't love me back, I'm certain I will die.

I knock.

No answer.

I knock again.

No answer.

I text him.

I know you're home. Please let me in.

No response.

Oli, PLEASE!!

No response.

I knock again then rest my cheek on his door. The tears fall hard. "Oli, please." I knock again. I'm not sure how much time passes, but I eventually peel my face off his door, and lug my bags across the street. Before I reach the top step I glance back.

Oli.

He's standing in his door way. If it's even possible to feel more pain today, I do. Looking at Oli with a glass bottle in one hand and his face somber ... eyes vacant, I die a little more. I reach into my purse and grab my phone. A moment later Oli pulls his out of his pocket and holds it up to his ear. He doesn't say anything, but I hear his breath and I swear I can feel it on my skin as a tingling chill spreads over me.

"I love you," I whisper.

He doesn't move, doesn't speak. My heart beats out of my chest and I feel like I'm falling.

The line goes dead. He puts his phone back in his pocket and steps outside. Taking a shaky step down, he sits on the top step. We stare at each other, but standoffs are for stubborn cowboys in westerns. I'm a hungry woman desperate for her man. I make the trek back across a distance that's too far between us. Tossing my bags on the step next to him, I straddle his lap. I can see the missing half of Jack Daniels glossed over in his eyes.

"You love me?" His words are slow with a soft slur.

I wrap my arms around his neck. "Completely."

His brow tenses as he tips his head to the side. "Why?"

I shrug. "I can no longer do the impossible."

"The impossible?"

"Not love you."

He closes his eyes and smiles.

"I'm not expecting you to say it—"

"I love you." He opens his eyes.

"I mean it. You don't have to say it."

"I love you."

"I'm serious."

He laughs and rests his forehead on my shoulder. "So am I."

"You're drunk."

"I am." He chuckles some more.

"So if in the morning you regret saying it then—"

His lips press to mine. He tastes like Jack and Oliver, the perfect cocktail. Releasing me, his forehead falls to mine. "No take backs."

With those three words, I do the only thing a girl in my shoes can do: I cry tears of joy in the arms of the man who *loves me*.

Oliver

I MISSED the sunrise this morning and that's okay; I didn't want last night to end. Vivian, naked in my arms, is all I can ever imagine wanting or needing for the rest of my life.

"Hey." I love her raspy morning voice.

"Good morning." I roll onto her and slide into to her with one smooth motion. Her breath catches and languid eyes disappear beneath heavy lids. I suck her cherry nipple into my mouth and graze my teeth over it as she arches her back and moans in pleasure. Unfortunately this won't take long; I've been hard as a rock for nearly an hour looking at her naked body. Pervert? Probably, but I don't care.

"Oli ..."

I love when she moans my name, it makes me thrust into her harder and faster. She clenches my hair and holds my head to her chest. The more I tease her nipples, the more she circles her hips and grinds against me.

"Don't stop, Oli, don't ever stop ..." She pulls my head to hers and takes my mouth like she's starving. Her long legs wrap around my waist and her nails anchor into my back.

A million words flood my mind, but when I'm inside her I can't speak, I can barely breathe. She's close, I can tell, because her head thrashes from side to side like she's willing it away, hoping it will last forever. I understand. My own body is at war feeling the nearness of it. I slow down and sometimes stop to let the feeling start to fade just to slam back into her, teasing that edge all over again. God, it feels so good.

I flip us over, letting her sit astride me. She struggles to hold her body upright as she sinks onto me—eyes closed, head back. I guide her hips and watch her breasts bounce as she finds her own pace. I'm so close to losing it just watching her, then she sends me over the edge with the unexpected; she pinches her own nipples then slides her hand down to where we're joined and brings herself to orgasm while digging her teeth into her bottom lip. I jerk my hips up once more and it's over. Damn! I can't believe how much I needed this.

"Oh, Oli ..." She collapses on my chest, breathless. "I love you."

I'm hers. She doesn't even know me yet, but I'm still hers. Uncertain eyes find mine and I can see the question in them, the fear that I was too drunk last night to remember. I brush her unruly hair away from her face. "I love you too."

Who needs to watch the sunrise? She's blinding me with a smile brighter than the most brilliant rays of sun. Her lips press to mine and her tongue slides in my mouth while she circles her hips resurrecting my dick still buried inside her warmth.

Interlacing our fingers she murmurs over my mouth, "Let's do it again."

I LOOK like a damn circus clown waiting for her to come downstairs. The second time in bed guaranteed a permanent smirk on my face today, but when she placed her hands on the shower wall and reminded me that I wanted to *fuck her in the shower*, that pretty much sealed the deal for the circus clown smile.

"Mmm, what's that smell?"

I try to tame my grin as she walks down the stairs, those sexy bare legs on full display beneath my T-shirt and wet raven hair hanging down her back and over her shoulders. Who am I kidding? Bozo it is. "Omelets, buttered toast, orange juice, and coffee." I pull out her chair.

She sits down and grabs my neck, pulling me in for a slow kiss. "Good morning."

I scoot her in and sit down across from her. "You have no idea."

She takes a sip of her juice. "Oh, I think I do. We should do this every day."

"Breakfast?"

She takes a bite of toast and smiles. "Sex, lots of sex, then yes, you making me breakfast in your boxer briefs without a shirt on." Licking the butter off her lips, lustful eyes fall to my chest and she smirks. "When I came down the stairs and saw you looking like this, I wanted to eat my breakfast off your naked body."

I choke on the bite I'm trying to swallow.

"You okay, Oli?"

Covering my mouth with my napkin, I nod while

fighting to clear my throat. In a world where guys brag and share stories, the events of this morning would be met with laughter and filed under big fish stories. Women like Vivian just don't exist in the real world. They don't look like her, act like her, and they certainly don't talk like her. In fact, I don't believe it myself. I half expect to wake up alone in my bed, covered in sweat with my hand fisted around my dick.

"I'm fine." I clear my throat once more and take a drink of juice. "So dinner at my parents' house tonight?"

There's that blinding smile again. "I'd love to." She takes a bite of her omelet. "Mmm, this is so good."

"Better than Boston Kreme doughnuts?"

She laughs. "Down boy, don't try to compete with the official doughnut of the Commonwealth."

"You do realize doughnuts are high on the list of the unhealthiest foods."

"Of course I know. I've been trying to cut back."

"You have?"

"Sure. Look at the clock. It's almost ten and I haven't had one yet. Now, the question you should have asked is if I like sex more than Boston Kreme doughnuts."

My forkful of omelet stops halfway to my mouth. "And?"

"Yes." She winks. "I like sex with you so much more. So if you're concerned about my health then I suggest you do your best to keep me preoccupied with the one thing that trumps the Boston Kreme."

I grin and mentally pinch myself because there's no way she just said that. "So we should treat this like AA. I'll be your sponsor. When you have a weak moment and temptation strikes, you call me and I'll meet you."

"You'll meet me for sex?"

I nod.

"Any time, any day?"

I nod. "I love you, so whatever the sacrifice, I'll do it. *We* can do this, babe. I realize it could take a long time and like most addictions, you may always struggle with it, but I'll do whatever it takes to help you through."

"You're a real gem, Oli." She bats her lashes at me and grins. "So on to the next issue. This might sound funny, since I practically sleep with you every night anyway, but I need a place to stay next weekend. Alex's parents will be in town for two nights before they leave for Europe. Normally, I would go to Kai's but since I ended things with him—"

"Wait. What do you mean you ended things with him?"

She tears the last piece of toast into little pieces. "Well, after what he said to you and then what he said to me, I told him we're over. I can't be his friend anymore." She looks up at me and I see her eyes fill with tears and a sad smile pulls at one side of her lips.

"What did he say to you?"

"He said he loved me and that he wanted to be with me. He said the words I've been waiting to hear for what seems like forever." She sniffles. "But I don't love him anymore and when I'm with you I question if I ever really loved him because what I feel for you is so much more than I've ever felt before." Using her napkin she dabs at her tears. "But it still hurts. In spite of everything, he's been my friend forever." She shakes her head. "Things just haven't been the same since the accident."

"What does that have to do with anything?"

Glossy green eyes look at me. "I was with Kai that night. We went camping and that was going to be our first night together. He stole a six-pack of beer from his parents and I had one, he had the other five. It was late and he wanted to get in the tent. I was having second thoughts, given his inebriated condition. He tugged the button to my shorts then he tried to remove my shirt. I backed away, insisting he stop. I tripped and fell backwards onto the coals of our campfire that had started to burn out. He landed on top of me and struggled to get off. I don't remember much after that, but later I was told that the people camping next to us saw the whole thing and rescued us before calling 9-1-1."

She releases a sob and I hurry to pull her into my arms. "He spent every night at the hospital with me until I was released. I promised him I would never blame him for it, but I do. It's not just the scars. I blame him for the way I feel about them. A year later we found ourselves alone at my parents' house and I wanted to have sex with him. I needed to know that he still wanted me that way. I needed to feel beautiful in his eyes." Another sob escapes and I'm torn between wanting to comfort her and rip Kai's heart right out of his chest. "All I saw in his eyes was ... pity. That moment ended our romantic relationship, but looking back, I think that moment ended our friendship. We've just been in denial over the past two years."

Cradling her face I wipe her tears and kiss her soft cheeks. She sniffles again. "So can I stay next weekend ... with you."

"No."

She physically deflates even more. I smile. "You can stay forever."

Her forehead wrinkles. "What?"

"Move in with me."

"What?"

I laugh. "You heard me. Move in with me."

Her eyes search my face like she's unscrambling a puzzle. "Are you serious?"

With those three words it hits me. No, I'm not. The

magnitude of my proposition starts to sink in. Where did that come from? What the hell was I thinking? Forever? Move in? *Shit!*

Eyes wide, she's holding her breath ... *I'm* holding her breath. "Yes, I'm serious."

She hugs me and squeals. Then her lips attack mine with purpose as her hand slides down the front of my briefs. "Boston Kreme me, Oli," she whispers with a naughty seductive voice.

Okay, this might work out after all.

CHAPTER FIFTEEN

COHABITATION

Vivian

I'M NOT sure what "the dream" is, but I'm pretty sure I'm living mine. Oliver asking me to move in with him, *forever*, has dissolved my reservations about us. Dr. Jekyll cannot ask someone to move in unless he intends to expose Mr. Hyde. Oliver's invitation feels like a promise—a promise to share everything with me, maybe not overnight, but soon.

"What is half your rent and utilities?"

Oliver gives me a sideways glance as he drives us to his parents. "Why?"

"I want to figure out how much I'm going to need to work when I start school in the fall."

He laughs. "I don't rent."

"Then what's half of your mortgage?"

He shakes his head. "You're not paying my mortgage."

"Then I should take care of all the utilities and groceries."

"No."

"Oli!"

"I asked you to move in with me because I want to be with you, because I love you." He squeezes my leg. "I wasn't looking for a roommate."

I entwine my fingers with his. "I'm not going to move in and mooch off you. I want to contribute."

"You can pay me back when you conquer empires after you graduate."

"I'm not living with you for free."

He smirks, keeping his eyes on the road. "I'm sure I can think of *something* you could do to earn your keep."

"Don't say sex. That would make me feel like a prostitute."

"Mmm, well we wouldn't want that. Maybe you could massage my aching muscles every night after I get done with my long labor-intensive work days. Naked, of course."

I laugh. "And that's not going to lead to sex?"

"I've never had sex with my massage therapists."

"Good to know, but how many of them have been naked while massaging you?"

His lips twist to the side. "Good point."

"Besides, I probably wouldn't be that good at it. I've never had a massage, so I don't have much to go on."

"You've never had a massage? Ever?" His brow furrows.

I shrug. "Nope. I don't think a lot of teenagers get massages and then the ..."

"The scars." He sighs.

"Yes, the scars. It's no big deal. I doubt either one of my parents have ever had a massage."

"Then that's another thing you should add to your to-do list after you accumulate your billions."

"You do realize it's not about the money."

"No?"

I roll my eyes. "Of course not. It's about making a difference in the lives of people like my parents. People who work for me will not work more than thirty hours a week. They will have generous pay, health and retirement benefits, and childcare. Then of course there will be fitness centers, healthy lunch options on site, sleeping pods to increase productivity, and who knows … maybe even chair massages. People will love working for me and as a result their enthusiasm and quality work will make my companies the best in the world."

Oliver's grin is enormous.

"What are you smiling at?"

"You. Just when I think you can't amaze me anymore, you do. I love listening to you talk about your future like that. You're so full of spirit and I have no doubt you will achieve everything you set out to do, a hundredfold."

"Thank you. That means a lot."

He winks at me.

"What about you? Are you going to retire co-owner of the Handy Hunk?"

"I'm not an owner, just a meager employee. Eventually, I will leave this glamorous job and move on."

"Practicing law?"

He lifts his shoulders. "Maybe."

"Hmm, I haven't seen you in a suit, but I'll miss those leather work boots."

He chuckles. "The boots? You like my boots."

I nod, digging my teeth into my lower lip. "You know how some men are about women in heels … nothing but heels? Well, that's your boots for me. I fantasize about you in nothing but those work boots."

He pulls into his parents' driveway. "The boots, huh?" He grins.

"Yep, *just* the boots."

"Might get the sheets dirty."

I blush. "We're not in bed ... at least not in my fantasy."

His eyebrows pull up. "We're not?"

I shake my head. "We're in the back loading area of The Green Pot. I'm in a sundress with flip-flops, no panties, and you fuck me up against your brother's work truck ... wearing only your work boots."

Oliver swallows—hard while adjusting himself. "Damn, Vivian. I'm going to walk into my parents' house with a boner."

"Sorry, I'll meet you inside."

"Wait! You're leaving me?"

I nod and open the door. "Giving you some privacy to *take care of things.*"

"Just give me a minute. It will go away on its own."

"I doubt that."

"Why do you say—"

I stand with my rear to the door and lift the back side of my dress. "Because I'm not wearing any panties tonight."

"Shit! What the hell—"

I close the door and giggle all the way to the house.

"Vivian!" Jackie hugs me.

"Jackie, nice to see you again."

"Where's Oliver?"

"Uh ... he's still in the car. He had to um ... *handle* something before coming inside."

"Oh, I hope everything's okay."

I grin. "I'm sure it's nothing."

"Well then, head out back. Hugh and Chance are out there."

"Can I help you with anything?"

"Not unless you want to chop veggies for the salad."

"I'd love to."

Jackie leads me to the kitchen and points to a strainer with carrots, peppers, and tomatoes. "A knife is in the top drawer and the cutting board is on the island." She slips on her floral apron and mixes something in a baking dish.

"What are you making?"

"Strawberry-rhubarb cobbler."

"Yum. I almost had a taste of it shortly after I met Oliver."

Jackie glances at me. "Almost?"

"Yeah, I hadn't had dinner and he offered me the leftovers you sent home with him, *except* the cobbler. He ate that in front of me, but let me lick the bowl."

"What? Where were his manners?"

"If you're going to tell the story without me, then don't leave out the important details," Oliver says, walking up behind me. "I offered her the last bite but she said no then practically gnawed my hand off after I stuck the spoon in my mouth."

I elbow him in the stomach. "I did not gnaw your hand off."

Jackie laughs and when I look up I see a sparkle in her eyes as she watches us and our playful banter. Oliver wraps his arms around me and nuzzles my neck as I continue to chop the veggies.

"Did you get everything handled in the car?" Jackie asks.

Oliver tenses his hold on me. "What?"

"Vivian said you had to handle something."

"She did, did she?" He pinches my sides eliciting a jump. "Yes, I *handled* it."

I bite my lips together fighting the grin that's dying to take over my face.

"Think you're pretty funny, huh? Just wait until I

handle you later," he whispers in my ear. "I'll be out back," he says to us both.

"Okay, sweetheart." Jackie winks at him.

We both watch him walk out back. "You're good for him." Jackie puts the cobbler in the oven."

"You think so?"

"I know so. When he moved back to Boston I was worried about him. The boy I once knew who was full of life, always cracking jokes, and driven to be a successful lawyer seemed to have vanished. He's coming back. I can see it a little more every day and I know it's because of you."

I blush. Oliver's been the one who has given me a life over the past month. I'm not sure I've done much for him, so Jackie's words touch something deep inside my heart and at the same time I feel sad for Oliver. "I know something significant happened while he was in Portland. That much of the puzzle has been pretty easy to put together. I haven't asked him about any of it and I don't plan to. I want him to tell me if and when he's ready. However, I know when it's on his mind. I see a different side of him, it's a mix of anger, insecurity, and ... I don't know, maybe grief?"

Jackie nods but doesn't respond. She just looks at me and her conflict is visible in the wrinkling of her forehead and the small creases along the corners of her eyes.

"Anyway, he asked me to move in with him, so that's a good sign, right?"

The conflict on her face explodes into all out shock. "He did?"

I nod and grimace. "It's too late now, but maybe I should have let him tell you."

Jackie shakes her head or maybe she's trying to bring herself out of shock. "No, you're fine. I won't say anything until he brings it up." She smiles but it's forced and I'm starting to feel uncomfortable.

"Here, everything's chopped. I'm going to use the bathroom before dinner. Do you need any more help?"

"Thank you, I think everything else is good."

Oliver

"Where's Vivian?"

She's in the bathroom, but she's been in there for a while. Maybe you should check on her," my mom says while walking past me, carrying out plates and silverware.

"Yeah, I will."

I stop at the door and listen, but I can't hear anything. "Vivian?" I knock.

"Yes?"

"Are you okay in there?"

"Yes. I'll be right out."

"Are you feeling sick or something?"

"No."

"Female *issues*?"

The door swings open. "*No*, I'm not having female issues, or the shits, or anything like that."

"Are you wishing you wore underwear?"

She rolls her eyes. "No!"

Damn! Why did I go there again? I'm already hard again.

She sighs. "I told your mom you asked me to move in. Then I thought that wasn't really my news to share with her. Are you mad?"

Men suffer from both types of ADD—Attention Deficit

Disorder and Acute Dick Dementia. The latter being the inability to remember anything that's said around us for at least five minutes after a sexual thought enters our brain, and if a new thought creeps in within that five minutes the clock starts over.

"Oliver? Did you hear me?"

"What? Yes ... no. You *have* to start wearing underwear, every day. Okay?" I adjust myself and her eyes follow my movement.

"What about your mom?"

"I'm quite certain she wears them. I don't think she's the type—"

"Oli! I'm talking about her knowing that I'm moving in with you."

"Oh." I pull her into my chest and kiss the top of her head. "I was going to tell everyone at dinner anyway, so it's no big deal. Why? What did my mom say?"

"Nothing really, but she looked shocked. I mean, before that she said I was good for you, but then I told her that you asked me to move in and her whole demeanor changed."

"I'm sure she's fine."

Vivian looks up at me. "Are you? It felt spur of the moment and we haven't known each other that long. I'd understand if you wanted to change your mind."

Hell yes I want to change my mind. Who wouldn't after a temporary lapse of sanity? The practical part of my brain wants to tell her to run and never look back.

"I'm not going to change my mind." I kiss her and the irrational part of me that asked her to move in returns and triggers my ADD response.

"We'd better go," she mumbles against my lips. "They're waiting for us."

"Let them wait." I suck her tongue and grab her breast with one hand while my other lifts her dress in the front.

"Oli, stop."

I slip my finger into her slick channel. "Are you sure?"

Her head falls against my chest while her hands grip my shoulders. "Yes ... I mean no. I mean ... oh ... God."

"Is that a yes?"

"No ... yes ... oh ... God." Her fingernails claim the top layers of my skin even through my shirt.

I add a second finger and rub her little nub with my thumb. It's sadistic of me, both to her and myself, but I can't stop.

"You two coming?" Chance yells from the back door.

"Oh God!" Vivian yells as I pinch her nipple through her dress and tug on it—hard. Releasing it, I cup my hand over her mouth.

"What's that?" Chance's voice echoes.

"In a minute," I yell back. "Are you close?" I whisper in her ear.

She fists my shirt and swallows while nodding her head, eyelids heavy.

"Good. I'll meet you at the dinner table." I pull out my fingers, kiss her cheek, then walk away.

"Oliver!" she grits between her teeth, but I don't look back.

Payback's a bitch.

CHANCE IS WAITING for me at the deck door. "I think you should ask Vivian to give the blessing before dinner," he says with a hushed voice.

"What?"

He rests his arm over my shoulders as we walk toward the table. "She just seems pretty religious."

"What are you talking about?"

"I heard her calling to our Lord."

I shove him away. "Are you drunk?"

"Not yet, but *oh ... God* I could be." His voice raises a couple of octaves.

I glare at him. "Not one word to her. You don't need to embarrass her."

He holds up his hands and shakes his head. "*Oh ... God*, no that's your job."

"What are you boys talking about?" Mom sits down at the table next to Dad.

"Nothing."

"Is Vivian coming?"

Chance chuckles and snorts like a perverted teenager.

"Yes she's com—on her way." I shake my head at Chance.

"There she is," Dad says.

She smiles at my parents and even gives Chance an endearing look. Me? I get nothing, not one glance. Standing, I pull out her chair. "Are you mad?" I whisper in her ear.

"I don't get mad, I get even," she says between gritted teeth.

If we didn't have an audience I would argue that what I did was getting even with her and that now we are in fact, even. End. Done. Final.

"How was Cape Cod? Thought you weren't coming back until Sunday." Chance knows all my buttons to push tonight.

"Vivian wasn't feeling well. I think she's still struggling with it tonight—shit!" I slap my hand against the table causing the glasses and silverware to rattle.

"Oliver, what are you doing?" My mom gives me a stern glare.

"Actually," Vivian interrupts with a fake grin while clenching my junk so tight under the table I doubt it's still in one piece, "Oli has trouble, well ... I'm just going to say it since you're his family and I know this is a nonjudgmental, safe environment. He can't sustain an *erection*," she whispers, "when there are other people in the house. So our romantic getaway wasn't feeling so romantic. That's why we came home early. I think he gets nervous or something. What do you think, Dr. Konrad?"

She did NOT just tell my family that I have ED, did she? My dad looks at me and I clench my teeth while prying her death grip off my crotch.

My dad grins and I'm not sure if Chance is even breathing he's laughing so hard. "Maybe you should come in for a physical, Son. ED can be a symptom of a more serious condition."

"Vivian's not wearing underwear." The words are out and I can't take them back.

Her eyes go wide as she gasps. Then they shrink into a menacing scowl. "Oli cut his head after he tripped while chasing me around his place *naked* because he was trying to *spank* me."

I throw in the towel and kiss her with my hands cradling her face. It's passionate and demanding and I don't stop until I feel her whole body surrender. The roar of laughter around us is accented with a nice round of applause.

Releasing her lips, I stare into her hypnotic green irises while still cradling her face as if we're in our own little bubble. "Vivian agreed to move in with me," I say with a soft voice.

She smiles and nods.

We both turn and I'm not sure if the watery eyes gazing at us are from all the laughter or something else; but in this moment, for the first time in over three years, I don't see it: pity.

"Man! I can't believe you stole my girl." Chance draws the attention away from us. More laughter fills the balmy summer evening air.

"You're still my backup." Vivian blows him a kiss.

"Well, I'm happy for you both." My dad raises his glass. "To Oliver and Vivian, may you never stop finding the humor in life."

My mom holds up her glass with one hand and wipes a few tears with her other. I know they are happy tears mixed with a few sad ones too. As much as she wants me to move on, I imagine she fears my past is unresolved and could destroy what I have with Vivian. Yet another self-diagnosis. It must be genetic.

"Will we see you two next weekend or do you have other plans for your birthday?" Mom asks.

Vivian looks at me with raised eyebrows. "When's your birthday?"

I shrug. "Friday, but it's not a big deal."

"Hmm." She puckers her sexy lips to the side. God, I wish I could read her mind. "Well, you're mine Friday but we'll be here for dinner next Saturday."

My mom beams. She's obviously pleased as Vivian sends an excited smile in her direction. "Perfect. I'll have all your favorites."

In what has become Saturday night tradition, we make our way to the chairs around the fire pit and crack open a few more bottles of beer and refill the wine glasses. I could stay here all night watching Vivian chat and laugh with my family like she's known them her whole life. There's such an undeniable feeling that she belongs here with me, with all of us. What doesn't make sense is the soul-crushing detour I took to get to her.

"I need to grab something out of my purse." She bends over and kisses the corner of my mouth then goes inside.

"She's amazing." My mom nods her head.

"She is." I take a swig of my beer.

"You need to tell—"

"I know." I try to control the sharp edge to my voice. She's just looking out for me, but I'm in too good of a mood to think about shit that doesn't matter tonight. My phone vibrates and I pull it out of my pocket.

Vivian: *I'm having an insatiable Boston Kreme craving!*
Me: *We're leaving.*

She walks out the backdoor, slipping her phone back into her purse.

I stand. "Thanks for yet another great dinner, Mom."

"Yes, it was wonderful." Vivian bends down and gives both of my parents each a hug.

Chance stands and pats me on the back. "You two heading home to say your prayers goodnight?" he whispers in my ear.

I can't help but grin as I smack him across the back of the head. "Shut up."

"Goodnight, Chance." Vivian hugs him and he lifts her off the ground.

I clear my throat as I watch the back of her dress ease up her legs to what I and now everyone else knows is her bare ass.

"Relax your balls, Bro. I'm just giving her a hug."

I grab her and pull her into me. "Hug's over, *Bro.*"

Chance's deliberate prodding is easy for me to ignore, except with Vivian. Another self-psychoanalytical discovery. Vivian was going to give her virginity to my younger, less complicated, surprisingly not as fucked-up brother, which makes him a permanent silent threat in my mind.

Walking down the driveway, she slides her hand into my back pocket. "You were an obnoxious tease tonight and if I weren't having such a Boston Kreme craving I would make you sleep on the couch."

Where to begin? As I open the car door for her, she looks at me with those innocent eyes, batting her lashes at me, baiting me. Looking around the dead neighborhood illuminated by the distant street lights and hearing only the buzzing and screeching of the nocturnal creatures; I pull her away, close the door, and open the back door instead.

"Get in."

"What?"

"Get. In."

She looks around as if doing her own assessment then slides in the backseat and moves to the opposite side as I get in back with her.

"Now," I begin while unbuttoning my shirt and unfastening my pants, "I'll get to the irony of you kicking me out of my own bed before you've actually moved in with me, in just a minute."

Swallowing, her chest noticeably rises with each labored breath as she watches me, eyes frozen wide.

"From now on you don't leave the house until I've inspected to see if you're wearing underwear." She tries to scoot toward the other door as my hand snakes up her leg, but she can't go any farther. "Do you understand?" I slide my middle finger into her very wet pussy.

She sucks in a quick breath.

"Do you understand?" I say with a firmer voice as I slip in a second finger.

Her eyes roll back and she nods, releasing a soft moan.

"Good. As for the *obnoxious* comment, I think you might have been self-reflecting. You drive me crazy—mad crazy, funny crazy, horny crazy ... just deliriously crazy. I think you want me to spank you."

Her eyes fly open.

"I think you like to see how far you can push me. Every word that crosses your sexy lips begs for my reaction. So if I'm sleeping on the couch tonight, you can rest assured that you'll be underneath me with my dick buried deep inside you."

With my other hand I slide her dress up to her waist and she bends her left leg letting her shoe slide off then rests her foot on the seat. I'm rock hard and dying to get inside of her. Freeing myself from my briefs, I slip my fingers out and guide my cock into her with a hard thrust.

"Oli!" I silence her with my mouth, and she slips her hands under the back of my shirt and claws my skin.

I'm done talking. I always am when I'm inside her. I can't think, I can't speak, and since the first day I laid eyes on her, I think I've been waiting to breathe. She's the exact moment I fall from the sky and emerge from the depths of the ocean—she's life.

"Oh my God, Oli, I love you so much!"

Her words ignite me as I pound into her beautiful body, intoxicated by her touch, her smell, her taste.

"I love you too, Bro. When you're done I'll be in my truck waiting for you to let me out of the driveway."

I freeze, which is easy to do when Chance's voice showers us like a bucket of cold water. Vivian's body goes rigid as she buries her face in my neck.

"Get the fuck out of here!" I look back not realizing I forgot to shut the door behind me as Chance holds up his hands. "Take your time. I'll be in my truck." He grins and walks back up the driveway.

"Shit!" I'm so pissed.

Vivian starts giggling with escalating hysteria into my neck. I start to pull out. "What are you doing?" She wraps her legs around my waist to stop me.

"What do you mean, *what am I doing*?" How can she ask me that?

"I'm not done."

"My brother just caught us having sex in my parents' driveway and you want to finish?" I can't hide the shock in my voice.

"I do." She kisses me and clenches her legs around me tighter.

"No!" I pull away. "I can't do this. My brother is sitting in his truck staring at us through his rearview mirror. Hell, he's probably called my mom and asked her to throw a bag of popcorn in the microwave for him to eat during the show."

"Mmm, popcorn sounds good too." She releases her death grip around my waist.

"You're drunk, aren't you?"

She pulls her dress down over her legs as I fasten my pants and button my shirt. "No, tipsy maybe, but not drunk." She opens the door on her side, gets out, and waves to my brother as she walks around to the passenger door.

I climb out of the backseat and wait for her to get in before I shut her door and give Chance the bird. I'm an idiot, she's trouble, and together we're ... *deranged*!

CHAPTER SIXTEEN
GHOSTS

Vivian

IN MY YOUNG naive world I like to believe that Oliver moved back to Cambridge to meet me. It's a fairy tale enchanted feeling that we were somehow fated to meet. In reality I know something bad happened to him while he was in Portland. I love him so the patient part is easy. However, I'm naturally an inquisitive person so the suspense, no matter how bad it may be, is killing me.

When we lie next to each other in bed, I sense him working up the nerve to tell me something, maybe everything. Then just as quickly as the moment comes, it vanishes and I'm left wondering when. When will he tell me what's behind that damn locked door? When will he tell me why we sleep on a flat mattress with no pillows? When will he tell me why he has a Harvard education yet spends all day playing in the dirt and working for pennies?

"Maybe you should see if Alex is okay with you leaving your bed here." Oliver says as we survey my empty bedroom with the exception of my childhood twin bed.

"What if we took it apart and stored it in your spare bedroom?"

"I already have a bed in there."

"I mean the other one."

He tenses staring at the bed then turns and walks downstairs.

That went well.

"Hey!"

He stops at the bottom of the stairs. I walk down and hug his back. "I'm sorry."

Turning, he runs his hands through my hair and stares at me with such pain I feel tears pricking the corners of my eyes and I don't even know why. I'm on the precipice of waiting for my world to begin and end at the same time.

"It's none of my business." He flinches and the last thing I want is to cause him pain, but I have. I reach up on my tiptoes and press my lips to his, then I wait. He moves his mouth with mine and all I want is for him to feel my lucid emotions. He is my forever even if I am nothing more than his now.

"Get a room," Alex says, coming in the front door.

"You're back early."

She hugs me. "Yes, we had to bring Kai back. He's a mess."

I let go and look at Oliver to see if he heard her, but he's too busy talking to Sean. They're both smiling. I wasn't sure how Sean would be toward Oliver since he and Kai are such good friends.

"I can't think about Kai anymore."

Alex gives me a sad smile. "I know." She gestures to the boxes sitting by the front door. "When you messaged me that you were moving in with Oliver I didn't think you meant this weekend."

I shrug. "I'm there all the time anyway and I don't have that much stuff so we decided to just do it today."

"You do realize you're going to have to tell your parents."

I nod. "I know. I need to tell my parents a lot of things."

Alex sighs. "I don't suppose you're going to keep paying me rent, huh?"

"Dream on. You're going to have to actually work with us at The Green Pot a little more often so your parents don't wonder why you're suddenly asking for spending money."

"Yeah, yeah, you're a traitor, you know. I took you in because you didn't have a life and you needed a hiding place for a few years *and* you told me I wouldn't have to worry about you bringing guys home or not being here to keep an eye on things for me. Now look what you've gone and done."

I flash her a wry grin. "Sorry."

Alex bumps my arm with her shoulder. "Whatever. Sex looks good on you."

The room falls silent and two sets of male eyes fall on us. "What are you two looking at? God! Typical men, the only time you're not selectively deaf is when the words sex, pussy, and tits are mentioned." Alex rolls her eyes.

"We just heard sex, babe. Did we miss pussy and tits earlier?"

"Shut up!" Alex marches over to Sean and he instinctively protects his balls. She punches him in the arm. "Help Oliver carry these boxes across the street so Flower and I can have a few minutes alone to compare the size of your penises."

Both Oliver and Sean divert their eyes to the boxes. Their nervous embarrassment is palpable. "I'm just kidding." Alex laughs. "We both already know whose is bigger."

Oliver looks at me with wild eyes, but all I can do is laugh.

"Come on, Flower." Alex locks arms with me and pulls me to the kitchen.

"You're terrible."

Alex opens a bottle of wine and fills two glasses. "Sean loves it."

"No, Sean loves you, he tolerates your crude behavior."

She takes a sip of her wine. "What about Oliver? What is there about you that he tolerates?"

"My insatiable sex drive."

Alex coughs and grins. "I knew it! I bet you're a real naughty little vixen."

I swallow my wine and smile.

"Oh my gosh, Flower! Are you into kinky shit? Sean is *so* not working for you ... *ever!*"

"It's not just about sex, it's sex with Oliver. It's ... life-altering and mind-blowing, like an out-of-body experience."

She shakes her head and takes another sip of wine. "An *out-of-body experience?*"

I nod and smile with a soft sigh just thinking about it.

"So while some of us are giving the nubbin a rubbin' after our man fails to get the job done, you're having a freaking out-of-body experience. That's great, Flower ... just great. Sean has got to up his game. Maybe we should try some of that spanking you and Oliver do."

"Shh ..." I look out to see where the guys are. "We haven't done that," I whisper. "At least not yet."

"Yet?"

I grin. "Yet. It's been a joke between us. I think that's all it's going to be, but I'm not sure."

"Yeah, well there's a little truth to everything. Men are animalistic by nature. About a year ago Sean pulled out early and spewed his spunk all over my breasts like he felt the need to mark me or some shit like that. I told him to clean it up or he'd be tasting my piss in his coffee the next morning."

I choke on my wine. "Did-didn't need to—know that." I clear my throat.

"Well, I'm just telling you so you can be prepared. One day it's a friendly pat on your bare ass, the next day he shows up with a sack containing shackles, an anal speculum, and a bottle of Sour Sin Sations Ravishing Raspberry lubricant."

"Sour Sin Sation—"

Alex waves a dismissive hand in the air. "Don't ask. My point is you need to remember that your perfect sex stallion is in fact a man, AKA a kinky bastard with fantasies that are just too unimaginable for such a young and inexperienced little flower."

"Anal speculum?" I blink in rapid succession.

"You're completely missing the point, Flower. Never mind, let's see if those boys are done hauling your stuff."

"I NEED to go visit my parents." I say while unpacking my clothes in Oliver's—*our* closet.

"Are you going to confess that you haven't been in school the past two years?" Oliver pulls out a pair of my I'll-be-a-virgin-for-life cotton panties and smiles.

I snatch them from him, giving him a glowering squint. "Yes *and* I think I should give them my new address and introduce them to my ..."

"Your what?" Oliver grabs my panties back and brings them to his nose. Alex is right, men are animals.

"My perverted boyfriend." I tug them away. "Fabric softener, they smell like fabric softener you freak."

He laughs. "So let's go next weekend."

"No, it's your birthday, but how would you feel about the following weekend?"

He tosses the empty box toward the door then plops down on the bed with his hands laced behind his head.

"Even better. I'm sure your parents want to see you on your birthday." He winks with a smarty-pants grin.

"How do you know my birthday?"

"I have my sources. When were you going to tell me?"

"Probably a week after you told me about your birthday."

"I wasn't going to tell you." He shrugs. "Because it's not a big deal."

"Well, then I was going to tell you a week after never. Now who told you?" I crawl on top of him and unbutton his pants.

Tilting his chin down, he watches me with a smirk. "Horny?"

I lick my lips and nod. "A name."

"Maggie told me a couple weeks ago. She said you'd never tell me." He unbuttons my shorts and unzips them.

I scoot off the bed and tug his shorts and briefs off then do the same to my shorts and panties.

"Never is a long time, but she might be right." I slip off my shirt and remove my bra.

He sits up and shrugs off his shirt then glances back at the alarm clock. "You do realize we had sex like twenty-five minutes ago."

I nod. "I could run and grab a doughnut instead."

He offers his hand and I take it. Pulling me onto his lap he sucks one of my nipples into his mouth while lining his cock up to my entrance, teasing it back and forth against my clitoris.

I arch my back and he sucks harder on my nipple, grazing his teeth over it as he releases it then does the same to my other breast. I love the feel of his tongue torturing my nipples.

"Make me come ... just ... like ... this." I close my eyes and let him bring me to a mind-blowing orgasm with just his tongue teasing the tips of my nipples and the warm, moist head of his cock sliding against my clitoris. "Yes ... Y-yeesss!" My cry is loud and uninhibited. He starts to slide into me but I scoot off the bed.

"Where are you—"

I hold up a finger and grin then go into the closet. A few seconds later I strut out wearing a black lace bra that does little to hide my nipples and a pair of black high-heel boots that zip up past my knees, and *no* panties.

"Oh. Sweet. Jesus." Oliver's breath is labored as his greedy eyes wash over my body.

I walk over to the dresser, the scene of the accident, and bend over bracing my hands on the edge. "What are you waiting for?" I ask looking back over my shoulder at him.

His emotionless face curls into a smile as his blue eyes find mine. He stands, then grabbing my hips, grazes his hard dick over my entrance. "You're every guy's fucking fantasy, you know that, right?" He plunges into me and the few photos of his family along with his watch and some loose change rattle on the dresser. A moan escapes his chest as he stills buried deep inside me.

"I only want to be *your* fantasy, Oli."

"Mission accomplished," he says through gritted teeth

then rears back and slams into me again and again, gaining speed and strength with each thrust.

Oliver

IT'S BRUTALLY painful how much I've come to love her in the past few weeks. I sit on the edge of the bed and watch her continue to put her things away in the closet and drawers I cleared out for her. She's back in shorts and a T-shirt, but my eyes still see her in those boots and lace bra. One thing's for sure ... I will never grab my wallet and watch off the dresser again without seeing her bent over grasping the edge asking me what I'm waiting for.

She has no idea how hard it was for me to look at her back today. Those scars represent how much she's really given herself to me, how much she trusts me. Vivian's all in, no holds barred, take me as I am, and I'm the luckiest bastard alive. She deserves the same and every time I think the words of truth, my truth, are ready to come out, they don't. I can't give them to her. It's like they're glued to my soul and it's only a matter of time before she rips them out of me.

"You're awfully quiet, Mr. Konrad. Too much sex today?" She grins while breaking down the boxes by the door, which is what I should be doing. Instead, I'm lost in my own world of self-pity.

I hold out my hand and she takes it, once again giving me everything with complete trust. Pulling her between my legs, I rest my cheek on her chest while feathering my fingers over the back of her legs. "I love you, you know that, right?"

"I do." She slides her fingers through my hair.

"Good, because someday you may question my love for you, but don't." I look up at her and I see the concern etched in the wrinkles on her forehead.

She moves her hands to my face, resting her palms on my cheeks. "O-kay."

"No matter what, I'm serious. Promise me you'll never forget how much I love you and how much I don't deserve you, but I'm selfish and letting you go is too impossible."

"Oli, you're scaring me."

I hug her tight as if I can physically draw her into me so we're connected in a way that nothing could ever separate us.

"Don't be scared."

She leans back and looks at me. "Are you dying?"

I laugh. "We're all dying, and when you don't wear underwear you kill me a little faster every day."

She rolls her eyes. "I'm serious."

"I am too." I grin. "But, no, I'm not dying any more than you are."

She steps back, opening the last box. Pulling out a fleece blanket, she tosses it on the bed next to me, then she pulls out a pillow and hugs it to her chest. Worrying her teeth over her bottom lip she stares at me. "I like to rest my head on a pillow when I sleep."

Fuck!

I swallow hard and shake my head slowly. "I can't."

"It's not for you, just for me—"

"I can't." I try to keep the anger out of my voice.

She steps toward me with the pillow, and I feel the sweat bead on my skin. "Vivian?" I hold up my hand and shake my head faster. She stops. "Remember what I just said to you?"

She nods.

I try to control my breathing and steady my voice. "Good, then you need to get rid of the fucking pillow before I tear it to shreds."

The woeful frown on her face guts me, but I can't change what's happening and I hate myself for it. As much as I want to put on an act and pretend the anxiety inside isn't eating me alive, I can't.

A few tears escape her eyes then she turns and puts the pillow back in the box and carries it downstairs. I can't breathe as sweat drips down my face. I shrug off my clothes and jump into the cold shower. Regret washes over me faster than the water.

I hate her. I hate her. I hate her.

CHAPTER SEVENTEEN
FOR YOUR PLEASURE OR MINE?

Oliver

WE GO TO WORK, eat, sleep, and even make love like it's the first and the last time. She's still her playful, funny, and sexy-as-hell self, as if I didn't nearly have a breakdown in front of her over a damn pillow. I try to smile at the right times and act engaged in our conversations. I'm living with the woman I love more than life itself, yet I'm miserable.

"Are you excited for your birthday tomorrow?" Lively eyes gaze up at me as we take the Red Line to work.

Shaking my head, I cup her ass and pull her close to me. "It's just another day."

She sucks in her lips biting them together. Then she whispers in my ear, "We'll see if by the end of the day tomorrow you're still calling it *just another day*."

And ... I'm hard. Just great.

"Thanks for the boner. This is my stop."

She kisses me and grins. "Love you."

"Mmm, you too." I turn to get off the subway and she smacks me on the ass. I whip around to see the devilish temptress in her eyes and catch a few snickers and grins from the passengers around her. As soon as I step off and the doors shut, I text her.

Me: *Paybacks are a bitch, my love!*
Vivian: *I hope so!*

CHANCE and I have started a new project at a park near the harbor. It's going to be a back-breaking day with over six tons of rock and fifty bags of mulch to haul by wheelbarrow.

"What's Vivian got planned for your big day?"

"She won't say."

"I bet it involves leather, whips, and icing on *her* cupcakes."

I dig the shovel into the pile of rock. "I don't think about her that way." *Lie.*

"Sure you don't. That's why you couldn't even get out of Mom and Dad's driveway before nailing her in the backseat of your car."

"And there it is." I shake my head and lift the handles of the wheelbarrow. "I was actually surprised and kind of proud of you for not mentioning it all week when I thought for sure you'd be razzing me about it on Monday."

"It is impressive, isn't it?" He tosses a couple bags of mulch over his shoulder.

"*Was*, it was impressive, but not anymore."

"Mom and Dad are worried about you."

"What's new?"

"They think you're going to mess this up by not telling her."

"I'm going to tell her. Everyone else needs to just butt out."

"When?"

I dump the load of rock onto the landscaping paper. "After we get back from her parents' house next weekend."

"Good call. Then they'll have a face to put with the name of the guy who broke their little girl's heart."

"I'm not going to break her heart!" There he goes pushing all the right buttons.

"Hey, man, don't get upset. I understand—"

"You don't fucking understand! Nobody does! You weren't there, you didn't see what I saw!"

Chance looks around to see if anyone's hearing me. He doesn't say anything ... for the rest of the day.

Vivian

"Oli?" I whisper while straddling him. "You're going to miss the sunrise on your big day, baby."

He flops his arm over his face. I take a mental picture of him hoping that in fifty years we're doing the same thing and that I will still remember this day. Kissing my way up and over the bumpy muscles of his abs, I pull his arm off his face. He squeezes his eyes shut like a defiant little boy.

"Fine." I crawl off him. "I'll be on the deck if you change your mind."

"Wait!"

I smile and don't have to turn around to know that he's opened his eyes. "You like?"

"Get back here."

I turn around so he can see the front of my sexy red lace

teddy connected to G-string bottoms. "I'll meet you on the deck."

"Vivian!"

I grin all the way to the deck. As soon as I open the door his hands are on my bare ass, caressing it.

"Have a seat, birthday boy."

He sits in the lounge chair and grins like I'm just about to make all his dreams come true ... and I am. The sky is still dark but there's a small line of light teasing the distant horizon.

"Have you ever had sex while watching the sunrise, Oli?"

He shakes his head as his eyes follow me. I spread his legs and kneel on the chair between them. "Good. Now, I believe you're thirty today, correct?"

He nods and his mouth goes slack as I release him from his briefs.

"Well lucky for you I don't have a strong gag reflex so you just sit back and watch the sunrise while I give you a thirty minute birthday blow job."

His breath catches as I take him in my mouth. "I-I don't know if ... I'll last ... thirty minutes."

I look up at him while my tongue makes a slow stroke to the tip. "Oh you won't, baby." I take him in as far as I can then suck and swirl my tongue around him as I release him. "But that's okay, I'll swallow and start over again."

THIRTY MINUTES, one quick, and two long orgasms later, Oli gets dressed while I make breakfast.

"Here, baby." I set his plate down as he takes a seat at the table.

"Mmm, smells good."

"Ground turkey hash and wheat toast. Coffee?"

"Please." He turns as I walk back to the kitchen and he's still staring at me as I return with two cups of coffee.

"What?" I raise a brow.

"Are you going to wear that to work?"

I look down at my red teddy. "Yes."

His eyes attempt to pop out of their sockets.

"Maggie said business has been a little slow lately so I thought I could stand out front, like a mascot, and draw in some new customers."

His toast falls from his hand back to his plate.

"Kidding, Oli." I laugh and shake my head. "Relax, I'm just kidding."

He struggles to smile as he continues to eat.

"You've been kind of quiet, even a little withdrawn since the *sunrise*. I sort of expected the opposite, I mean ... you enjoyed it, right?"

He chuckles looking down at his plate. "Yes, it was enjoyable and unexpected."

My appetite vanishes. I can see something is bothering him. There's really nothing more humiliating than dressing up in lingerie and sucking a guy's dick for a half hour only to be given the cold shoulder and told it was "enjoyable." A good movie or dinner with friends is *enjoyable*, an epically long birthday blow job deserves a better adjective.

I stand and take my plate to the kitchen. "Well, I'm glad you *enjoyed* it. I'm going upstairs to get ready for work."

"Vivian?"

I stop midway up the stairs. "Hmm?"

"Is something wrong?"

I don't know, you tell me!

"Nope. I'll be down in a few minutes." I turn and sulk my way to the closet.

"Enjoyable, I eat three servings of your cum for breakfast and all you can say is it was *enjoyable*!" I mumble to myself as I shimmy out of this stupid, itchy, expensive piece of nothing.

I've never wanted to lump Oliver into the "typical man" category until today, on his birthday of all days. I can't even chew his ass out for being so insensitive—maybe tomorrow. I wonder what the waiting period is for yelling at someone for acting stupid on their birthday.

"Let's go." I fake a smile as I grab my purse.

"Thanks for breakfast. It was incredible!" He slips on his boots by the front door.

Potatoes and turkey are incredible, but a thirty minute blow job is enjoyable? I'm rethinking my plans for him later. Maybe we'll order in and I can knit while he scrubs the kitchen floor again. That's probably *enjoyable* too. We walk down the front steps and head toward Harvard Square.

"I was thinking of taking you out tonight, but now I'm wondering if you would rather stay in and order takeout?"

He wraps his arm around me. "Sounds perfect."

Of course it does. Thirty must be the new fifty. I should have gotten him loafers and a cardigan for his birthday. It's possible I have a bruised ego taunting me. It's also possible that he's already bored with me. Maybe Alex is right. Oliver may want to spice things up between us, which seems ridiculous since we are still in the early honeymoon stage of our relationship. I suppose I could pick a few things up and try them out on him tonight. He's probably had more blow jobs than I care to imagine so this morning was just an extended version of an all too familiar routine.

"What's going on in that beautiful head of yours?"

Oh nothing. Just making a mental note to Google sex toy shops when I get to work.

"Nothing, nothing at all."

Our morning is busy, well, at least in the illegal cash sales. Maggie and her VIP customers have spent most of the morning sorting out the fine details of everything that's wrong with our government—campaign financing ... blah, blah, blah ... corporate government ... blah, blah, blah ... and, of course, the need to legalize marijuana.

"Some of your customers don't look sick anymore, yet they keep coming in. What's up with that?"

Maggie laughs. "Look at how long I've been in remission, but I still smoke a joint before bed every night. Don't knock it until you've tried it."

"Are you suggesting I try it?"

"Absolutely! This could be a real kick-ass year for you, Viv. Sex, pot, and Harvard."

I open a new box of gardening gloves and refill the display. "With my luck it would be sex, pot, jail, and no Harvard."

"Pish posh, I'll send home a couple for you to share with your birthday boy tonight. Just don't smoke them on the subway or your front door steps and you'll be fine."

"I sort of had something else planned for tonight. I don't know if it should be mixed with pot."

"What's that, sweetie?"

I giggle and shake my head. "I can't believe I'm saying this to you, but what the hell. I was planning on picking up some *toys* to try out."

"Shoot." She waves her hand at me. "I've seen it all ... and used most of it too."

My jaw takes a nosedive to the floor. "What!"

"Don't look so surprised. Before I was into scarves and wigs I was quite the naughty little minx."

"Maggie!"

"It's true. Ask me anything."

"I-I ... well—"

"Are you thinking something geared toward his pleasure or yours?"

"Uh ... um ..."

"Never underestimate the power and pleasure of a good strap-on penis. I'd recommend a beginner kit and start small unless he has experience in this area. Maybe check with him before you buy anything. They don't usually allow returns. Oh, don't forget ... lots of lube."

Is she high? Am I? I can't imagine how Oliver would react to a text asking him if he's had a dildo or strap-on penis stuck up his ass, and if so what size can he accommodate?

"Now if you're thinking something less expensive may I suggest his-and-her pleasure vibrators. Once again, lots of lube especially if you get one for your G-spot. I'm guessing Oliver is *pretty well endowed* so your little vagina that hasn't been broken in yet may not easily allow both him and the vibrator at the same time. But once you get both in ... wowza! Let me tell you, it's serious amazballs!"

Oh. My. God! This conversation is not really happening. I'm going to wake up soon with sweat dripping down my body and I'm going to laugh hysterically at this weird dream my mind has conjured up.

"Yeah, maybe we'll just stick to the weed for tonight. With the no return policy and high price tags, I'd hate to make a hasty decision without checking something like uh ... Consumer Reports or Good Housekeeping."

Maggie hands me the last pair of gloves and I punch them with the pricing gun and slip them on the rack. "Okay, but if you'd like I could see what I have in my basement. I'm sure I have a box or two with a nice assortment of everything. I could throw it all in the dishwasher for a good cleaning and Lysol anything with a battery pack."

I grin. "We're good. I'm sure the new stuff is BPA and phthalate free now and then there could be recalls. So ... we'll stick to the weed for tonight." It's insane that by this point in our conversation smoking marijuana seems innocent, almost normal, compared to everything else.

"Suit yourself. You know where to reach me if you change your mind."

Um ... yeah, that won't be happening.

CHAPTER EIGHTEEN
CROSSING LINES

Oliver

I'VE NEVER BEEN the jealous type, until Vivian crashed into my life. Three years for someone my age is a long time to go without sex. Now I've been handed this incredible sexual genie in a bottle who turns my fantasies into reality. The problem is ... every time she puts my dick in her mouth all I see is Kai. Her mouth on *him*.

"Hey, birthday boy!" Vivian greets me at the door with an enthusiastic hug and a long sensual kiss. "How was your day?"

"Not as good as this." I kiss her again. "But it was okay."

"Hmm, well I have dinner—Indian, and I picked up a cake. I know your mom is going to bake you one tomorrow so I'm not even going to try and compete with her."

I untie my boots and slip them off then remove my sweaty T-shirt. "I'm going to take a quick shower. Care to join me?"

She stares at my chest and then she does her signature

lip lick, like she wants to devour me. Thirty's not feeling too bad today.

"I'd love to, I mean *really* love to, but if I do, we both know it won't be a quick shower and dinner will be cold." She blows me a kiss from the kitchen. "I'll make it up to you later."

I shrug and turn taking the stairs one slow step at a time while unfastening my jeans and easing them over my hips exposing part of my ass. "Your loss."

"Nice briefs, babe. At least one of us is wearing underwear today."

I try to play it cool but damn if she didn't just beat me at my own game. "Did I mention I'm going to staple them to your ass if you don't start wearing them?"

"You may have."

I mumble a few indiscernible expletives and head to the bathroom for a very cold shower. An ocean of thoughts flow through my mind and the chaos in my brain is almost nauseating. I'm uncontrollably in love with Vivian. In such a short amount of time she's infiltrated my thoughts, cast a spell over my body, and wormed her way into the deepest part of my heart. A day without her would feel like a lifetime without a breath, an eternity without light.

As I pull my T-shirt over my head and comb my fingers through my wet hair, I play with the words in my head. The words that she needs to hear, and she will—soon. I chuckle, but it's not born of pleasure; it's pain and utter disbelief of the sadistic irony of what's to come. What will I say to her parents next week? "Hi, I'm the guy who is crazy about your daughter but as soon as we leave here I'm going to crush her because it's unlikely that a twenty-two-year-old, even one as smart as your daughter, can wrap her head around the reality of my past." Yeah, that should go over well.

I spot Vivian shoving her feet into her flip-flops and slinging her purse around her shoulder as I come down the stairs.

"What are you doing?"

She looks up at me and her eyes are red, cheeks tear-stained. "I have to go. I'm so sorry."

"What's wrong? What happened?"

Watery eyes look up at me as I pull her into my arms. "Beth died." She sobs.

"Who's Beth?"

"Kai's sister."

I tense at the mention of his name.

"Sh-she was in—a car ac-accident."

"I'm so sorry." The words come out automatically because I feel her pain and I want to take it away.

"I have to go." Her broken voice is just above a whisper.

"Where?"

She steps back, wiping her cheeks with her fingers. "Hartford, with Kai. I'm driving him back in his car because he's in no condition to drive. Alex and Sean will come Sunday and I'll ride back with them after the funeral on Monday."

"I'll come with you."

"No ... Kai doesn't need that, or this ... *us*." She sighs.

I fight to keep my emotions controlled. "I thought things between you two were—"

"Jesus! He just lost his sister. I've been his best friend forever. Now's not the time to get into this! What is your deal with him?"

My head jerks back. "*My* deal with him? Are you serious? My deal is that ever since we went to Cape Cod all I can see is his dick in your mouth. That's all I could see this morning. It's all I—"

"Oh my God! I knew it. I knew something was wrong this morning. *Unbelievable*! I spent over a hundred dollars on lingerie and sucked your cock for over thirty minutes swallowing *every time* and all you thought about was Kai?" She backs up closer to the front door while shaking her head, face tense.

"Viv—"

"Don't! I gave you all of me. I gave you something no other man has ever had. I gave up a sixteen-year friendship for you. I shared the most painful part of my past with you and what have you given me?"

I can barely breathe as the blood runs cold through my veins.

"What happened in Portland? Why are you so afraid of pillows and what in God's name is behind that locked door upstairs?" The anger in her voice is raw ... unrecognizable.

I take a step back. Her words become a distant echo.

"Nothing? Is that all you've got? Fine then. I'll be in Hartford with my best friend grieving the loss of his sister, a sister I thought of as my own. So if the only thoughts that you have to share are ones of pathetic jealousy about some other guy's dick in my mouth, then I think this..." she gestures her finger between us "...was a huge mistake."

Tears drown her cheeks and I hate myself for it. In this moment I realize how fucked-up I am because not a single word escapes my mouth as I watch her walk out the door.

Vivian

"You didn't have to drive me home," Kai speaks, ending a half hour of silence.

"I did. It's not safe for you to drive when you're so distracted."

"Your *boyfriend* okay with you driving me home?" He keeps his gaze out his window.

"Yes." I lie because I don't want him to know what happened. The heavy weight on my heart from the loss of Beth has only been compounded by leaving Oliver. I don't even have to say the words aloud for the tears to sting my eyes. That's what I did, I left Oliver. In the moment I was running on adrenaline-driven emotions, and the reality of what I said and what he *didn't* say has not hit me yet with full impact.

"Sean said you moved in with him."

"How are your parents doing?" I refuse to continue talking about Oliver and me.

Kai lifts his shoulders. "Sarah said Mom's a mess but Dad hasn't cried yet. Denial, I guess."

Kai's older sister, Sarah, is an emergency ER doctor in Hartford, and she was working when Beth was brought to the hospital. I can't even begin to imagine what that had to be like for her.

"How about Sarah?"

"She's staying strong for Mom and Dad."

He shakes his head. "I just can't wrap my own head around it." His voice cracks.

I reach over and take his hand. He looks over and squeezes mine and doesn't let go until we reach his house.

"Coming?" I ask as I open my door.

Kai stares at the house like he's seeing it for the first time. "I don't know if I can handle walking through the front door and not hearing her voice."

Beth was six years younger than Kai, and she had the most enthusiastic spirit.

I wipe a few stray tears. "I know, Kai."

Opening his door, I offer my hand and he takes it. I lead him up the front walk and his grip on me tightens as we get closer.

Silence. I expect to hear his parents or Sarah, but it's dark and silent.

"Where are your parents?"

"They're staying with Sarah. Dad said my mom can't even sleep in the house right now."

I nod and flip on the entry light. "Well it's late. I'll call you in the morning, okay?"

"Don't go." His eyes are bloodshot, his voice weak. "I don't want to be by myself."

"Kai—"

"Viv, I need my friend tonight."

"Okay," I whisper and then the wish list begins. I wish Beth were here telling us about her latest crush. I wish Kai and I had never been more than friends, which would make it easier to always be friends. I wish Oliver were the one leading me to his bedroom. I wish I knew Oliver, all of him. And since everything I want is so far from reality, I'm going to go ahead and wish for flying unicorns, my own private island off the coast of Australia, and world peace.

Kai kicks off his shoes and collapses onto his bed, staring at his ceiling.

"I'm going to use the bathroom."

He nods, not looking at me.

After washing my face and finger brushing my teeth, because I didn't bring in my bag from the car, I crawl into bed next to Kai. He turns and faces me. We stare at each other in silence—maybe like there's nothing to say, but more like there's everything to say but the words are just too painful.

As I start to drift off to sleep, my phone rings.

"Hello?"

"Hi." My heart skips a beat with one word because it's one word from Oliver.

"Hi," I whisper.

"Were you sleeping?"

"Just about."

"Listen, I'm—"

"Who is it, Viv?" Kai asks sending my world into yet another disastrous tailspin.

"Are you *sleeping* with him?" Oliver's icy voice pierces my ears.

I grimace and take a deep swallow, sitting up and turning my back to Kai. "His parents are not here and he didn't want to be alone so—"

"So you're sleeping with him?"

I stand and walk out of the room without looking back at Kai. "Don't do this," I whisper, leaning my head against the wall in the hallway.

"Don't do what? Be pissed that your idea of comforting your ex-boyfriend is to sleep with him?"

"Yes, Oli, *sleep* with him. I'm not sucking his dick or anything like that. I'm lying next to him in bed, fully clothed, so for one night he doesn't feel completely alone in the world."

"You're so naive."

"Excuse me?" I've never felt the age difference between us before now. He's treating me like a child.

"You're not a doe-eyed virgin anymore and he's not your five-year-old buddy down the street who doesn't think of you as a girl."

"It's not about that. This is a simple case of you not trusting me. Do you know how that makes me feel?"

He sighs. "I trust you, Vivian, it's him that I don't trust. He manipulates you. Have you forgotten why you ended things with him last weekend?"

"This is different. His sister died."

"Yes, she did and that's terrible. You drove him home. Make him a casserole or send flowers and a card, but don't fucking crawl into his bed!"

"You're being a jerk!"

"Yeah, well I won't even say what sleeping with him makes you."

I press end and shut off the power to my phone.

"Viv?" Kai calls from the bedroom.

I close my eyes and wipe the tears. I'm so sick of the pain and anger, but more than anything ... I'm sick of men.

I HAVEN'T HEARD from Oliver in two days. Then again, I only turn my phone on as needed. He could leave me a message but he hasn't, and that in itself says a lot. Kai's dad has come back home to stay with him, although his mom is still at Sarah's. Kai wonders if she'll ever come back home. The past two nights I've stayed with my parents even though Kai wanted me to stay with him. One night was enough since his dad is there now.

"You should bring your bed back home so when you come to visit you don't have to sleep on the couch," Alex says as we get dressed in our traditional black mourning attire.

I lean toward my vanity mirror and apply some mascara. "Yeah, about that ... I think I'm moving back across the street if you haven't already rented out my room."

"What?" Alex's voice escalates.

"I didn't want to mention it in front of my parents when you and Sean arrived last night, but Oliver and I aren't getting along right now." I will myself not to get emotional while applying my makeup.

"Flower, what happened?"

Dabbing some blush onto my cheeks, I look at her reflection in the mirror. "Secrets, jealousy, and Kai happened."

"I get the Kai part. Oliver couldn't have been too thrilled to see you rush off on his birthday with your ex-boyfriend."

"Yeah, that started it but then he called when I was at Kai's Friday night."

"And?"

I sigh. "And he was pissed and basically implied I was being a whore."

"What? Why?"

"Because Kai's parents were at Sarah's and Kai didn't want to be alone so I stayed the night."

"So, why would he be pissed about that? It's not like you slept with him."

"No, I didn't *sleep* with him as in have sex with him, but I slept beside him in his bed, like friends."

"What the hell, Flower! Why would you do that?"

"What?" I turn toward her. "We didn't do anything. He was grieving the loss of Sarah ... we both were."

"That doesn't mean you sleep in his bed. You just moved in with Oliver. That should mean something."

I cross my arms over my chest. "What's the big deal? You're acting like Oliver and it really hurts that nobody trusts me."

"Flower …" Alex's voice flows like honey. "I don't think you're looking at this the right way. How would you feel if Oliver had a female *friend* that had once been his girlfriend and her sister died so he stayed with her … in her bed? Would you think it was appropriate?"

"Yes." *NO!* The internal chastising begins. How could I not see it through his eyes?

"Flower …" Alex cocks her head to the side.

"God, I'm so stupid." I turn back to the mirror. Yep, that's what stupid looks like.

Alex zips the back of my dress and adjusts my necklace. "Innocent, trusting, and maybe even a little naive … but not stupid."

Naive. From his lips it felt like a hurtful lie, from hers it's the painful truth.

"I have some fences to mend."

Alex nods with a sad smile, slips on her black heels, and offers me her hand.

CHAPTER NINETEEN
MRS. KONRAD

Vivian

How is it that Oliver can choose not to disclose his past, let me move in with him, not share what's behind that stupid locked door, and avert all discussion about anything that makes him uncomfortable, yet I am always the one apologizing? I've spent the entire ride back to Cambridge going through my speech in my head. There will be an apology on my part, but there will also be disclosure on his.

It's after nine at night by the time we arrive home.

"Good luck, Flower." Alex hugs me. "My door is always open if he kicks you out."

With a roll of my eyes, I laugh. "Go ahead and lock your door tonight. No worries, I've got this."

Sean hugs me. "Do your worst, Viv, and if all else fails take off your clothes."

As if on cue, Sean gasps for air as he hugs his gut and buckles his knees. Alex adheres to the strict motto. "Spare the junk punch, spoil the boyfriend."

"Get your ass inside instead of talking through it.

Flower isn't going to take off her clothes like some pathetic bimbo to make her apology more believable. Now go!" She points to her red door and Sean scampers off like an injured animal.

After he's inside she turns to me. "You're totally going to have to strip, but then you make sure you milk the upper hand. Got it? Work that hot body of yours and by morning he'll be confessing like a Cardinal with a room full of altar boys. Now go!"

I open my mouth and she presses her finger to it. "Go!"

Lugging my bags up the stairs, I look back once more before opening the door. Alex gives me the shoo signal so I go inside. There's a small light on in the living room, but I don't see or hear Oliver.

"Oli?"

No answer.

I drop my bags and walk upstairs. No Oliver.

Going back down the stairs I call his name again. No answer.

There are no notes on the counter and his car is out front, but it's possible he's walked somewhere or he could be with Chance, but he doesn't usually leave on the lights. I walk past the patio door and freeze when I see a shadowy figure out of the corner of my eye. Opening the door, I spot him reclining in a chair with his back to me and the porch light off.

"Hey, didn't you hear me?"

"I did."

I step out on the deck. He doesn't look at me.

"Why didn't you say something?"

"I don't think there's anything left to say." He holds up a familiar bag, but still doesn't look at me. "You need to take this and the rest of your stuff and leave."

I take the bag from him. "You're kicking me out?"

He nods.

"Because of a little weed?"

He turns with bug eyes. "A little weed? You have an illegal drug in your possession. I'm not getting involved with a pothead! Maybe you're going through some college experimental phase, but I'm not."

"I'm not a pothead you idiot! I've never smoked it, ate it, bonged it, or whatever the hell people do with it. I brought it home for your birthday to share."

He laughs with insane hysteria. "To share? This was my birthday present? You bought me marijuana for my birthday?"

"I didn't buy it and it's not your present. Maggie sent it home with me after I told her you were acting weird Friday morning."

He sits up and runs his fingers through his hair while shaking his head. "Where did Maggie get this and why were you telling her about us?"

"What do you mean *where did she get this*? She's been growing it since she was first diagnosed with cancer years ago, hence the name, The Green Pot! And I have to talk to someone about us because you sure as hell don't want to talk about anything."

"I can't do this." He stands and brushes past me.

"You can't do what?" I follow him into the house. "Us? Pot?"

"Either ... both." His back is to me, hands resting on his hips, head bowed.

It hurts to breathe. The pain in my chest is crushing. "I came home, or here..." I shake my head "...I guess I don't even have a home anymore." I blink back my tears. "I was going to tell you that I was sorry. Nothing happened between me and Kai, but staying with him was wrong, and hurtful, and ... *naive*. I was going to ask you to share your past with me, to trust me with all of you the way I've trusted you with all of me. There was so much I wanted to say, but now ... I see that it doesn't matter."

The tears can no longer be blinked away. I sulk to the door and pick up my bags, but I don't turn back to look at him. "So I guess the only apologies you want to hear are these ... I'm sorry I'm too young and stupid and that for one night I was going to smoke a joint just to see what it was like. I'm sorry you can't be intimate with me without envisioning some other guys cock in my whore of a mouth. I'm sorry for all the times I've embarrassed you, but please, *please* don't ask me to be sorry about us." A strangled sob escapes as I grab the doorknob. "I'll ge-get the rest of my stu-stuff tomorrow ... when you-you're g-gone."

Oliver

SHE'S GONE and I said nothing ... absolutely nothing. My condo feels empty just like my heart and my life again. I've reached the point in this relationship that I no longer know who I'm trying to protect, her or me. My heart thunders in my chest when there's a knock at the door. *She's back!*

I open it.

Smack!

The sting on my cheek is more shocking than painful as I stare down at Alex and her fiery scowl.

"You're a fucking moron to let her walk out of your life. I hope I'm around to see the misery on your pathetic face when an amazing guy that deserves her snatches her up and you're left with nothing!" She stomps back across the street and gives me the bird before closing her door.

The cheap shrink in my head, the one that usually shows up at times like this, must be on vacation. I've got nothing. I need to rationalize that I don't deserve her, that we're both better off without each other. I'm too old for her and my past is not something she deserves. In a month she's going to be in college and I'm floundering around with my brother and a dwindling savings account. The best of me is gone and the best of her is still on the horizon.

I shut off the lights and collapse onto my bed—my lonely bed. Then it hits me. That's it. I'm the sunset, she is the sunrise, and the only thing between us is a world of darkness.

I bolt up from the bed. Crap! I've fucked up!

It's a little after eleven, but I see lights on through their windows. No doubt a male-bashing fest has ensued since Alex physically assaulted me. Crossing the street feels like breaching the frontline and all I'm armed with is "I am the darkness and you are my light?" If I don't come up with something better than that I might as well shove a sword through my own chest. I've already used up the gold standard, "I love you." Now what? I want you? I need you? The sex is amazing? *Yeah, that's the one.*

I knock on the door and pray the right words will magically find their way from my mouth to her ears. Alex answers with a smug grin.

"Come back for round two?"

"Where is she?"

"Flower is ... *busy*. Maybe you should come back in the morning."

I push the door open easily overwhelming her attempts to keep me out.

"Oliver!"

I scan the main level then head up the stairs; a pungent odor fills the air. Opening the door to Vivian's room I'm greeted with bloodshot eyes and a lazy smile.

"Oli," she says before taking another drag of her joint then coughing.

I take the joint and toss it in the coffee mug on the floor next to her bed. There's also a box of sugar cookies, a bag of chips, and a bowl of pistachios on the floor. She plops back on the bed and closes her eyes.

"You must be feeling pretty smug, Mr. Konrad." She giggles. "You nailed it. I'm a pothead. Maggie was right ... don't knock it until you've tried it."

"Let's go." I lift her off the bed, cradled in my arms.

"Put me down! I'm not going with you!" Her attempts to kick and flail are weak and pathetic.

I wasn't planning on going the caveman route, but then again, I wasn't planning on her being high either.

"Alex!" she yells as I carry her to the door.

Alex hops off the couch and comes at me.

"Back the hell off!" I glare at her.

She gasps as if no one has ever put her in her place before, then she does something I'm not expecting. She opens the front door and grins.

"Take care of her."

I pause only for a moment then nod as I take a now passed-out Vivian to my place.

She needs a shower and her teeth brushed to rid the smell of marijuana from her body, but right now I don't care. I lay her on the bed and remove all of our clothes. A single thread is too much separation when I have such an intense craving to feel the touch of her skin against mine. I wrap my body around hers and let myself drift off to sleep in peace, a peace that will evaporate in the morning. Tonight, however, I just need this ... I need *us*.

Vivian

I'M RETHINKING the weed idea. Foggy head, pulsing brain, and it must be one hundred degrees in here. Here? Where am I? What time is it? Why can't I move?

The heavy feeling on my chest lifts as I remove the arm draped over me. I'm naked and so is Oliver. Great. I know we didn't have sex; that I would remember. *Pervert!*

Easing off the bed, being careful not to wake him, I look for my clothes. After getting dressed, I tiptoe downstairs. It's four-thirty in the morning so I'm going to leave before the sun, and Oliver, rise. Apparently we need to talk, but not naked in his bed. I look for my shoes but don't see them. Reaching for the doorknob, I notice a pile of mail on the entry table. What catches my eye is the return address on the corner of an envelope sticking out from the middle of the pile. It's from a hospital in Portland. The fine print below the name reads: Mental Health and Chemical Dependency Care.

Walk away!

I can't. My curiosity has morphed into a monstrous need to know about Oliver's past. I rip open the envelope. The cover letter explains the enclosed information is an emergency contact update for a Caroline Konrad.

Mark the "No Changes" box, sign and date if all the information is still correct.

The next page has Oliver's name, address, e-mail, phone number, and relationship to patient.

Husband.

Bile races up my throat leaving a wake of acidic burn, and my heart pounds with anger as my blood runs toxic. Somewhere in my heart or soul I have to be crushed beyond words, but right now my mind is a volcanic eruption of anger and unfathomable rage. I think I could kill him.

Taking the stairs two at a time, I'm in his room within seconds ... and then it begins.

"You have a fucking WIFE!" I think he startles awake, but I can't tell for sure because all I see is red. One picture frame, then another thrown in his direction. A bookend, a vase, his shoes, a clock, all shattering and banging against the wall, his headboard, and even him.

"Vivian!" He stumbles around trying to find his balance in the midst of the debris coming at him.

I yank one dresser drawer out and heave it in his direction, then the next, and yet another until clothes are scattered everywhere and he's charging at me.

"No!" I yell, grabbing the back of the empty dresser and tipping it forward to block his approach. I run into the hall ripping framed art and pictures off the wall, leaving a wake of broken glass behind me. Down the stairs I run into the kitchen flinging open cupboard doors.

"Bastard!" I repeatedly throw glasses, plates, cans, and jars in his direction. "You're a fucking liar! How could you?"

"Vivian! STOP!" The roar of his voice can't compete with the hurricane of deafening emotions in my head.

Shot glasses. Whisky bottles. Coffee mugs.

Clank! Bang! Crash!

I'm running out of ammunition, then I glance up and see the pots and pans hanging from the suspension rack. Climbing onto the island, I grab two at a time from their hooks and hurl them at Oliver. Sometimes I hear the crash of my miss, other times I hear a thwack and a few expletives when my aim is perfect. After the last pan has been launched, I see a bloodied Oliver lumbering toward me. I look behind but there's no escape, so I leap with every last bit of energy I can muster and take him to the ground.

Thud!

Darkness.

B*EEP ... beep ... beep ...*

A flash of light and distant echoing bring me out of my sleep. I can't remember where I fell asleep. Alex's? Oliver's? Maybe I smoked too much pot again. God, I really am turning into a pothead.

"Flower?"

"Ouch!" I squint trying to open my eyes, but the pain in my head feels like it's paralyzing my whole body.

Alex flickers into focus. "What happened?"

"You ... *fell* and *other* things." She grimaces.

"Fell?"

"Well, sort of jumped or leaped ... from Oliver's counter. You have a concussion, and stitches in several places along with numerous cuts from the glass they had to remove from various parts of your body, especially your feet."

The pain in my head and now everywhere else multiplies one hundredfold as the flood of memories rushes back. *Oliver is married.*

"The doctor said you can go home this morning. All of your injuries are minor. There's just a lot of them, so you're going to have trouble getting around for the next week or so.

You must have been pretty pissed and running on pure rage to not realize you had so many shards of glass impaled in your feet."

"He's married." My voice sounds like the words are ripping through my throat. The anger has taken a backseat to the emotional pain and ... Oh. My. God. It hurts so bad. My vision clouds as the tears overflow down my face.

"Oh, Flower. I'm so sorry." Alex holds my hand with a gentle touch and as I try to squeeze hers, I feel the pull of bandages against my skin.

What have I done to myself?

"For what it's worth, he doesn't look any better than you do, except he doesn't have a concussion. He sat with you all night, against my better judgment, but I made him leave this morning before you woke. I think he and his family are in the waiting room."

Another sob escapes and Alex blots my face with a tissue. "I don't want to see them ... any of them, ever again."

"Do you want me to call your parents?"

"No! They ... they wouldn't understand. I haven't told them about Oliver."

"Okay, well, Sean will be back soon. I sent him to get you some clothes that weren't covered in blood."

"Good morning, Vivian."

I sniffle and look up.

"I'm Dr. Bennett. I just talked with Dr. Konrad and he said you're a close friend of their family so I came in early to get you checked out and hopefully back home soon so you can rest and heal." He swipes his finger across his iPad then hands it to the nurse and starts examining me.

"We're not friends."

Dr. Bennett shines a bright light into my right eye. "No? Hmm, sorry I must have misunderstood."

He blinds, pokes, and prods me then messes with his iPad again. "Well you're going to be fine. If you need something for the pain, Tylenol or Advil should work."

I nod. "Thank you."

"My pleasure. Get some rest."

Just as Dr. Bennett and the nurse exit the room, Sean comes in with a bag. "Hey, Viv. I brought you some clothes. Oliver gave me the key to his place. He's out in the waiting room and wants to see you."

Alex helps me sit up to the side with my feet dangling off the bed. "Can you give him a message for me?"

"Sure," Sean replies.

"Tell him to fuck off."

Sean looks at Alex then back at me.

"You heard her ... go." Alex motions with her head.

"Can we have a moment?" All three of us look to the door where Oliver stands. He has a black eye, fat lip, and stitches on his chin.

Good!

"Never mind, Sean, I'll tell him myself. Fuck off, Oliver!"

"Just five minutes. Please." He steps inside the room.

Alex rests her hand on my knee. "Just give him his five and then I'll take you home. Okay?"

I hesitate. I don't want to see him, and I sure as hell don't want to talk to him, but I want to go home so I nod once, staring down at my feet.

"We'll be right outside."

Oliver shuts the door behind them and comes closer to me. I see his brown Sanuk shoes and bare legs, but I don't look up.

"Vivian—"

"I hate you," I whisper.

"I know."

"Four minutes left."

He squats down resting his hands on either side of me so I'm forced to look at him. "I'm so very sor—"

"Three and a half minutes." I grit through my teeth.

He sighs. "Caroline is legally still my wife. She's suffering from ... *severe* depression and she's suicidal. I filed for divorce over a year ago, but given her mental state, a quick divorce is not an option. I love you. I want to be with you and I was going to tell you—"

I laugh. "You were going to tell me? When? Before you took my virginity? Before you let me fall in love with you? Before you asked me to move in with you? WHEN, OLIVER?" The emotional pain wars with the physical pain, and the anger I'm feeling is intensifying both. I'm exhausted. I feel empty, except for the tears. Damn the tears ... the endless river of tears.

He rests his cheek on my bare leg and I feel the surrender of his touch against my skin. It's a cruel reality when the touch that healed me becomes the flame that burns me.

"Time's up," I whisper then sniffle as I fight to breathe.

With a slow turn of his head, he brushes his stubbly face against my legs then presses his lips to my skin. I squeeze my eyes shut wringing out more tears, trying to hold my breath, but the emotions are too powerful. Instead, my body shudders as soft painful whimpers escape against my will.

"Bye, my love."

I feel him leave, but I can't open my eyes. I'm blinded by tears, blinded by emotions ... I was blinded by love.

CHAPTER TWENTY
MENDING

Vivian

THERE'S NOT a cell in my body that isn't screaming with pain, of course none more than those of my heart. I've been home from the hospital two days and today is the first day Alex has left me to run some errands. The tender wounds on my feet have me hobbling like a toddler, and the pain is off the charts, although I don't let on to anyone else. I don't like that type of attention ... never have.

Maggie has banned me from working for the next week, minimum, and money is going to get tight, but I haven't told her or anyone else. I also need to get my stuff moved out of Oliver's place, and although Alex and Sean have offered to do it for me, I've refused. Pride is a real bitch.

Oliver should be at work so I decide to go retrieve my stuff. It takes me fifteen minutes to make it from my door to his, counting rests on the stairs and both curbs. The last few steps to his front door bust open several cuts on my feet, so I drop to my knees. Now would be a good time to accept defeat, retreat, and ask for help. That's what a normal person would do in this situation. I've never been normal.

My roller derby kneepads would come in handy right now, but they're back in Hartford at my parents' house. Still, my hands and knees have fewer cuts than my miserable feet, so I opt to crawl my way through this mission. After unlocking his door, I slide the key back in my pocket and crawl into his house. Thankfully, he's cleaned up after my rampage so I don't have to navigate through a war zone to gather my stuff.

"Ugh!" I moan as I crawl to the stairs. Resting my head on the bottom step, I take a few deep breaths before proceeding up the stairs like an injured dog. I collapse at the top, sucking in as much air as I can, sweat beading on my brow. I didn't expect this to feel like a marathon, but it does.

An hour later, I have all my stuff shoved into three big bags, 2 of which are Oliver's. My whole body throbs and I'm pretty sure blood is oozing from several of my deeper cuts. I scoot the bags down the hall, nudging them with my head then sending them over the edge of the top step, tumbling to the first floor. My hands hurt, my feet hurt, my knees hurt, and yet I need to navigate down the stairs. Maneuvering to my butt, I stick my feet out in front of me and slide down the stairs.

"Ouch! Shit! Oh! FUCK!"

THUD!

It's time to waive the white flag. I can't do this. My phone is at Alex's, but maybe she'll come looking for me when she gets home. I grab the wood banister and pull myself up to a sit on the bottom step. Releasing a big sigh, I open my eyes.

Oliver.

He's sitting on his couch with his legs propped up on the coffee table and his arms crossed over his chest.

"Hello," he says in monotone voice.

"How long have you been here?"

"Awhile," he replies.

"Longer than me?"

He nods.

"Did you see me come in?"

He nods and I flush with humiliation, if that's even possible at this point.

"I ... uh ... was just getting my stuff."

"I see that." He still doesn't move. "Would you like some help?"

"I've got it."

He nods.

I can't stop staring at him. He looks worse than he did after the spanking incident. Cuts and bruises scattered all over his face.

"You not working today?"

He shakes his head.

"Me neither."

He nods.

I can't believe how awkward this feels. He lied to me and I'm royally pissed at him, yet his reserved demeanor actually makes me feel sorry for him. How does he always make me feel like I'm the one who needs to apologize for something?

"Well ... I'll just be ... going now."

He nods.

Stop with all the nodding!

I'm the martyr like in one of those war movies, the ones where the soldier with a severed arm and shrapnel in his legs and torso manages to drag himself and three other men off the battlefield to the safety of a bunker. I stand and try to mask my grimace by looking down. I probably couldn't carry all three bags in a healthy state, so why I think I can do it now when carrying my own body weight is excruciating in itself, is beyond me. I bend and grasp the strap to one bag and lift it to my shoulder. The weight of it tears at the cuts on my hand. I suck in a breath between clenched teeth.

"Sure you don't want some help?"

"I ... I've got ... it."

I grab the second bag and the pain has me seeing white. My eyes water from the exertion. Okay, I'm crying ... but oh my God it hurts! I take a shaky step toward the third bag and a sob escapes. I cough, trying to mask the sounds of my agony.

The weight on my shoulder is lifted. I look up. Oliver has my bags. He sets them back on the ground then scoops me up in his arms while shaking his head. "You're one stubborn woman."

"What are you doing?" I try to wriggle out of his arms as he carries me upstairs.

"You're getting blood on my floor."

I wrap my arms around his neck and rest my cheek against his chest because honestly ... I'm too exhausted to protest. I hear his own muffled grunts with each step, and it just now occurs to me that he too probably has wounds on his feet.

He sets me on his bed without making eye contact and limps into the bathroom. I plop back and close my eyes, praying for the pain to subside. The bed dips as he sits on the edge and grabs my foot. In slow motion he unwraps the gauze bandaging. I hiss in a breath as he touches one of my cuts.

"It's just a salve, it shouldn't hurt."

"Everything hurts," I reply with a grimace while draping my arm over my face to hide my wimpy tears. I'm drowning in humiliation. Once again ... why should *I* feel this way?

After treating and rewrapping both of my feet, he leans back next to me and rests his hands on his chest with his fingers interlaced. Being with him and yet not really *with* him is like dying a slow death. His presence in my life has felt as natural as the breath in my lungs. Losing him feels like losing the part of myself that has made me feel alive. What's left when the part of yourself that *feels* everything is gone?

Oliver is not mine; he never really was. The circumstances don't matter. There's a woman at a hospital in Portland who bears his name. Caroline Konrad. *Why are you there and what happened to you and Oliver?*

Oliver

Iᴛ's unfathomable to think I don't have the right to love someone. However, the morning I woke to the shrill scream of Vivian's voice saying the one word I hadn't been able to say, *wife*, I knew I didn't deserve to love her. There's just one problem. Loving her is not a choice. It's automatic like the beat of my heart, the breath in my lungs, and the earth giving way to the sun every morning.

My emotions for Vivian cannot be defined by words which makes explaining my actions impossible. It's absurd to think that the perfect touch or right look will say it for me, but I have to try. I rest my hand on the bed between us and our pinky fingers touch.

She doesn't move.

I inch my fingers over the top of her hand until mine rests on hers.

She doesn't move.

That's it. One touch, albeit so small, feels like everything. She didn't move her hand, she's allowing my touch, my *words*, like she hears me.

"Why?" she whispers.

Why what? Why the touch? Why am I married? Why did I not tell her earlier? Why is life so unfair? It doesn't matter. The answer is the same for it all.

"I don't know."

Her hand fists under mine, her body begins to shake, and then she sucks in a shaky breath. I did this to her. Turning, I pull her into my arms as she breaks down. Her hands fist the front of my shirt.

"I don't want to love you anymore," she cries.

"I know." I kiss the top of her head and let her lose her emotions to me. They cut deep and I welcome the pain. It's a reminder that what we had was real, our love was real, *life* with Vivian was real.

I'm not sure when she stops crying or when we fall asleep in each other's arms. I'm awake again and she's next to me, her head resting against my chest. If there's truly a God, then I have to pray that he allowed my heart to whisper all my unspoken emotions. I'm not sure what it really means to bare my soul, but for this woman ... I'd give my last breath.

"Oli?" Her voice is barely a whisper. I rest my cheek on her head.

"Hmm?"

"Tell me about Caroline."

God, the pain is crippling. "We met in college. Married

right after graduation and then moved to Portland. Her family is there and that's where she grew up."

"Why is she depressed and suicidal?"

The lump in my throat expands to an unbearable size as I feel my pulse begin to race.

"Oli?"

I try to swallow past it. "Our ... um..." I try to clear my throat and fight back the emotions that have been haunting me for so long "...our baby died."

Vivian gasps and looks up at me with her hand covering her mouth. I divert my eyes to the ceiling and blink back the tears. I don't want to lose it ... not now ... not in front of her.

"Oh my God!"

I nod and keep looking up, blinking at a furious speed, fighting the fucking tears.

"Oliver, oh my God!" Her hands slide up and cradle my face. The undeserving touch is nearly as painful as the words I could barely speak.

"Flower? Are you here? Oliver?" Alex calls from downstairs.

I sit up and hobble into the bathroom shutting the door behind me. Leaning back against the door, I run my hands through my hair. "Fuck!" I hate this. Memories like this never disappear, but I wish they would. Sometimes I think I need a damn lobotomy. I'd gladly give up the good memories to get rid of the bad. I splash some cold water on my face and go back into the bedroom.

"Hey." Alex greets me with a wary face, then looks at Vivian sitting on my bed. "What's going on?"

Vivian glances at me with a sad smile then looks at Alex. "I just came to get my stuff. I didn't know he was here. My bags are downstairs."

Alex nods. "You shouldn't be walking this far yet."

Vivian scrunches her nose. "I know, it was stupid. I should have waited for you."

"Yes, you should have. I'll carry your bags home, and then I'll come help you back across the street."

"I'll get her."

"Your feet—" Vivian starts to protest.

"They're fine." I scoop her off the bed.

"Okay then..." Alex shrugs and walks toward the stairs "...I'll get the bags."

I feel her intense gaze on me the entire walk to their place, but I don't meet them. "Upstairs or down?"

"Leave her down," Alex answers before Vivian has a chance to respond.

I set her on the couch, but she keeps a hold of my neck until I look at her. "Oli—"

"Remember that look of pity?" I whisper, reaching up to move her hands from my neck.

She nods.

"I don't want it either."

She nods again.

"I'll be around if you need anything. I'm not working again until next week."

"She won't." Alex stands by the door holding it open, no doubt waiting to slam it on me as soon as I step out.

Slam!

Just as I thought.

VIVIAN LOOKED miserable today crawling around on her hands and knees. It was probably a real dick move not to help her sooner, but at the time I questioned which was going to be more painful—seeing me or her dealing with her physical injuries. I think it was a tie.

I imagine her smoking pot or inhaling pain pills to ease the misery. Jack is my best friend when it's time to numb the pain. He has been for the past three years. Vivian took over for Jack for a while, but she's not at arm's reach any longer. I know she's just across the street, but when the loneliness sets in she might as well be on another planet.

My phone chimes and I should be asleep since it's approaching midnight, but I'm not. Instead, I'm still on my deck, drowning in a sea of misery and Jack. Apparently I'm not the only one who can't sleep.

Vivian: *Can't sleep. Thinking about earlier, not pity just … thoughts.*
Me: *Can't sleep either. Not sure what else to say.*
Vivian: *Sorry I trashed your place.*
Me: *That's pity. You weren't sorry before we talked earlier.*
Vivian: *You're right. I'm still pissed and I get a sadistic pleasure out of seeing your scarred face and gimpy walk.*
Me: *That's better.*
Vivian: *Now I don't know what to say so … goodnight.*
Me: *Goodnight, my love.*

I erase it and retype the last part.

Me: *Goodnight, Vivian.*

This afternoon wasn't a forgive and forget moment. I'm not stupid. My confession gave me a stay of execution, but I have a sick feeling the worst is yet to come. Once the magnitude of what has happened to us over the past week settles in, she's going to see how fucked-up my life really is … how fucked-up I really am. And she's going to be gone from my life forever.

* * *

Vivian

I AM ALMOST twenty-two years old and I mean it as in *only* twenty-two years old. Yet I am dealing with a relationship situation that seems like something from a motion picture drama or out of a fictional book. Seriously! I just found out the man I imagined living with forever is married *and* had a baby that died. That is a crap load of emotional baggage to deal with for anyone, let alone a twenty-two year old who, until recently, still had her V card and has never seen the inside of a college lecture hall or even been on an airplane.

I need to know more, but I'm not sure why. Morbid curiosity? Maybe. Will it change anything? Doubtful. I don't know how it could.

"What was going on with you two when I showed up yesterday?" Alex hands me a cup of coffee.

I take a sip. "He told me something."

"And ..."

"And I'm not sure it's my place to share it with you."

"You cannot be serious. The guy just broke your heart. He lied to you ... humiliated you, but you feel obligated to keep some secret for him?"

She's right. As tragic as his past seems to have been, he could have ... *should* have told me before our relationship got so serious. But I understand that it takes a serious connection to open up to someone about something so personal, so heartbreaking, so *life-altering*. I've been there. I get it.

I bite my lips together and nod. "His secret is on a whole different plane of awful and tragic than mine has ever been, so yes, I feel obligated to keep it, respect his trust."

"Flower, you amaze me, but not necessarily in a good way. I think it takes a while after you lose your virginity to really find that seasoned tarnish that can only come from being screwed in more ways than one. You, my dear, have a ways to go."

I laugh. "You should have majored in philosophy."

"I'm just looking out for you. Nothing good can come from being with a married man, and he knows it too. That's why he never told you. You're young, Flower, you need to experience the world—lots of sex with lots of guys."

"Says my monogamous friend. What makes you think I'm going from virgin to slut? Oliver was different, the exception. I can't imagine being with anyone else." I sigh. "I also can't imagine being with him anymore either. Maybe I'll go back to Virginville. It really wasn't so bad there."

"Liar."

I grin then look down as it fades. "I love him."

"Loved."

"No, I love him still—always. The pain doesn't take away the love."

"And the love doesn't take away the pain."

I nod and wipe a stray tear. "I wish I would have met him first."

"Before his wife?"

"Yeah."

"That would have made you what? Fifteen? Sixteen? Can you say statutory rape?"

"You know what I mean. I thought I came with a lot of baggage, but Oliver's a damn cargo ship compared to me."

"That bad?"

I close my eyes and lean back. "That bad."

ALEX AGREED to work for me until I can stand on my own two feet, *literally*. I'm supposed to go home for my birthday weekend tomorrow, but now I'm trying to figure out how to physically get there and what my explanation will be to my parents.

I hate that I can't control the excitement I feel when my phone chimes with a text from Oliver. He hurt me, and my heart has that painful memory, but my body didn't get the memo.

Oliver: *How are you feeling today?*

Me: *Fabulous, LOL, you?*

Oliver: *Like someone tried to murder me in my own home.*

Me: *You probably deserved it.*

Oliver: *I did.*

Me: *Contemplating the trip home tomorrow. Would it be weird if I crawled at the train station?*

Oliver: *Not in Boston, but maybe in Hartford.*

Me: *Wondering what I'll tell my parents?*

Oliver: *May I suggest the truth? Lies can be BAD news!*

Me: *Point taken :(*

Oliver: *Why don't you take my car?*

Me: *I couldn't. What if something happened to it?*

Oliver: *It's insured ... like everything in my house was.*

Me: *Low blow.*

Oliver: *Sorry. I think I'm the one that broke the only irreplaceable thing that day.*

Me: *?*

Oliver: *Us.*

I exit the message screen and toss my phone aside. Where the hell am I? I love him. I hate him. I want to have some self-respect, to stay angry at him, but he lost a child. He has some serious emotional issues *and* he's still married. Do I sever all ties with him? Can we be *friends* or *neighbors*? Then there is the burning question—why is he divorcing his wife? She lost her baby. I'd probably go insane too. It doesn't make sense.

CHAPTER TWENTY-ONE
NAKED BOOTS

Oliver

KEY. Lock. Door.

I still can't open my eyes, but I slide inside the room and collapse down the wall hugging my knees to my chest. The sweat surfaces in an instant. Heart racing, body shaking, the memories still cut too deep. It didn't make sense then, and it doesn't now. I just hate her so much.

With each labored breath, I squeeze my eyes shut tighter until all I see is Vivian. Her innocent smile and those loving eyes looking up at me like I'm the reason they dance with life. My life, they dance with my life, and without them I'm not sure I can feel alive. My pulse evens out and I relax my eyes, cracking them just enough to see the blurry white outline. I can't. Fumbling for the door knob, I fight to get out of the room. I can't breathe. There's no oxygen in here ... no life.

I need a life again. I need Vivian.

Me: *I'll "pick you up" at 8 a.m., we'll stop for donuts and coffee on the way to your parents' house.*
Vivian: *?? Not taking you to meet my parents.*
Me: *Why not?*
Vivian: *Um … because they'll wonder why I'm bringing my married neighbor home with me.*
Me: *Tell them because he's crazy-wild-beyond all words in love with you. AND he'll do ANYTHING to prove it!*
Me: *Vivian?*

Nothing.

I expect a response, at least a "screw you" or *something.* There's a knock at my door. *Something!*

"Prove it." Vivian stands with her weight shifted to the outer edges of her bandaged feet and slippers.

"How?" I try to contain my grin because her lips are tilted into a frown and her eyes are tensed into a challenging scowl.

"Carry me upstairs."

My dick hardens. I may be banged up a bit, but *this* I can do. I'll go all night if that's what it takes. Dear God, I hope that's what it takes. I scoop her up in my arms and kick the door shut. Bending down, I try to kiss her but she turns away.

"Not yet."

She's playing hard to get, making me work for it. Challenge accepted.

"Stop," she says before we get to the bedroom. "Put me down."

I ease her to her feet and she hobbles back a few steps. "Prove it."

I hope she's asking me to fuck her against the door and

not open it, but the nauseating sensation in my stomach tells me I'm not that lucky.

"It's all or nothing, Oli. You said *anything.* No take backs?"

Am I ready for this? No. Can I let her go? No.

I suck in a deep breath and release it with a slow nod. "No take backs." I lift the cobalt vase and dump out the key. Sticking it in the lock, I pause before turning it. The thought of opening it paralyzes me as much as the thought of losing her. "Can I ask you for a favor?"

She crosses her arms over her chest. I'm pushing my luck. "What?"

I rest my forehead against the door and close my eyes. "You go in, but when you come out we don't talk about it until we get back from your parents' house this weekend."

"Why?"

"Just ... *please,* Vivian." I hate the desperate sound of my voice, but that's what I am. Right now I'm so desperate.

Her hand rests on my back. "Okay."

I sigh and turn the lock, but I don't open the door. "Take your time. I'll be waiting out here."

She furrows her brow as I step back and move to the side so I can't see in the room when she opens the door. Her hand turns the knob with painful slowness, like she's fisting my heart, squeezing it unbearably tight. I close my eyes and lean back against the wall as she steps inside and closes the door.

There's a good chance she comes out and says "no fucking way" then leaves my ass. I'm a normal guy in every aspect of my life except this room. A teddy bear or Barbie fetish would probably be easier to handle than this. I've never chewed my nails, but right now I'm biting the hell out of them. How long has she been in there? What is she doing or thinking? There is a window; it's possible she's halfway to Hartford by now.

The door opens rescuing me from my thoughts or maybe torturing me with the anticipation of her reaction. I'm not sure which yet.

Shit! She's been crying. A sad smile pulls at her beautiful lips and she sniffles. "So 8 a.m. tomorrow?"

I nod once.

She holds out her arms. My wrinkled forehead isn't doing a good job of hiding my confusion. "Carry me downstairs."

My dick, that decided to take a nap when she chose door number one, perks up. My brain sends the silent message that he will not be needed at the moment. I feel his disappointment, I really do, but this was a small victory and I have to believe our patience will pay off … eventually.

"This is good."

I stop at the door. "I'll carry you across the street.

"Nope, I need to practice walking, even if it does still hurt."

"But you had me carry you up the stairs."

She shrugs. "I just like the feel of being in your arms. But I don't need to look completely helpless to the rest of our neighbors."

I set her down and she leaves her arms wrapped around my neck. "See you in the morning," she whispers and kisses the corner of my mouth like she didn't just see something very disturbing upstairs.

"In the morning …" I release her hand one finger at a time as she takes a cautious step out the door.

Vivian

I'm GIVING myself a three-day reprieve from my troubles and Oliver's. It's not possible to make the memory of his reveal vanish from my mind, but I'm hoping my parents and my birthday will help distract my thoughts. The anger is gone. It's been replaced with pain ... his pain. He's filed for divorce for reasons that are still unclear, but he chose to leave her before he met me. He technically never lied to me, he just didn't tell me everything. And I feel with absolute certainty that he wanted to, but the words were too painful to speak.

"Alex?" I knock on her bedroom door then start to open it. "I'm leaving—oh my God! I'm—uh-uh—sorry." I exit as fast and unexpected as I entered.

What the hell?

"Hey, Flower, sorry about that. I forgot you were leaving this morning. Happy birthday, by the way. I have a present for you on the counter downstairs." Alex ties the satin straps to her red robe and closes the door behind her.

I can't look her in the eye. "Yeah, um, so I'm taking off and ... I'll be back uh ... later."

"Flower, don't be embarrassed. You were the one who inspired us."

"What?" I whip around.

She bites her bottom lip and nods. "The whole spanking thing. I think it's kinda *in* right now. So Sean and I decided to spice things up."

I swallow hard. "He had you handcuffed to the bed facedown and blindfolded."

She waves a hand in the air. "Oh that's nothing new. I thought you must have heard the sound of his palm slapping against my bare ass a few minutes ago. It's kind of hot."

My cow eyes refuse to blink. "He's wearing black leather chaps, a cowboy hat, and *nothing* else," I whisper with a shouting exertion.

She grins. "I know, it's new. What do you think?"

I shake my head like a dog, trying to erase the memory. "I think I need to get out of here."

"Have a good time!"

"Um yeah, thanks, you too ... I guess." I lug my bag down the stairs surprised to do it without much pain. Alex brought home a box of second skin pads last night and they make walking so much easier.

"Don't forget your present," Alex yells down the stairs.

I grab the gift bag and my purse off the kitchen counter then hustle out the door.

"Good morning, birthday girl." Oliver stands right outside my door holding a single red rose.

He takes my bag and hands me the flower while giving me a chaste kiss on the cheek.

My grin beams out of control. "Thank you."

"Shall we?" He motions to the steps.

We cross the street and he opens my door. A box wrapped in beautiful floral paper adorned with a wide pink bow is on my seat. "Oli ..."

He picks it up and holds my hand while I get in then hands me the gift and walks around to his side.

"Ready, my love?"

Love? Am I his *love*? Yes, I believe I am.

I smile and lean over. He meets me half way. "I'm glad you're coming with me."

"Me too." He kisses me and then starts to pull away.

I grab his shirt and hold him to me. My tongue brushes his upper lip and he opens his mouth. Our kiss deepens and a moan escapes me. My God what is happening? It's like my whole body came alive and I'm in desperate need of him, like *now*! His cologne, minty breath, and clean-shaven face are driving me crazy. My mind screams that it's too soon, but my body pleads its case with the winning argument: It's my birthday!

"Oli—" I mumble against his lips. "We should go ... inside."

He pulls his head back. "What?"

I'm breathless. "Let's go inside. I need ... you."

"Sex?"

I nod trying to catch my breath while fumbling to unbuckle my seatbelt.

"Whoa, wait..." he latches my belt back again "...What's gotten into you?" He sits up straight and starts the car.

"Nothing, that's just it. I need *you* to get into me, Oli."

He grins and pulls out onto the street. "I like you like this, but you can wait a couple of hours until we get there can't you?"

I squeeze my legs together. "You mean a couple of days. My parents are not going to let us sleep together."

He slams on the brakes, thankfully no one is behind us. Resting his arm on the back of my seat, he looks behind us and reverses back into his spot with the speed and precision of an indie driver. His seat belt is off and he makes quick strides to my side. I no sooner get unbuckled and he has my hand, dragging me up his front steps.

Door slams. Pants unfasten.

He drops to his knees and slides his hands up my bare legs under my cotton skirt. Curling his fingers into my panties, he pulls them down.

"Sure, *now* you're wearing them." He looks up at me and grins.

I run my fingers through his hair with a coy smile pulling at my lips.

Leaving my panties on the floor, he skims his hand back up my legs. "What does the birthday girl want?"

I want you to tie me up and spank me. Holy crap! How did that thought invade my mind? Damn Alex! Now all I can think about is being handcuffed to the bed and spanked.

"What's it going to be, Vivian?" His voice is thick with lust.

I stare down at him pursing my lips to the side, trying to hide my naughty-thoughts grin.

"Tell me."

The words are on the tip of my tongue ready to jump off. They want to play, but I pull them out of the game and send in a different lineup. "Just ... do something to me that you've never done with anyone else."

He raises a brow and smirks. "But it's *your* birthday."

"I know, so make it unforgettable."

He grins.

"But hurry ... I'm a little ... *desperate.*"

"Yeah?

I nod.

"Well, maybe I should take the edge off for you first."

"The edge?"

"Mmm hmm." He lifts my left leg over his shoulder. "Are your feet okay?"

"Yes," I answer through a breathless pant.

He slides my skirt up to my waist and swipes his tongue along my slit once real slow. I let my head fall back against the wall. "Yes ..."

He does it again and stops when my hips jerk.

I open my eyes, look down at him, and grab his hair.

"You're supposed to be taking the edge off not keeping me teetering on it in angst and misery."

Keeping his eyes on mine, his entire mouth covers my sex and his tongue doesn't stop until I feel completely ... satisfied.

"Oli ..." My eyes fight to stay open as my jaw goes slack.

"Yes?" He wipes his mouth with his arm and smiles as he sets my foot on the ground and kisses his way up my body taking my dress with him. He sucks in my nipple and it jolts straight to my sex.

He grins and lets my dress fall back over my body then bends down to pick up my panties.

"Here." He hands them to me. "I'll meet you in the car."

"Wait, what are you doing?"

He walks to the pantry. "It's a surprise, now get your sexy ass out to the car."

"Okay, okay, bossy."

I wait in the car and a few minutes later he comes out with a brown bag and puts it in the trunk.

"What's in the bag?" I ask when he gets in the car.

He laughs. "For the last time, it's a surprise, now open your gift. We have two more stops to make before leaving town.

"Whe—"

"Uh uh ..." He holds up his finger. "Damn, woman! Just let the day happen and stop being such a nosy control freak."

I roll my eyes, untying the pink ribbon before removing the wrapping paper. In the box is a messenger bag.

"For school?" I grin.

"Yes. It's custom made. I picked the floral pattern for the center panel and red and white for the sides. It made me think of your tattoo. Well, and you work at a greenhouse and Alex calls you flower. Sorry, they didn't have a cannabis pattern as an option."

"Shut up." I shake my head and laugh. "It's perfect. I love it and I'll no doubt be the coolest freshman on campus." I lean over and kiss his cheek. "You do realize Alex doesn't call me flower because of my tattoo or my job?"

"Oh?" He gives me a quick sideways glance.

"It was because I was a virgin. Not sure why she's still calling me it ... since I'm not." I look over at him.

Oliver keeps his eyes on the road as his lips curl into a roguish grin. "Sorry. I blame myself for that." He squeezes my leg.

I laugh and squirm out of his grip. "You should."

Our first stop is appropriately Dunkin' Donuts. It's our second stop that has me confused.

"The Green Pot? Why are we here?"

"I need to borrow something from Chance." Oliver pulls around back next to Chance's truck. "Stay here I'll be right back." He gets out, takes the bag from the trunk, and goes inside. A few minutes later he knocks on my window, startling me. I was checking out all the compartments to my new bag and getting excited for my first day of classes like I did in high school. He opens my door.

"What are we—" I look down and see he's wearing his leather work boots. "Why are you—"

"Get out." Oliver offers his hand and I take it. He leads me around to the side of Chance's truck facing the brick wall of the alleyway building. Shrugging off his shirt, he smirks.

I look all around us, feeling a little nervous when the

realization hits me. He drops his shorts and boxer briefs and steps out of them.

"Oli!" My eyes bug out. "Oh my God, you're not seriously going to—"

His lips crash against mine as he pulls up my dress and lifts me up pressing my back against Chance's truck. I'm still sans panties and before I can even catch my breath, he plunges into me. "Oh God!"

His fullness drains my lungs, and he doesn't give me a second to acclimate before he lifts me up and lets me fall back onto him. Pinning me against the truck with his body, his hands slide to my breasts. His thumbs dip under the material and rub over my taut nipples.

"Is this how you imagined it?" His breath scorches against my neck as he sucks and bites at my skin.

"Yes ..." I moan, meeting him thrust for thrust while holding onto his bare shoulders and digging the heels of my feet into his hard, muscular ass. I arch my back and he exposes my nipple sucking it into his mouth. "Oli!" He drags it through his teeth and repeats with the other side.

"Harder!" *What the hell? Did I just yell that?*

His mouth moves back to mine as he grips my hips and slams me onto him, hitting the most sensitive spot. I rock my pelvis, finding the perfect edge of pleasure as my clit ebbs and flows against his skin with the sensual tide of his pelvis.

"You're everything," he murmurs against my lips while taking my hands above my head and interlacing our fingers. "No take backs..." he speeds up his pace "...not ... ever." I squeeze his hands and whimper into his mouth as fireworks explode in the most incredible birthday celebration ever. He stills, keeping me pinned to the truck. "Oh dear God that was ... fucking incredible." His labored breath washes over my skin and my head collapses onto his shoulder.

"Happy Birthday to me." I giggle.

He eases me to my feet and opens the driver's side door to the truck. "Here." There's a wad of napkins in his hand. "I don't think gravity is going to be your friend."

I grimace with a little embarrassment, taking the napkins and wiping between my legs. He bends down to pick up his shorts and briefs.

"Wait."

He looks up.

"Just stand there a minute." I grin and let my eyes explore his naked body and boots. Firm muscles bronzed by the sun, messy copper hair, brilliant blue eyes, and those abs … I could run my tongue over them and give myself another orgasm. Oliver is so sexy it's not even fair.

He tilts his head to the side, waiting for my eyes to find his again. "Are you done?" I wet my lips and smirk. "Not really, but I'll finish the tour later."

He pulls on his briefs and shorts. "You just want me for my body. Do you know how it makes me feel when I see you looking at me like eye candy? I'm a person, you know, with real feelings."

"You're right. I do just want you for your body, and if you don't stop getting your pretty face scarred up, I'm going to have to throw a brown bag over your head when we're having sex."

"Get in the car before I swat your ass, birthday girl."

Did he just threaten to spank me? "You're all talk, Mr. Konrad." I look back while sashaying to the car.

He looks at his watch. "We still have ten minutes, Ms. Graham. I think that's plenty of time to rosy up that fine ass of yours."

I stop and look over the top of the car at him as he pulls on his shirt while flashing me a suggestive raise of his brows.

"What do you mean we have ten minutes? Are we being timed?"

"You could say that." Oliver lifts a leg up and pulls off one boot then the other before tossing them in the trunk and retrieving his shoes.

"Get in ... We'll save the corporal punishment for later."

I slide in the seat and glare at him. "Who's timing us?"

Oliver starts the car and pulls out of the parking lot. "Chance."

I gasp. "You told Chance?"

He grins. "I told him I needed to borrow his truck for twenty minutes no questions asked, and I also needed him to keep Maggie occupied inside during those twenty minutes."

"Did you tell him why?"

"Sure. I told him I needed it to do a favor for my *neighbor* before I left town with you."

"But ... I ... when did you call him?"

"My God, you're full of questions. I called him after I sent you out to the car. That's when I grabbed my boots as well." He looks over at me. "What?"

I shake my head. "Nothing. I just love you. That's all."

He holds my hand, circling his thumb over my skin. He's so beautiful and easy to love. I know this same strong hand holds my heart and with the slightest flinch he can crush it.

"I love you too." He gives me another glance. Honesty radiates from his soft smile that crinkles the corners of his eyes every time he looks at me. I try to imagine the things those eyes have seen because they radiate the emotion from a thousand lifetimes. Sometimes all I see in the depths of his blue eyes are oceans of unshed tears and a permanent void that was once filled by something ... *someone* very special.

CHAPTER TWENTY-TWO
MEET THE PARENTS

Oliver

I'M NOT sure who that guy was back at the greenhouse. Exhibitionist is not a word I've ever used to describe myself. The man I am with Vivian is not the same guy that came home from Portland, or even the same guy that left Boston over three years ago. The changes I see in myself are subtle, well ... most of the time. Caroline would have shuddered at the idea of sex in any place but our bedroom or the couch. I'm not sure she ever fantasized about me or sex at all. If she did, I'm certain she would *never* have told me.

Vivian slips off her shoes and rests her feet on the dash. "Is this okay?"

"What?"

"My feet on your dash because you got a funny look when I put them up here." She wiggles her toes.

"I was just looking at the pads on the bottom of them."

"Second skin. Alex brought it home last night. Talk about a lifesaver."

I nod. "I was wondering ... Was your reaction the other

day typical? I mean, do you often *lose it* like that in the face of adversity?"

"And by 'face of adversity' you mean finding out the man to whom I gave my virginity, and to whom I declared my love, is married? If that's what you mean then yes, my reaction would be typical—irate, out of control, somebody's going to die. Now, the answer to your other question, 'do I often *lose it*' would be no. So don't lie to me anymore, keep your dick in your pants except when I request you take it out, and don't ever wear a cowboy hat in the bedroom. If you can follow those simple rules, you shouldn't have any problem staying on my good side."

"Cowboy hat? I take it you're not a country fan."

"It's an embarrassing story that I don't need to think about right now." She turns on the radio. "Ooo, I like this song. Gotye, 'Somebody That I Used to Know.'"

She wails out a few lines about being screwed over then she giggles as I shake my head and change the station.

"Oh, leave it. How perfect ..." The same cringe-worthy voice goes into seductive lyrics about big birthday balloons.

"Hey, what's wrong with Katy Perry?" She yells in a whiny voice as I switch stations again.

"Katy's great. You, my love, sound like a donkey in labor."

"Oh my gosh! You shit! I can't believe you ..." She punches my shoulder then folds her arms across her chest and stares out her window.

"What? You just told me not to lie to you, to keep my dick in my pants, and not wear a cowboy hat. What rule did I violate?"

"Just shut up granny driver."

"Granny driver?"

"Yeah, granny driver, drop the hammer for goodness

sake. I don't want to spend all day in the car with your *honest* insults."

"This, coming from the girl who plays with two sticks and a ball of yarn all day. But I love it when you get sassy with me. As long as you're not throwing shit at my head, I think your fieriness is hot as hell."

"Yeah, well, cool your balls, buddy. I'm not sure bestiality is legal in Connecticut. Hee haw!"

"I didn't say you were a donkey, I said you sounded like one, and for your information I believe it is legal in Connecticut. So don't be surprised if I try to mount my favorite ass later."

She tries to keep her somber face, but she can't hold it in. We both fall into a fit of laughter. I glance over and she's wiping tears from her eyes and can't stop giggling.

"Mount your favorite ass?" She continues to laugh. "That's just great. You called my singing an ass in labor. Jeez, Oli, how romantic. You sure know how to woo a girl."

"I aim to please."

———

THE DRIVE here was two of the most enjoyable, nonsexual hours of my life. I love the easy conversations we have and the playful banter. Vivian has a facial expression for every emotion, and I could spend the rest of my life counting and memorizing them. Calling her smart, sexy, and funny sounds like such a cliché, but that's what she is with me. An uncontrollable smile here, a wink there, the brush of her fingertips along the nape of my neck while I'm driving ... it's all the little things with her that add up to the best moments of my life.

"KISS, Oli," she says while opening the door. I lean over

to taste her cherry lips and she shakes her head. "The acronym, dummy: Keep It Simple Stupid. I'm going to tell them everything before we leave, but there's no need to back the dump truck up to the front door. You're my neighbor. We've been dating this summer. You worship the ground I walk on ... just the basics, babe, stick to the basics." She winks. *Ah, there it is.* Then she smiles. *Another favorite.*

I meet her at the front of the car and offer my hand. She takes it and leads me up to the door. No need to argue with her little jabs. Truth—I do worship the ground she walks on.

"Vivvy!" her mom squeals pulling *Vivvy* into her arms. "Happy birthday, baby girl."

"Thanks, Mom."

She looks back at me and takes my hand again, pulling me into the house. "Mom, this is Oliver ... my boyfriend. Oliver this is my mom, Lydia."

"Pleased to meet you, Mrs. Graham." I shake her hand. She looks between me and Vivian with an exuberant grin and wide eyes.

"Lydia, please. So *boyfriend*, huh?"

"I hope so." I look at Vivian and her cheeks turn pink.

"You get in a fight?"

I laugh. "More like a home invasion."

"Oh dear! Did they catch the person who did it?"

I feel Vivian's scowl. "Yes, as a matter of fact they did."

"Well I hope they get the punishment they deserve."

Vivian coughs then clears her throat. "Where's Dad?"

"Working, sweetie. He'll be home for dinner. Looks like I'll be setting three extra place settings instead of two."

"Three?" Vivian leads me to the back porch where her mom lets a dog inside.

"Rosenburg!" Vivian ditches me and picks up the little white fur ball. "I missed you." She nuzzles her face into his fluffy coat. "Oli, meet Rosenburg." She hands it ... *him*, to me.

"Rosenburg ... interesting name."

"She named him after the founder of Dunkin' Donuts. Crazy girl." Lydia shakes her head. "Have a seat." She gestures to a padded gliding bench.

"Thank you." I sit next to Vivian. "Didn't know you had a dog ... a dog named *Rosenburg*." I smirk at her. "Your doughnut obsession is worse than I thought."

She winks. "It'll be fine. I'm in therapy now."

My dick twitches, feeling ready to give her some more of that *therapy*.

"She gets her insane metabolism from her father. It's not fair. I gain weight just thinking about food." Lydia gives Vivian the stink eye.

"You could have fooled me." I smile.

Lydia shares a familiar blush that I've seen on Vivian's face a thousand times. She's not as tall as Vivian and her curves are more prominent, but she has those green eyes and black hair with a few streaks of gray all pulled back into a bun.

"I like him, Vivvy."

Vivian tucks her feet underneath her legs and leans into me. "Yeah, he's okay."

"Vivvy, what happened to your feet?"

"Uh ... stepped on some broken glass ... um, helping Oliver clean up after the *invasion*."

"Yes, I told her I would clean it up, but she wouldn't listen."

"Tell me about it. She's a stubborn girl, but we're still real proud of her. Can't wait to see her walk across that stage in two more years."

Vivian clears her throat. "So, um, you didn't say who the third person is who's coming to dinner."

"Oh, Kai of course."

I'm not sure if Lydia can see the steam escaping from my nostrils, but it's there. Vivian knows it's there. Her body tenses against mine.

"Uh, why did you invite Kai?"

"I can't believe you're asking me that. He's your best friend. He's home for another week or so. And his sister just died. Did I mention it's your birthday too? Oh speaking of ... your cake's in the oven. I need to go check on it."

Lydia goes back inside and Rosenburg jumps off my lap and follows her.

Vivian straddles my lap facing me with a nervous smile. "Are you mad?"

No, I'm fucking livid!

"At whom? You, when you didn't know. Your mom, who didn't know about me until today? Kai, because his sister died?"

She brushes her lips against my neck and kisses my ear. "So basically you're pissed, but you don't know where to aim the blame," she whispers.

"Basically."

"Vivvy! Get off that boy. I taught you better than that. How rude of you to invade his personal space." Lydia brings out a tray of beverages.

Vivian rolls her eyes and climbs off my lap.

"Can I offer you a drink, Oliver?" She holds the tray out in front of me.

"Yes, thank you." I take one of the small Dixie cups filled with red liquid.

"Vivvy?" She offers a cup to her.

"Oh my God, Mom! You made Kool-Aid for us? We're adults not seven-year-olds taking a play break."

I take a sip to hide my grin. *This is not just Kool-Aid!*

"I know, sweetie. I'm just teasing you. Take a sip."

Vivian hesitates then brings the cup to her lips like something's going to jump out and bite her. "What is this?"

"Kool-Aid cocktail. It's Tropical Punch Kool-Aid mixed with fresh lemon juice and dark rum."

Vivian shrugs. "Mmm, not bad."

Priceless. It's the only description for this moment—the dog, the spiked Kool-Aid, the "personal space" invasion, and *Vivvy*. The crazy part is we've been here for only thirty minutes. Adding in dinner with my nemesis and Vivian's college confessions to her parents is going to make this a memorable weekend.

Vivian

OLIVER'S FAMILY IS *NORMAL*, I think. They have refined social skills, yet they are far from pretentious. Even the last night we had dinner with them and acted like a couple of tattling children they handled the situation with humor and love. My family ... not so refined. I was raised by two hard-working and very loving parents. We struggled to make ends meet, but I never felt like I truly wanted for anything. My parents never fought over money in front of me. In fact, they rarely fought at all. So I have to give them a free pass when it comes to being overprotective and sometimes embarrassing.

"There's my birthday girl."

"Hi, Dad." I give him a big hug as he walks in the

back door. He's the only other man in my life that makes me feel short. My dad is a towering six foot six with a shiny head that he's shaved bare for the past ten years since he started going bald in his mid-thirties.

He releases me with his gaze falling over my shoulder. "And who is your friend?"

I step back and wrap my arm around Oliver's back. "This is Oliver."

Oliver offers his hand and my dad shakes it. "Nice to meet you, Mr. Graham."

My dad, the gentle beast, smiles. "Call me Rod."

Oliver nods.

"Rodney, Oliver is Vivvy's *boyfriend*," my mom calls from the table where she's setting the dishes for dinner.

"Boyfriend, huh? Well what does your boyfriend do?"

Oliver grins. "I work with my brother. He owns a handyman business. This time of year it's mostly land-scaping jobs. In the winter he does snow removal and home repair."

"A man who's not afraid to get a little dirt on his hands and apparently can take a punch." My dad nods toward Oliver's face. "I like you already. You'd never catch pretty boy down the street doing manual labor or getting in a fist fight."

My dad has never been a huge Kai fan. His opinion has always been there's something wrong with a boy whose best friend since kindergarten is a girl.

"For your information, Oliver has a law degree from Harvard."

Oliver lifts his shoulders, giving my dad a guilty smile. "Don't hold it against me."

My dad chuckles as he walks past him and pats his

shoulder. "I won't. But it makes sense now. Vivvy likes guys in fancy suits."

I shake my head and wrap both arms around Oliver's waist. "Shows what you know, Dad. I happen to be quite attracted to guys in *boots*."

Oliver wets his lips and I can see the lust in his eyes as I feel something firm against my belly.

"I should go bring in our stuff from the car."

I grin knowing he needs to get out of the house before he embarrasses himself in front of my parents. "Need help."

"Nope, I've got it."

Oliver heads out to the car while I snag the mixer beaters from my mom. "So, what do you think of Oliver?" I swipe my tongue over the frosting.

"He's handsome, that's for sure."

I giggle. "I know."

"I wonder if he's too old for you. How old is he?"

"He just turned thirty—not too old for me."

"I'm only looking out for you, Vivvy. I know how important your career goals are to you and someone Oliver's age is probably looking for a wife and children. Something a twenty-two-year-old girl in college should try to avoid."

God, if she only knew. "Oliver's not planning on marrying me, or having children, or ruining my career."

"Well that's not great either. Why are you wasting your time with a guy who's not planning on marrying you?"

I laugh and shake my head. "Jeez, Mom. There's no pleasing you today."

"Your mom just wants the world for you." My dad bends down and kisses me on the top of my head.

"Done. Just so you both know, I've never been happier than I am with Oliver."

The back door opens. Oliver has bags slung over both

shoulders and in both hands as well. I may have over packed.

"Here, let me help you with those." My dad offers, taking the bags from Oliver's hands.

The gift bag from Alex falls on the floor. There's a buzzing noise that gets louder as a ... Oh. My. God! A *vibrator* rolls onto the floor.

Let me die. Right here. Right now.

As soon as I recover from my crippled state of embarrassment, I bend down and shove it back in the bag with the tissue paper while fumbling with the switch.

I'm crimson. My mom's eyes are huge and her hand is cupped over her gasping mouth. Oliver purses his lips to hide his naughty I-can't-believe-you-brought-a-vibrator smile. And thankfully, my dad has a confused look on his face. I'm quite certain he has never seen a vibrator.

"Uh ... here." I take the bags from my dad. "We'll just ... um ... take these upstairs."

Ducking my head, I bolt from the kitchen.

I toss the bags on the daybed in my old bedroom that my mom's converted to her sewing room. Oliver presses his body against my back, brushing my hair off to one side. Soft lips caress my neck.

"Am I failing to meet your *needs*?"

I close my eyes and giggle. "I can't believe Alex got me a vibrator for my birthday."

"So it's your first?"

"Yes ... well ... no." I feel the red heat surface on my skin again.

He turns me toward him. "No?"

I shake my head, staring at my feet.

"Well we'll have to check it out later."

My head jerks up. "What? *We*?"

Oliver grins. "Sure, why not?"

"Well—I-I ... ugh! Don't do this to me at my parents' house." I brush past him and grab my purse. "I'm going to be a pathetic horny mess by the time we get back home."

"What?" He chuckles. "Did you just say *horny*?"

"Yes, as in ... you're going to tease me all weekend with your dirty talk and sexy..." I wave my hand in the air "...ways."

"Vivvy? Don't forget the rules. No boys in your bedroom."

"The door is open for heaven's sake!" I yell down to her.

I send off a quick WTF-thank-you text to Alex as Oliver slides his hands around me squeezing my ass. "I'm going to feel like a teenager this weekend, sneaking around trying to avoid getting caught," he whispers in my ear.

"Whoa, no. There will be no sneaking around—not now. After the vibrator incident, my mom will be on high-security alert. I wouldn't be surprised if she decides to install hidden cameras around the house."

Oliver laughs. "What is she going to do? Ground you?"

"She might." I mock bite my nails with a frightened look on my face.

Oliver grabs me and gives me a dizzying kiss. My fingers claw into his back as all sense of control obliterates under his tempting touch.

"Vivvy? Kai is here."

Splash!

There's the cold water being dumped on us.

I rest my hand on Oliver's chest. "Thank you."

"For what?"

"For being amicable with Kai tonight."

He laughs. "Have you been talking to my mom?"

"Why?" I look up at him.

"Because you're messing with my mind. Thanking me in advance so I subconsciously feel the need to live up to your expectations of me."

A wink from me, a shake of his head. I love this man.

As MUCH AS I want Oliver here with me this weekend, I'm not looking forward to my birthday dinner with both of them. Of course my parents have no idea what's gone on over the past few weeks, and I hope it stays that way.

"Can you get the door, Vivvy?" my mom calls from the kitchen as the doorbell rings.

"Sure." I hand Rosenburg to Oliver. They've been bonding over the past few hours, but I haven't worked up the nerve to ask him if he'd consider letting me bring him back to Cambridge. I wanted to take him with me when I originally left home, but a dog would be a red flag to Alex's parents that I live there.

"Hey, Kai."

"Please tell me you borrowed his car and he's not actually—"

"Here? I am." Oliver's voice startles me. I turn. He's standing behind me, holding Rosenburg.

"Oliver," Kai says with a smug voice as he walks past us both toward the porch.

I take Rosenberg from Oliver. "You know how much I love you, right, babe?"

He gives me the stop-buttering-me-up smirk. "Yeah, I know." He kisses me and I fist his shirt to make it last a little longer.

"Uh hum ..."

I let go of Oliver.

"Your mom wants to see you in the kitchen," Kai says.

I rub my lips together and nod. "Be nice," I whisper while passing Kai.

"Watcha need, Mom?"

She leans against the counter with her hands planted on her hips. "You and Oliver are living together?" I can tell from the tension in her neck that she's struggling to keep her volume under control.

"No. Why are you asking me this?"

"Because Kai said he hasn't seen you much lately since you moved in with Oliver."

Thanks, Kai ... asshole!

I look up at the ceiling and exhale an exasperated breath. "We were for a little while, but we're not now."

"So you've had sex with him?" she whispers, glaring at me.

I laugh. *No, Mom, we just sleep in the same bed, holding hands.* "Yes, I've had sex with him. Good grief, I'm an adult."

"So he knows about your back?"

"Yes, he knows about my back!"

She startles. "Keep your voice down, Vivvy."

"He loves me, Mom. He thinks I'm beautiful and more than that ... he makes me *feel* beautiful in a way I never have before. When I'm with him I don't think about school, or my past, or marriage and children." I bite my lips together and blink back the deep emotions that can only come from thinking about Oliver. "He's my simple perfection. I like *me* with *him*."

"Dinner ready?" My dad furrows his brow while peeking his head around the corner.

My mom nods, still staring at me. "Yes, tell the guys to come eat."

"You know I just want what's best for you, Vivvy."

"Oliver ... Oliver is what's best for me." I speak the truth. I know in a part of my heart that wasn't alive until I met Oliver that he was meant to be with me. I just wish I knew what to do with the pain of his past. A past that's still part of his present, *our present.*

"Okay, Vivvy." She sighs and hands me a dish of steamed veggies. "But you're still not sleeping with him under this roof."

No problem. Oliver and I don't do much sleeping when we're together anyway. I smirk. "That's fine." I've never considered myself a rebel, but the more she treats me like a child, the more I want to take Oliver upstairs and do *very* adult things with him in my boy-banned room under my parents' roof.

We make it through dinner without any bloodshed. My parents ask me about school under the scrutinizing looks of both Oliver and Kai. I think if it were just Oliver here I would tell them. Sometimes it feels like Kai is waiting for me to fall on my face so he can come to my rescue, so he can keep me needing him. Not anymore.

"Oh my gosh, Mom! You didn't need to put candles on my cake."

"Yes, I did. You deserve a wish, Vivvy."

Mom sets the chocolate cake with vanilla frosting in front of me. I look around the table at the people who mean the most to me, even tattletale-half-the-time-I-want-to-kill-you Kai. Taking a deep breath, I give Oliver a sideways glance and a wink before blowing out all my candles and wishing for ... *nothing.* I already have everything I could ever want.

I blow them all out with one breath. Oliver rests his

hand on my leg and leans over. "Happy birthday, my love," he whispers in my ear and kisses my cheek.

"Our little girl is twenty-two. Where did the time go?" My dad smiles while shaking his head.

"Twenty-two … how old is your wife, Oliver?" Kai silences the room.

Oliver's grip on my leg becomes painful.

"Wife?" My dad clenches his jaw.

"Get out, Kai." The anger inside me builds to an explosive level. I should have never taken him home after his sister died. Cracking the door for Kai is like cracking the door to a bull's pen. If given the chance he will trample me every time.

"Kai's not the one with the wife, Vivvy. Why are you kicking him out?"

"You're right, Mom." I glare at Kai. "He's not the one with a wife. Kai's just the one who got drunk and wouldn't take no for an answer the night I tried to escape his advances and fell into the hot coals."

My parents look at Kai and the smugness evaporates from his face. "Viv, you swore you'd never say—"

"Say what, Kai? The truth?"

I could have predicted it—he's tearing up. Unbelievable. He should have majored in theater, not pre-med.

"Vivvy? Kai? What's going on?" my mom asks with a wrinkled brow.

"The truth?" Kai shakes his head. "That's real rich coming from you."

The legs of Oliver's chair screech against the tile floor. "I think you've said enough." He stands and clenches his fists.

"What are you going to do? Hit me again? Is that what put your wife in the looney bin?"

Smack!

"Oh my gosh! What are you doing?" my mom yells, scrambling to get to Kai, who looks close to unconscious on the floor with his chair tipped over and blood oozing from his nose.

I didn't even flinch because I expected Oliver to knock him out the first time he made the wife comment. Once is risky. Twice is just stupid. My dad hasn't moved and his eyes are on me. The anger is obvious, his anger with *me*— my lying, my "disappointing" choice in men.

"Rodney, help me get him up." My mom presses a napkin to Kai's face.

My dad shakes his head. I'm sure the only reason he helps Kai up is so he won't have as much blood to scrub out of the grout later.

I look around, but I can't find Oliver. "Oli?" As I start toward the stairs, I see him coming down them with his bag in hand. "Where are you going?"

He pulls his wallet out of his pocket and hands me a fifty. "Here's some money for the train."

I don't take it. "What are you doing? I don't want your money. Where are you going?"

"Home." He keeps walking.

"I don't understand. You're just leaving me here?"

"Yep." He opens the front door and heads to his car.

"Oliver, stop!"

He shoves his bag in the backseat and then gets in the driver's seat.

"Stop!" I grab the door before he shuts it.

"I'm so sorry. Kai's an asshole. But I stuck up for you, for us. Why are you leaving and punishing me?"

He rests his hand on the top of the steering wheel while looking out the windshield. His unwillingness to look at me is painful. "You told him I'm married. You told him Caroline is in a mental hospital!"

I jump at the angry snap of his voice. "I didn't." I shake my head and wipe a few errant tears.

Now he glares right at me. "Bullshit! I'm sure you couldn't wait to call him after you got out of the hospital."

"I'm not lying. I didn't tell him." I keep shaking my head like this is a bad dream. "Alex must have told Sean and he probably told Kai, but it wasn't me."

"It doesn't matter. It's none of their business, it's none of your ..." He pauses.

"*Excuse* me!" I draw in a deep breath. "It's none of my what? Business?"

Oliver closes his eyes and shakes his head.

"*You* have some nerve. I was in the freakin' hospital! Broken in every sense of the word thanks to you keeping your past hidden from me. So excuse the hell out of me for confiding in Alex. But don't you dare invite me into your bed and tell me you'll do anything for me then turn around and say it's none of *my* business." I slam his door and start walking down the street because there's no way I'm going back in the house with Kai and my parents.

"Vivian!"

I keep walking.

"Stop." Oliver catches up and steps in front of me.

I stop. "You'd better knock me off my feet because right now anything less than that isn't going to work. I'm so sick of everyone making me feel like the pain in my heart caused by other people is somehow my own fucking fault. It's not my fault I have this embarrassing, mauled skin on my back that makes me look like a mutant. It's not my fault you have a wife and didn't tell me. And it's not my fucking fault Kai told everyone tonight!"

There's an echo of several dogs in the neighborhood barking. I'm sure my outburst has riled them up.

"You're right." Oliver sighs with downcast eyes and a sullen face.

I wait.

Nothing.

"No." I shake my head and start to brush past him. "Not good enough."

"Wait." He steps in front of me again.

I stare at his chest, clenching my jaw.

"I'm trying so hard not to regret my past, as awful as it's been. But when I'm with you it's so hard to do. I let my mind imagine a world where you've always been mine ... a world where you don't see your imperfections through *his* eyes, but your divine beauty through mine. Then I think of the pain that won't go away ... my pain, Caroline's pain ... Melanie's pain. And I wonder if time was worth it. Can I be that person who doesn't believe in divine purpose and meaning? Can I call fate bullshit and wish my child never entered this world because the pain with which she left it ... left me is too great? I don't know what to do with the pain and anger." His voice breaks and so does my heart. "You're the very best thing that's happened at the very worst time. I feel like I'm in the middle of the ocean and you're my life raft, and sometimes I get so frustrated that we're not making it to safety fast enough. I find myself blaming you for it, but it's only because I fear my weight, the weight of my past, is going to take us both under."

He cups my face with gentle, loving hands, and tilts my head up. "What if we're sinking?"

I place my hands over his and close my eyes to the anguish etched in his face. "What if we're not?"

I LET him go back to Cambridge, not because I want to, just because I need time alone with my parents.

"Young lady, where have you—" My mom pauses as I close the front door and look at her with red swollen eyes.

"Can you just..." I wipe away my tears "...treat me like an adult for once. I need a friend more than a mom right now. So can you? Can you be both tonight?"

My dad hugs me and kisses the top of my head then does the same to my mom before going upstairs. She looks at me for a moment then nods and opens her arms. I fall into her embrace and weep. All of the emotions I can't share with Oliver come pouring out—the fear that we could be sinking, the insecurity of knowing that he has a wife and it's not me, the meaning of what I saw behind the locked door.

"You love him."

I nod between sobs.

"Tell me about his wife."

"I-I don't know. They l-lost their b-baby and she went ins-sane or something."

"Oh, Vivvy ... he had a baby?"

I sniffle. "A daughter ... Melanie."

She leads me into the kitchen and I sit at the counter while she makes us tea. "He's leaving his wife for you?"

I shake my head. "He filed for divorce before we met."

"Why?"

I suck in a shaky breath. "That's just it. I don't know and I'm so afraid to ask."

"Does he see her much?"

"She's in Portland. That's where they moved after he graduated from Harvard."

She hands me a cup of tea and sits across from me. "What happened to Melanie? SIDS?"

I shrug. "I don't know. I haven't found the courage to ask him. But I have this very unsettling feeling it wasn't SIDS."

"What makes you say that?"

"I don't know it's just a ... feeling."

"Can I give you some advice as both your mother and a friend?"

I nod.

"Ask what you need to ask and decide sooner verses later if you can make the time and emotional investment in Oliver and his past. You have two years left of school and I'd hate to see anyone or anything derail your dreams."

I grimace. "Yeah, about that ..."

CHAPTER TWENTY-THREE
RIPPED OPEN

Oliver

I OFFERED TO STAY, but she told me to go. Leaving felt cowardly, like I was abandoning her in the middle of a huge mess. Kai has impeccable timing. Of course I know it's not fair to blame him for the timing of his sister's death, but nonetheless it dragged Vivian away on my birthday. His announcing my wife to her family on her birthday ... unforgivable. He must like having my fist stamped on his face. Dear God I hope Vivian is too smart to give him another chance.

"What'd you think of her parents?" my dad asks as we row along the river just after sunrise.

I grunt as my oars grab the water. "I like them. They're a little overprotective, but I suppose that's to be expected since she's an only child."

"Yeah, that and I'm sure they feel responsible for her burn accident. Every parent feels responsible for what happens to their children even if they have no control over it."

I nod but don't respond.

"Shit! Oliver, I'm sorry. I didn't mean to—"

"No, it's fine. I ... I know what you mean." I stop for a moment and sigh. "It's probably about time for me to stop expecting everyone to act like my life in Portland didn't exist. Vivian knows part of it and when she gets home later I'm going to tell her the rest."

"Oliver that's ... Have you talked to your mom about this?"

I shake my head. "I trust Vivian. I don't need Mom to tell me if or how to tell her. This is something I have to do by myself."

"What about Caroline?"

I shrug, trying to dismiss the tensing hatred that takes over my body every time her name is mentioned. "What about her?"

"You're still married to her. Responsible for her."

We pull the boat out of the water. "No, I'm not. She's Doug and Lily's problem, not mine."

"Oliver—"

"The papers have been filed, and it's just a matter of time before it's official."

"You loved her once."

"Dad! I'm not doing this with you!" I slam my oars in the boat.

He rests his hand on my shoulder. "I just want you to be prepared for the unexpected. You're a lawyer. I shouldn't have to tell you that circumstances can change."

Resting my hand on my hip, I look at my feet and nod with a sigh. "I know."

From my dad's lips to my life, what are the chances? There's a message on my phone after I get out of the shower. Doug Welch, my soon-to-be ex-father-in-law wants to talk to me. He has a *favor*, but he wants to talk in person, as if I have time to fly across the country on a whim. Not happening. I delete the message.

Vivian will be back in a few hours. That gives me a small window in which to get my shit together. I promised her answers and that's what she's going to be expecting. The door upstairs has to be opened and I need to face my fears ... face my reality. The problem is I can't get the sound of Doug's voice and his message out of my head. What's his favor? Why does he think we have to talk in person?

It may only be nine in the morning, but I think this day calls for an exception so I grab a beer. Three beers later I pour a glass of Jack and head upstairs. Inverting the cobalt vase, I wait for the key to fall out. Nothing. Where the hell is the key? I try to turn the knob, but it's locked so I bang on the door ... The door that I've not wanted to open, until now. I step back and kick it, but it doesn't budge. It's possible the alcohol is robbing my strength or my common sense.

Pulling my phone out of my pocket, I call Chance.

"It's nine-thirty on Sunday, dipshit, what do you want?"

"I need an ax."

"Okay, Paul. Shall I bring my blue ox too? What the hell do you need an ax for?"

I lean back against the wall and slide down while laughing. "Funny, you're real funny today."

"Jesus! You're drunk and it's not even ten o'clock."

"Yeah, well what's that saying? It's five o'clock somewhere."

"She dump you again?"

I empty the last few drops of Jack into my mouth. "Who?"

"Viv."

"No. Why?"

He chuckles. "Uh … no reason. I'll be there in twenty minutes."

After two trips back downstairs to refill my rocks glass, I come up with a brilliant idea. I bring the bottle upstairs with me. Genius … pure genius. My Harvard education is totally paying off.

"Yo, Bro … where are you?"

"In my house."

Chance chuckles, coming up the stairs. "No shit."

"Where is it?"

"What?"

I sigh. "The ox, stupid … I—jeez, I mean the ax." I purse my lips together and squint at the door. "Although I bet an ox could take that door down too."

"What's behind the door? Dude! You have a fucking dead bolt on the door. What on Earth?"

I let my head thump back against the wall and close my eyes. "I know. I'm pretty messed up. Don't tell Mom." I laugh.

"Where's the key?"

"It's in my pocket. I just thought it'd be more fun to bust it down with an ax." I think my speech slurs, or maybe it's just my hearing making everything sound slow and muffled. My eyes are so … very … heavy.

"Oliver?"

I'm tired … too tired.

"Oliver?"

"Hmm?"

"What's behind the door?"

The world's fading ... "Melanie."

Vivian

A WISPY, free feeling floats inside me on the train back to Boston. I had a transcendent moment with my parents yesterday. All my fears of how they would react to my lies and deception vanished. The words came to me without hesitation. I saw so much love and understanding in their eyes mixed with their own anguish and guilt. As much as I tried to convince myself that I was protecting them by lying about college, the truth is ... I was protecting myself. I didn't want to face their disappointment in themselves for not making enough money, or watch them continue to feel pity for me. The tears were plentiful, the moment was raw, but in the end everything was out, and I feel closer to my parents than I have ever felt before.

Now I'm dying to see Oliver. I miss him. All I can think about is leather work boots and his hot, naked body pressed against mine. His smile ... I love his smile, especially when it gets so big both dimples appear. I'm sure if I could see past my complete infatuation with him, I'd see his flaws. Maybe he has some birthmark I haven't discovered, or the veins in his hands are too prominent. It's possible he walks pigeon-toed, but I haven't noticed. Oliver can't be perfect, I know that, but he's perfect for me.

Chance's truck is parked behind Oliver's car on the street. Alex's car is there too, so I decide to take my bags home since attacking my man in front of his brother might not be good etiquette.

"Hey, Flower! How was your weekend?"

I drop my bags on the floor by the stairs. "What are you doing?"

"What do you mean?" She glances over her shoulder at me.

"I mean, you're cooking and..." I glance at the cooling racks filled with cookies. "...baking."

"Yeah, so?"

I take one of the bite-sized sugar cookies and pop it in my mouth. "Are your parents coming or something?" I mumble over a mouthful.

"No. I'm just getting back into practice. I haven't done much in the kitchen for a while."

I raise a single brow at her. "You're acting too weird, even for you. What's going on?"

She turns and licks some cream sauce off her fingers, lingering when she gets to her left ring finger.

"Oh my God!" I grab her hand gawking at the huge princess-cut diamond.

"I'm getting married!"

I can't peel my eyes off the mammoth rock. "Yeah you are. Holy crap, where did Sean get the money for this?"

"It was actually from a necklace that his grandfather gave his grandmother. Sean had it put into this platinum band. You like?"

I pull her in for a hug. "It's incredible. I'm so happy for you."

"Good, I hope you still feel that way when I tell you that you have six months to plan the best bachelorette party ever, Maid of Honor."

"What, me?"

She rolls her eyes and turns back around to the stove. "Duh, of course you."

"Why so soon? Are you pregnant? I knew that outfit-thingy he was wearing the other day would get you into trouble."

"Yeah, Flower. I got pregnant on Friday. Saturday he drove to Jersey to get the diamond, had it mounted and sized on Sunday, and proposed right after I peed on the stick this morning." She laughs. "No, I'm not pregnant. His older brother will be back from Africa for a week over Christmas. Remember I told you Dillon's in the Peace Corps?"

"Yes, I remember."

"Anyway, Sean decided he wanted to seize the rare opportunity of having his whole family here so he proposed."

"So you're not pregnant?"

She laughs again. "No, Flower, I'm not pregnant. But you'd better make nice with neighbor boy because once I move in with Sean…" she turns and gives me a sly grin "… well, *officially*, then my parents are selling this place."

"Speaking of neighbor boy. What the hell kind of birthday present was that supposed to be?"

"Ahh, it's the deluxe version of the model I bought for you right after you moved in. I have one too. Isn't it a-mazing?"

"Well, I wouldn't know. Once it fell out of the sack and onto the floor in front of my parents and Oliver, I sort of lost the mood to try it out."

"No way!"

"Way … as in *way* embarrassing. I've been having the best sex of my life so why did you think I would need that?"

Alex chuckles. "Flower, first, you've been having the *only* sex of your life, so technically it's the best and the worst. Second, it can be used as an adjunct to all the kink you and neighbor boy have already been doing."

I bite at the peeling skin on my lower lip. "That's what Oli alluded to as well. So, how does that work. I use it in front of him? He uses it on me? I use it on him?"

"Yes, yes, and yes. You guys into anal?"

"What?" I gasp.

She shrugs while draining the pasta. "It was just a question."

"Anal me or anal him ... or ... ugh, never mind! No to both anyway. How could you even ask me that?"

"Don't knock it until you've tried it. Maybe you should watch a little guy-on-guy porn. It's hot as in capital H.O.T. It might change your mind."

"You are definitely Maggie's niece. Are your parents into this *stuff* too?"

"Ooo, yuck, gross! Why did you say that? Now when I see them it's all I'm going to think about."

Yeah, like my images of her tied to her bed and Sean in chaps and a cowboy hat.

"Think about what? Your mom wearing a strap-on penis? 'Spread 'em, Mark. You've been a naughty boy.' 'Harder, Annabelle!'"

"STOP!" Alex squeezes her eyes shut and sticks her fingers in her ears while stomping her feet.

I laugh. "That's for not locking your door before the rodeo." I steal another cookie. "I'm going to unpack then go see Oliver."

"I'm going to vomit then have a voluntary lobotomy!" She slings a sticky piece of spaghetti at me as I head toward the stairs.

I skip down the front steps. Glass scars? What glass scars? A pang of disappointment hits me when I see Chance's truck still there. Maybe he'll take the hint and leave when he sees me salivating through labored breaths at his brother.

"Hello?"

Nothing.

I hear voices as I near the stairs. They become clearer as I tiptoe my way upstairs.

"I think you should stop drinking."

"Why?"

"Well, once you pass out the party is over."

"I didn't pass out ... I took a nap."

"You passed out."

"How would you know? You're wasted too." Oliver chuckles.

"I'm not drunk."

"You broke your ax on my door."

"Okay, I'm a little wasted."

"Viv-i-an's going to be here ... soon. You should go."

"You should let *her* go. You're fucked-up and you're just going to break her heart."

"You're right—"

"He's right?" I turn the corner at the top of the stairs, startling both of them. "Is that what I heard you say?" My jaw clenches while I squint at him. "I thought we had this conversation! Stop jerking me around. Either you want to be with me or you don't. But I'm fed up with you acting like some martyr willing to give me up even if it kills you just because you think it's best for me. Either you're in or out! So what's it going to be?"

He struggles to stand up, but falls right back down on his butt. Chance laughs.

"What's so goddamn funny? What's wrong with the

two of you? Why are you both sitting in the hall, drunk off your asses, in the middle of the day?" I look to my left at *the door*. There's an ax stuck in it with the handle broken off. I pull the key out of my pocket and dangle it in front of them. "Seems a little less destructive than an ax, don't you think?"

Oliver goes to grab it, but I pull it away. "Why do you have my key?"

"I slipped it in my pocket the other day and forgot it was there. I have it now because I was planning on returning it. Now answer me."

He squeezes his eyes shut and shakes his head as if that's going to help him sober up. "What was the question again?"

"Ugh! Are you keeping me or cutting me loose? Why are you both drunk? And what the hell is the meaning behind the pillow with a photo of your dead daughter sitting on top of it in the middle of an otherwise empty room?" I point to the door.

Chance looks at Oliver. "Bro, you kept the pil—"

"Get out!" Oliver grits through his teeth.

"That's so fuc—"

"GET. OUT!"

Chance crawls to his feet and stumbles to the stairs.

"Don't you dare drive home," I say to Chance, still glaring at Oliver.

"I'll call for a ride," he replies on his way down the stairs.

Oliver bows his head and rubs his temples. "My head is killing me. So pick one."

"What?"

"Pick the question that matters most right now."

I kneel down between his bent legs. He looks up at me with heart-wrenching emotion in his glossy blue eyes.

"Are you letting me go?" I whisper with such fear of his answer smacking me in the face.

"Never."

I nod. "Okay then." Releasing a sigh of desperate relief, we embrace like we're holding on for life.

***

My back screams in protest while my body temperature approaches boiling point. We're still in the hallway. Oliver has half his body draped over mine and his head is on my chest. I'm not sure how long we've been asleep, hopefully long enough for the alcohol to clear his system.

"Oli?" I whisper, running my fingers through his hair.

He mumbles something.

"Oli, wake up."

He lifts his head just enough to see my eyes. "Thank you."

"For what?"

"Choosing me."

I smile. "I think it was the other way around."

"No, when you chose us over my past ... you chose me."

"I'll always choose you. No take backs, remember."

"No take backs." He grins and rolls me on top of him. "You didn't let me finish earlier." I close my eyes when his lips brush across mine. "I should let you go, but you've become my sunrise. I need you when the darkness threatens to take over."

"When is that?"

"Always."

Oh, Oli ...

Our faces are as close as they can be without actually touching.

"You're staring at my freckles." I rub my nose against his.

"Because they're so damn cute."

"Shut up. Dimples are cute. Freckles are spotty, patchy, and messy."

"Messy?" He laughs.

"Yeah, like I'm messy right now and sweaty. I need a shower."

"Bath?"

I grin and nod.

We fill the tub ... too much, thanks to us both being incapable of keeping our hands off the other when we're naked.

"We're going to have a mess to clean up by the time we get out," I say as I ease in the water between his legs. I love his deep claw-foot tub.

"We'll add it to the messy list with your freckles."

"Ha, ha!" I lean back against his chest and skim my fingers over his legs.

"So how did the weekend go?"

"Great, actually. I feel free. The painful weight of lying to my parents for the past two years has been lifted. They felt bad that I thought I needed to protect them from the truth, but they weren't mad."

"And your adulterous boyfriend?"

I laugh. "They think we're both insane, but they get it."

"Get it?"

"Yeah, why?"

"How much did you tell them?"

"I told them your wife is mentally ill because your baby died. It's tragic and something I'm sure you don't want the whole world to know, but they're my parents and I had to explain the situation."

He doesn't respond.

"Are you mad?"

He wraps his arms around me and kisses the top of my head. "No ... I'm not mad."

After twenty minutes of silence and the dropping water temperature evoking goose bumps, we get out. I wrap my towel around myself and comb through my hair while Oliver goes into the bedroom.

"You're awfully quiet," I say while grabbing one of his T-shirts from the drawer and slipping it on.

He sits on the edge of the bed in just his briefs with his head bowed. "I'd been working late ... a lot. Being the youngest lawyer at the firm meant long hours. We both knew that when I took the position. That's the reason I looked for a job in Portland, so her parents would be close by to help when the baby came."

He's telling me everything and I can't move. I want to sit next to him, hold his hand ... something, but I'm frozen in front of the dresser, just feet away from him, completely paralyzed.

"She went into labor at five in the morning two weeks before her due date. They ended up doing a C-section. Melanie was tiny but so..." his voice cracks "...strong." He shakes his head. "God, she was so strong. Caroline had a tough recovery, but her mom stayed with us to help out. The partners at the firm insisted I take a week off and work from home. I thought we were good, tired and exhausted, but good."

Silence settles over the room. I don't know if he's looking for the right words or the right amount of courage. Forcing my body to find its own courage, I move closer and kneel on the floor by the bed, resting my head on his leg. His hand moves to my hair and he runs his fingers through it in slow methodic strokes.

"I went back to work, but her parents came to help every day over the next couple months. They encouraged her to take a shower, a walk, even run an errand or two just to have a break. One day she would scrub the kitchen floor then the next she didn't want to get out of bed. Her doctor said it was postpartum depression, fairly common. Her mom thought she was starting to hallucinate, but I never saw that side of her. Then again, I wasn't home much. Melanie was usually asleep by the time I got home, so my only interaction was when she woke in the night, but even then Caroline was usually up. She hardly slept."

He laughs, it's a painful, maybe even an angry laugh. "It wasn't postpartum depression, it was postpartum psychosis. Did you know that point one percent of women get it? And even then, less than five percent of that *point one percent* are suicidal or ..." He swallows and takes a deep breath.

I can't move ... I can't breathe. I know where this is going. It's the sickest feeling I've ever had in my life. It's worse than waking up in the hospital with third-degree burns. It's worse than hearing about Sean's abusive past. It's even worse than the news of Kai's sister dying. One blink and my tears release. They flow freely down my face and onto Oliver's leg.

"Less than five percent of ... Point. One. Fucking. Percent. Her parents had driven down to visit her brother in Salem, just for the evening. I made sure to be home by dinner. I brought food and flowers. It was going to be our special night together, just the three of us."

His tears fall to my cheek. I look up at him and the pain on his face is like someone's ripping him apart and he can't stop them.

I shake my head. "Don't." I need him to stop.

"It was quiet ... too quiet. So I went to our bedroom."

"Oli, stop." I release a sob and grab his tear streaked face. "Please."

He just stares at me like he's looking through me, not even seeing me. "They weren't there. I thought ... I thought maybe she was in the bathtub. The floor ... so much blood ... she was lifeless."

"Oli ... don't do this." I cry.

"I called 9-1-1 and went back down the hall to unlock the front door. That's when I saw them." More tears fall from his glazed-over eyes. "Her feet ... they were bl-blue." A break in his voice and a single sob ... it's a dagger to my heart.

My forehead falls to his chest and I cry so hard. He places his hands over mine still on his cheeks.

"She was in h-her crib with a p-pillow over her head." He releases another strangled sob.

I crawl up onto his lap and press my wet lips to his. "No more, Oli! No more." I mumble between sobs against his lips.

He nods, resting his forehead on mine and holding me tight in his arms.

CHAPTER TWENTY-FOUR
BARED TO BOSTON

Oliver

I GAVE Vivian the version of the story that showed the monster in Caroline. There's the version where I'm a monster too. The one I've never told anyone. It's the version that includes my thoughts that night ... my regrets. I regretted calling 9-1-1 because Melanie was already dead and Caroline was still alive. *Monster.*

It's almost midnight. We've both been in and out of sleep but never leaving each other's arms. The most incredible woman in the world found me ... *me!* Someday I could wake up and discover she is in fact, just a dream. But for now I'm holding on to her with the intensity of a lifeline.

"Do you miss Rosenberg?"

I love her ... I fucking love her more than I ever thought humanly possible. We haven't said a word in six hours, not since I finished reliving my past, hopefully for the last time. Yet, she just knows to ask me about something as random and mundane as her dog.

"Can't say I've given him much thought."

She brushes her fingernails over my chest in the same repeated pattern. "Well, I think he took a real liking to you."

"Mmm, I guess I'll have to go visit him again."

"Yes, *or* maybe he could come here ... for a visit."

"Uh ... yeah, sure ... I guess."

"Really?" She looks up at me resting her chin on my chest.

I shrug. "Sure. Why not?"

"Thanks, babe." She leans up and kisses me. "I'm hungry."

I chuckle. "It's past midnight."

"Well, all my tummy knows is that we missed dinner." She climbs out of bed and looks over her shoulder. "You coming?"

"You're serious?"

"Mr. Konrad, I'm always serious when it comes to food." Her voice fades as she heads toward the stairs.

"I don't have much food in the house." I catch up to her at the bottom of the stairs.

"I should run across the street and see what Alex left for me. She was making the yummiest pasta with a cream sauce and the whole place smelled like sugar cookies which were to die for."

"And you left that for me?"

She opens the refrigerator. "I know, what was I thinking? Jeez, Oli, *not much* was an overstatement. You have nothing." She opens the pantry and grabs a nearly-empty jar of peanut butter and a bag with bread. She pulls out the bread. "Heels ... figures."

"I'll stock the kitchen just for you tomorrow." I pull her hair away from her neck and kiss her soft skin.

"Where are your plates?" she asks while opening and shutting the doors to the empty cabinets.

I step back and hop up on the island with my hands folded in my lap. "Funny you should ask. I haven't had a chance to replace them since the *home invasion*."

She turns toward me, licking the peanut butter off the knife. "Oli ..."

I shake my head and reach for her arm, pulling her between my legs. "Don't. I don't want you to be sorry or feel bad or regretful. I should have told you long before you found out."

"But—"

I press my finger to her lips. Her eyes fill with tears. "No buts. Just because I've shared everything with you doesn't mean you're supposed to give me a free pass. I love you, Vivian, and I knew it long before I said it. So I should have told you then. I should have told you everything."

She nods while I wipe away the few tears that have fallen down her cheeks. "Just let me say this once, Oli. I need you to hear it. Okay?"

I feel the desperation in her voice. "Okay."

She draws in a slow breath then releases it as she sets down the knife and takes my hands in hers. "What happened to your family is unimaginable. I still can't comprehend it. But you have some issues that aren't going to disappear by simply ignoring them."

I look away then close my eyes.

"You have to deal with what's behind that door. I can deal with you having pain, Oli. People live with pain, but that's not pain. That's torture. And eventually it's going to destroy you."

She squeezes my hands and I open my eyes. "So, stock your kitchen." She steps back and grabs her sandwich. "I like crunchy by the way, this creamy crap is lackluster."

We both smile.

"I'll meet you for breakfast and let you take me to dinner. If you're lucky, I'll indulge you in a slumber party on the weekends, but I won't move back in with you or make a commitment to a future with you until that door is opened and the walls are painted yellow. I want my single bed in there and a desk to use for my school work. And when I come to bed with you in *our* bed I want to lie on my pillow after you've made love to me once and fucked me twice." She winks. "I need the Oli that I fell in love with. The guy who bought me my first bikini and gave me my first orgasm—the guy who let me lick my Boston Kreme donut off his—"

"Vivian!" I adjust myself. "I get the point." My body is at war. She's talking about my past and essentially telling me to get my shit together or we don't have a chance, but at the same time she's eating, and my dick knows that my brain views her eating much the same as watching porn.

"Sorry, babe. But you get what I'm trying to say, right?"

"Yeah, I get it." I grab her wrist and take a bite of her sandwich. "I need to get it together and you like to lick food off my body." I mumble over a mouthful.

Vivian giggles. "Your words, not mine but close enough." She feeds me the last bite. "We should grab a couple of cookies before we go back to bed."

"I don't have any cookies."

"I'm talking about the sugar cookies Alex made." She grabs my hand and pulls me off the counter.

"She's probably asleep."

"There's a key under the planter."

"I'm in my underwear and you're not wearing anything but my T-shirt."

"Come on, Oli. Don't be such a spoilsport. It's just

across the street and who's going to see us at this hour?" She opens the door.

"So responsible people are considered spoilsports?" I follow her out the door.

"There's responsible and then there's stuffy and boring. Live a little, Oli." We look in both directions then streak across the street. "Her car is gone anyway. She must have gone to Sean's after dinner."

I keep a lookout for cars while she lifts the planter. "Hmm ... it's not here. Man! I bet cowboy Sean forgot to put it back the last time he used it. Idiot!" She tries the door but it's locked.

"We'll do cookies tomorrow, my love. Come on ... it's a little breezy out here in nothing but my skivvies."

"Fine!" She pouts as I pull her back across the street.

"Maybe we should go upstairs and do a doughnut intervention, but call it a cookie intervention tonight." I look back at her and smirk while grabbing for the doorknob.

"I suppose." She continues to pout. Those must be some amazing cookies over there. For the first time since we've been together she's treating sex like a subpar consolation prize.

"What the hell?" I jiggle and tug at the knob.

"Did you lock the door?"

She shakes her head. "You were the one who shut it."

"Dammit!" I bang my fist against the door.

"Just use your spare key."

"I gave my spare key to *you*." I try to keep my voice calm but it's a challenge.

"Well, why'd you lock the door then?"

"I didn't! Chance must have turned the lock when he left and I didn't check the lock before we decided to *live a little*."

"Oh, so now this is my fault?" She plants her hands on her hips.

I shake my head. "No, it's just ... it doesn't matter. We need to figure out what we're going to do."

"Well, it's after midnight so we can't take the T."

I mimic her stance and bend toward her so we're eye level. "Really? You think the reason we can't take the T is because it's closed? Not possibly, hmm let's see ... because we're *practically naked?*"

She looks down at her shirt or *my* shirt. "It's no shorter than some of my dresses."

"You're not wearing underwear."

She gives me the wide-eyed and-your-point-is look. I stare up at the sky and shake my head some more then look back at her.

"It's white and your nipples are not and ... it doesn't matter anyway! You may gallivant around town in short dresses and no underwear, but I don't go anywhere in just briefs."

"I still don't see how this is my fault."

I grab her and lead her down the steps. "It's not worth arguing over. It doesn't change anything."

"Where are we going?"

"Chance's. Unless you know someone closer."

"That's like a thirty minute walk."

"Forty, if we avoid the busy streets and guess what? We're going to avoid the busy streets."

"My second skin patches on my feet will never hold up walking barefoot on concrete and cobblestone."

"Tell me about it. Mine won't either ... oh that's right, only one of us has cushy little padding on our cuts."

"Babe, I detect a hint of sarcasm in your voice."

"No, really?"

She pulls her hand out of my grasp and stops, folding her arms across her chest. "I'm not taking another step until you apologize for your grumpiness."

One thing is for sure: This woman brings out every emotion humanly possible.

I hold my arms out to the side. "Look at us? We're passing-one-cop-car away from getting arrested for indecent exposure and you want me to *apologize* for my grumpiness?"

She nods.

I rub my hands over my face and groan. "Fine! I'm sorry for not being happy about our situation. I will try to enjoy this leisurely walk to my brother's place in my *underwear* a little more. Happy?"

She takes my hand and we continue to walk. "You could stand to work on your apologies."

I think I taste blood, I'm biting my tongue so hard.

"I wish we had some money on us. Do you think any of the Dunks around here are open all night?"

Laughter vibrates through my chest. I can't hold it in. "I don't have any reason to know if one is open at this hour. Although I'd be surprised if there isn't one of their gazillion locations open all night. Why the hell do we need so many anyway? There are two at the train station within like twenty yards of each other. I just don't get it."

"A lot of Dunkin' Donuts are franchises and by contract if you open one you have to open another within a year. But the reason they can do that and keep so many open is the concept of a business cluster. A geographically concentrated group or *cluster* of businesses that share similar markets. It's like seeing a McDonald's and Burger King next to each other. It's not so much about giving the consumers a choice, it's about the demand for burgers and fries—enough to keep both businesses in business. So with a huge coffee demand why wouldn't Dunks be on every corner? More concentrated locations means convenience, shorter lines, and happier customers. If they're going to share customers with the coffee place up the block or across the street, why not keep it in the family and let it be with another Dunkin' Donuts? It's called transfer of sales."

Yep. She's a one-track mind business geek. Just when I think she's losing it tonight, she goes off on business clustering 101.

"I'm impressed and surprisingly a little turned on. Like the day I came back from rowing and you were reading the business section of the newspaper with your black-framed glasses. I like it when you get the fuck-me schoolgirl or naughty teacher thing going on."

"Lovely, Oli. I hope my economics professor gets as aroused as you by my contractionary monetary policy paper. It should guarantee me an A."

"Fuck! Stop, Vivian." I adjust myself.

"Oh my gosh! That actually turns you on?"

I shrug. "Intelligence is sexy."

"Wanna do it in the alley?" She gestures with her head toward a dark alleyway off to our right.

"No, I don't want to do it in the alley."

She tugs on my hand making me stop. "Are you sure about that?" She grins looking at the bulge in my briefs.

My cock is trying to break free. "It's just because we're talking about it."

Grabbing my hand she presses it between her legs. "So you don't want to put *that* in *here*?"

I swallow. My heart pounds in my chest. Of course I want to bury myself inside of her. I hate it when my dick doesn't understand bad and inappropriate timing.

I pull my hand back. "We're not doing this."

"Okay, lead the way with your iron rod ... stud."

"You're trying to bait me and it's not going to work." I continue ahead, trying to will my dick to just ... take a nap or play dead. I see headlights coming toward us. "Crap! Hide!" I pull her back and into the alley.

"Well ... since we're here now."

"No." I peek around the corner, keeping Vivian behind me, and look for any other cars.

She slips her finger under my waist band and tugs me back. "Just a quickie."

"No." I smack her hand away.

"A blow job?"

"What? No!"

"A hand job."

"No!" I tug on her hand to get going but she yanks her hand away.

"You could go down on me."

"Vivian Graham! Let's go!"

An eye roll and a pouty lip, but she follows. "You are so getting replaced with my new vibrator."

Vivian

ONE OF THE things I love about Oliver is his maturity. One of things I hate about Oliver ... his maturity. Come on, it's one o'clock in the morning. Who is ever going to see us in a dark alley? Good grief, he's walking down the sidewalks of Boston in his underwear like a damn Diesel model and he expects me to keep my hands off the merchandise? We're about two blocks from Chance's and he's banned me from so much as holding his hand—possibly because I try to rub it against my girlie parts to entice him.

"My feet hurt, Oli."

"We're almost there."

"I can't make it."

"Yes you can."

"You're going to have to carry me, babe."

He stops and turns around. I'm a few feet back, shoulders sagging, back hunched—total puppy dog eyes.

"Fine, but behave."

I reel in my enthusiasm, releasing just a small appreciative grin. "Thanks, babe." I jump on his back, and I have to bite my bottom lip to keep a moan of pleasure from escaping as my bare, wet sex rubs against his flesh. He has to feel it. I'm not just moist and sticky, I'm a dang Slip N' Slide.

His long strides turn into a rhythm. *Friction. Release. Friction. Release.*

"Oh God ..."

"What?"

My forehead falls to his shoulder. "Nothing." My voice is breathy. I try to keep my body still, letting him do all the work ... all the unintentional teasing. But there's nothing I want more than to rock my hips into him. I have never been this horny. I picture us on my birthday, him slamming up into me over and over against Chance's truck.

"Yes!" The word escapes before I can stop it.

"Yes, what?"

"I see his bu-building ... We're almost th-there."

"Think you can walk now?"

"No! More ... I mean ... keep going."

"What the hell is wrong with you?" He releases my legs and I almost cry as I drop to my feet.

"You have sweat on your brow. Why are you sweating? I was the one carrying you, not the other way around."

I squeeze my legs together.

"Do you have to go to the bathroom?"

I grimace and shake my head. "I was really close to ... and now you've left me hanging and—"

"Close to?" He reaches around and feels his back. "Were you *getting off* on me?"

My grimace intensifies as my skin takes on heat and a nice rosy color.

He rubs his fingers together. This is monumentally embarrassing. "Well ... did you finish?"

I shake my head.

"Were you close?"

I nod.

He turns. "Hop back on then."

"What? No ... no way. I'm not going to just hop back on and hump your back the rest of the way down the street."

Oliver shrugs. "Suit yourself. I was only trying to help." A cocky smirk plays across his face.

I send him my meanest glare. "If you really wanted to help me you would have left me with an exfoliated back from the brick alleyway wall and a sated vagina."

"Oh for crying out loud, not this again. I'll do you as soon as we get home. Deal?"

Why the nerve ...

I breeze past him. "Think again, buddy! You won't be *doing* me until I'm good and ready. And that won't be anytime soon!" *It will be soon.*

After streaking our way up the desolate alley, Oliver stands right in front of me. I move a little to the right, he moves a little to the right. I move left, he moves left. Finally, I shove him.

"What are you doing?"

"My brother doesn't need to see you in that." He knocks on the door.

"It's dark out, Oli. So unless he pours a bucket of water on me, I don't think you have any reason to worry."

Oliver knocks again, this time a little louder.

"Dude! What the fuck?" Chance looks like a bear emerging from its cave after a long winter. A bear with a loosely tied sheet around its waist. "Where are your clothes, Bro?"

"It's a long story so don't ask, but we got locked out. I need you to grab your key to my place and drive us home."

"Well I would except my truck is still parked along the street in front of *your* place, dip shit. I figured you'd pick me up for work in the morning. Don't you remember? We had too much to drink? I took the T. Did you two walk here?" Chance looks at me for a second too long and Oliver tries to shield me from his sight.

"Yes, we had no other choice. Alex is gone and so is the spare key to their place. Obviously neither one of us has a phone on us, so we had to walk here."

"Why didn't you drive my truck. Would have been faster and less ... streak-showish."

"I don't have your keys." Oliver pushes him aside, grabs my hand, and drags me in the house. He tosses me a blanket from the couch. "Cover up," he mouths.

I roll my eyes and wrap it around me.

Chance shuts the door. "The keys are in the truck, under the floor mat where I always keep them."

"You don't lock your truck?" I question.

Oliver drops his head. "He never locks it ... the idiot."

"I'm the idiot? I think my brother, who knows I always keep my truck unlocked with the keys under the mat, is the idiot for traipsing his half-naked girlfriend through the streets of Boston in the middle of the night."

"Someone was a little muddled in the head tonight," I murmur.

Oliver's head snaps up. "You're still trying to pin this one on me?"

I give him the if-the-shoe-fits smirk and head tilt.

"*Hey, Oli ... I'm hungry. Hey, Oli ... let's get some cookies. Hey, Oli ... we don't need our clothes. Hey, Oli ... don't be such a spoilsport. Who's going to see us at this hour?*" Oliver mimics me with his best high-pitched voice.

Chance laughs. "I'm going back to bed. You two can have the spare bedroom, or there are blankets in my closet if you get your ass kicked to the couch, Bro."

"Thanks, Chance." I smile, but Oli ignores us both.

"So ... I'm going to use the bathroom then go to bed."

Oliver grabs my blanket from me, wraps it around himself with his lips in a firm line as he lies down on the couch without a single word. *Yep, he's peeved.*

"You can sleep in the guest room with me."

He doesn't say anything. Clearly, him sleeping on the couch is my punishment, not his. I sulk up the stairs, use the bathroom, and crawl into the lonely guest bed.

My monkey brain won't let me get to sleep. I can't stop thinking about Oliver downstairs, mad at me. Then memories of how our whole evening started begin to replay in my head. Caroline killed Melanie ... Suffocated her with a pillow ... the pillow in that locked room. I remember the pain in his eyes, the feel of his watery emotions on my cheek, and I still hear the echo of his sobs. And now, I go to him.

It's quiet down here. I can't tell if he's asleep or not. I tiptoe my way through the family room to the couch. Just as I start to contemplate whether I should say something or tap his shoulder, he lifts his arm holding up the blanket—inviting me in. The room is dimly lit by the light from the fish tank, reflecting shadows in his eyes. We stare at each other, my body resting on his.

His lips twitch and I think he's about to say something, but instead he kisses me.

Match. Strike. Flame.

He sits up never letting go of my lips until he pulls my shirt off. I moan with the touch of his mouth on my breasts, arching my back into him. He fists my hair and tugs hard while assaulting every inch of my skin from breasts to lips. I lace my fingers through his hair and rock my pelvis against him. A vague memory of my intentions to deny him as a punishment fades into oblivion as he leans me back on the couch and removes his boxer briefs. He doesn't wait. The animal in Oliver takes over. Pushing my right knee up toward my shoulder he sinks into me. We both moan.

He pauses, looking at me with such intensity, then pulls back and slams into me, over and over. I want this feeling to last, but my body is in desperate search for a release and there is nothing I can do to stop it. I bite my bottom lip with blood-drawing intensity and thrash my head back and forth willing myself to hold on just a little bit longer. Oli takes my hand and sticks my fingers in his mouth, sucking them and swirling his tongue around them. Then he moves my hand between us. I circle my fingers, slick with his saliva, over my clitoris. Closing my eyes I imagine it's his tongue. He picks up his pace and my fingers circle faster. His lips find mine and we both fall over the edge together, our moans muffled and captured by our deep kiss.

"I love you ... just so ... completely."

His words grab me and hold me in another dimension that's beyond the reach of the rest of the world. It's our world where time stands still, yet together we grow and connect, our love intertwining into something so beautiful.

"My love for you, Oli, has no depths. It's effortless and forever," I whisper with tears in my eyes. The emotional impact of the night has caught up to the moment, and the infinite love I have for Oliver is overwhelming.

Bliss ... it's all I see in his soft, endearing smile. We cocoon ourselves in the blanket and fall asleep. Our paths to each other have been brutal and unforgiving, but I would do it all over again if it meant I'd end up in these same arms.

CHAPTER TWENTY-FIVE
GO

Oliver

Rosenberg came to visit two weeks ago ... and he's still here. Vivian's parents were going to be out of town for the weekend to celebrate their anniversary. I've offered to drive Rosenberg back to Hartford, but Vivian hasn't wanted me to go without her, and she's been too *busy* to go. She also hasn't moved back in yet. However, she's been kind enough to leave Rosenberg with me to keep me company. *How thoughtful!*

When she's not working at the greenhouse, she's helping Alex and her mom plan for the wedding. I can't help but wonder if Vivian has the white gown 'til-death-do-us-part dream. She's never mentioned it and neither have I. My life is still preoccupied with the demons behind that door that's still locked. Hence the reason Vivian is not living here.

Then there's the incessant phone calls and texts from Doug, pleading with me to come to Portland. Most of the time I let it go to voicemail, but as of lately, I've been answering just to tell him to stop calling, then I hang up. His persistence and the desperate tone of his pleas cinches the already existent knot in my stomach. I feel like he's a ticking bomb ready to ruin my life like his daughter tried to do.

"Rosenberg? Oli?" Vivian calls, and in that order, as I pull the lasagna out of the oven. That fluff ball rates way above me; it's pathetic and embarrassing.

"He's on the couch licking his balls."

She comes up behind me and slides her hands up under the front of my shirt. "And you?"

"I can't bend that far. I tried the other day, hoping you'd love me as much as the mutt, but I just can't quite reach."

She giggles with her lips pressed to my back. "I mean what are you doing?"

"Making dinner."

She rakes her nails down my chest as I slice the French loaf. "I can see that, silly. It just looks like a lot of food for the two of us."

"I know, we're having company."

"Oh, who?"

"Your parents. They're taking Rosenberg home tonight since you've been too busy to go with me to take him back."

I glance over my shoulder to see the look on her face. Wide eyes and a gaping mouth ... just as I suspected.

"You called them? About Rosenberg?"

"I called them to see if they wanted to have dinner with us. I just *assume* they'll take Rosenberg home with them. Why wouldn't they?"

"I ... well ... it's just ..."

I turn and lean against the counter with my arms

crossed over my chest. "You seem to be stammering. Do you have something to tell me?"

She releases a heavy sigh. "Rosenberg is my dog. I was supposed to bring him with me when I moved to Cambridge, but I couldn't have him at Alex's since I wasn't *living* there, so to speak, and my parents have been asking for the past two years when I'm going to take him. My dad's threatened to drop him off at the local shelter and I don't think he really would, but some days I'm not so sure."

She's not giving me a press release. When we picked Rosenberg up two weeks ago I had this feeling he wouldn't be returning home. It may have been the two thirty-pound bags of dog food, or all three of his little beds, or the large basket filled with every toy he owns that filled my car. Regardless, there were red flags everywhere and I'm not as stupid as Vivian apparently thinks I am.

"So he's staying here?"

She nods.

"Indefinitely?"

Another nod.

"So you live with Alex and Rosenberg lives with me?"

Shrug. Pause. And finally ... another nod.

I turn back around and start chopping lettuce for the salad. "Well, then it's a good thing that my parents are the ones coming for dinner and not yours."

"Oliver Konrad!" Her voice shrieks behind me. "You tricked me, set me up just to watch me squirm."

"Wow, it must feel maddening to have someone *trick* you into something. I can't imagine what that must feel like."

Vivian smacks my ass.

"Damn, woman! You're always asking for it." I set the

knife down and lunge for her. She squeals and runs into the living room. The only thing separating us is the couch with her fluff ball on it yippity-yapping.

"It was just a joke. I was being playful."

Her plea for leniency falls on deaf ears. "I know. I like jokes, and I like to play too."

Vivian's eyes dart from left to right. It's a fun cat and mouse game. I'm toying with her because she has no idea that I could hurdle this couch and have her pinned to the floor before she could so much as blink.

"You're burning the bread!"

I look behind me and she Carl Lewises her way around to the entry. I'm on her tail, chastising myself for being so gullible with her burning-bread decoy.

"Oli!" she screams just as the doorbell rings. Leaping toward the door, she opens it and squeezes outside hiding behind my unsuspecting parents. They look at each other then at me.

"Mouse in the house?"

"Not a mouse! Oliver's trying to spank me."

Oh, for the love of Pete! Why is she always sharing this information with my parents?

"Oliver." My dad cocks his head to the side while my mom purses her lips to control her grin.

They step inside, still shielding Vivian from me. "This is odd behavior considering we never spanked you when you were a child." My mom puts her arm around Vivian.

I squint at Vivian wearing her smirky face, all huddled into my mom. "I have to finish up with dinner. Help your-selves to some wine or beer."

"When did you get a dog?" my dad asks.

"I didn't. In fact, I'm not sure why he's here. Some sort of squatter, I guess."

"Rosenberg is my dog." Vivian scoops him up and nuzzles her nose into his fur. "He came for a visit and when I saw how Oli took an instant liking to him, I didn't have the heart to send him back to my parents'."

My dad rests his hand on my shoulder while I cut the lasagna. "Funny, I didn't realize you were a dog fan."

I give him a sideways glance. "Funny, neither did I."

I don't know if my dad knows what it means to be pussy-whipped, but whether he knows it or not, it's what his grin says.

Dinner is filled with light conversation, good food— thanks to yours truly—and sexy glances between me and Vivian. Banter is our foreplay. The sassier she gets, the more I want to thrust her on the counter, spread her wide, and indulge in her body until she's screaming my name. At least that's tonight's fantasy keeping me semi-erect throughout dinner.

"Thanks for bringing the strawberry-rhubarb cobbler. It's my favorite." Vivian winks at my mom as she takes a bite then pulls the spoon across her lips with slow seduction. I'm fully erect now.

"When do classes start?" My dad changes the subject, probably because her sensuality with the spoon doesn't go unnoticed by him either. After all, he's still a guy.

"Ten days and I'm so excited!"

"She already has her bag packed." I squeeze her leg under the table.

"What can I say? I've always loved school. I was the girl who got the perfect attendance award at the end of the year. I was student body president, on student council, the year-book team, and all the fundraisers I helped organize raised the most money."

"I'm in love with a financial geek."

Vivian elbows me and my parents laugh. "I'm not a geek..." she shrugs and takes another bite of her cobbler "... okay, I might be a little geeky."

"Well, we look forward to watching you blossom." My mom reaches across the table and squeezes Vivian's hand.

I can speak from experience. Watching my girl known as, Flower, bloom in my presence has been life changing.

Vivian

Four days. I'm giddy with excitement. Alex and Sean think I'm crazy, but they've been enjoying the college life for two years. They're the Disney World employees just showing up for another day's work. I'm the five-year-old waiting in line for the gates to open to the Magic Kingdom.

"How are the bachelorette party plans coming along?" Sean asks while lying on the floor with Rosenberg snuggled onto his chest.

"Why? Are you jealous that Alex is going to have a kick-ass party while Kai, at best, pays for a skanky stripper old enough to be your mom to jiggle her wrinkled cleavage in your face while porn plays in the background, *and* he serves you and your friends warm beer from a keg?"

I'd like to say that Kai and I are being amicable about being the best man and maid of honor, but we're not. It's turning into the War of the Roses – Wedding Edition and the wedding is still five months away.

"For your information we're going to Atlantic City."

"Yep ... that has class written all over it."

"Do I need to separate you two?" Alex calls from the kitchen. She's agreed to bake her cookies and banana bread at Oliver's so he and I can savor the smell for the evening. Admittedly, it's an odd request, but Alex is used to my quirky ideas.

"When is Oliver going to be here?"

"Soon, so finish up and get out."

"I love you too, Flower."

Okay, it's not just the bakery-fresh aroma. I want to make Oliver think I've been the one baking up a storm.

"How much of this am I leaving behind?"

"Full batches and loaves. If you leave six cookies and half a loaf it's not going to be believable."

"So, Oliver digs your deception?" Sean smirks at me.

"I'm not cheating or stealing ... I'm just making myself more appealing for one evening. He cooks all the time and I'm quite certain both he and his family think I lack in domestic skills—"

"Because you do." Alex laughs.

"Because I didn't waste my time in school taking frivolous classes like home ec."

"I think it's called family and consumer science now."

"Shut up, Sean." Alex and I both chime together.

"I didn't learn how to cook in school."

"I know, Alex, your mom taught you. My mom didn't have time to teach me when I was younger."

"That's why I'm here for you, Flower." Alex hugs me and takes off her apron. "I'm leaving you with the mess, that should make it more believable."

"Thanks, I owe you one ... for a change."

"True." Alex blows me a kiss as her and Sean leave.

I take my time cleaning up the kitchen and just as planned, Oliver walks in while I'm in the middle of doing dishes.

"Wow! Something smells delicious." He slips off his

boots and washes his hands in the hall bathroom.

"You're a mess." I grin, looking at his ripped jeans covered in dirt and his gray T-shirt that looks more like a deep charcoal.

"I am. We worked hard today." He kisses my cheek and grabs a cookie off the cooling rack. "Mmm ... so good."

"You like?"

"Yeah, why wouldn't I? They're amazing!"

I bite my lip to keep from grinning too big. Oliver presses his body to my back, sliding his hands over my hips and around to my front, fisting my skirt while drawing it up my legs.

"You need a shower, babe. You're all sweaty and dirty."

"Mmm ... maybe when you're done with these dishes you can wash me."

"Maybe you should think about rewarding the baker."

He kisses my neck and presses his erection into me even harder. "I don't think Sean would like that."

"What?" I grab the towel and turn around.

Oliver has already undressed me with his eyes and my body begins to feel naked under his hungry gaze. He kneels in front of me and slides his hands up my bare legs.

"What does this have to do with Sean?"

He pulls my panties down my legs while wetting his lips. I'm wet too, but I also want answers.

"Well, you said I should reward the baker, and the tone of your voice implied something naughty. I imagine Sean would be pretty pissed if I tried something like that with Alex." He starts to push my skirt up my legs.

I grab his hands. "Why do you think Alex is the baker?"

He laughs and kisses my hand, running his tongue up to my wrist. "Because she texted me to tell me I have shitty cookie sheets."

"Damn her!"

Oliver chuckles. "But I'll give you an E for effort."

I glare at him, but he continues to move up my legs. "Or instead of an E, I could give you an O." His mouth covers my sex and his tongue teases my clitoris.

"Oh God ..." I close my eyes and clench my fingers in his hair.

O's ARE SO MUCH BETTER than E's. If that makes me sound like a vowel snob, then so be it. I received my hard earned O in the kitchen, and Oliver received his in the shower. The cookies and banana bread were probably unnecessary. Lately Oliver has been coming home ready and eager to devour me with barely so much as a hello. I'm not complaining, but I wish he'd put some of that energy and love for me into himself.

He still hasn't mentioned or made an effort to deal with the room upstairs. I haven't brought it up either. As with everything, I'm trying to let him do it on his own time. Apparently my promise to move back in with him when he does deal with it, is not the incentive I'd hoped it would be. Disappointing? Very.

"We should get some dinner before we go into a sugar coma." Oliver suggests as we finish off the first loaf of banana bread.

"Well, I'm exhausted from baking all day..." I wink and grin "...so maybe we should go out for dinner."

"Indian?"

"You read my mind, Mr. Konrad."

"Grab your shoes. I'll go throw on a shirt." He kisses me then heads upstairs.

"Bye, Rosenberg. Be a good boy for Mommy." I kiss him and shove my feet into my pink Nikes.

The doorbell rings just as I sling my purse over my shoulder.

I open the door to a man and a woman, maybe in their mid-fifties, staring at me with inscrutable faces. She smooths her shoulder-length auburn hair like it's a nervous habit. His forehead below his peppered buzz cut wrinkles with what can only be confusion.

"Can I help you?"

They look at each other and then back at me. "Does Oliver Konrad live here?" he asks.

"Yes. He's upstairs. Can I tell him who's here to see him?"

"What the hell are you doing here?"

My body tenses and an eerie tingle runs along my spine from the iciness of Oliver's voice.

"We just want to talk, Oliver," the woman says with a soft shaky voice.

"I don't have anything to say."

"We do," the man replies.

It seems improbable that this could feel any more awkward.

"You must be Vivian?"

I look at the woman and nod as Oliver wraps a possessive arm around me. "You'll have to excuse me. I'm at a disadvantage here."

"Sorry, Jackie told me about you. She said you and Oliver are really happy together."

"Um, yes, we are." If Oliver's mom told this lady about us, I assume she's a relative or family friend.

"I'm Lily and this is my husband, Doug. We're Caroline's parents."

Oliver's grip on me intensifies. I'm not sure if he's trying to hold me or himself together.

"Oh, wow, I thought you lived in Portland."

"We do. We flew out here to talk to Oliver."

I look up at Oliver. His jaw pulses as he keeps his death glare on them.

"Well, come in." I step aside, feeling a slight resistance from Oliver's body against mine.

"Thank you." They make their way to the living room.

"I'll be over..." I motion with my head in the direction of Alex's "...if you need me."

"I think it would be best for you to stay," Doug calls from the couch. "This now involves you too."

Oliver shakes his head and nudges me toward the door.

"Maybe I should stay, then?"

"No."

"Oli—"

"There's nothing they have to say that you need to hear."

"We need you to come back to Portland." Doug's voice makes Oliver's body shake with anger.

"I think I'm staying," I whisper and walk past Oliver to sit on the love seat adjacent to the couch where Doug and Lily sit.

Oliver lumbers into the room and sits next to me. He's seething with rage and I'm sure my decision to stay isn't helping the situation. He takes my hand. I squeeze it tight hoping what little strength I have left after Doug's comment will transfer to Oliver. I have this sick feeling he's going to need it more than me.

"Caroline has been asking about you." Doug continues. "Lily and I tried to explain that you've filed for divorce, but she's in denial. Then we told her that you moved back here and since then she's tried to commit suicide again. She said if she loses you too, then she has nothing to live for."

I wish I could read Oliver's mind. We've never discussed his feelings for Caroline. What does hearing this do to him? I remember the night he shattered his phone and now I wonder if it was a call about Caroline that set him off.

"You do realize she'll probably never see the outside of that facility again, right?"

"Yes, we know it's a long shot, Oliver, but we're her parents and you're her—"

"Nothing. I'm her nothing. Husband, only by law, but that won't be for long."

Doug nods and Lily wipes a few tears. "Before you left they had started to reduce her meds. The doctors were optimistic that she might make a recovery given enough time. Now she's..." Doug's eyes start to fill with tears "...she's a shell, an empty vessel and ... we just want our daughter back."

Oliver releases my hand then rests his elbows on his knees with his head bowed into his hands. "I don't know what this has to do with me."

"She needs you!" Lily's kept emotions burst with a desperate plea.

Doug hugs her to him and strokes her back. "We think she'll come back around, at least to the daughter we recognize, if you're there. If she thinks you haven't abandoned her, she might find the will to do the therapy again, and start interacting with others. She might find ... the will to live."

"I can't ... I ... won't."

"Oliver, please! Once she's doing better we'll be able to explain to her that your marriage is over and she'll be better equipped to handle it if you give her some sort of closure instead of just abandoning her. Can't you do this for her? For us? For ... Melanie?"

I feel Oliver's rage a split second before it erupts. "Get the fuck out of here! Don't you dare ask me to help Caroline for my dead daughter's sake! She suffocated her with a pillow! Do you get that? A two month-old baby, killed by her own mother! Why in God's name would I try to help Caroline now if I didn't want to help her then?"

Oliver's words are a brutal slap to Doug and Lily. Their faces contort into painful grimaces.

Oliver stands and paces the floor with his hands on his hips. "That day ... when I found her ... my biggest regret was calling 9-1-1. You don't know how bad I wanted to take the knife that was in her bloodied, limp hand and shove it into her ruthless heart."

Lily sobs as Doug helps her to her feet. He opens the front door and turns. "I don't even recognize you, Oliver. You're not the loving man our Caroline married." Doug's gaze shifts to me. "Good luck, Vivian. You're going to need it."

Oliver

Vivian sits idle in the chair, holding Rosenberg. I don't understand why she's still here. I just admitted the one thing I never imagined admitting—I wanted Caroline to die.

But it's more than that. I didn't want to stand by and watch her bleed out. I wanted to *kill* her.

She stands. Here it comes, the goodbye that will send me spiraling into the personal hell from which I had just started to emerge. I press my palm to my chest to keep my heart from leaping out after her; it knows she's the rhythm to which it beats.

I close my eyes as she approaches the door where I stand. Of all the mental images I will forever have of Vivian, her walking out my door ... out of my life, cannot be one of them.

Her hand on my cheek, so gentle, tears me apart. "I'm taking Rosenberg out to go potty. Then we'll go eat. Okay, babe?"

I open my tear-filled eyes and suck in a shaky breath so desperate my lungs have a physical flashback to the day I was born.

She wipes her thumb under my eye as her lips curl into a tight, painful smile.

"Vivian—" I try to swallow back my emotions.

"Oli..." she tilts her head to the side "...no take backs. Remember?"

I'm paralyzed by her love. I know if I move I'll wake from this dream, so I stand still—completely still—and pray this moment lasts forever.

"Come on, Rosenberg." Her voice fades as she walks outside.

I stop the chanting in my brain. It's always the same one. *You don't deserve her. You don't deserve her ...*

And I replace it with two words repeating over and over. *Thank you! Thank you ...*

"Ready, babe?" She sets Rosenberg down and grabs her purse.

I can't stop staring at her. It's the craziest thing. Part of me feels like I'm seeing her for the first time. The other part feels like I've known her my whole life—that part I call my heart.

"I'm ready." I hold out my hand, and as certain as my morning sun stealing the darkness, she takes it.

***

"OLI?" Her angelic voice brings me out of my sleep. I kiss the top of her head that rests on my chest. "I think you should go to Portland."

I scoot over and turn on the lamp. We both sit up facing each other.

"Why would you say that?"

She looks down and traces the pattern of the sheet with her finger. "I think you need closure."

"I need my divorce to be finalized."

She looks at me. "It's more than that."

"It's not." I shut the light off and flop back down with my arm over my eyes.

She reaches over me and turns the light back on. "Yes, it is. Oli, you lost a child, and whether you want to believe it or not, you lost your wife that same day."

"I—" She puts her finger over my mouth.

"Not because you wanted her to die, because in that moment the Caroline you married was lost forever. I know you, Oli. You would not have married her if you didn't love her. And when people lose the ones they love, it hurts. You can't let go of the pain until you let yourself feel it first. I know it's awful and unimaginable, but you have to acknowledge it. You have to *feel* it. I don't think you can do that here, thousands of miles, clear across the country from Caroline, and the reminders ... the memories of Melanie."

I sigh, resting my hand on her leg. "If I go. Where will that leave us?"

She leans down and kisses me, her lips so soft, her touch so achingly familiar. "Hopelessly in love and desperately missing each other."

I grin. "I already miss you." I roll her over and take her body like it's mine to touch, mine to love, mine forever.

CHAPTER TWENTY-SIX
MILES APART

Vivian

Three days ago I told Oliver to go to Portland. He talked it over with his family and they agree it's what he needs to do. Two days ago he made the decision to go. Yesterday I broke down in Alex's arms and told her I regretted telling him to go. Today he's leaving.

"I want you to move in."

I laugh as I towel dry my hair. "You're leaving today. I don't think it matters now."

Oli zips his suitcase and holds out his hand. He leads me down the hallway, stopping in front of *the* door.

"Chance will come by next week and put on the new door."

My brow furrows. "What are you talk—"

Oliver opens the door.

Yellow.

The walls are yellow with charcoal and white-striped curtains. There's a desk against one wall, bookshelves on the opposite wall, and my bed in the middle with a new floral quilt and ... pillows, lots of decor pillows.

"Oli..." I step in the room and turn in a slow circle "... when did you ... I can't believe ..."

He pulls me into his arms and smiles down at me. "I don't know how long I'll be in Portland, but I do know that being so far away from you is going to feel like my heart is living outside of my body. The one thing that will get me through it is knowing that you're here in *our* house waiting for me to come home."

He brushes his lips over my falling tears. "Will you be here?"

Don't go!

"Yes, I'll be here." I hug him, clinging to this man I love with all my being, and dying a little inside.

"I expect great things from this room." He showers my nose and cheeks with kisses like he's trying to kiss all of my freckles. "Lots of hours studying, straight A assignments, a few naughty videos that you'll send me ..."

"Mr. Konrad, I would never!"

He squeezes my ass. "I think you would and I hope ... *really* hope you will."

"We should go."

Oliver glances at his watch. "I'm afraid you're right."

***

OLIVER DRIVES us to Logan International. I've had a slow building of emotions threatening to ruin our goodbye.

Hold it together. Hold it together.

He gets his suitcases out of the trunk and hands me his keys with a smirk.

"I know, don't wreck it." I hold out my hand.

"I was going to say don't kill yourself or anyone else."

"Ha ha."

He sets the keys in my hand then closes his hand around mine. Our eyes meet. "I'm going to try and get back to you as soon as I can."

I nod because I can't speak. He holds my face in his hands and kisses me. Our tongues brush together as our lips move in sync. One last embrace follows our long kiss goodbye.

Hold it together. Hold it together.

"I'll talk to you soon."

I nod, holding my breath, strangled by my emotions.

We share one last sad smile before he turns and walks toward the doors. I get in the driver's seat and start the car. My stomach churns with nausea and my heart feels heavy and tight like it's suffocating. I place my hands on the top of the steering wheel, rest my forehead on them, and I cry. My door opens and I suck in a startled breath, looking up.

Oliver. He shakes his head and bends down pulling me into his arms. I sob. It's ugly and painful, but I can't hold it in any longer.

"Let it go, my love, let it go," he whispers in my ear, stroking my hair.

"It h-hurts s-so bad."

"Shh ... I know it does. I feel it too."

He doesn't rush me like he has a plane to catch, and he even ignores the occasional horn that honks behind us. Oliver's love is patient and it makes his departure even harder to handle.

He wipes my tears as I sniffle. "Don't hide your feelings from me, not ever. Okay?"

"O-k-kay." I grab a tissue out of my purse and wipe my nose. "Why'd you c-come back."

He smiles. "Because I had this feeling you needed one last hug."

My lips curl into a tight, painful smile. His words manage to wring a few more tears out of my puffy, red eyes.

"Vivian, I love you more than you could ever imagine in a million lifetimes. Don't ever forget that, okay?"

"K ... I love you too, Oli."

"More than Boston Kreme?"

"Yes." I laugh and kiss him.

"More than my mom's cobbler?"

"Yes." Another kiss.

"More than Rosenberg?"

"You're pushing it, buddy."

"There's my girl. Sweet and sassy, just like I like her." He kisses my forehead then stands. "Say bye to the fur ball for me."

I roll my eyes as he shuts the door. He places his hand flat on the window and I do the same. One last, sad smile. I see the unshed tears glisten in his eyes right as he turns and walks away.

"Bye, Oli." I choke out as I look in the rearview mirror and watch him disappear through the glass doors.

OLIVER NEVER INDICATED how long he might be in Portland and I never asked. I knew it would just be a guess on his part, and I didn't want to set myself up for disappointment if it took longer. Measuring the time in weeks is probably unrealistic, months is what I imagine, and anything beyond that is too painful to think about right now.

I know Alex is probably waiting for me. We're supposed to meet with a band that may play at their reception. But I need a few minutes alone to ... I don't know—miss Oliver some more.

"Rosenberg," I call, opening the door. Slipping off my shoes, I look up. "What's ... going on?" My parents are here and so is Alex, Sean, and Maggie. "Is this an intervention?"

"More like a prevention." My mom hugs me.

"Yeah, Oliver called yesterday and asked if we could all plan on being here for you after he left today." Alex grabs my hand and gives me the familiar sad smile that's been going around today. "I guess he didn't want you hiding in the closet, curled up on the floor wearing his T-shirt with your nose nestled into an old sweatshirt that smells like him."

Everyone laughs at Alex's comment.

"I don't think you need to worry about that." I laugh.

They should definitely worry about that. It's number three on my Oliver-left-me-a basket-case list—right after washing my hair with his shampoo and dry humping the sheets on his side of the bed.

"Good to know, but we're still taking you out on the town for the day," Maggie says.

"Out on the town?"

"Yes. Oliver won't be in Portland for almost eight hours so while you're waiting for his call we're heading out to see the best of Boston like a bunch of tourists."

"The Tea Party museum and Freedom Trail," my dad says.

"Mike's cannoli and duck boats," Sean chimes in too.

"Maybe we'll head to Newbury Street for some school shopping, compliments of my parents." Alex gives me a wicked grin and holds up a *black* American Express card.

"I don't know ... I start school tomorrow and I don't really feel like—"

"We're under strict orders from Oliver ... Staying here is not an option, even if we have to drag you along." Sean winks, giving me a wicked grin. We fight like siblings most of the time. I'm sure he'd love nothing more than to drag me around Boston by my hair.

"Fine."

EXHAUSTED. That's the only word for my mental and physical state. As promised, we did the whole tourist thing and took in as much of Boston as we could in one day. Had I not been thinking about Oliver the whole time it would have been a great day. Although I've lived here for over two years, I've never taken in all of Boston and its rich history. We finished off our day at Oliver's parents' house for dinner. Being with them made me feel closer to him. It was bitter sweet too. I'd imagined we'd be together when our parents met for the first time. They seemed to get along well and our moms even exchanged e-mail addresses and phone numbers to keep in touch, more like keep tabs on their kids.

The house is lonely and quiet without Oli. I'm grateful Rosenberg is here to keep me company. I'm not on the closet floor, but I am wearing Oli's T-shirt, snuggling with Rosenberg on Oli's side of the bed waiting for him to call. Tomorrow will be my first day of college. I hope it's the distraction I need from Oliver and not the other way around.

My phone vibrates and I answer it with a pathetic teenage girl eagerness.

"Oli?"

"Hey, sexy."

My whole body melts into the sheets as I sigh from the sound of his voice.

"Just got off the plane and I'm waiting for my luggage. How was your day? Anything exciting happen?"

"Nope. After I dropped you off, I came home and curled up in a ball on the closet floor, wrapped in your clothes, and sobbed until I fell asleep. In fact, I just woke up."

"What? You mean nobody—"

"Yes, babe. I'm officially an expert on all things Boston. I have ten bags of clothes from the most expensive stores on Newbury Street, guaranteeing that I'll be the best-dressed freshman on campus tomorrow; that is if I can fit into them after the meal your mom made for everyone tonight."

"I just didn't want you—"

"Oli?"

"Yes?"

"Thank you. It was the most considerate thing anyone has ever done for me."

"I love you."

"I love you too. If it's even possible, I think I love you more now than I did this morning."

"I miss you. It's taking everything I have to not march over to the ticket counter and buy a ticket back home to you and just say to hell with the rest of this."

"You're going to make me cry again so just stop."

"Sorry."

"So, I never asked. Where are you staying while you're there?"

He sighs. "Since I have no idea how long I'll be here, I'm staying with Caroline's parents for now."

"Oh ... is that ... I mean, a good idea? Can you handle being around them all the time?"

"They both work, so it will only be in the evenings and weekends."

A twinge of something hits me. Jealousy would be ridiculous; it's not exactly that. It feels a little like insecurity. Maybe it's just uncertainty. I'm uncertain of how I feel about Oliver immersing himself in his past. And at this moment, just for tonight, I don't want to talk about it.

"Rosenberg's claimed your side of the bed already."

"Is that so? Well, that fur ball hadn't better get too comfortable. I'm not sharing you with anyone when I get home."

"That is ... if you can tear me away from my love affair with higher education."

Oliver chuckles. "You're such a geek. A sexy geek, but geek nonetheless."

"You're just jealous that I've always loved school, unlike some kids who get so nervous they wet their pants on the school bus." I bite my lip to keep from laughing.

"Low blow. I see my mom has been running her mouth. For the record, I was six, over-hydrated, and the bus driver hit a huge pothole."

I let out my giggles. "What about your first day of Karate? Your mom said the kid next to you slipped on the puddle you made and knocked out his front tooth when his face met the stack of boards behind you."

"That's it! You're banned from seeing my mom ever again."

"Too late. She's already put me on the Saturday night dinner VIP list."

"That's ... just ... great." His voice is muffled and I can envision him rubbing his hand over his face in frustration. "My luggage is here, and it's later there so you'd better get some rest before your big day."

"You're right, babe. We can finish discussing your urinary incontinence issues later."

"No. That subject is closed. Locked. Never to be discussed again."

I laugh some more. "I like hearing about young Oliver. It takes the sting out of missing you so desperately."

"If you miss me, call me. We can even video chat, but for God's sake … don't talk to my mom about me."

"Oli?"

"Yes?"

"I love you and thank you for today."

"You're welcome. I love you too. Play nice tomorrow."

I grin. "I will."

I CAN'T SLEEP. Rosenberg's snoring, I miss Oli, and I'm worried my alarm won't work which would make me late for my first day of classes. After a long shower, drying my unruly hair, and putting on my new, holy-crap-these-are-expensive True Religion jeans and a sleeveless Guess T-shirt, I dab on a little makeup and whip up some brain food. Oli would be proud. I have two eggs on whole grain toast and fresh squeezed orange juice.

I love my new bag filled with all my favorite things: razor-sharp pencils, spiral notebooks, crisp folders, and a new iPad mini from Jackie and Hugh. A kiss to Rosenberg, a deep breath, and I open the door to my new adventure.

"Say cheese, Flower!" Alex, still in her bathrobe, is at the bottom of the front steps taking picture after picture.

"What are you doing?"

"Getting pictures of my girl on her first day of college."

"Why aren't you dressed?"

"Puh-lease. Only freshman nerd girls schedule eight o'clock classes."

I stick out my tongue. "Whatever."

"Do you have apples for your professors?"

I keep walking and flip her the bird.

"Love you too, Flower. Oh! And don't touch John Harvard's shoe, or any other part for that matter."

"Yeah, yeah ... I know what happens at night."

Tourists love to have their picture taken next to the John Harvard statue. His left shoe is worn and shiny from so many people touching and rubbing it for good luck. Students walking by cringe and laugh because they know what happens at night: Students, often times drunk, piss all over it. Kai and Sean have done it ... more than once, and my guess is Alex has too.

As I walk to campus via the shady tree-framed streets and cobblestone paths, I feel the shift happening in the direction it needs to go. School takes my mind off Oli, well ... more like easing the pain of missing him. I'm certain for as long as I live Oli will always be on my mind.

I RECEIVE four texts from Oli today:

How's it going, smarty pants?

What are you wearing? Hope it's sexy. Feel free to lie to me if it's not.

Maybe avoid the John Harvard statue.

I think we should have sex in the stacks when I get home.

Okay, so apparently another tradition or rite of passage besides defacing John Harvard is having sex in the stacks at Harvard's Widener Library. Yeah, I don't see Miss Perfect Attendance/Student Body President joining that elite group of students. But now I'm wondering if Oli is part of that group.

Me: *Almost home, missed Rosenberg … and you, of course. No to sex in the stacks. Might piss on John Harvard. I mean … does any human really deserve to be idolized to the point of having a statue made of them?*
Oliver: *Won't even address you missing the mutt more than me. I will change your mind about sex in the stacks. And if you're going to piss on John, take the mutt with you. He'll show you how it's done. BTW, as your attorney, I really should not condone such behavior.*
Me: *My ATTORNEY? Being in Portland has already helped you. Shall I shine your shoes and press your shirts for your return? No need to take Rosenberg. I have a Go Girl. It's a firm NO for the stacks, no mind changing.*
Oliver: *No comment. Go Girl? And there will be something firm for you in the stacks when I get home, but it won't be a NO.*
Me: *Home.*
Oliver: *…*

I'm not sure what his ellipsis means. I unlock the door and start to say Rosenberg's name when my breath catches in my lungs and my words are stolen. The whole lower level is filled with bouquets of white and "crimson" roses. And before I can even move, I hear the click of a camera.

"Alex!" She grins and takes more pictures of me.

"Did you—"

"No, no ... I'm just capturing the moment. It's all Oliver."

Setting my bag down, I pull one of the roses from a vase and smell it.

Click. Click. Click.

"How did you get in here?"

"I have a key and I keep it under our entry planter with ours. Oliver suggested it. I understand why I needed the key, but his suggestion to keep it under our planter is weird."

I grin. Alex hasn't heard that story yet.

My phone vibrates. It's Oliver and he's sent me a picture with a message.

Oliver: *My new screen shot for my phone.*

The picture is of me smelling the rose. The one Alex just took.

"You're sending pictures to Oliver?"

She snaps a few more of me. "Yep. That's what I've been hired to do."

Me: *Why are you having Alex paparazzi my every move?*
Oliver: *Missing your touch is almost unbearable. Missing every-thing else too, would kill me. Love you.*
Me: *Tears ... love you more!*
Oliver: *Nice try, but not possible. Call me later when you're alone.*
Me: *O ... kay?!*

"How were your classes? Any cute guys?" Alex flops back on the couch and twirls her hair around her finger.

"Last I heard, you're engaged and I'm ..." I gesture to the embarrassingly romantic display of roses surrounding us.

"I didn't ask if you scored us dates for the weekend, I asked if there were any cute guys in your class. You know ... on the likely chance that the lecture gets boring, you can strip the hot guy sitting in front of you with your eyes and dirty mind."

I toss the rose I grabbed earlier at her. "For starters, there is no one sitting in front of me. I have to sit in the front row for my recorder to pick up everything clearly. And you've seen Oli, he's..." I sigh "...perfect."

"I love that your definition of perfect is a guy much older than you with a tainted past and a wife in the looney bin."

"I feel bad for her." I sit on the floor next to Alex with my legs crisscrossed. "Does that make *me* crazy?"

"You feel bad because of what she did or where she's at?"

"Both. She didn't choose to lose her sanity. Can you imagine what it would be like to not have control over your thoughts or to not be able to distinguish reality from illusions? She's sick, really sick and ..."

"Oliver left her?"

I nod. "The problem is even if I can't imagine it, I understand why she did what she did. I also understand why Oliver despises her so much, but it makes me wonder where couples draw that line. I mean ... when you and Sean get married will you vow to love each other through sickness and health?"

"No, absolutely not. Our vows are going to be more like the reading of a hypothetical prenup. 'I promise to love you in times of acute, non-antibiotic resistant illness and health as long as you don't try to pass it off as a beer gut and man boobs.' His will be similar except instead of beer gut and man boobs it will read saggy tits and bingo wings."

"AKA, you too are in love with a damaged man who loves you something fierce?"

"Basically."

CHAPTER TWENTY-SEVEN
INSANITY

Oliver

I never imagined returning to Portland. Then again, I never imagined moving back to Boston. When Caroline and I moved here, I fell in love with everything: the people, the view, the mountains, and the less-than-two-hour drive to the beautiful Pacific coast. We had a great house, I had a promising job, and we were getting ready to start our family —our future.

Now the view isn't so spectacular, and I think I prefer Boston Harbor to the Pacific coastal beaches. The city feels too congested, and I don't recognize the people. Since I've met Vivian, everything outside of her blindingly beautiful aura seems dull and boring.

I went to see Caroline today. Mental hospitals have to be the epitome of boring. If a patient's not truly insane going in, they will be before too long. It's fairly quiet except for the occasional outburst that's dealt with by quick hands and a syringe filled with a magical sleep-it-off-until-you're-ready-to-knock-this-shit-off potion. Every activity is planned with military regimen. There's a short window of visiting hours, especially for Caroline, and so today there weren't any breakthroughs, at least while I was there. She was heavily sedated, coming in and out of sleep for the first half hour. Then they brought in her dinner with plastic silverware, customary for suicidal patients. She didn't eat and she didn't speak—not one word. I didn't say anything either. I went to show her I'm here, but my presence didn't seem to encourage her. I left feeling angry and regretting this trip after only one day.

An hour ago, a nurse called and said Caroline ate all her dinner after I left when the nurse told her I'd come back tomorrow, but only if she ate. Apparently, she hasn't eaten in three days, so now I'm the saintly miracle worker. Fucking fabulous. Whatever, eat, taper off your meds, admit you fucked up, and face the consequences. Then accept we're over and let me get the hell away from you.

The anger I have inside is brutal. For a while I thought it was fading, but seeing her today I realized it was just time and distance buffering my raw emotions. I didn't recognize her and not just because she looks horrid from the meds, lack of sun, and ripping out half of her own hair. It was her eyes. There's no life in them. It's as if her body is a vessel with a heartbeat, but her soul is gone. I think that's what happens when you take someone's life. Maybe that's what happens *before* you take their life. Everything good in you has to leave, and then you're nothing but a human machine acting without emotion. At best, she'll get rehabilitated enough to not want to kill herself or anyone else, but I don't believe she'll ever be able to love or have genuine emotions for another human ever again.

I'm staying in Doug and Lily's walkout basement. One of the reasons I agreed to stay here is because there's a separate kitchen and bathroom so I can avoid them for the most part. They, of course, were elated about the nurse's call and offered one too many I-told-you-so looks for my taste. So now I'm waiting with impatient frustration for Vivian to call me. I'm already having withdrawals from her and I need to hear her soft voice filled with sexy seduction that makes me hard every time she says the words *Oli* or *babe*.

Me: *Are you alone yet?*

I wait a few minutes and just as I'm ready to send another message my phone chimes.

"You're killing me."

"Miss you too, babe."

And ... I'm hard.

"So how was your first day?"

"Amazing. Except I pressed pause instead of play on my recorder during my math class."

"You recorded a math class?"

"No. Aren't you listening? I *tried* to, but I didn't get it recorded."

I chuckle. "That's what I meant. You *tried* to record a math class?"

"Yes, *Alex!* I record all my classes," she says with mock annoyance.

"When do you have time to listen to them all again?"

"Duh ... while I'm sleeping."

"What are you wearing?"

"What?"

"You had an amazing day, you've reconfirmed your nerd girl status, enough pleasantries, now what are you wearing?"

"Your T-shirt."

"Hmm ... in the back of the closet are my dress shirts. Put one on then pull your hair up, get your black framed glasses and then bring your laptop to your bed and we'll Skype."

"Why—"

"Just do it."

"Um ... okay."

I slip off my pants and shirt and lie back on my bed. A few minutes later her live picture appears on my screen. With one look I'm hard as a brick and I can tell this won't last long.

Her grin is bright and huge. "I want to kiss the screen."

"Me too. Unbutton the shirt."

She scoots her computer off her lap onto the bed between her spread legs. *Perfect!* Her lips part and her tongue eases out to wet them as she works the last button. Alluring eyes look up at the screen through sexy glasses and a few strands of her hair hang down from the messy pile on top of her head. "Like this?"

I slide my hand down my briefs and fist my erection. Her eyes follow my hand then she looks back up in wide-eyed surprise.

"Let me see your breasts."

She glances back down at the screen. I slide the front of my briefs down so she has a better view. I can see her breaths coming quicker, almost feel her nipples hardening, and I can definitely taste the slick sweetness between her legs. Vivian pulls the sides of my shirt back with slight hesitation until her perky breasts with pebbled nipples are fully exposed.

I swallow and wet my lips while my hand slides along my erection. "Vivian, how do you like me to touch you?"

She drops her chin to her chest and stares at herself. Then bright emeralds peer at me over black frames. I have to slow down my hand. The vision before me is college professor porn.

Vivian moves her hand to her stomach then eases it up to her breast like she's touching herself for the first time. She looks down and squeezes it while drawing her thumb down over her nipple. Okay, I thought this was a good idea, but I was wrong. I want to crawl through the screen and devour her. This sucks ... really, really sucks.

Her other hand does the same thing and when I see her eyelids close and fight to open again, I squeeze my hand and moan in both agony and pleasure. She bends her knees and spreads her legs wide.

My hand speeds up.

"See anything you like, Mr. Konrad?"

"Fuck, Vivian!"

"I miss your lips *here*." She slides her hand down her stomach and between her legs. "Mmm ..." She moans and closes her eyes.

I'm so close.

"And I miss your tongue *here*." She presses two fingers to her clitoris and moves them in slow circles. "Oh, Oli ..." Each word is a drawn-out pant.

I slow down again and try to hold off, but it's killing me. I close my eyes to let the tension ease a bit, but her soft pants and whimpers don't allow much of a reprieve.

"Oli, don't stop."

I open my eyes to Vivian with one hand on her breast squeezing and tugging at her nipple and her other hand still low on her stomach. Her two fingers are alternately pulsing in rapid succession.

"Ol-Oli … oh God … Oliver!" she yells my name as her head falls back and her knees collapse together.

It only takes a couple more pumps before I release—stomach muscles tensing, teeth digging into my lower lip.

God, I love technology even if I hate missing her.

THE DAYS HAVE BLURRED into weeks and I'm starting to wonder if time exists. Is anything changing or am I stuck in limbo where Vivian is busy with school and working a few hours a week at The Green Pot while I'm trying, with little success, to get Caroline to … what? That's just it. I don't have a damn clue. She may never get better. I think Doug and Lily are grasping for something that's just an illusion—wishful thinking, but not reality.

I need to work, but not just for the money. I need to feel like I'm making a contribution and doing something more than watching Caroline eat dinner every night while chanting she loves me. Yes, that's the new development. She loves me. It's ridiculous, unbelievable, but mostly pathetic. Since I've been here those are the only three words she's said to me. I think it's the meds, but who knows and who really cares? Not me.

Her doctor is going to adjust her meds and get her back in therapy now that she's showing improvement and isn't suicidal any more. I'm not a doctor, but where he's "seeing improvement" is beyond me. Improvement would be moving past her half-ass suicide attempts and just getting the job done. There's no need for her to be using up air that other people could make better use of. *Obviously the monster in me is still alive.*

Visiting Sturgeon, Wallace, and Faye, the law firm I

used to work at, was not on my Portland to-do list. Unfortunately, plans have changed. Valerie Wallace is due with twins next month and the other partners and myself were planning on absorbing her work load while she takes maternity leave. I'm sure my leaving has made the load that much heavier for Sturgeon and Faye.

"Oh my gosh! Oliver!" Samantha, the receptionist, calls as I walk into their office. She waddles in her tight skirt and heels to give me a hug. She turned fifty this past spring, but between her time in the tanning bed and years of smoking she doesn't look a day over seventy.

"Hey there, Samantha."

"What are you doing here?"

"I was hoping to talk with Brice. Does he still mark off an extra half hour after lunch for a nap?"

"Oh, honey ... you know that's just hearsay."

I laugh. "No, it's *I've seen*, not hearsay. I've walked into his office on more than one occasion and seen him hunched over, drooling on his tie."

"Well, Cindy said he has sleep apnea so I'm sure he's just exhausted by one."

I glance at my watch. "So are you stalling or are you going to let me sneak in on him?"

She shoos me toward the hall. "Have at it, but if he asks, I wasn't at my desk when you arrived."

"Deal."

Brice Sturgeon is third-generation law school. His grandfather practiced until he was eighty-two, but his dad took early retirement at sixty-three after a triple bypass. Brice and his twin sister, Valerie Wallace, took over the family practice seven years ago and brought their friend from UCLA law school, Mitchell Faye, in with them.

"Knock, knock, wipe your drool and stash your porn."

"Oliver Konrad, what the hell are you doing in town?" Brice shoves his half-eaten sandwich back in its sack, stands while wiping his mouth, and offers his hand.

I shake his hand and take a seat opposite him. "Wish I could say sightseeing, but unfortunately that's not the case."

I look around his office. "You found another Ivy League sucker like myself to come work for you?"

Brice, Valerie, and Mitchell never tried to hide the fact that they hired me based on my Harvard degree. Brice said my diploma would look good on the wall and lend confidence to potential new clients. I just needed a job and an established client base. We were a good match at the time.

"Nah, preppy boys like yourself don't like to navigate off the East Coast. Most of your breed are just a bunch of mama's boys with a trust fund."

"Well I haven't been notified about mine. That's why I'm here."

"Oh?"

"I'm in town for a while. Unfortunately, I think it's going to be longer than I originally expected. Caroline's parents want me to stay here until she gets ... better, of sorts."

"Better? You do realize—"

I hold up my hand. "You don't have to tell me. I'm fully aware of her chances of ever getting out of there or having anything resembling a normal life. I'm doing this for Doug and Lily and ... I guess my own closure or something." I rub my hands over my face. "I don't know."

"So you need a job?"

"Not a job. I'm not staying. Just work. I need something to keep me from going crazy myself and some income until my magic trust fund becomes available wouldn't be bad either."

Brice grins and tosses a whole stack of files on the desk in front of me. "Have at it. Valerie's here maybe two hours a day before she has to go home and elevate her swollen feet. As you know, she has a lot of female clients that would bend over backwards to work with you—figuratively and literally."

I grab one of the files and open it. "I'll start on these next Monday if that works. I need to go back home and pack up my stuffy suits and shiny shoes."

"Yeah, I heard a rumor you've been helping your brother plant shit."

I stand. "Yes, that's his business tagline. 'We plant shit.'"

Brice pulls out his sandwich and props his feet up on the desk.

"Looking forward to it, preppy."

I shake my head. "See you Monday."

***

As EXPECTED my news isn't going over well with Doug and Lily.

"You can't leave. She's just started to come around again," Lily says.

"It's just for the weekend. I'll tell her I'm leaving for two days and that I'll be back."

I start down the stairs, tired of having this argument with them.

"She won't understand," Doug calls after me.

"Then she probably won't notice that I'm gone for two flipping days!"

Every day I wonder what I'm doing. I found out after Caroline was admitted that Lily has struggled with depression most of her adult life and even takes medication for it.

The genetic factor was there. *That* would have been helpful to know when I married my pregnant wife. So naturally Lily is extra sensitive about ... *everything*. I not only have to baby step my way around Caroline, I have to with Lily as well. I hope I can accomplish whatever the hell it is I'm supposed to be accomplishing here and get out before I lose it with one or the other.

I contemplate calling my parents and letting them know I'll be coming home this weekend, but I want to surprise Vivian, and to be honest, my mom is not to be trusted. A poor trait for a psychiatrist, but I think in her professional life she abides by her oath and keeps information in strict confidentiality. Maybe I should hire her and tell her my childhood secrets, then I could sue her for breach of confidentiality every time she tells Vivian about the weak bladder I had as a child.

I'm considering calling Alex. She's very protective of Vivian, and she and I have had a few stern words since the news of Caroline came out, but Alex has been great about sending me photos of Vivian and making sure all of my surprises are in fact, a surprise. I think I've managed to beg, steal, and crawl my way back onto her good side.

"Make it quick. I'm on my way to class."

"Alex, I need a favor."

"Big surprise. What now?"

"I'm coming home this weekend—"

"Oh my gosh! Vivian is going to freak out. She's been missing you so much and—"

"Alex!"

"Yes?"

"I coming home *just* for the weekend. I'll be flying back out here Sunday afternoon."

"Oh ... that sucks."

"Tell me about it. Anyway, you're the only one who knows I'm coming home and I'd like it to stay that way. But I need you to make sure she's home Friday night. It will ruin the surprise part of my visit if I have to hunt her down when I get home."

"That shouldn't be a problem. She doesn't go anywhere except to work with Maggie on Saturdays. I'm talking total nerd girl. She studies *all* the time. She got her first B the other day and ate a dozen Boston Kreme doughnuts ... in one sitting."

I laugh. "She told me about the B, but not the doughnuts."

"Of course she didn't." Alex chuckles.

"I'll let you go. Thanks a million. I really do appreciate all you've done."

"You know I do it for Flower."

"I know, she's lucky to have you. Bye, Alex."

CHAPTER TWENTY-EIGHT
SURPRISE

Vivian

I LOVE SCHOOL. If money weren't an issue, I'd make a career of it. And right now without it, I'd fall apart missing Oliver so much. We text and talk on the phone everyday and on the weekends we have Skype-X—sex via Skype. Oliver has tried to engage me in it during the week, but he's apparently forgotten the demands of college. It's also possible that he was a student like Alex or Sean, here for the degree and not necessarily the knowledge.

I've made some friends, good ones, the kind who sit in the front row and record all the lectures. A few of them have been asking me to join them for open mic night at one of the local pubs. I've graciously declined until today. Weekends are lonely for me, even with all the studying I do. There's too much time to miss Oliver, especially living in his house and sleeping in his bed. So I've accepted their invite and I plan to drink too much wine, piss on Johnny H. on my way home, then drunk dial Oliver to see if he wants to get naked on Skype with me.

It will take more than a few drinks to get me up on stage. Oliver ruined karaoke for me since the Katy Perry-donkey-in-labor comment. It was harsh, especially considering how much I love to sing. I'll get over it … eventually.

"Flower?"

"Upstairs," I call from the bathroom, contemplating wearing my hair up or down.

"Whoa, look at you! Hot date?"

I grin pulling out my hair clips, opting to wear it down. "Hardly. You'll be so proud of me. I'm going out with some friends tonight for open mic night."

Alex deflates. "You are?"

"Yep." I apply some lip gloss and rub my lips together.

"I don't think that's such a good idea."

"What? You've been telling me for weeks to get my ass out of here and have some fun … to 'let my hair down.' Look…" I point to my hair "…hair down, and I'm going out."

"Sean's coming over and I'm making dinner, then we're going to watch a movie. I was hoping you'd join us."

Raising a brow, I smirk. "You were?"

"Yes, of course."

"Hmm, karaoke with my new single friends or third-wheel dinner and a movie with my friend and her fiancé, which will no doubt end in you two making out in front of me through the whole movie? No offense, but I'm going out."

"What can I do to make you stay?"

"What is your deal? Is there a bomb threat I don't know about?"

"No."

"Have you had a premonition about tonight?"

"Not exactly." She squints and purses her lips.

"Then I'm going out and there's nothing you can do to stop me."

I grab my black heels.

"I can't believe you're wearing that."

I look down at my fitted, red strapless dress that ends just above my knees. "Why? Does it look bad?"

"No, you look like a freaking model. I was surprised when you bought it, since it shows part of your back."

I turn and look at my back in the mirror. The upper branches reaching toward my shoulders with red and pink buds are visible even with my hair down. I shrug. "I don't care. Oliver thinks I'm beautiful and since he's been in my life ... I'm starting to believe it too."

I think Alex has tears in her eyes, but she hides it well with a few rapid blinks. "Come here." She opens her arms to me and I hug her. "Flower, you're the most beautiful person I know ... inside and out. Go have fun."

"Thanks, Alex."

"What bar are you going to?"

"Not sure. Chelsea hasn't messaged me the info yet."

"Well, text me when you find out. You know, in case we have to come pick up your drunk ass."

"Thanks, *Mom*, I will."

THE FOUR OF us find a table close to the front, just right of the stage. Chelsea, Felicia, and Tess have fake IDs; it never occurred to me that my new freshman friends are two years younger than I am and not of legal drinking age yet.

"Your tat is incredible." Tess brushes my hair away from my back.

"Thanks."

"That had to hurt like hell. I chickened out getting a small butterfly on my shoulder," Felicia says.

"It took several visits to complete. The pain wasn't too bad." I spare them the details of the inspiration for the tattoo being the real pain.

"Drinks?" Chelsea stands.

"Whisky sour."

"Lemon drop."

Chelsea looks at me. "Sam Adams, thanks." I hand her a ten.

"Ooo, dibs on the guy with wavy black hair at the table behind us," Felicia leans in and whispers followed by a giggle.

"Whatever, I've already got eyes for backwards ball cap guy by the stage." Tess stares and bites her lip.

"See anyone that catches your eye, Viv?"

"Not really." I haven't told them about Oliver. I'm not sure how to explain our current *situation*.

"Not really what?" Chelsea hands us our drinks.

"We're trying to find a guy for Viv. Tess and I have already spotted our prey." Felicia points out the two guys to Chelsea.

"Nice." Chelsea nods her head. "I'm keeping my options open. This place is going to be packed in a few hours. I think my guy has yet to enter the building."

"Maybe he's coming with Viv's guy." Tess and Felicia laugh.

I nurse my beer over the next hour to pace myself. Being the oldest in our group has made me feel like I should be the responsible one too. Chelsea has sung once, but Tess and Felicia are still deciding what they want to sing. I'm too sober to even look at the playlist.

"Viv?" Tess yells over the music. "You have to get on the list. Hurry up and pick a song."

I sigh, staring at my empty beer bottle. "Okay." I go get another beer, okay two, and I put my name on the list. By the time I get back to the table, three guys have pulled up chairs and joined our group.

"Viv, this is Mike, Lance, and Troy." Chelsea introduces us.

The guys all seem polite, so I sit back down and start on my second beer as the roar of the crowd picks up with the start of the next performance. My new friends work their flirt overtime while I make out with my beer bottle. By my third beer, I have a confident buzz going and I decide to quit since my name will be called soon.

My phone vibrates in my purse. I assume it's Alex checking up on me even though I sent her the location of my whereabouts earlier. It's a text.

Oliver: *Hey, baby. What are you up to tonight?*

I focus on the screen and type slowly ... My dexterity is a little impaired.

Me: *Hi, babe! At a bar with friends.*
Oliver: *Bar? What kind of bar?*
Me: *One with people, alcohol, and music. LOL!*
Oliver: *Not karaoke, hopefully.*
Me: *Not funny and yes maybe.*
Oliver: *Yes, funny! Want to sext with me?*
Me: *Not now ... when I get home.*
Oliver: *Are you refusing me?*

"Who are you texting, Viv?" Chelsea giggles. "Your

imaginary boyfriend?" The small coed gathering at our table breaks out into laughter. Yes, I'm the loner.

"Yep, my imaginary boyfriend." I giggle to myself because everything is funny after three beers.

Me: *Gotta go. I'm up soon!*

I slip my phone back in my purse and try not to think of Oliver and his naughty texts that I'm missing out on.

"I think you're next, Viv!" Tess squeals.

I start to stand as the announcer comes to the mic, but he doesn't announce me. He announces some guy. *Konrad Rosenberg.* Amazing name, I think to myself as I sit back down.

"Hey, I thought you were next?" Felicia asks.

I shrug. "Some jerk probably slipped a twenty to the announcer so he could budge in front of me."

The piano starts as a voice comes in with the first note.

"Ron Pope's 'A Drop in the Ocean.' I love this song!" Tess jumps up and down in her seat.

My head is a little fuzzy, but the voice is familiar. I squint to see who's singing it, but they're standing back behind the corner of the stage and all I see is a shadow.

"Holy shit!" Chelsea says.

"Dibs!" All three of my new friends call as the performer steps into the light.

I think I could faint. It's been almost eight weeks since I've seen him and he's here. I can't believe he's here! To hell with the song, my friends, or the crowd, I stand. "Nope, he's mine." Squeezing my way through the crowd, I worm a path to the stage.

Oliver watches me the whole time as he continues to sing. Tears sting my eyes as I get closer. I feel like an army wife running to her husband as he steps off the plane. I know our time apart doesn't even compare to that, but eight weeks has felt like an eternity without him. I'm almost there and he hands the mic to the announcer while the music continues to play.

"Oli ..." I fall into his embrace and hug him with everything I have as he lifts me off my feet.

Tears flow. Lips collide.

The crowd erupts into crazy cheers with lots of whistling and clapping.

"Hi, gorgeous." He sets me back on my feet and brushes away my tears.

"You're back."

He smiles. "Let's go home. I'm not sharing you tonight." He steps off the stage and holds out his hand.

I take it and follow him through the crowd. As we pass my table, I tug on him to stop. Grabbing my purse off the chair, I grin at the gaping mouths and jealous smiles aimed at me.

"I'll explain Monday." I wink at the girls and follow Oliver. "Why didn't you tell me you were coming?" I fist his shirt and pull him to me as we step out onto the sidewalk.

He kisses me and it's mind-numbing, shooting stars, and a grand finale of fireworks all at once. I despise the three blocks between us and home, specifically our bed.

"And ruin the surprise?" He rubs his nose against mine.

"I can't believe you did that in there. Oli, you can seriously sing."

He interlaces our fingers and leads me down the sidewalk. "Well, one of us should be able to."

"Oh my gosh! I thought you did that to serenade me, a romantic grand gesture. But you did it to block me from singing!" I punch him in the arm.

He chuckles. "I was serenading you. The fact that we left before you got a chance to sing was just a happy coincidence."

I pull my hand from his and stomp ahead of him.

"Miss Graham, if you don't stop strutting your sexy ass like a pendulum in that dress and those shoes, I'm going to have to take you into the alley and show you how desperate I am for you right now."

My insides melt with his words, and I hope the evidence of that doesn't start running down my leg since it's a panty-free night for me. I didn't want them to get in the way if the freshman initiation pissing opportunity presented itself.

"Sorry, *Konrad Rosenberg*, your threats need to be more believable."

"Are you a little tipsy, Vivian? It doesn't look like you're walking too straight."

"No, I'm just artificially confident and chemically relaxed." I laugh at my own joke. It was a good one; at least after those three beers it sounds funny to me. "Eee!" I squeal as he grabs my waist and pulls me into the alley.

Oliver pins me against the wall with his body, his warm breath heavy on my face. The carnal need in his intense eyes and firm lips evaporates all humor between us. Strong hands slide down my arms and around to my ass. He squeezes it with a sudden jerk toward him. His arousal nudging my abdomen.

"Oli—"

He presses his mouth to mine and our tongues explore with determined strokes. My hands tug the button on his jeans until it's released. The zipper follows and my hand kneads and strokes him through his briefs as he rocks his pelvis into my touch. He moans into my mouth with deep intensity.

His hands clench my dress, yanking it up once. I hum into his mouth with untamed anticipation. He grips my dress lower and yanks up one more time, completely exposing me from the waist down.

I wait for him to chastise me for my lack of panties, but he doesn't. His right hand moves mine off his erection. He releases himself and with his left hand he hitches my leg to his waist and thrusts into me.

"Oh God!" I yell, letting my head fall back as his invasion stretches the part of me that's forgotten the capacity of his touch.

Oli grabs the back of my head and pulls my lips to his again, muting my cries. I grip his hair holding him with just as much need while releasing small whimpers. I've missed him so much his touch is almost painful. Our bodies are starving and can't get close enough—can't find that release fast enough. He moves in me with the speed and determination of a race horse coming around the last turn. His upward momentum collides with my downward descent, sending a crescendo of pleasure through my body. My mouth goes slack, my standing knee buckles, and he digs all his fingers into my legs slamming me onto him one last time while pressing me to the wall.

"Oh shit ... that ... was ..." His head falls to my shoulder as his labored lungs search for oxygen. He dots a trail of feathery kisses up my neck, stopping at my ear. "I've missed you like doughnuts would miss coffee."

I laugh, wrapping my arms around his neck. "I've missed you more, like peanut butter would miss jelly or hot chocolate would miss marshmallows."

He grabs my other leg and hoists me up around his

waist and kisses me again, taking his time, savoring this moment. "My love…" Oli looks at me with soft eyes and a growing smile. "I've missed you like my heart would miss its own beat."

***

Oliver

RAVEN HAIR FANNED out on a *pillow*. I never imagined I could love the sight of a pillow again. I was wrong. Vivian magically makes everything … better. Twenty-four hours ago I was three-thousand miles away and miserable. Now I'm *me*. Oliver, who loves rowing and dinner with friends and family. I'm the boy who dreamed of playing for the Red Sox from the moment I got my first baseball glove. I'm the guy who wants to call up his buddies from college and see if they want to play basketball in the park. This Oliver wants to hold on to the woman next to him *forever*.

I trace her tattoo as she sleeps on her stomach. Then I kiss every cluster of buds that I know hides her scars. But I don't see them and I can't feel them. It's become impossible for me to see anything but a beautiful, radiant woman through and through.

"Good morning, babe." She rolls toward me so her back is against my chest.

I wrap her in my arms and kiss the top of her head. "It's the best morning."

She traces gentle circles on my arms with her nails. "Can I ask you something?"

I laugh. "You just did."

"I'm serious."

"Yes. You can ask me anything."

She pauses. I feel the weight of her question before she ever asks it.

"Why can't you have children anymore?"

I release the breath that I've been holding. "Because I did some stupid shit after what happened."

"Like drugs?"

"Like selling almost everything we owned and burning what wouldn't sell, like our wedding album, and all our other photos, except for one."

"The one of Melanie?"

I nod against her shoulder as I kiss it.

"So are you saying all the heat from the burning caused damage to your sperm like a hot tub or something?"

I chuckle. "No. It's true about losing a child: It's the ultimate loss. At the time I knew only one thing for sure—I never wanted to experience that again. So I got a vasectomy."

"Do you regret it?"

"I regret making rash decisions at the time, even if they weren't all wrong decisions."

She turns in my arms to face me. "Was the vasectomy a wrong decision?"

I let myself fall into her eyes because I know somehow all the answers I'll ever need are in there. "It was if you want to have children with me."

"Do you want to have children with me?"

I kiss her forehead. "I want you and there isn't anything I wouldn't do for you."

"That's not an answer."

My lungs deflate, she does that to me—strips me down, exposes my weaknesses, and takes the part of me I don't willingly give.

"I can't imagine ever wanting children again because I

can't look at a baby right now and not see Melanie. But the only thing that's more unimaginable than that is living without you."

She kisses me, awakening my whole body. I have to remind a certain part that this is a serious moment and it's not being called into action despite the mixed signals percolating through my mind.

"I love you and I'm so glad you're home." She nuzzles into my neck. "Mmm ... it was a slow torture, but I didn't want to say anything. I didn't want you to feel rushed or conflicted. But now that you're home I can say it..." she kisses her way down my chest "...I was miserable." Her tongue teases over my abs. "God, I missed you."

My dick hardens under her touch. She strokes me a few times with a desirous grin on her face, eyes locked on mine.

"Vivian ..." I need to tell her.

"Hmm?" She sits up and straddles me.

"I need..." my thoughts begin to drift as she guides my hands to her breasts "...to tell you..." I squeeze her perky tits in my hands, circling my thumbs over her nipples. "...something." My words are nothing more than a strained whisper.

She sinks onto me with a soft moan. "What's that, babe ... mmm ..." She closes her eyes as I fill her.

"Nothing ... it's *nothing*."

I'LL ADMIT IT, I'm such a guy. Sex trumps everything. The few times I've managed to resist her seductress temptations can only be described as aliens taking over my brain. I should have called and told her my plans. The surprise, while priceless, was not worth the pain I'm going to cause.

"Where are you going?"

She slips on her clothes and pulls her hair back. "I have to work today, but just until one."

"But I just got here." What the hell! I sound like a whiny kid.

"I know, I'll make it up to you later and tomorrow, and the next day, and the next ..." She winks and blows me a kiss.

I sit up in bed, running my fingers through my hair as I sigh. "Vivian, I'm not staying."

She peeks around the corner with her toothbrush in her mouth. "What do you mean?" She mumbles over a mouthful of toothpaste suds.

I slip into my shorts and stand at the entrance to the bathroom. "I'm just here for the weekend. I needed to get a few things ... I leave again tomorrow."

She freezes with the toothbrush still in her mouth and stares with a blank expression at my reflection in the mirror.

"I'm sorry, I wanted to surprise you. I should have called and told you before I came home."

Her eyes fall to the sink. She spits and tosses her toothbrush in the cup.

"Okay, I'll just see you later then." She squeezes past me without making eye contact.

I grab her arm. "Vivian ..."

She yanks it from my grip. "No, it's fine. Maybe we can go someplace nice for dinner or something. I have to go. We'll talk later."

I chase her down the stairs. "Vivian, wait!" I push the front door closed just as she opens it. "Don't, please don't do this."

Her forehead thumps against the door and her sobs fill the air.

"I'm so sorry." I turn her around and pull her into my

arms. She doesn't hug me back. Instead, she keeps her hands over her face.

My anger inside is fueled by her tears. Caroline is a lost cause and maybe I am too. I'm so fucking confused.

"I'm s-sorry." She pulls away and shakes her head while wiping away her tears. "You don't need this."

I turn and take a few steps away with my hands planted on my hips. "Dammit! Stop apologizing. This is not your fault. This is me all me! My fucked-up life is sucking everything out of you. I wish..." I look to the ceiling, releasing an exasperated breath "...I wish I could just let go."

She sucks in her quivering lower lip and swallows hard. "I have to go."

My head falls, shoulders slump, and the door bangs shut.

Vivian

IN THE OFF-SEASON The Green Pot closes at noon on Saturdays. Most days Maggie and I stay until one cleaning up and chatting. Today I don't feel chatty.

"Spill it, Viv."

"Spill what?" I ask, carrying in the mums from the sidewalk.

"You showed up late this morning with puffy eyes and you've been sulking ever since."

"Oliver's back."

"Sweetie, that's great ... isn't it?"

"He's leaving again tomorrow."

She stamps the back of the checks. "Well, at least he came for a visit, right?"

I frown. "He came back to get some stuff. The visit part is just a perk, if you can call it that."

"He came back to see you, Viv. There's nothing he forgot that he can't pick up in Portland, except you."

"You think so?"

She crooks her finger at me. I mope over to her.

"Come here." She hugs me. "I know so. He loves you and being away from you has to be killing him. Besides, I've been so proud of you the past couple of months. You're doing great in school, you still find time to help me out, and until today, I haven't seen you be anything short of your jovial self."

I step back and tug at my lower lip with a grimace. "Yeah, well it's sort of been an act. I'm pretty driven so the school and work part has been easy, the jovial part ... not so much. Honestly, I've been miserable on the inside. Life without Oliver is dull and lifeless. I shine when he's here. I feel confident by his side and beautiful in his eyes." I laugh. "I know it sounds so pathetic. I shouldn't need a man to have that."

"You're right, you don't need a man, Vivian. But life sure is a lot more fun with them."

We both laugh.

"Thanks, Maggie. You're the pep-talk queen."

***

"Rosenberg," I call, opening the front door. I look up as Oliver walks down the stairs holding him. Rosenberg barks and runs to me after Oliver sets him down.

"Hey," he says with a sad, I-know-I've-hurt-you smile.

"Hey." I pick up Rosenberg.

"Are we on for dinner at my parents' tonight?"

"Yeah, whatever you want." I slip off my shoes and go into the kitchen for a drink.

"Are you mad?"

I draw in a breath and hold it while my brain formulates the politically correct answer. "No, I'm not mad."

Yes, I'm mad and I'm not sure why or even who I'm mad at. Oliver, for having a past? Myself for falling in love with him? Caroline? Her parents?

"Don't lie. I know you're mad."

I set Rosenberg down and shake my head. Men are idiots; I swear it's as much a part of the Y chromosome as their penis.

"Well if you *know* I'm mad, then why ask?" Sarcasm drenches every word.

"What do you want me to do?" He shoves his hands in his pockets.

I grab a glass and fill it with water. "I want you to do whatever it is you need to do, and I can't tell you what that is because I don't know." I take a sip of water. "Talk to your mom or get help from someone else. Stay in Portland until Caroline gets better—"

"She won't get better."

"Then stay there until your in-laws are happy or until you can find closure! I don't know, Oli!" I slam the glass down on the counter.

His brows tense. I close my eyes and pinch the bridge of my nose. "I have some studying to do before we leave later." I walk past him to the stairs with my little lamb, Rosenberg, following me, Oliver too.

I walk toward our closet to change my clothes. The hanging bags on the bed catch my attention. They're not zipped up yet so I can see Oliver's suits and dress shirts in them. Near the foot of the bed are his ties and dress shoes. "You going to church in Portland?"

"Work."

I stop just inside the closet and turn toward him. "Work?"

"The firm where I used to work ..."

I nod once.

"...one of the partners is going on maternity leave soon, and I'm going to help out. Make some money and find a way to occupy my time during the day since I can't go see Caroline until later in the afternoon."

My heart leaps into my throat. "How long will she be on maternity leave?"

"I'm not sure. She's having twins so my guess is at least twelve weeks."

Turning, I suck in a shaky breath which is incredibly hard to do since his confession just punched me in the gut. I pull off my T-shirt and push down my cargo pants.

"You're so beautiful." His voice is a breath away as his hands ghost down my arms.

I step away and grab a pair of jeans and a sweater. I dress with quick moves and turn to him. "I have to study."

He eyes the entire length of my body and nods. His face goes slack as he rubs the back of his neck. Disappointment radiates from him. *Join the club*, is all I can think.

CHAPTER TWENTY-NINE
FOR YOU

Vivian

PAIN BREEDS vulnerability and right now, as Oliver drives us to his parents' house, I'm feeling unimaginable depths of both. There's a wall of awkwardness between us that feels impenetrable. Neither one of us knows what to say or what to do. It's as if we're marking time in silence, waiting for yet another goodbye.

His words from this morning linger like poison—*"I wish I could just let go."* Let go of what? Me?

Oliver shuts off the car and walks to my side. I get out before he reaches the door. He stops and sighs, as if my refusal to accept his chivalrous gesture is a slap in the face. Too bad.

He offers his hand—*that* I take. I'll always take it, even when it wears a glove of heartache and pain.

Oliver stops before opening the front door and cups my face in his hands. "I choose you. I love you. No matter what happens you need to know that. If you don't want me to go, then say the words and I'll stay. It's you I love, all that matters is you."

I nod through the sincerity of his words. It's never been a question of Oliver's love for me. There's no choice to be made. We claimed each other months ago—no take backs. I'm waiting for him to realize he's more than the sum of the events of his past. I'm waiting for him to tattoo his scars with something beautiful and not be afraid to show it to the world. I want to give him what he gave me, but I don't know how and it kills me.

His lips press to mine, and I swear I can feel the heaviness of his heart in the way they cling to me.

"Let's go." I smile and nod to the door.

He waits, eyes searching for something. Certainty? I rub my thumb over his bottom lip that stole some of my gloss.

"I can smell the grill, babe, and I'm starving. Let's go already."

He gives me a full double-dimple grin and opens the door.

"Vivian!" Jackie tosses her apron aside and pulls me in for a big hug.

"For Christ's sake, I can't win." Oliver shakes his head. "I've been gone for eight weeks and it's 'Vivian!' like you didn't just see her last week."

Jackie grins while releasing me. "Come here, baby boy."

He gives her a half smile as she hugs his chest. Then he attempts to glare at me but fails miserably. "You and your dog are giving me a complex."

"Son, good to see you." Hugh walks in from outside and hugs Oliver, *first,* hopefully giving him a little ego boost.

"Vivian." He hugs me and kisses my cheek.

"Where's Chance?" Oliver asks.

"He's squeezing in a 'quick date' before dinner." Jackie

waves her hand in the air. "That boy is never going to settle down."

Oliver and I look at each other. I'm sure both of us are wondering if she realizes *quick date* is code for getting laid.

"He just hasn't found a girl like Vivian." Hugh hands Oliver a beer.

"Well, don't tell him that. He'll tell you he laid some claim to her before I showed up and stole her from him." Oliver takes a pull of his beer. "It's all I heard all summer."

Everyone laughs.

"How's he been doing with business?" Oliver asks.

Jackie, Hugh, and I look at each other and grin.

"You haven't heard?" Hugh raises a brow.

"Heard what?"

"He's hired someone part-time."

"That's great."

We all grin again.

Oliver looks around at us. "Am I missing something?"

"Ronnie is young but has lots of experience from growing up around family in the construction and trim-carpentry business. Just what Chance was looking for going into the time of year that indoor home projects are more in demand." Hugh grins waiting to see if Jackie or I want to finish the story.

"Chance hired Ronnie via e-mail correspondence. Ronnie's résumé was too good to pass up. It's probably even better than Chance's." Jackie smirks.

"So ... what's the deal? Is he a real dick or something?"

We laugh at the unintentional humor in Oliver's question. Jackie and Hugh smile at me as if they're bestowing the pleasure of the big reveal to me.

I take a sip of my wine. "That's just it, babe. There is no dick to Ronnie, AKA Veronica."

Oliver's jaw drops. "No way!"

We laugh. "Oh yes, way." I nod and giggle.

Oliver's grin widens. "Man! I can't believe I've missed out on all this. So have you met her? What's she like?"

"We haven't met her yet, but Maggie has. Veronica did some shelving work for her at The Green Pot. Maggie said she's *very* attractive, smart, and has a quick wit that knocked Chance down a couple of notches every time he came by to check up on her."

Oliver stares at me with a deviant grin. I can see the cogs turning in his head, no doubt concocting a huge ration of shit to deal out in small increments to Chance all evening.

CHANCE CALLS to tell us he's skipping dinner but to save him some dessert. That's code for his date has offered him an encore performance.

"So how long are you staying?" Hugh asks.

I know Oliver has stayed in contact with them since he's been gone, so the conversation about Portland has been kept to a minimum so far.

"I fly out tomorrow." He keeps his eyes on him while I glance up from my plate and then back down.

"Will you be home for the holidays?" Hugh continues.

Jackie gives him a stern cease-and-desist look. I'm not sure if it's that she's a woman, mother, or psychiatrist, but she has spot-on intuition to when a conversation becomes uncomfortable. Hugh doesn't catch the look.

"I'm not sure yet." I feel Oliver's eyes shift to me, but I still don't look up.

"Well I'm just happy to hear that you're putting that

degree of yours to use again. Working with your brother was never going to be a career."

The table shakes and I know it's from Jackie's foot connecting with Hugh's shin. The wince on his face confirms it. I risk a peek at Jackie and she gives me a polite you're-welcome-dear smile.

"How are your parents, Vivian?" Jackie takes a bite of caramelized squash.

"They're really good. My dad got a job with a larger company. It's actually four ten-hour days, no weekends, and better pay."

Oliver tilts his head. "When did this happen? You never told me."

I shrug. "Last week. I tried to call you but you didn't answer. Then when you called me back, we … well …" My eyes go wide as I clear my throat.

Oliver's eyes match mine in understanding while Jackie fights her own smile of understanding. This is getting embarrassing. Time to change the subject.

"Hey, hey, hey!" Chance comes through the door and into the dining room with a cocky smile and … oh my God! His pants are not zipped and I'm afraid to stare long enough to be sure, but I think he's going commando.

"Hi, sweetie. I was just getting ready to get the pie." Jackie gives him a hug on her way to the kitchen.

Okay, so she doesn't notice.

"Good to see you, Bro." Chance pats Oliver on the shoulder.

"You too, man."

Chance walks around the table to me. "Viv, lovely to see you as always." In true Chance fashion, he takes my hand and kisses it while smirking at a scowling Oliver.

I, however, couldn't care less about the stupid kiss.

Chance is standing at my side with his exposed area inches from my face, talking to Hugh about a new truck he's looking into purchasing. I stare at Oliver until he squints his eyes at me. Nudging my head in Chance's direction, my eyes widen. Oliver stares at me then gives a quick glance to Chance and back to me. I exaggerate my head and facial signals. He looks at Chance again and flinches.

"Ah, man! Zip it up, Chance. That's disgusting. Get it away from Vivian."

Chance looks down and laughs while zipping up. "Sorry, I rushed over here after..." he looks at Hugh and clears his throat "...my *date*."

Hugh puts his fist over his mouth and clears his throat. "Have a seat, Son. And next time spare us all and take a quick glance in the mirror before joining us for dinner."

"So how's it been going in Portland?" Chance asks while sitting down.

Jackie, once again, saves the day as she brings in the pie. "Tell Oliver about Ronnie."

Chance grunts as Oliver laughs. "You replaced me with a woman, huh?"

"I'd hardly call her a woman. She's basically a man who lost his penis."

Everyone laughs except Chance.

"I heard she's quite attractive." Oliver says.

"I hadn't noticed." Chance takes a bite of pie.

"Bull shit! Man..." Oliver shakes his head "...she must be something. I've never seen you worked up like this before."

Chance waves his fork in the air. "I'm not worked up. In fact, I should have fired her ass by now."

"For what?" Oliver asks.

"Insubordination."

I cough. "Sounds like Chance is an alpha male."

"Would you like to find out?" He wiggles his brows at me.

"Would you like to go on your next date with all your teeth?" Oliver says through clenched teeth.

"Enough, boys. I'd like to know what happened to the respectful young men we raised." Jackie gives them both a tightlipped, disapproving glance.

Hugh stands while looking at his phone. "Well, if you find them, sweetheart, let me know." He smiles. "I have to go into the hospital."

Oliver and Chance walk their dad out while I help clear the table with Jackie.

"You know if you ever want to talk, I'm here." Jackie takes the plates from me and sets them in the sink.

"Thank you." I blink back the tears. All day I've felt on the verge of losing it. My emotions are eating me alive. "I just wish I could help him, that's all."

"Ah, sweetie, you are. I wish you could see that. He would not have gone back to Portland had he not met you."

I look up and laugh because that's not too comforting right now.

She takes both of my hands and squeezes them. "I know this has been hard for you, but trust me when I say that Oliver is finding his way back to you. Even if he doesn't recognize it, that's what he's doing."

I shake my head and swallow back the emotions. "Well it feels like one hell of a detour."

"It is and I hope and pray with all my heart that you both have what it takes to survive it. Not very many couples have what you two have. It's not just love, it's friendship and respect. You laugh and play together and the passion between you is enough to make a momma like myself blush."

We both smile.

"It helps to talk, and in case you haven't heard, I'm a pretty good listener."

I grin and hug her. "Thank you, I'll remember that when I hit my blue moments again."

"Call me anytime, okay?"

I nod.

"What's going on in here?" Chance asks as he and Oliver come back inside.

"Girl talk," Jackie answers.

I dab my fingers to the corners of my eyes while seeing the concern on Oliver's face.

"We're taking off, Mom." He hugs her.

"Have a safe trip, Oliver."

Chance gives him a hug too. "Let me know when you're coming back to work for me. I'll cut the vagina with a hammer loose."

"Nah ... it's too much fun hearing how much she busts your chops."

Chance grumbles something under his breath.

Oliver holds out his hand. "Shall we?"

"We shall."

***

Oliver

THE PAIN in her eyes floods me with guilt. More guilt. I swear I'm drowning in it. Melanie, Caroline, her parents, my parents, Vivian ... it's overpowering me in every direction.

We feed Rosenberg and head upstairs. There's a sadness between us that's hard to ignore. I miss her laughter. I got a mild version of it tonight, but not like I remember. The Vivian I fell in love with is cute and sassy with a carefree attitude and a penchant for doughnuts. I haven't seen her eat a doughnut in months. Maybe I'm wearing her down too much. Everyone has a breaking point. I'm afraid Vivian has been so giving or *flexible* with me that she could break and it would be so subtle I wouldn't notice until it's too late.

"I need a shower." Her voice is barely audible as she passes by me in the closet carrying her robe.

"Want some company?"

"It doesn't matter."

My head drops—hell, my whole body slumps. When did anything between us not matter? I shrug off my shirt and remove my jeans and briefs.

The steam from the shower pours out as I open the door. Bloodshot eyes look up at me through inky wet hair.

"I can still see your tears."

Her beautiful face contorts like a knife is being driven through her body. "I don't want to say goodbye again." A sob escapes with her last word.

"I'll stay." I take her in my arms and let the water drown my own tears. This woman is *everything* in a world I was convinced was filled with *nothing*. And maybe that's it. Maybe apart we are nothing and together we're everything. Is it really that crazy to think that in a world with over seven billion people, it's quite possible we weren't meant to live alone—that maybe, just maybe, we need each other?

"Oli..." she looks up at me and presses her palms to my face "...love me."

I close my eyes and cover her hands with mine. And then ... I *love her*.

My lips seek hers with magnetic touch. She's all I ever

taste. My hands melt into the curve of her breasts until she arches her back. Her skin, it's all I ever feel.

"Oli ..." She whispers my name. It's all I ever hear.

I lead with my hands and follow with my lips, taking the slow journey down her body—feeling, tasting, memorizing. Kneeling, I pull her to me and she eases onto me with slow, agonizing perfection.

"Love me." Her soft words echo in my ear as she wraps her whole body around mine.

I'm at war with myself. My body wants to move with hers, giving and taking pleasure to the likes of which I've never experienced before, or will ever again. My heart ... it wants to hold her in idle perfection ... *forever*.

She moves against me, her body begging for our perfect pleasure, and my body wins over my heart. I taste her lips, suck in her sweet tongue, and knead her breasts.

"Look at me, Vivian."

She opens her eyes, water raining between us, a few drops clinging to her long lashes. As I rock up into her, deeper every time, her cherry lips part and her tongue slides along her lower lip. The warm staccato of our breathing mingling between our mouths.

Vivian's eyes leaden as I rub her clitoris.

"Stay with me, baby."

She pulls them open again. "Oli ..."

I need this. I need to see something other than pain in this woman's eyes. I need to see passion, love, life ... *us*.

Gripping her hips, I grunt from deep in my chest and bury myself in her so deep I swear I just lost my mind and it may never be found again. Every muscle tenses as I still, releasing into her. Exhausted, I rest my forehead against hers. We share weak smiles before our heavy eyelids surrender.

Vivian ... sprawled out on her stomach, *diagonally*, across our bed, naked, sated, and mine. Until this moment I hadn't realized that I'd been holding my breath for eight weeks. How did I do that? How does one live without breathing? How could *I* possibly live without *her*?

I've traced her tattoo so many times in the light of the moon I think I could recreate it with my eyes closed. Her fun and witty personality brings a spontaneous smile to my face even when I'm alone. Her beauty is the brightest star in my sky. And the sex is—indescribable. But *this* ... tracing flower buds and counting freckles, I'm in Heaven. Vivian is my heaven.

"Wondering what I looked like before all that ink and the nasty scars it hides?"

"Shh..." I kiss her shoulder. "It's two in the morning. Go back to sleep."

She rolls to her side and kisses my chest. "It's okay. Sometimes I try to imagine what the pre-Caroline Oliver was like."

I twirl a lock of her long hair around my finger. "And?"

"And I can't. Which makes me think that I wouldn't have been part of that life." She places the palm of her hand on my chest, over my heart, and spreads out her fingers. "So I don't go there anymore, because a life without Oliver Konrad isn't a life at all."

I swallow past the suffocating feeling in my throat. When Vivian opens her heart and shares such raw vulnerability, it's like a vice around my chest. She has no idea how fierce my need to protect her is. The unbearable part for me is when I feel like the biggest danger to her is me and my past.

I go for a mood lightener. "Yeah, well I've never tried to imagine you before me. Probably because I still wake up every morning and question whether I dreamed you. And when I realize you're my real, it's like winning the lottery every damn day of my life."

She giggles. "Lottery? Pfft ... whatever. You must mean scratch tickets."

"Nope. I'm talking the sole winner of the Mega Millions ... every day."

She ghosts the pads of her fingers over the thin patch of hair on my chest. "Oli?"

"Hmm?"

"Remember when you came to The Green Pot and needed some more plants that day we were really busy?"

"Yes."

"Remember how long the line was and I let you budge and got you what you needed without having to wait?"

"Yes."

"Remember I told you that you'd owe me a favor?"

I chuckle. "Yeah, I remember."

She looks up at me with an inward gaze. I can feel her heavy thoughts like a barrier between us.

"Go back to Portland."

I shake my head before her last word. "I said I'm staying."

"You need to go back."

"Vivian, no, I don't want to go back. Caroline doesn't need me, her parents just think she does. But the truth is they're as delusional as she is."

"Oliver, you need to go back for you."

"What does that even mean? Have you been talking to my mom?"

"You owe me."

I clench my hair then rub my hands over my face, releasing a sarcastic laugh. "I *owe* you? Really? You're trying to trade cutting in line for sending me back to Hell? No, I won't. Yesterday morning, yes, I was going. Even last night at my parents' house I planned on going. But I saw the pain in your eyes, Vivian. Hell, it's dark in here and I still can see the goddamn pain in your eyes! I'm not going. Period."

She rolls on top of me, our faces a breath apart. "Oli, don't you see? The pain you see in my eyes is *for* you not *because* of you. Get on the plane tomorrow, but not for Caroline, or her parents, and not for your job, but for you, Oli. And if you can't do that..." she blinks and her tears fall to my cheek "...then do it for me."

I don't want to go. When I said I was staying it was for me as much as her. But when a man loves a woman the way *this man* loves *this woman*, there's nothing I wouldn't do for her. To the front of the battle line, the end of the earth, to my last breath ... That's how far I will go for her.

"For *you*, my love, only you."

CHAPTER THIRTY

YEP

Vivian

Another Monday, another school day, another day to miss Oliver. It's been six weeks since he boarded the plane to Portland, six weeks since we made love until the sun peeked over the horizon, six weeks since he soothed me to sleep in his arms, and six weeks since he left me asleep in our bed and walked out the door without a goodbye.

After he agreed to go back, for me, I had two more requests. One, that he'd make love to me until we both fell into a post-coital coma, and two, that he'd leave without a goodbye. Missing him is like a dull pain; when I'm studying or sleeping, I don't notice it so much. But the goodbye ... it's a slow, cruel torture.

We talk and text every day, even if it's just a quick I love you. Oliver has been working for the firm during the day and visiting Caroline in the late afternoons into early evening. Her progress is slow but noticeable. They've changed her medications and she and Oliver have been able to have random conversations about the food she's served or a show that's on the television at the hospital. Neither have talked about Melanie or the events that led to that tragic day.

I still go to Oliver's parents' every Saturday night, and sometimes my parents drive out to join us. While Hugh is out rowing on Sunday mornings, Jackie comes over for coffee. This is when we have our heart-to-hearts about Oliver. She assumes Caroline is talking through Melanie's death with the doctor in her private sessions and discussing her ongoing struggle with depression in group sessions. Oliver still refuses to see anyone or even talk to Jackie about any of it. I fear he'll start to slip away from me and everyone else who loves him if he doesn't.

"My mom wants to get these wedding invitations mailed out, but you haven't given me Oliver's address in Portland."

"Just send it to his house. I'll relay the details." I set down my menu. Alex and I discovered we both have a break between classes on Mondays that hits right around lunch time. I'd planned on using it for study time at the library, but she insisted we use it for wedding planning over burgers and fries ... okay, salad for her. Although at this point there's not much left to plan.

"My mom thinks that's poor etiquette, since he's basically living in Portland."

"Well he's still making the mortgage payment here and I hope to God he still considers this home." I slap her hand. "Why do you order a salad and then steal half of my fries. Just get the freakin' fries."

"Can't. I have to fit into my wedding gown."

"Sooo ... my fries are void of calories?"

"Yep. They only have the power to make the person who ordered them fat." She pauses mid-chew with half the fry still sticking out of her mouth. "Shit! Look at you, Flower. You're a junk food addict with a bony ass. Everything in the universe has to find balance. So if these fries aren't making you fat then..." she spits out the fry "... dammit! I'm not going to fit into my dress and it's going to be all your fault!"

"My fault?"

"Yes, you're a terrible influence on me. Would it kill you to get a salad once in a while? Skinny people die too, you know?"

"I eat salad."

"When?" She stabs a piece of lettuce like she's spear fishing.

"Almost every day." I laugh. "When you don't finish yours because you eat too many of my fries."

She wrinkles her nose and squints at me. I giggle and take a huge bite of my hamburger; ketchup and grease dribble onto my plate.

She grabs her phone and snaps a picture.

"What the heck?" I protest through a mouthful of sandwich.

"All you celebs forget the paparazzi is just waiting to capture your embarrassing moments."

"Are you seriously still sending pictures to Oliver?"

She smirks. "I am now."

As I TRENCH my way through all the required reading for this week, I get a text from Oliver. I was expecting a call or even better, some Skype-X.

Oliver: *Having dinner with Brice & Mitchell. Talk to you tomorrow.*
Me: *I'll be up, call me when you're done.*
Oliver: *It'll be late your time. Tomorrow. Night, my love.*

And there I go ... deflating like a leaky balloon. It's one night, I know that. However, lately our phone conversations have been cut short, usually by Caroline's parents or one of Oliver's clients. Our messages have been less consistent, and Skype-X hasn't happened for several weeks. Next week is Thanksgiving and Oliver has yet to purchase a plane ticket.

I have zero leverage to be angry with him or even to have a pity party for myself. Oliver is in Portland because I told him to go. I imagined him sorting through his issues with Caroline and her family, or visiting Melanie's grave. The naive but hopeful part of me dared to imagine him getting some help for himself too. But what I didn't envision was dinner with the partners, lunch with clients, and less and less communication with me.

Me: *Love you <3*

Wait.
Wait some more.
Needy.
Nervous.
Going crazy!
I read two more chapters then check my phone. Nothing. I brush my teeth and wash my face. Nothing. Then just as I crawl in bed with Rosenberg and my English assignment, my phone vibrates.

Oliver: *Yep!*

Yep? YEP! His response to I love you is *yep?*

I'm angry ... really angry. Swiping my finger across my phone screen, I contemplate calling Alex, but I know she's at Sean's tonight. Then I consider calling Jackie. She told me to call her any time about anything. But what would I say? *Hey, sorry to wake you, but Oliver said "yep."*

Yeah, she might start charging me if that's the type of craziness I start calling her about.

***

THIS MORNING CALLS for extra coffee. I really need to treat sleep like it's of vital importance to my body. Maybe I can catch up over the holidays. Yeah right, dealing with Bridezilla and a bachelorette party. Sounds like I'll be getting lots of sleep.

I take Rosenberg out once more before I head off to class. Grabbing my bag, I notice I missed a text from Oliver this morning.

Oliver: *Good morning. Watching the sunrise and thinking of you.*

Ugh! I ignore his message until I can decipher if my mood is forgiving and cheerful or begrudging and spiteful. As I head out the door, messenger bag slung over my shoulder and my insulated cup of coffee in the side pocket, I decide to be somewhere in the middle.

Me: *Okay*

My unstoppable smirk shows my inward satisfaction.

Oliver: *Are you in class?*

Me: *Nope*

Oliver: *Are you okay?*

And here comes payback ...

Me: *Yep*

My phone rings.

"Hi." I answer in the most diplomatic voice I can muster.

"Have I done something wrong?"

I answer without answering. My hesitation says it all.

"Am I supposed to know what I did?"

I look ahead. My building is approximately fifty yards away, so I can either lie and play the immature relationship game—hang up and be pissed all day ... still immature—or lay it all out in plain sight.

"I was disappointed when we didn't get to talk last night, which I can live with. But then you said *yep*."

"Yep?"

"Yep."

"You said yep to me this morning."

I sigh. "Because you said it to me last night. I was making a point."

"When did I say yep to you last night? And what point were you trying to make?" I feel the exasperation in his voice.

"I said I love you and you texted *yep*. My point is that nobody likes to be told yep!"

"It's just an informal word for yes!"

"Well it was the wrong response, Oliver! I love you is a statement, not a fucking question!" I cringe the moment I realize people are staring at me. I'm really not the girl who throws around f-bombs in public. Veering onto the grass, I hide behind a large tree trunk.

"Vivian I ... I'm sorry. I was in the middle of dinner last night and trying to text you while fielding questions from Brice and Mitchell. I didn't mean to—"

"Stop." I blow out a long breath. "It's not your fault. I overreacted. I've been a little stressed lately and I just ..." I'm dying to say the words I feel, *I miss you*, but I don't. "I'm sorry. I have to get to class."

"Vivian?"

"Hmm?"

"I love you."

I smirk and roll my eyes, feeling embarrassed, ridiculous, and in spite of my scholarly surroundings, a bit stupid.

"Yep."

Oliver releases the most genuine and spontaneous laugh that erases all the tension from the past five minutes.

AT FIVE THIRTY there's a knock at the door. It's a delivery guy from my favorite Indian restaurant, compliments of Oliver. An hour later there's another knock on the door: a flower delivery guy. I set them on the counter and read the card.

I read that fifteen roses means "I'm truly sorry, please forgive me." So I sent you eighteen because three means "I love you."

~ Oliver

After the initial ah-I'm-the-luckiest-girl-ever moment

fades, I chastise myself for my childish, insecure, teenaged girl behavior. He has to wonder if he's trading one completely unstable woman for another. I pray to God he hasn't told anyone about our argument and his guilty need to apologize. I can just imagine that conversation.

"Hey, Oliver, why the grand gesture?"

"I texted Vivian the word 'yep.'"

If that doesn't say psycho alert, then I don't know what does.

I know he's probably with Caroline, but I can't resist shooting off a quick text.

Me: *I'm not worthy.*

I'm surprised by his immediate response.

Oliver: *Tell me about it. I just got the photo. You have some serious explaining to do!*

My breath catches as my mind reels with confusion.

Me: *What photo?*
Oliver: *We'll talk later.*

His left-field comment makes it impossible for me to think about anything else. Photo ... *what* photo? I've been out to the bar a few more times with Chelsea, Felicia, and Tess, and we all took goofy pictures with our phones, but I was never with another guy or doing anything that should upset Oli.

Time drags on while I reread the same page in my book over and over. Finally, like a stay of execution, my phone vibrates. Oli sent me a photo ... *the* photo. Then it rings.

"Oh my gosh! You shit, I thought you were mad."

"I am mad."

I put him on speaker and stare at the photo that Alex took of me at lunch yesterday—the one that makes me look like a rabid animal attacking a hamburger. It was so good, but even I have to cringe looking at the ketchup-laden grease dripping from it.

"You do realize my dad's a cardiologist, right? If this got out it would be such an embarrassment to our family."

I laugh and even though he can't see me, my face flushes.

"I think it was a turkey burger."

"Vivian."

"At least that's what I ordered, but come to think of it, the waiter may have mixed up my order and I didn't have time to wait for him to correct it—"

"Love, you can't lie worth shit."

I laugh.

"You asked me about Thanksgiving a while back. I'm afraid I'm not going to be able to come home. I'm really sorry."

He just stole the smile he put on my face ten seconds ago.

"Why not?"

"Doug and Lily think my absence on the holiday would be bad for Caroline, and the workload I've taken on is more than I expected."

"How are you doing, Oli?"

"Me? I'm fine, why?" The confusion in his voice is disheartening. "I mean, sometimes it's frustrating waiting for Caroline to make a noticeable improvement. Her parents say they see it, even her doctors say she's doing better, but I don't see it. I just wonder how long it's going to take."

"How long what's going to take?"

"For her to understand."

"Understand what?"

I hear the frustration in his sigh. "To understand the ramifications of what she did and that she needs to let me go!"

My body goes rigid. His icy voice holds so much bitterness and unleashed anger.

"I'm sorry ... I didn't mean to—"

"Oliver, it's fine."

"It's not fine. The whole reason I'm here is to protect you from all of this shit. That's why I never mention it."

"But if you want to talk about it—"

"No! I don't want or need to talk about it. I just ... I just need you. I need you to tell me about your day and Rosenberg, and the wedding plans that are driving you crazy. That's the life I want and if I can't have it right now, I at least want to imagine it, if only for a little while every night on the phone with you."

I wipe the tears he can't see. He doesn't want my pity. I get that. I've been there. But Oliver is stuck. He's in this dark hole and he can't find his way out. And it doesn't matter how many helping hands reach down to pull him back into the light, because he can't see them either. So I do all I can. I give him a glimpse of the life he's chasing.

"I don't think my English instructor's first language is English. I mean, really? Shouldn't that be some sort of requirement? Rosenberg has taken a real liking to your old running shoes. How crazy is that? Aren't dogs supposed to have a heightened sense of smell?"

Oli laughs and if there weren't thousands of miles between us I'd swear he's laughing through his own tears.

"Alex is the typical Bridezilla, only to be trumped by her mom's wedding OCD behavior. Which, by the way, if you're an etiquette snob then you might as well know now that your invitation is being sent to your house here."

I pause. He doesn't respond.

"You'll be at the wedding, right?"

"I'll be there. I wouldn't miss seeing you dressed to the nines for anything."

"Well, Mr. Konrad, the feeling is mutual. You flew off with all your sexy suits. I have yet to see you wearing one. I'm wondering if it will replace my leather work boots fantasy."

"Fantasy? You can't call it a fantasy if you've lived it. And as I recall, I made that fantasy a reality." His voice drops a notch to fuck-me-against-the-truck sexy, and I have to squeeze my legs together.

"Yes, you certainly did. Goodnight, Oli. Love you."

"But we were just getting started."

"Exactly. If I don't go now, I'll never get this chapter read."

"Cold shower it is. Goodnight."

CHAPTER THIRTY-ONE
PHONE SEX

Oliver

I'm in Hell and I can't tell anyone. So if I don't make it out I hope Vivian knows that this was how far I was willing to go for her. My time with Caroline is accomplishing nothing, except feeding my hatred for her. How can she be so self-absorbed? Her refusal to make real progress is just for the attention. She probably knows I'm leaving as soon as she's stable again, which means I'm not the incentive to get better that her parents think I am.

The job is the only thing that's saving me right now. But even it's starting to wear on me. Too many people know about my past. It didn't make national news, but it was a big deal around here. I have clients with their own problems, who think their four-hundred dollar an hour time spent with me should be used to console their wounded attorney. If I didn't know better, I'd think Brice and Mitchell are giving me all the female clients just to see if I break.

Today, the day most people pause and give thanks, I'm with Caroline, Doug, and Lily. Nothing beats Thanksgiving during visiting hours at a mental hospital. Caroline looks quite pleased that I'm here and in turn, so do Doug and Lily.

"How are Mom and Dad?" Caroline asks.

I look at Doug and Lily then back at her. She must be digressing, delusional again, because she can't recognize her own parents.

She stares at me. "Oliver, your parents, I asked how they're doing."

My fingers dig into the arm of the chair as my jaw clenches. I'm used to people baiting me. I've experienced it with my job. Hell, I've counseled clients on how to stay calm on the witness stand during cross-examination, but all that knowledge and self-control is lost. I can't find it in the very moment I need it most.

"*Mom and Dad?*" I grit through my teeth.

"Oliver—" Doug stands.

I hold up my hand to stop him.

"When you gave them a grandchild, my mom said you could call them that."

"Oliver," Lily pleads in desperation.

I ignore her.

"But I'm pretty damn sure that you lost that privilege when you suffocated their granddaughter with a fucking pillow!"

My chest heaves with contempt as I stand over her. Caroline brings her knees to her chest and cries, breaking the silence I caused among the other patients and visitors. The more she cries the less I hear. The blood pulsing in my ears is deafening.

I'm being ushered out by some guy in white scrubs, but I'm not resisting. In fact, by the time we reach the main floor I'm sprinting out of the building. The automatic doors open as I approach and the cool fall breeze greets me. My lungs draw in air with marathon exhaustion as I hunch over with my hands on my knees.

I hate her so much.

THIS WAS a mistake of epic proportions. I should be in Boston sitting around the dinner table with my family ... with Vivian. Instead, I'm weaving through traffic in a race to Doug and Lily's in a fucking rental car. Why didn't I drive my car out here? Oh that's right, because I wasn't supposed to be here this long!

Staying with them is no longer an option. I have to get the hell out of here. I pack my bags and drive to an extended-stay hotel. What I really want is to purchase a one-way ticket back to Boston and say goodbye to Portland forever. I need nothing more than to crawl in bed with Vivian and let the rest of the world fall into oblivion. However, what I'm going to do is stay just long enough to make sure Brice and Mitchell can handle the clients I've taken over for Valerie that will require longer services.

"Hey, happy Thanksgiving!" Just the sound of her voice alone takes the edge off.

"Happy Thanksgiving to you too. I really needed to hear your voice."

"Is everything okay?"

I fall back on the hotel bed and close my eyes. "It is now."

"I figured you'd still be at the hospital."

"She wasn't having a good day, so I left early." I'm a cowardly ass for lying. I don't know how I'm going to go back home and tell Vivian that all this time away from her has been for nothing.

"That's too bad. I was hoping for your sake she'd have a better day."

"Are your parents there?"

"Yes, our moms are in the kitchen making magic. I just stuck the pies in the oven."

"*You* made the pies?"

"Thanks for the vote of confidence, babe. Yes, I made pumpkin and pecan."

"Are they baking or reheating?"

"Baking, you idiot. Your mom helped me make the perfect crusts and my mom supervised the filling stage. So as long as the timer on the oven doesn't fail, I will have bragging pictures to send to both you and Alex."

"I'm impressed and so bummed that I'm not there."

"Me too. We all miss you and can't wait to see you."

It hurts to breathe. God, I miss her. Our first Thanksgiving together is our first Thanksgiving apart.

"Miss you too. Is Chance behaving? Is he fully dressed?"

She laughs. "He's on his very best behavior because he brought a guest."

"What? On Thanksgiving?"

"Ronnie."

"No way!"

"Yes, way. You know he hired her via email. Well, that's because her family lives in Ohio. She's going back home for Christmas but decided to stay in Boston for Thanksgiving so Chance invited her."

"How's that going?"

"Let me just say it would take more than an electric carving knife to cut through the sexual tension."

"What?"

"I'm serious. I'm kind of horny just from being around them."

"Fuck! Vivian! Is anyone listening to you?"

I have to adjust myself because the idea of her being horny makes me hard as steel.

She giggles. "No, I snuck off to the guest bedroom for some privacy and because the TV was too loud."

"Sooo ... you're alone?"

"Mmm hmm."

"And horny?"

"Mmm hmm."

I'm a fucking disaster. My mind is all over the place. I just lied to the one person I swore I'd never lie to again, but in spite of it all, I'm still a guy and I *need* this.

"Lock the door."

"Already did."

"God, I love you."

"I'm wearing a light pink lace push up bra and matching thong."

Sweet, sweet Jesus. I didn't even have to ask what she's wearing. I'm not sure I've ever seen her this anxious, and the crap part is I'm not actually *seeing* her. Dammit!

"What are you wearing over that?"

"Nothing, babe. I removed my sweater and jeans while we were talking about the pies."

Oh fuck me, this is not happening. I unfasten my jeans and slide them down enough to free myself.

"Oli ... I'm so wet for you."

I pump myself several times. She's not even giving me a chance to say anything. All I can do is close my eyes and imagine her naked body astride mine, slamming down onto me with relentless need, taking control just like she's already doing.

"Lick your lips, Oli. Can you taste me? Oh God. I can see you, babe. I can see your head buried between my legs. How do I taste?"

"Sweet, you always taste so sweet. Where are your hands?"

Her breath is slow and heavy in my ear. "My breasts. I'm squeezing and oh ... oh God ... pinching my nipple. I love it when you pinch and drag your teeth over my nipples." I hear her moan. "It's like ... it's like a bullet of pleasure to my sex."

I pump my dick harder and a little faster, circling my thumb over the head several times. "You make me so hard, I want to bury myself in your warm, wet pussy."

"Oli ... oh God!"

"Can you feel me?"

"Yes."

"Are your legs spread wide for me?"

"Yes."

"Are your fingers wet?"

"S-so wet." She pants.

"Slide a finger in for me."

"Oh ... yes."

"Now pull it out and circle your clit."

"Ung ... yeesss ..."

I clench the sheet with my other hand.

"Make yourself come. Do it now."

"I-I ... I'm c-coming! Oh dear God!"

I thrust up into my hand and stroke myself letting my release squirt onto my shirt. "Oh, shit ... holy hell ..." I pant as my heart catapults from my chest. My head falls back as my breathing slows.

"Vivian? Are you in there, sweetie?"

Fuck, nothing like my mother's voice to yank me back into reality.

"Uh ... yes. I'm in here."

"Are you alright, sweetie? I thought I heard you yell something."

"Um ... no. I was uh ... laughing. I'm talking to Oliver."

"Oh, well open the door. I want to talk to him."

If this woman loves me she will not open that door—

"Oh my, are you feeling okay? You look like you're burning up. You even have perspiration on your brow."

Kill me now. My parents are both Harvard-trained doctors. It's not going to take my mom long to diagnose Vivian with an acute case of phone sex fever.

"Oli, your mom wants to talk to you."

"Am I on speaker?"

"No."

"Good. Have a wonderful dinner, send me pictures of your pies, and know that I have not come this hard in months. Love you."

She giggles. "Love you too, Oli."

"Oliver?"

"Hi, Mom."

"Are you coming home for Christmas, honey?"

"I'm not sure yet. I'm trying to wrap things up here, and I don't want to miss Alex and Sean's wedding so I can't make any promises yet."

"What do you mean 'wrap things up?'"

"I mean making sure Brice and Mitchell can finish up anything that I can't before I leave to come home."

"And Caroline?"

"She's fine." Another lie and to my mother. I'd say I'm

fast-tracking my way to Hell today, but since I'm already there what does it really matter?

"*Fine?* Really?"

"You should know better than anyone that she'll never be the same again, but her doctors think she's improving so my job here is done."

"And you?"

I sigh. "What does it matter what I think? The doctors are the experts."

"Oliver, I'm not asking what you think. I'm asking how you're doing. Have you made any progress?"

"I'm not the one in the mental hospital."

"Oliver ..."

"Yes, I'm fine, great, fabulous. I'll be home by the wedding so life couldn't be better."

"Have you gone to Melanie's grave?"

"Yes." Lie.

"And?"

"And she's still dead."

"Oliver!"

I fist my hair. "I'm sorry. I just don't need this from you."

"I love you, Oliver. I want my son back. He's found an amazing girl and I'd like to see him get his happily-ever-after. So don't waste your time out there. Do what you need to do so you can come home."

Do what I need to do? Stupid psychobabble bullshit.

"Yep." I cringe after the word falls out. Please let her react better to my "yep" than Vivian.

"Happy Thanksgiving, Oliver. I love you."

"You too. Tell everyone hi for me."

"I will."

I toss my phone aside. Yeah, sure *Happy Thanksgiving.*

It's been a real peachy day. The best part of it is evidenced on my shirt. The rest ... Caroline—I still hate her.

Vivian

IT's HEARTBREAKING that Oliver feels the need to lie to me, and equally so that he has to do the same with Jackie. What Oliver doesn't know is that Lily called Jackie after he was escorted out of the hospital. It must be a motherly thing; she was worried about him and wanted us to know what had happened. She called a second time when she got home and discovered he and all his stuff was gone. That was about ten minutes before he called me. Funny how he never mentioned any of it. So now we know he's had a breakdown and he's no longer staying with Doug and Lily. What we don't know is where he *is* staying or what frame of mind he's in.

The phone sex wasn't planned, and honestly I didn't think he'd be interested after what had happened earlier. But I've been studying like a crazy woman, and Oliver's been so busy, my body needed a release. Then Chance showed up with Ronnie and I caught them in the hallway making out. Not like, we've-been-having-sex-but-are-just-messing-around making out, it was, you've-been-frustrating-the-hell-out-of-me-for-months-I'm-dying-to-fuck-you-for-the-first-time making out. He had her shoved up against the wall, you're-under-arrest style, and he was grinding his crotch against her ass while massaging her sex through her jeans. They didn't see me and it's embarrassing to admit that I hid behind the Ficus tree and watched him give her an orgasm, but it's true. So when Oli called I was hot and bothered and already on the verge of having my own orgasm.

"These pies look amazing!" Jackie smiles while cutting them.

I've taken at least a dozen pictures of them because she's right, they do look ... well, like somebody else made them.

"Did Oliver say when he'll be home?" Chance asks.

I shake my head.

"For sure by Alex and Sean's wedding," Jackie answers to my surprise.

"He said that?" I glance over at her.

"Yes." She nods.

"What about Christmas?" My mom asks.

"He's going to try..." she looks at me with a sad smile "... but he didn't sound as confident about it as I'd hoped."

My posture sags and I'm sure everyone else sees it.

"Maybe you should fly out to Portland as soon as you're done with classes," Chance suggests.

Jackie and Hugh scowl at him.

"What?" He takes a sip of water. "Oliver's the best version of himself when he's with Vivian and maybe he needs a little reminder of what he's missing."

"He needs to find something I can't give him."

Jackie nods with pain in her eyes. "Closure."

I nod back.

"Who cares? Go out anyway and surprise him. He has to be missing you something fierce."

"I can't afford it." I look down at my pecan pie.

My dad's hand covers mine. "Yes, you can."

I look up and he winks at me.

"Consider it your Christmas present from me and your mom."

My parents have struggled financially for so many

years. I want to turn down his offer as I've done so many times before, but I can't. Yes, I'm dying to see Oliver, but right now I know how much this means to my dad and that alone is the reason I accept his gift.

"Thank you." I hug him with tears in my eyes and then lean the other way and hug my mom.

I look at Jackie and see the concern etched along her face. She's worried about Oliver's emotional state, and she's worried about me being in Portland with him so close to the source of his pain.

I smile at her. "I've got this."

It's faint, but she smiles back.

CHAPTER THIRTY-TWO
SMACK

Vivian

THE DAYS between Thanksgiving and the start of my winter break fly by. When I'm not in class or studying, I'm helping tame the Bridezilla. How Alex is managing to pass her classes and prepare for her wedding at the same time is way beyond my comprehension.

"You're going to be back for my bachelorette party, right?"

I laugh. "Yes, at least that's what my round-trip ticket says."

"And he still doesn't know you're coming?"

I pile my folded jeans into my suitcase. "Not unless you've blabbed or sent him pictures of me packing."

"Then how are you going to find him since he still hasn't confessed that he's no longer staying with Caroline's parents."

"My plan is to show up at his work."

Alex hands me my sweaters. "And if he's not there, what's your backup plan?"

"I'll turn around and fly back to Boston."

"What?"

I laugh. "I'm kidding. I don't have a backup plan. If he's not there, I'll think of something. Maybe an airplane banner over the city that says *Oliver Konrad, where are you?*"

Alex chuckles. "Nice, Flower, go with that one."

I zip my suitcase and lug it off the bed. "Don't leave your sneakers out where Rosenberg can get them."

"Don't forget your ID." Alex follows me down the stairs.

"Don't forget to check the front step for delivery packages."

"Don't forget to make it home for my bachelorette party."

I slip on my coat and grab my purse as Alex does the same. "Don't forget it's poor etiquette to kill the groom during a Bridezilla rage." Alex holds the door open for me as I kiss Rosenberg goodbye. "And don't forget to give Rosenberg his present from me on Christmas."

She shuts the door behind us. "Don't forget how weird I think it is that you treat that mutt like a human being."

Traveling two days before Christmas ... crazy. Showing up unannounced in a new city ... beyond crazy. I hope wherever Oliver is staying there's room for me—I didn't make hotel reservations. On the cab ride to his work my nerves kick in. As unimaginable as it is, *what if* he's not happy to see me? Maybe he's really busy and I won't be the exciting surprise I'm imagining. Then there's Alex's scenario: He won't be there and I can't find him.

After paying the cab driver, I wheel my suitcase up to the gray building entrance. I find Sturgeon, Wallace, and

Faye, *22nd floor*. When the elevator doors open an older lady with silver-streaked ginger hair and yellowed teeth gives me a welcoming smile.

"Welcome to Sturgeon, Wallace, and Faye, how may I help you?"

"I'm Vivian Graham, here to see Oliver Konrad."

She looks at her computer screen with her lips pursed to the side.

"I don't have an appointment. I'm a *very* close friend and I'm here to surprise him."

My comment elicits a once-over look and another polite smile. "I'm sorry. Mr. Konrad is out of the office and I'm not sure if he'll be back in today. He had an out-of-office meeting with a client at one."

I nod while strumming my nails on the counter. *Dang! What's my plan B?*

"Do you have his cell number?"

I sigh. "Yes, it's just ... I wanted my arrival to be a surprise."

She shuffles a few papers around on her desk. "I take it you and Mr. Konrad are *close?*"

I smirk. "Yes, you could say that." A warm blush creeps up my neck.

She rolls her blue eyes up to me. "As in ... *really* close?"

I glance around to see if anyone else is hearing our conversation, then look back at her with narrowed eyes. "Yes, *really* close. Why?"

She clears her throat. "Well if it were me, I'd ask to use Mr. Konrad's office, to make a phone call or something like that." Now she scans the room and lowers her voice, leaning in toward me. "Then I'd lock his door, close the blinds, and take a picture of myself to send to him." She winks. "You know ... one that says *come hither*."

My eyes widen. I'm not sure whether I should be offended by her unprofessional behavior, or grateful for what really does seem to be a brilliant idea.

She sits up straight again and taps at her keyboard. "But that's just what I would do."

My body remains a statue, maybe for a minute maybe for five, I'm not sure. Finally I suck in a breath of courage.

"I didn't catch your name."

She smiles. "Samantha."

I offer my hand and she accepts with a dainty shake.

"Well, Samantha, I was wondering if it might be okay if I used Mr. Konrad's office to make a private call?"

She stands and smirks. "You got it. Follow me."

After securing the lock and closing all the blinds to the hall windows, I look around his office. There are two brown leather wingback chairs, a mahogany desk, his chair, and a few file cabinets. I walk to the large window overlooking the city. It's an incredible view of Portland, including the Willamette River. The building across the street has tinted windows so it's just a random guess as to whether or not someone can see in here. I'll risk it.

Oliver is a tidy guy so it doesn't take much to clear a spot on his desk. I slip out of my jeans and sweater then position myself on my side with my head resting on one arm while I hold out my phone with the other and take a few shots. They're not too bad, wish it could be from a little farther back but I think asking Samantha to take it for me might be crossing some line, even if my intuition is that she'd do it.

I pick out the best shot—cleavage, thong, my tongue wetting my upper lip, and just enough of his desk that he will *know* it's his desk. Then I send off a text.

Me: *Hey, babe. What's up?*
Oliver: *Grabbing a late lunch. Just got done with a meeting. What are you doing?*

I send the picture with a message: Not much. Just waiting for my attorney to get back to his office.

Oliver: *WTF!!!!!!*

I should just be nice and wait for him to get here, but what fun is that?

Me: *It's chilly in here. My nipples are so hard. Maybe I'll just rub them.*

I wait a few minutes.

Me: *I've never had sex on a desk. Do you think I should lie down flat with my legs spread or bend over the edge with my ass in the air?*

It's only been a few minutes, but I hear his voice outside the door.

"Are Brice and Mitchell gone for the day?"

"Yes, Mr. Konrad."

"Then you can leave early, Samantha."

"Are you sure?"

I giggle, knowing she's just messing with him.

"Positive. Have a good holiday."

"You too, Mr. Konrad."

The doorknob jiggles then I hear his key slide in the lock.

"Merry Christmas, Mr. Konrad." I greet him with my sexiest voice.

He smirks while his eyes peruse my nearly-naked body sprawled out on his desk. Oliver in a suit is a spontaneous orgasm. Oh. My. God! He moves toward me like he's on the prowl. I swallow hard. Move over leather work boots, you've forever been replaced with this image. There is nothing sexier than a guy loosening his tie with a predatory look in his eyes.

"Sorry I'm late, Miss Graham. I wasn't aware you were added to my schedule." He removes his jacket, tie, and shirt with calculated patience. He's teasing me ... tempting me, and he damn well knows it. "But I'm glad you waited and now that I'm here ..." He tugs my legs and brings me to standing. Tracing a finger over the swell of my breasts he smirks again then works the belt and zipper of his pants. "... We should start with a *debriefing*."

I look up at him, my body tingling, heart pounding. He rests his hands on my shoulders and turns me toward the desk. Placing his hand flat on my back, he nudges me forward until I'm bent over his desk, resting on my elbows.

I hear the clink of his belt buckle as his pants fall to the floor. I squirm as he pulls down my panties. Looking over my shoulder at him, I grin, but his face is stone.

He steps his leg between mine, forcing me to widen my stance. I tense as his right hand touches the bare skin of my ass.

He rubs small circles. "Would you say you've been *naughty* or *nice* this year, Miss Graham?"

I don't realize I've been holding my breath until my answer comes out as a timid squeak. "Nice."

Smack!

"Shit!" I yell as my mind races to catch up. Holy crap! He just *spanked* me! It was hard but not painful, and my reaction was from the shock of it, not the feeling.

"Now see..." he rubs the same area he just hit "...I disagree. Looking back, I recall several incidents which landed you on the naughty list."

"Oli ..."

"Now, now ..." I close my eyes as I feel his lips on my back. "In the spirit of the holiday, I'm still going to grant you your wish."

"What's tha—ahhhh!"

He slams into me then stills. "Me," he whispers in my ear.

And then it begins—the slapping of our skin, labored breaths and desperate moans, the squeak of the desk, and eventually my loud scream of ecstasy.

"I can't believe you spanked me," I mumble against Oliver's lips between kisses as we ride the elevator up to his hotel room.

"I can't believe you liked it so much."

"What?" I shove his chest as he chuckles.

He shrugs. "You did. I watched your face while I did it and after the initial five seconds of shock, I saw the corners of your sexy little lips turn up into a *smile*."

"It was a grimace, you idiot! The corners of a person's lips curl up when they grimace too, not just when they smile. Jeez, you're a sadist."

The elevator doors open and I stomp off with purpose leaving Oliver behind with my suitcase.

"Left," Oliver says as I come to the T-intersection of the hall.

I turn left like I already knew that—although of course I didn't.

"Back here," he says with a chuckle as he slides his key into the door of a room I passed ten strides ago.

I stop and let out a sigh then turn and sulk back to the door Oli's holding open for me.

"You liked it," he whispers with a taunting edge to his words as I walk inside the room.

"Shut up! I did not."

He scoops me up eliciting a squeal then tosses me on the bed and straddles my body. "So what brings you to the West Coast, Ms. Graham?"

We had sex on his desk, got dressed, cuddled in his chair, had sex in his chair, got dressed, then made out like teenagers on the drive to the hotel. What we haven't done is talk about ... anything.

"Sex. I flew in for sex." I look at the imaginary watch on my wrist. "I fly back out in an hour."

"Funny girl, huh?" He pins my hands above my head and kisses me.

"God ... I've missed you." There, I've said it. I miss him, all the time—every hour, every minute, every second. Now how do I tell him to make things right and come home to me?

"Well, not anymore. You stole my surprise by showing up here." He wiggles his brows. "*Not* complaining. I'm coming home the day before the wedding ... for good."

I try to make my outward smile hide my inward sadness. Oliver doesn't know that I already knew he was planning on coming home. He also doesn't know that it breaks my heart that all his time here in Portland was for nothing.

"Well, say something!"

I open my mouth then shut it. "That's amazing!"

"Vivian, my love..." he shakes his head "...remember, you can't lie worth shit. My mom told you, didn't she?"

I grimace and nod. Oli flops over on the bed next to me. "God! Typical shrink. They only keep your secrets if you pay them."

I laugh. "*Shrink?* That's your mom you're talking about."

"Well, either she's terrible at keeping secrets or you hypnotize people with your mesmerizing eyes until they tell you all their secrets." He turns on his side facing me. "I've gotten lost in them many times, it could go either way, so I'll give her the benefit of the doubt."

"Whatever." I look around the hotel room and see if I can make my next statement more believable. "So, why the hotel room?"

"Oh, Doug and Lily were having family in for the holiday and since I was going to be leaving soon anyway, I just decided to get a hotel room."

I'm not sure if Oli's a good liar or not. I knew the truth before I asked so I can't say for sure.

"Well, lucky us." I roll on top of him and yank his tie that's hanging in a loose knot around his neck. "I like you in a tie. I'm thinking for my next birthday, just a tie and boots ... in public, of course."

"Are you trying to get me arrested?"

"Oh, Oli ..." I work the buttons of his shirt. "You're such an enigma, all stuffy and we're-not-having-sex-in-public one minute and the next you're screwing me in an alley or bending me over your desk and spanking me. I think you're a bad boy by nature and a bore by nurture."

"A bore?" He slides his hands under my shirt and unfastens my bra.

"Yes, you grew up with money and manners—*boring*."

He laughs while sitting up and pulling off my shirt. "I guess I'll have to try and be less of a *bore*." Bending down he sucks in my nipple and bites it, *hard*!

CHAPTER THIRTY-THREE
BROKEN

Oliver

Vivian coming all this way to see me is the best gift ever. When we're together the world is perfect again. It doesn't matter that we're not with our families, or that we wake up in a hotel room on Christmas morning. She's all I need.

"So since I fly out tomorrow are we staying in bed all day?" Vivian asks as she feeds me an orange wedge, part of our Christmas morning room service in bed.

"It's where we've been for the past two days. Works for me." I smirk, sucking the juice off her finger.

"What time will you arrive in Boston on Friday?"

I "accidentally" drop a dollop of Greek yogurt on her nipple. She rolls her eyes as I clean it up with just my tongue. "Five Boston time."

"So you'll make it for rehearsal dinner?"

"I should unless I get delayed."

She nods and stares at me with lines of tension along her face, as if she's trying to figure something out.

"Are you going to see Caroline today?"

Her question blindsides me. "No."

I feel her judgmental eyes on me, so I focus on the toast I'm buttering to perfection.

"You can. I'll be fine here by myself for a while."

"No need."

"When's the last time you saw her?"

I shrug wishing she'd drop it. "It's been a little while."

"So she's doing better?"

"She's in a mental hospital with a family history of depression and doped up on a million meds. It's only going to get so good, Vivian." I close my eyes and sigh. "I'm sorry ..." I detest the unnerving feeling of anger that over-powers my resistance.

She rests her comforting hand on mine. I open my eyes and look at her. I hate lying to her. I hate Caroline for putting me in this position. Why can't she just get better and let me go or stop fucking failing at her pathetic suicide attempts. "I haven't seen her since Thanksgiving."

"Why?"

What the hell?

"What do you mean *why*? I just told you I haven't seen her since Thanksgiving and your reaction is why?"

Vivian's eyes widen as my volume escalates.

"You should be shocked or angry, but you're not. You knew didn't you?"

"Oli—"

"Don't Oli me, Vivian. You knew, didn't you?"

She shakes her head.

"Who told you? Did Caroline's parents call you? Did my mom find out? She told you, didn't she?"

She continues to shake her head.

"Tell me!" I swat the tray of food off the bed sending the plates and glasses crashing against the wall and floor. Vivian cups her hand over her mouth as tears ... fucking pity tears fall from her eyes.

"Why? Why didn't you tell me? Why didn't you tell me to come home?"

"You weren't ready."

"What the hell does that mean?" I stand, slip on my pants, and pace the floor, rubbing my throbbing temples. "Ready for what?" My voice breaks.

She kneels on the bed, pulling the sheet up to her chest. "Ready to deal with your past. Oli ... you kept the pillow that was used to ..." She can't say it. Of course she can't. It's too morbid.

I shake my head. It feels like the whole fucking world is caving in on me. What did I do? I'm the victim. She killed Melanie and left me with nothing. Why does everyone think I'm the one with the problem? I hate her ... she's turning everyone I love against me, making me seem like the crazy one.

"She killed her, not me."

"Oliver—"

"No, she killed her. I was working ..." I shake my head. "I wasn't there."

"Oliver—"

"She did it. She took everything from me. God ... I hate her so much!"

"Oliver, stop!"

I hold out my hand to keep her from touching me. "No. Why is this happening? Why is everyone blaming me?"

"Oliver, please ..." I hear Vivian's sobs, but I don't feel her. I don't feel anything.

"What does that mean?" I squeeze my eyes closed. "Tell me! What does that mean?" I open my eyes and Vivian is reaching for her phone. No fucking way. She's not calling anyone, not until she tells me. I grab her phone and throw it into the wall shattering her screen. She's shaking like a leaf. What's her problem? No one's making her feel crazy. No one's telling her to deal with her past.

"Oli—"

I grab her shoulders and shake her. "My wife suffocated my baby girl with a fucking pillow! That's my past, I can't change it! So would you please Tell. Me. What the fuck do you mean, Deal. With. My. Past? How in God's name do I do that?"

She cries.

I see it, but I refuse to hear it.

She pleads for me to let go.

I don't.

And then she wrecks me with two simple words.

"Forgive her."

I release her and stumble backwards. It feels like she shot me in the heart.

"It's not h-her f-fault. She was s-sick." She sobs.

I stare at familiar eyes, but I don't really see her. A voice ... I hear her voice, but I feel numb, completely numb.

Vivian

I think I broke him. Oliver's experienced the unimaginable in his life, but I've never thought of him as broken—until now. His eyes are on me, but his gaze goes through me. I want to crawl to him and hold him in my arms, but I'm scared. He's shown me a side I've never seen before, and I'm not sure he recognizes me or even himself right now.

I move with caution to the edge of the bed and ease onto

the floor, keeping the sheet wrapped around me. He's several feet away, slumped against the wall. "You said it yourself, Oli—less than point one percent. It was a tragedy. That's all it was ... an awful tragedy."

His whole body is stone-cold still and void of all emotion. I wish I could have a tiny glimpse into his mind right now. I wipe my eyes and wait. I don't want this wrenching moment to be our first Christmas together, but time is running out. Oliver is getting ready to leave Portland with the same hatred and resentment he's had for years. The crippling emotions that have held him hostage since that fatal night are threatening to steal the rest of his life.

Hating someone does that to you. It's a virus that infiltrates your life and takes hold of everyone that matters to you, then it rips them away one at a time until you're all alone, empty, and dead inside. Hatred breeds resentment and murders happiness. It's opportunistic and will suck the life out of you until you're nothing but an empty shell.

That is ... if you let it.

I can't watch Oliver fall victim to it any longer. My love for him is too strong. I will sacrifice us to save him.

"Oliver?"

He finally blinks and I see him recognize me as his eyes start to focus, but his expression remains lifeless.

"Go home."

His words shatter me inside, but I refuse to let him see it. I swallow back every single emotion that's threatening on the surface as I stand and get dressed. *He'll come back to you.* Jackie's words strum through my head, but they don't give me comfort. Looking at him now, I'm not sure he'll ever come back to any of us.

I gather my stuff and zip my suitcase. Oliver doesn't

even flinch. I set my suitcase and purse by the door and grab my broken phone. Then I hunch down in front of him.

He closes his eyes. "I'll wait for you at home." I lean in and press my lips to his forehead. "But only for forever." I press my palm to his cheek and move my lips to his ear. "No take backs, Oli."

I find a cheap hotel near the airport to stay the night. Luckily my phone still works even though the screen is cracked into jagged lines and chipped pieces. It's Christmas so I imagine both my family and Oliver's are enjoying their own festivities and time with loved ones. As much as my heart needs comforting and my mind needs reassurance, I don't call anyone. One day isn't going to make a difference except to ruin someone else's day. Mine and Oliver's is enough.

I'm not giving up on him. I could never do that. He told me to leave and I'm giving him space. My love is his—it's unconditional, patient, and waiting for his return. Sometimes the only way to hold on to someone is to let them go. I regret nothing. Melanie's tragic death cannot be erased, it cannot be forgotten, and it cannot be ignored. He laid her tiny body to rest and gave her brief, but no less important, life necessary closure. Now he needs to do the same for himself. Oliver needs to lay his anger and hatred to rest. Forgiveness is letting go and letting go is painful. It's not something we do for others; it's something we do for ourselves.

I PUT on my clown face. Alex is getting married in three days, and I will not let her see how crushed I am on the inside. Jackie and Hugh are the only ones who know what happened on Christmas in Portland with Oliver. As his parents, they needed to know that he's hit bottom and that I can no longer help him. Jackie boarded a plane yesterday for Portland ... I'd hoped she would.

"You didn't do anything lame like book pedicures and dinner at some family restaurant by the harbor, did you, Flower?" Alex squints at my reflection in the mirror as I curl her hair.

"Yes, that's why the invitations said masquerade ball attire." I roll my eyes.

"Will there be a naked guy? There better be, it was my only stipulation."

"Will there be a naked girl at Sean's bachelor party tonight?"

Alex laughs. "I can't believe you're even asking that. Kai's in charge ... I'm sure there will be more than one naked girl."

"And that doesn't bother you?" I pin up some of her spiraled curls as she puts on her mascara.

"Hell no. They're strippers, not prostitutes."

I raise a brow and smirk.

"Well ... okay, you never know what Kai will do, but I trust Sean."

"You should. He adores you."

"Wow, that's quite the endorsement considering how much shit you two give each other."

I shrug. "It's all in good fun. Now let's get your dress and mask on."

"Eek! I can't believe you got everyone masks. This is going to be so much fun!"

We put on our party dresses. Alex's is light pink lace and satin, and her laser cut butterfly mask is white. The rest of us girls will have black masks. My dress is a gold strapless chiffon with a short skirt and my hair is pulled up exposing the top of my tattoo. But who cares? I'll never look at myself the same way again: It will always be through Oliver's eyes —beautiful.

"Oh my God ... look at you!" The eight other girls dressed in cocktail dresses and black masks on the party bus greet the bride-to-be with enthusiastic squeals.

I take a deep breath. I can do this. Maybe tonight is what I need to forget about Oliver, even if only for a few hours.

"Thank you all for reading your invitations!" I look around at eight girls with naked lips, then I hold up a bag filled with tubes of lipstick and pass it around. "Everyone gets a different color and don't try to find something subtle and elegant. They're all obnoxiously bright and wild."

More squeals, clapping, and bouncing ensue as we add the finishing touch to our hot, sexy, here-comes-trouble look for the night. I can do this ... I can forget about Oliver.

I CAN'T DO THIS. I can't stop thinking about Oliver. Even after three beers and four shots, all I see is him. The party bus takes us to a club in the theater district and the bare ass shaking six inches from my face is Oliver's. So I do the only thing I can ... I spank it.

"Now who's on the naughty list?" I giggle.

His jiggly glutes come to a firm halt. Then he turns and stares at me with wide-eyed shock. I adjust my mask thinking that it's causing my blurred vision, but it's not. I was wrong. The guy ... Mr. Shaky Buns—not Oliver.

"Miss?" A guy in a black suit taps my shoulder.

I look up.

"I have to ask you to refrain from that type of interaction with the performers. If you'd like to pay for something more *hands-on* I could arrange for a private room."

I look at Mr. Shaky Buns. He grins and winks at me.

"I'm ... uh ... good. Sorry."

"Oh my God!" Alex collapses on my lap with her hands around my neck. "You spanked him!" She closes her glazed-over eyes and laughs.

The night continues on in similar fashion. My mind is altered by alcohol and Oliver ... not a safe combination for the unfortunate citizens of Boston that encounter our rowdy group. We leave our stamp—lip stamp—everywhere we go: doors, mirrors, tables, booths, DJ's, strippers, and unsuspecting bystanders.

It's three a.m. by the time the bus drops off the last bridesmaid before taking me and Alex home.

"Best. Bachelorette. Party. Ever!" Alex leans against me as the bus approaches our place. Her eyes fight to stay open as her tongue gets in the way, slurring her words.

I kiss her forehead, leaving my purple stamp next to the eight other colorful lip prints on her face, then I take a picture of her. "I'm glad you had fun. Now ... time to sleep."

We both stumble off the bus in a giggly fit and call it a night or *morning*.

CHAPTER THIRTY-FOUR
FORGIVENESS

Oliver

Fucking hangovers! I should be used to the pounding headaches and the taste of monkeys shitting in my mouth by now.

Prior to my move to Portland three years ago, the last time I was this intoxicated was my freshman year of college. Since the move back to Cambridge, I can't even count how many times I've felt like I do right now.

"Welcome back."

I try to peel open my eyes. It feels like sandpaper against my pupils. "Blinds."

"Nope, they stay open, dear."

"Mom?" I sit up and rub my temples.

She hands me a glass of water. "I should be upset that you've been binge drinking for the past two days, but had you been in your right and stubborn mind you might not have told me where you were staying."

"You called?" I take a sip of water. Jeez, my mouth tastes like shit.

"Thirty-two times. The thirty-first time you finally answered and told me your room number. The thirty-second time you told me the name of the hotel in exchange for me, and I quote 'fucking off'."

I cringe.

"Of course there's more than one Hilton here in Portland, so after several misses and weird looks when knocking on the right door at the wrong hotel, I finally found you. Lucky for me I knocked on your door a whole five minutes before you passed out. Otherwise I would have been calling the authorities with reason to believe my son was in danger of injuring himself."

"Why are you here?" I finally make eye contact.

"Because I'm afraid you're going to hurt yourself." She folds her hands in her lap.

"God, I'm not suicidal." I shake my head.

"That's not what I'm talking about." She stands and walks over to the bed and brushes her fingers through my hair. "You're going to lose another person in your life that you dearly love. And it's going to wreck you beyond repair if you don't figure this out soon. I've given you three years to work through this and you haven't. I wanted you back home with us but not because you were running away, Oliver. It should have been because you were moving on."

"I can't ... I don't know what to do." Even though she's my mom, I hate that these stupid tears sting my eyes and she's here to witness me like this.

"Yes, you do."

"She killed my baby." I suck in a shaky breath but can't hold it, not anymore. A sob cuts through me and she pulls me into her like she did when I was a little boy. That's what I feel like, a lost child.

"She killed her baby too because she was sick, Oliver, so sick. Caroline couldn't see Melanie. Her mind wouldn't let her see anything but the pain. She was putting an end to the pain."

"Oh ... God! It hurts so bad." I sob with excruciating pain seizing every part of my body.

"I know it does, sweetie, I know ..." She rocks me in her arms and so many thoughts and emotions that I've never allowed myself to think and feel crash into my heart like a wrecking ball.

***

I MET Caroline Sue Welch at the campus bookstore. She was working behind the counter and I was immediately drawn to her curly blond hair and rich hazel eyes. I was three people back in line and she kept peeking up at me while trying to help other customers. She was innocent and flirty. I was young and horny. When it was my turn in line, she gave me her address and phone number, in case I had any questions about *The Story of My Life* by Clarence Darrow, the book I was purchasing. A week later I called her up and asked her to dinner. Over margaritas and guacamole in a loud Mexican restaurant, I found out she had never read *The Story of My Life* by Clarence Darrow.

I have a million wonderful memories of Caroline. Everyone loved her, including me. But she's gone and I don't know where she went or what took her from me. The woman before me is a stranger—a stranger in my Caroline's body. I wonder when I lost her or if she tried to tell me. Did I not see the signs? Did I not hear her fading voice?

"What do you want, Oliver?" Her hazel eyes are the

only part of her body that reminds me of that day in the book store. She's twenty-seven but her malnourished body looks thirty years older.

"I'm sorry."

She tilts her head. "What do you mean?"

I fight past the three years of emotion that have been stuck in my chest, climbing up my throat, and threatening to steal my breath.

"I didn't know ... I didn't see it. The doctors said it was common, but I should have seen it. A man should know when his wife is slipping away. I worked too many hours. I wasn't there enough." I swipe away a stray tear.

She looks away, a million miles out the window with an expressionless face. I'm not sure she even hears me. Maybe she never will. I start to stand. This feels like a waste of time. My Caroline's gone.

I walk to the door and it hits me. This is the last time I will ever see Caroline. I turn. She's still looking out the window.

"Caroline?"

She turns.

I feel my lower lip start to tremble as I blink back the tears. "I forgive you."

Those familiar hazel eyes fill with tears, but I walk away before they fall.

I DON'T KNOW if I'll ever be able to convey the gratitude I have for my mom. Only now, as we wait to board our plane to Boston, does the impact of her love over the past three years really resonate with me. She's a fixer, as a mom and a psychiatrist, yet she stepped aside and let me fall apart over the last three years. Maybe she knew that's what I needed, maybe she didn't. Either way, it had to have taken an incredible amount of strength and love to watch in silence.

"How can you be so quiet?" I ask, sitting next to her in the terminal.

She reaches over and takes my hand. "There's nothing left to say. I'm in awe of your courage. You made peace with Caroline and you said a proper goodbye to Melanie. Oliver, my dear, you came to Portland a victim and you're leaving a survivor." She squeezes my hand and smiles.

"Do you think I'm the first person to leave a pillow by a headstone?"

She laughs. "Maybe."

"You know a raccoon or something is going to take off with it."

"Probably." She shrugs. "The birds and squirrels take off with the flowers."

I nod. "How'd you know to bring it?"

"You chose to give it to me instead of throwing it away, so I knew that meant you trusted me to know what to do with it. Honestly, I didn't know what that was until Vivian came back from Portland."

I stare at her for a moment then sigh. "This is so inadequate but right now it's all I can think to say, so ... thank you."

My mom smiles as her eyes tear up. "You're welcome." She dabs the corners and sighs. "Isn't it amazing that the Weeping Cherry tree near her grave finally bloomed this past spring?"

I smile thinking about Vivian and the scattering of cherry blossom buds inked on her back. "Yes, some things are just ... amazing."

After we board the plane and take off, I feel ... free. My

mind relaxes on my favorite thought ... Vivian. I was cruel to her, and my actions were abhorrent and by all rights, unforgivable. And if she's still waiting for me it will be a miracle, but that's what she is to me ... a miracle.

CHAPTER THIRTY-FIVE

BLISS

Vivian

T HE FORECAST WAS FOR SNOW, but Alex called in a favor with the big guy and agreed to apologize for all her Bridezilla outbursts if he granted her a day of sun. Wish granted. The ceremony at the church was perfect. Alex looked like a princess that walked straight out of a Disney fairy tale and Sean won me over when he cried during his vows.

Everyone gathers outside of the church on this sunny but very chilly December day to toss rose petals at the happy couple. They drive off in a Rolls Royce and the wedding party crowds into a stretch limo.

"You look amazing," Kai says as we're wedged so close I'm half sitting on his lap.

"Thank you," I mumble without looking at him.

"Kai, you look devastatingly handsome in that tailored suit and tie." Kai mocks in a high-pitched voice.

I don't want to smile because I'm exhausted from faking

my emotions over the past two days, but his comment elicits an involuntary one.

"What's that? An actual smile ... wow! Does this mean we can call a truce, a ceasefire for the evening?"

"I think we've had a ceasefire since rehearsal dinner last night. Otherwise you'd be dead."

One of the other groomsmen pours and passes around champagne. Kai hands me a glass. "Go easy, Viv. I'd hate to have to take advantage of you later in your inebriated state."

"You're a jerk."

"I'm just kidding. You used to be able to take a joke."

"You used to be my friend."

"Ouch."

Ouch is right. I would never have imagined that Kai and I would not be in each other's lives. My mistake was falling in love with him. His mistake was not letting me go. Now it feels like we've been ripped apart by circumstances and the wounds are too jagged and raw to ever heal and be the same again. That seems to be what's happened with us over the past two years, physically and emotionally.

"Well, *old friend,* would you mind getting off my lap?" Kai says with a snarky edge as the driver opens the back door.

I gather the long skirt of my strapless metallic gold lace dress and ease my way out of the limo. The icy December breeze cuts into my bare skin as I try to keep my wrap over my shoulders. We enter the State Room and take the elevator to the most spectacular view of Boston's skyline. A massive window wall is the backdrop to large round tables adorned with white linens, brilliant rose topiary center pieces, and twinkling candles—all covering a mahogany floor. I can't even fathom the dollar figure behind this wedding.

"Shall we?" Kai offers his arm as we make our way to the head table.

I take it, and we follow the rest of the wedding party. There must be five hundred or more people here. I don't think I know one percent of them. I'm definitely going to need more than the glass of champagne from the limo to stand up in front of all these strangers to give my toast.

Alex and Sean are introduced and the crowd claps and whistles as they enter the Great Room. The band begins to play while dinner is served. I'm starving but my nerves cripple my ability to eat. I look out at the sea of people hoping to find a familiar face, a go-to during my speech.

Nothing.

Maybe I'll just look at Alex ... that's not good either. I promised her no tears, but that will never work if I'm looking at her the whole time. I wish Oliver were here. He soothes all my nerves and with just one look he gives me confidence. Missing Oliver is hard, but not knowing if or when I'll see him again is like a slow death. The temptation to call him has been overwhelming the past several days, but I can't. He'll come to me when he's ready.

God ... I hope that day comes.

I didn't write down my speech and as my turn approaches I'm starting to regret it.

"Next, we'll hear from the maid of honor, Vivian Graham."

I stand as I'm handed the microphone. Yep, I might pass out, definitely not enough alcohol.

"Hello." The crowd falls silent. "A month or so ago I thought up this great speech that summarized our relationship over the past two years and it included all the reasons Sean is the luckiest guy in the world to give you his name." Sean grins at me and kisses Alex on the cheek. "But recent events in my life have made me rethink what I wanted to say to you both, so ... here it is, simply and sweet." I take a nervous sip of my champagne then suck in a courageous breath.

"I hope every day you take each other's breath away. I hope every kiss feels like the first but ends like the last. I hope you always see the best versions of yourselves reflected in each other's eyes." I look at Alex while my own emotions derail my thoughts. "But mostly, I hope you wake up every morning next to each other because there's no place in this world you'd rather be, instead of having nowhere else to go. May you always be each other's home."

I raise my glass and the band starts in as applause and clinking glasses echo in the air. Alex and Sean cut the cake and have their first dance. In spite of my suggestion to skip the wedding party dance, claiming that it was unoriginal, we have it and I'm forced to once again breach my comfort zone and dance with Kai.

"Do you think we'll ever be friends again?" he asks as the band plays "Maybe I'm Amazed."

"I don't know if we know how to be friends anymore." I shrug. "Nothing lasts forever."

"Such a cliché." He shakes his head.

"Yeah, well, cliché seems to be the term that's used when someone doesn't want to admit the truth."

"So Oliver isn't your *happily-ever-after*? You don't want that to last forever."

"Oliver grounds me in the moment. When I'm with him I don't think about tomorrow or next week, and I sure don't think about forever. I don't try to quantify my love for him or our time together. I just want to *be* with him and if along the way time passes, so be it."

"Did I not ground you?" Kai asks as the song comes to an end.

I give him a sad smile as he releases my waist. "No. I always felt like I was floating ten feet off the ground ready to fall and hoping you'd see me ... hoping you'd catch me. But you never did."

"Viv, I'm ..." Kai winces and shakes his head as the power in his voice fades.

"Kai?"

He gives me a slow glance.

"In spite of where we ended ... I forgive you, for everything."

Kai's mouth opens but no words come out. He nods and I turn and worm my way off the dance floor. I suck in a shaky breath and blink back the tears. Forgiveness breathes life into a weakened soul.

FREE-FLOWING LIQUOR, a stellar band, and the best view of Boston—all mine for the next three hours. I should have a nice buzz and be living it up on the dance floor with the other bridesmaids. Instead, I'm sitting at the head table, alone, rearranging cake crumbs with my fork and thinking of Oliver. I haven't heard from him or Jackie since she left for Portland. Alex has consumed my every minute until now. I grab my phone from my handbag but there are no missed calls or messages. So I do what any lonely girl in my shoes would do ... I get another piece of cake.

The lead singer of the band starts to talk. "This next song is a special request dedicated to anyone still eating cake."

I freeze with my fork in my mouth, scanning the room. Am I the only one still eating cake?

Then the music starts: "A Drop in the Ocean" by Ron Pope.

"You are, you know ..." A tingle of hair-raising chills flows across my skin as his words whisper along my neck. "... You are my heaven."

I didn't realize how many tears I'd been saving for him—until this moment.

"You're here," I whisper, turning my head with slow ease.

Oliver holds out his hand, and of course ... I take it. "I'm here for you. God, I'm so sorry—" He pulls me into his arms.

"Don't ... don't apologize." I shake my head and cling to him.

I try so hard to control the emotions that detonate inside, no longer able to be held back by the overwhelming need to do right by Oliver. This is my selfish moment. I just can't keep it in another second.

"I—I didn't know if—you'd come back."

He leans back and looks at me, brushing away my tears with the pads of his thumbs. "I had to let something go. But it wasn't you ... never you."

I smile and so does he ... two dimples. But then mine fades.

Oliver cups my face. "What is it?"

My face wrinkles with concern. "Did you ... forgi—"

He presses his lips to mine, silencing me—holding me. As he releases me, he rests his forehead on mine and nods.

We say our goodbyes to Alex and Sean, who both insist us two 'lovebirds' get out of here. I feel a pang of guilt being the maid of honor that leaves before the bride and groom. But I need Oliver now, more than anything or anyone else.

He leads me toward the elevators. "By the way, you make that dress look beautiful."

I giggle and shake my head.

"Even with the frosting smeared down the front." He glances back over his shoulder with a smirk.

"What?" I stop and look down. "Dammit!" I rub the chocolate frosting with my thumb, but it only makes it worse.

Oliver chuckles. "Don't worry about it. You won't be wearing it much longer."

My insides begin to heat as we maneuver our way through the sea of tables and people. I take the opportunity to drink in my sexy man in his suit, but my eyes stop, glued to his ... *leather work boots.*

"Oliver?"

"Yes?" he calls back.

"What's up with the boots?"

"Patience ... you'll see."

"I HAVEN'T WORKED out in a while. Do you think I'm looking flabby?" Oliver asks.

Looking over my shoulder, I bite my lower lip and shake my head.

"Is my tie straight?"

I nod with an enormous grin, my body screaming for the teasing to stop.

"What about my ass? Do these boots make my ass look big?" Oliver turns and flexes his firm glutes at me.

I begin to drool. "Oliver!"

"Yes, my love?"

"Now!"

He grins while crawling onto the bed. "So what made you think of this?" Lifting my hips, he slides his erection between my legs, teasing my clit.

I'm on my knees, bent forward with my wrists hand-cuffed to the headboard—the handcuffs were in my brides-maid's goodie bag, compliments of Alex.

"Um, nothing really. Ahhh!"

Oliver slams into me and pulls my hair back. Who *is* this guy?

As he works into a steady pace, he releases my hair and grabs my hips with the occasional reach-around to stimulate my clitoris.

The cuffs, although fur covered, bite into my skin. It's pain and pleasure. It's sexy and erotic. It's demanding and playful ... It's me and Oliver—unpredictable, indestructible, and inseparable.

Skin to skin, heart to heart, in his arms is my home. Everything else I do in my life will just be what I accomplish in a day to get back to Oliver.

"Oli?'

"Hmm?" His chest hums against my ear as our tired bodies search for sleep.

"Why did you keep the pillow?"

Loving fingers trace my back. "I wanted her last breath."

EPILOGUE

Oliver

5 Years Later

WHAT HAPPENS when a business geek from Harvard meets an engineering geek from MIT at Dunkin' Donuts? Bloom Pods.

Before either Vivian or her MIT friend, Anne Gade, received their degrees, they both became millionaires. Bloom Pods are sleep pods revolutionized. They have therapeutic lighting, essential oil diffusers to stimulate the pineal gland, music, white noise or nature sounds, chair massage options, and a cover that's a virtual screen with every imaginable scenery choice. It's so realistic that even people with claustrophobia can use them with ease. Fifteen minutes in a Bloom Pod feels like hours of physical rejuvenation. They've infiltrated all major cities, now common in corporate buildings, fitness centers, and mental hospitals.

Since graduating a year ago, Vivian has expanded her wellness corporation, Idle Bloom, beyond Bloom Pods. Now that marijuana is legal in all fifty states, she has hired a group of doctors and scientists to head up The Green Pot Project. They're conducting long-term research studies on all the health benefits of marijuana, including cannabinoids effect on reducing inflammation and preventing scar tissue after severe burns.

As for me ... I've managed to sleep my way to the top. The CEO of Idle Bloom has a thing for tall guys in ties and work boots, so now I head their legal department. My office is next to the boss lady's with an adjoining door. We schedule time for a private meeting every day and some-times our pressing *needs* require two meetings to remedy the situation.

We live an unconventional love story. She won't marry me because she wants me to know that she's with me by choice, every day, no matter what. I won't stop proposing because I want her to know that if marriage is the ultimate symbol of commitment and love, I'll never stop wanting her —all of her—forever. We're the only two that understand how devastating it would be if I stopped proposing or if she ever said yes. Every day we share mad love, crazy emotion, and unforgettable passion. We are the best thing that ever happened to us.

Vivian

So I'm not the next Amazon, and Dunkin' Donuts still has my undying loyalty, but I have a great job and employees who love working *with* me—as promised, four day work weeks and weekends off. I do it all for the challenge and satisfaction of knowing I'm making a difference. The money doesn't matter, in spite of the eye roll I get from my accountant every time I request pay raises for my employees. The money and *things* have not changed me. I'm still the simple girl who fell hard for a guy that changed everything.

I won't marry him ... Okay, I would, but why? We don't plan on having children, as taboo as it sounds. Although after my commitment to lifelong virginity, I'm a bit more reserved about saying never. Somehow with Oliver in my life anything feels possible. For now, we spoil Chance and Ronnie's two boys and Alex and Sean's six-month-old daughter.

I like introducing Oliver as my boyfriend, just like I like showing off my tattoo, and driving my car so fast Oliver's bladder considers reverting back to his younger years. Maybe I'm a rebel or maybe I'm just not a conformist. Either way, it doesn't matter. No two people could love each other with any more fierce intensity than what Oliver and I share every day.

"I can't believe you're doing this." I smile, looking over at Oliver with his shirt off.

"Me? What about you?"

"I'm a pro, but you're a virgin."

"Stick, pinch, burn ..." He grins.

I smirk. "I should never have told you that."

He's done before me.

"Let me see."

He lifts his arm so I can see the black tattooed script along the side of his torso.

No Take Backs

"What do you think?"

"Perfect."

"You think so?"

"Absolutely. I'll see it every time I cuddle under your arm."

When I'm finished, Oli looks at my lower back. It's official. I have one *bloomed* cherry blossom tattoo. Next to the round O-bloom are the letters *l* and *i*, *Oli*. He sighs. "Marry me?"

"Nope."

We both laugh while the tattoo artist looks on with an amused grin.

I used to think time stood still when we were together. He was afraid to look back and I was afraid to look forward. Now I realize during all those perfect moments that seemed to stand still, we were healing and growing, loving and learning in the light of each other's hearts ... We were two souls in *Idle Bloom*.

The End

ACKNOWLEDGMENTS

My greatest thanks will always be to my family. You are *the best*! I know everyone says that, but in my case it's the honest truth. You are the gatekeepers to my sanity, my cheerleaders when I question my ability, and the grounding center of my world every single day.

Thank you, Mom, for believing in me and spending so many hours proofreading my manuscript. A special thank you to my sister for your late night proofreading with Cameron in your arms. It will be priceless to see the look on his face someday when he finds out mommy nursed him while reading sexy novels. Thank you also for reminding me that our mom is crazy for thinking there's too much sex in my book. My readers owe you a special thanks, too!

To my best friend, Jyl – Boston was legendary! Thank you for letting me tagalong to do research and whale watching, while you sat in medical conferences all day. I love that we still make each other laugh until we cry and now probably even pee a little. Yep, we're going to define forty as fabulous!

Thank you to my editor, Maxann Dobson, from the

Polished Pen. I love being your student and I hope I never stop learning from you. I smile every time a review acknowledges how well my books are edited; and it happens a lot!

Thank you bloggers for supporting my journey. Your endless promoting, reading, and reviewing has changed the way people read books and find authors like myself. It's a true pleasure to share my passion for romance books with you. I have to mention a few that have made a lasting impression on me over the past year. Sandy from The Reading Café, you are the Twitter queen! Tara from The Lustful Literate, thank you for the constant kind words of encouragement. Diane from Tometender, you win the award for making my books sound, quite possibly better than they are in your enthusiastic and poetic reviews. Grace and Michelle from After Dark Book Lovers, I loved every minute of your ranting while reading the Holding You Series. If that makes me sadistic, then so be it! Elusively Ella, thank you for befriending me on Goodreads and sharing advice and opportunities for me to find connections and new readers. Finally, the thank you that will always feel inadequate but it's all I have, goes to The Rock Stars of Romance. Your love for books and the authors who write them is just insane. Lisa, oh my, there really are no words. You taught me book lingo when I first came to you, not even knowing what a blog tour was. You invited me to "pick your brain" an offer you're probably regretting by now, but that brain of yours has helped me immensely. I'm sure if you've kept all the messages we've shared over the past year you could publish it under comedy because I'm pretty sure I've vented about everything from the weather to my perimenopause symptoms. I just cannot say enough about how absolutely wonderful, kind, and generous you've been. Thank you!

To my amazing readers, I am eternally grateful. You have allowed me to pursue my true passion and that is a gift everyone deserves but few ever receive. The personal messages I get from some of you make my heart swell and my tears flow. You justify all my late nights, early mornings, and tedious research, AKA reading lots of books! Thank you!

Thank you Jenn Beach for the beautiful new cover and formatting.

ABOUT THE AUTHOR

Jewel is a free-spirited romance junkie with a quirky sense of humor.

With 10 years of flossing lectures under her belt, she took early retirement from her dental hygiene career to stay home with her three awesome boys and manage the family business.

After her best friend of nearly 30 years suggested a few books from the Contemporary Romance genre, Jewel was hooked. Devouring two and three books a week but still craving more, she decided to practice sustainable reading, AKA writing.

When she's not donning her cape and saving the planet one tree at a time, she enjoys yoga with friends, good food with family, rock climbing with her kids, watching How I Met Your Mother reruns, and of course...heart-wrenching, tear-jerking, panty-scorching novels.

www.jeweleann.com